WE IS ME
UPSIDE DOWN.

DOUG MCPHILLIPS

Also by Doug McPhillips

Other Visionary Stories

NOVELS.

The Sword of Discernment.
Santiago Traveller.
I Prophet.
Masters at My Table.

POETRY.

From Darkness to Light.
Awake to my gutted dreams.

ALBUMS.

Country Camino.
Santiago Traveller.

Doug McPhillips 2020.

ISBN 9780645264500.

Authors references throughout this book.

This book is a work of fact and maybe fiction. All characters in this novel are real. Any re-semblance to actual events or locales or persons, living or dead, has been considered with poetic licence as I so recall. Where poetic licence is used to turn fact into fiction or visa versa, names have been changed to protect the innocent.

To my legitimate family
and the not so.

Some memories are not included here
and are best forgotten.

FORWARD:

Memories come flooding back to near to the beginning, like a capitulation of progressive images on a screen in front of me. It seems I have been born with a majestic power of recall or maybe its just a vivid imagination that I have developed the ability for people, places and things in my mind, in chronological order from the time of my birth until the present day. It is a handy tool, as I can scan images and lock into any 'picture in time' and recall the events surrounding it. I am under no illusion that my ability to recall the past does not apply to the majority of humanity, it does. It's just that I can go back in time and see these vivid pictured events as far back as my first breath of life as clearly as I see the present day and in that I reckon I am a tad unique.

I know of no other person in my lifetime who is blessed with this gift, talent or curse; depending on ones viewpoint. No one I know that has the ability to go back to their beginning and see it all like it's the present. It has served me well over a life time bringing to me from time to time employment opportunity, love of nature, feelings of happiness and episodes of heightened enthusiasm of predetermined goals and equally times of the deepest darkness and despair. In a single day I may experience joy, sorrow, pain and the suffering of a once torment soul. The recognition that feelings are not facts and the images conjured up from past ritual or present day living experiences I accept as normal for me and do not take these images nor myself to seriously, nor do I see them as a roadmap for living an extraordinary life. My recall ability has, more often than not, felt more a curse than blessing as I recall events or imaginary pictures that often interfered in the everyday comings and goings of an ordinary life. It is then I am driven by impulse that suddenly catapults me into a fourth dimensional universe of creative ideas and imaginings. It is then I am plagued by a work ethic that deprives me of sleep, unsettled eating patterns that adversely effect my mental, physical and spiritual health. For it is for me a time of exhausting and endless pursuits of ideas and action that from an output prospective works well for a time; that is until I ultimately run out of battery and have to rest, switch off from the mad mind and relax. Once rested a drone like existence prevails for a time, until I happen upon an idea for another book or a song and it is then that I am back in picture land and some kind of creative madness.

When I moved this way I am in a danger zone of maybe hours of research on relevant subject matter or a frantic writing spree that may last for hours and even days. So it is with this thought in mind that I have slowed it all down to go back to the beginning now to my earliest memories and were they have led me to the present day. This book I choose to write in chronological order as a picture post card of ideas spring forth.

[1]It is my intention here to select events and stories I recall that appear relevant to me and that may prove beneficial in some small way to you the reader. It is hoped that what I choose to write about here will inspire your very own creativity that may lead you to a point of telling your tale of real life or imaginary experiences or to use the facts of your on life today, to weave a story worthy of the best you have to offer. Whatever may transpire in reading this book may it come to be for you a source of inspiration and happiness, which is the ultimately that anyone can wish for. So I trust as I write these lines that the masters of your dreams and aspirations bestows upon you the special gifts and opportunity that one may be granted to write, record, journal or sing or whatever may prevail for you that will bring you love, health, spiritual wealth and the very best of intent for a better life. In my case the events of my childhood granted me a love of nature, real and imaginary friends, the spirit of hope and aspirations for a better life. What transpired to date has shaped me into who I am and what I am becoming. The lessons of this my life has taught me that I am more than what I had formally imagined. For I came to discover that it is not all about who I was as me, nor who I am as me now. Rather it is the discovery of a real higher power in my life; the realisation that it is about being lead more than doing the leading. Yes, I come to believe in a power greater than self that turned the old me upside down. In fact I am no longer a Me but a We, upside down. So my journey begins here with the known known Doug and as you will see in the snippets of images I choose to recall that I slowly but surely evolve into the We known not me known. For this 'two in one flesh' is influenced by an all powerful ego self which needs to be curtailed from time to time to allow the power of the higher self to take command and do its work. This is for my betterment for I am a better person now, who lives a more fulfilled life with WE is ME upside down. Now read on.

CONTENT:

God got the job to run the show before me, eons before I became a twinkle in my Fathers eye and a seed implanted in the womb of my Mother. In hindsight thou, I wonder if given the choice again would he or I have chosen the path I took in coming here in the first place. I have had the free will to make my own choices ever since I reached an age of reason. The wisdom of having lived a long earthly life has taught me a lot and to a great degree nothing. To digress any further here may take you dear reader away from this my story. So I now leave it at your discretion to take from these snippet of my life, the people I have known and events I have chosen to recall to determine if the words herein are of some benefit to you for which you may well use in your progressive realisation and wisdom or just completely disregard.

- -

CHAPTER 1.

THE POWER OF A FIGHTER

The physiotherapist sat for a moment after listening to me rant and rave, not for the first time, about my earliest most painful memories. He had asked me to recall my most painful childhood memory that had a dramatic effect on my life to this day. I quickly scanned my memory bank recalling events that had caused me the most pain and a flash of enlightened perception came to me. The power of a photograph memory of people places and things from my earliest days were triggered by emotional feelings, sights and sounds that back then I could not understand until now. I recalled a clear picture of my birth, my mothers inability to nurture, the women in the next bed happily cuddling and feeding her baby. Mum was emotionally void of all feelings from the moment I was born. She could not react to feed me and her milk dried up within days of my birth. She cared but was void of emotional bondage in a nurturing way. In hindsight now as an adult, one might say she was in a constant state of depression from the moment of my birth and I felt it then and am reminded of it from time to time when I portray such symptoms. Mum had hurriedly taken me to a surrogate mother to feed my empty belly. Cath O' Rooke had big boobs and I suck merrily away to fill my empty belly. Of such women I still feel a great attraction but not for the same reasons.

I was born on the other side of midnight, at the beginning of Spring 1944, one year earlier than the end of World War 11, almost to the day. It was a significant learning curve year for the world at large , but the war had little effect on a kid in far away Australia in his first year of life. Unbeknown to me back then but given to my ears later, conversation around the neighbourhood dinner tables often broached the subject of the end of the War in Europe which seem to end with a whizz and a fizz in the Spring of 1945. On the other hand, 'The War in the Pacific' was a cessation of mighty proportion. A final death knoll happened when Colonel Paul Tibet's and crew of the leading United States B-29 bomber 'Enola Gay' dropped its payload of an A-Bomb known as "Little Boy" on the industrial city of Hiroshima, Japan in the dawn light of 6th August 1945.

The Uranium A-Bomb exploded with an energy force equivalent too 16 kilotons of TNT over the city, missing its main target of military communications, for weapons, boats and planes assembly and troop deployment, but wiping out other key military locations. Some 70,000 plus people were killed by the blast and as many as 20,000 military personnel too. The prime target job completed by the leading B-29 Bomber, the weather reconnaissance aircraft teams returned to base for they were low on fuel. The remaining aircraft equip with blast measurement instrumentation headed from Kokura to drop their payload over the industrial area of that city as its was the back up bombing team.

Finding the city encased in cloud, they continued on to Nagasaki with the intent to drop their A-Bomb backup weapon of mass destruction over the small industrial area there. Major "Chuck" Sweeney instructed his crew to open the bombing hatch of 'The Great Artiste' B-29 but as they approached Nagasaki was not visible from the air due to cloud cover, so being low on fuel elected to drop the 4.5 Ton A-Bomb 'Fat man' on a hunch that they were on their industrial city target. They knew they would not get home due to low fuels so at 11 a.m.on August 6th 1945 'Fat Man' plummeted down on the city of 200,000 souls of whom more than 70,000 would die, many without a trace. They had missed their prime target too and the bomb exploded over the residential area. The blasts of those bombs set in motion a fear that has resinated throughout the decades of my childhood to present day manhood. Cold War is a noun meaning 'a state of political hostility between countries characterised by threats, propaganda and other means short of actual warfare'

The Cold War that followed WW11, primary between the USA and the USSR, raged on until 1991 with the fear and threat of Nuclear War forever mindful in the loins of both sides after the Japanese episode. We the child of the late 40s and early 50s were conditioned by education to this fear as much as present day and the likelihood of future wars and terrorism. The Korean War, The Vietnam War, The Falklands War, the present day war in the Middle East and the continued tears of terrorist attacks of 9/11 proportions, all serve to keep up this threat of fear of a pending Nuclear War, which right now is a greater threat than ever before, in a world mad on building up Nuclear arms on the ground, under the sea and in space too. I don't even know why I am repeating this now, but looking back it seems to have more historic value for me than my life at that time.

So to continue with my childhood. Whilst my conditioning at home, at school and in the workplace became a matter of fact in the long run, my prime fear back in those early years before the age of reason was off loneliness and isolation. Mum's nature was to act on impulse as this seem to be a perfectly normal reaction fro the sufferer of depressive mania. Back then, long before capping and teeth implants were first thought of, dentures were all the rage. One of Mums first actions after my birth was to go to the dentist and have all her perfectly healthy teeth removed for the implant of this new fad, false teeth. She had no trouble persevering with the top dentures staying put in her mouth but could not stand the discomfort of the bottom set, so she just left them in the bathroom cabinet were they remained indefinitely. Mums face could light up with a smile at the slightest inkling of attention to her. This had the effect of her artificial teeth appearing as a Colgate like smile at the top of her mouth, whilst the bottom jaw protruded to what appeared as defiance, hiding the toothless gums from appearance to the naked eye. The friendly smile hid a tormented mind that had been damaged from her childhood. Grandmother Mary married George Cooper giving birth to 15 children from her teens to mid forties. She contracted cancer after seven children, lost two in childbirth and gave birth to seven living children after the cancer off the womb was diagnosed.

Mum was one of the latter seven. Grandmother Mary was advised by her doctor to have a full hysterectomy which would have prolonged her life. Mary (nee McCormick) Cooper was having none of this. She was a strict Catholic and in her mind it went against God's law to have the womb surgically operation to remove the uterus. She decision to keep on having children which was in my favour, for if she had off proceeded with the hysterectomy I would not be here today. Grandmother died before I was born of cancer, she was only forty five. My early memories of being left alone in a cage like pen whilst my mother seemingly busied herself with household chores, was normal for me. They were hard times after WW11 and creating garden beds, growing vegetables, cleaning, washing clothes and cooking meals and preserving fruit to give to the the nuns or feeding the priest when he called to administer his view of the 'Holy Spirit' my mother considered her priorities in lieu of the burden of a child.

I have since learnt that this was similar to most Mums of that era, the difference being that I was was only picked up and man-handled to perform, smile, dance and laugh at her beck and the call for strangers. After the 'acting' was over and I was no longer the centre of attention, I was placed back in the pen. It is no wonder I grew up to believe that the only way to make it in life was to fake it and perform.

As I sat there with my eyes closed and on the advise of the physiotherapist I continued my recall of childhood events as more fear based pictures came to light. I was watching my father swim a swollen river to help save the contents of a friends house and hoping against hope that he would not drown as a consequence of his actions. I was much relieved when he return to me safely on the shore. Many years later he drowned near that river location under the influence of alcohol and although I was an adult and married at the time, I felt a string had been cut inside me when I received the news. I never felt that way with my mothers parting some twenty years later, but I had made peace with her by then. I had weathered many a storm with my father at my side and he had always had my back and supported me through thick and thin despite his alcoholic nature he was my everyday hero as a child. Dad went on to prove himself as a successful businessman, entrepreneur, philanthropist and engineering genius. I watched him rise to the top of the heap and slowly decline into full blown alcoholism and prescription drug abuse. It was a sad state of affairs but I have been through much worse since my dysfunctional childhood and that is why I ended up on the psychs' couch. Apart from my painful family recall that I had discussed with the quack seated opposite, the memory of the drowning of by best childhood friend when at the beach together. Another repeated fear came with the teaching of Latin by a one eyed priest who stood over us kids cracking a stock when we misunderstood a latin verse. This rated rather high in my priorities of painful memories. "Mea Culpa, Mea Culpa, Mea Maxima Culpa," but I did manage to learn the Latin.

Of course the physical abuse of the Sisters of (no mercy) nuns and Marist Brothers at boarding school also rated high in my painful memories of v childhood , but not as much as the one event that had the biggest impact and the deepest memory recall- the death of my Uncle John who at just fourteen died of heart failure. I was present at the time and from that day and for days after his death I was lost, alone, bewildered and heartbroken. That is until I realised there was another way to live. I was just five at the time and could not comprehend the impact of death over life.

I began to tell the story of John's death to the engrossed physiotherapist. How he had fallen from his bed after stretching out to put a boxing glove on the hands of a neighbouring child. John suffered from rheumatic fever from birth which so often rendered him bedridden. Despite his pain he was always cheerful and had a barrage of young female teenagers at his beck and call when at his worst in illness. Once he regained his strength thou, he was out and about attending school, riding horses, entering buck jump events and riding bulls at the local Rodeo and of course there was always boxing. Every one loved John and especially the girls and I loved him more than life itself. John told his stories to any listening ear of the greatest of boxers, mostly local aboriginal champions, who made the big time, great champions like Dave Sands, Freddie Dawson and Ron Richards. To colour his stories he made cardboard cut outs of the heroic sportsman and reenacted the fights that he heard on radio using the cutouts whilst convalescing. He taught me to shape up as the champs did and he arranged an under six years of age boxing tournament in our back yard with him as referee. I was pitted by him against a much taller and strong boy at the time and took a walloping. It was his way of toughing me up for later life.

John Cooper seem to have an insight into personalities and perhaps knew that he would not be around for much longer and I would have to stand up and be counted sooner rather than later. When he became too sick to walk, Mum carried him too and from the old toilet can 50 metered out the back yard. There was no sewerage back then and no toilet paper either. We used old pieces of newspaper to wipe our bums when the butchers paper from the weekly meat wrap was all used up. The highlight of 'taking a dump' was when the 'dunny' man would come once a week to remove the full can and replace it with a clean one.

Dad would leave him a couple of 'bob' (two shillings) at Christmas and Mum would wrap him up a piece of Christmas cake as a bonus and leave it at the toilet door. Dad always seem to be at work and John was my male mentor when Dad was absent. In the depth of John's illness Mum would wash, fed and clothes him. It was no mean feat for a women off small frame as her domestic duties also included collecting wood from the wood heap and carry a pile to store in a box in the kitchen. Dad's only domestic duties otherwise seem to be sharpening the axe, cutting wood for the fire from a pile stacked out back and knocking the head off a chock or two, plucking the feathers and cleaning the bird for Sunday lunch.

There was no plumbing or drainage in those days and cooking was done with lard of which the excess ended up down the drain collecting in the grease trap under the house below the kitchen floor. My duties included collecting eggs from the chicken coop but Mum who always seem to be there to do most of the chores. To get water back then it meant pumping it by hand from an overflow underground stream to the surface to an above ground tank. No doubt Mum was relieved to see it rain as it save her all that pumping and carrying water and nature would then replenish the tank outside our backdoor and revive the vegetable patch. An old chip heater need to be filled at the head of the bath tub and once fired up the water would heat and a tap at its base could be turned on to add hot or cold water to a bath. It was standard practice to have no more than a few centimetres of water to bathe in as it was consider a precious commodity.

The water was brought to boil for cooking as well as washing our cloths by hand. The practice of boiling the old copper up to wash, wringing the clothing by hand then pegging all out to dry on a propped up cloths line out in the back yard was the norm for my mother. As the song of the times went: "Monday is washing day... is everybody happy, you bet your life we are." Every day of the week there were full time chores to do and we all took it in our stride believing that it was how it was meant to be. Mum was absolutely devoted to her young brother and in his case I was never jealous of her affection for him instead of me. It all went with the territory as I now believe it was meant to be.   I feel sure my Dad spent so much time away from home building his empire and drinking with mates as he like me had figured he didn't fit in at home.

He considered himself completing his duty as father, breadwinner and provider and that as as far as he could take it. John, like my Dad when he was around, was my life blood for living. All that changed the day John died and my life changed forever. It did for both Mum and Dad and for me until the time of my adulthood and the getting of wisdom. It was somewhat of a coincidence that Dave Sand's the greatest of all boxing champs of the time and brother of a family boxing dynasty died not long after their greatest of his promoters, my Uncle John parted this earth. Dave was born at Burnt Bridge, near Kempsey, a stones throw from were I lived with my parents and my Uncle John. Not far either from the Kirkpatrick dairy farm where son David donned a slouched hat, picked upon a guitar and performed at the local agricultural shows and become a renowned Australian country music singer using the handle 'Slim Dusty." Slim's claim to fame and greatest hit at the time, repeated on country radio was "The pub with no beer' for which he paid five quid to local poet and song writer Gordon Parsons. Slim sold over a million copies of that record whilst all that Gordon got was enough money to buy a few beers and gratitude from Slim who included him in his touring Slim Dusty shows around Australia for a long as I they were on the road. More to be said on that story on another occasion, but I digress.

The fighting Sands brothers between them contested 494 official fights, with 302 wins (209 by knockouts), 327 draws and 163 losses during their boxing careers of the late 1940s and early 1950s. The Sands brothers were heroes too many an Australian boy growing up in the 1950s and Dave was the hero of us all. By far the greatest of the boxing champs Dave who was at the time Australia's most popular sportsman. He was an athlete that would rival Mohammad Ali with an unbeatable left hook, lightening speed and foot work in the ring second to none. At the time of his tragic death in a trucking accident at Dungog in 1952 he was ranked number two for Raging Bull Jake Motta's title just behind 'Sugar' Ray Robinson for the world Middleweight title. Dave had beaten an American boxer at the old Rushcutter's Bay Stadium and was found sitting on his suit case at Central station after the fight eating a meat pie. He was catching the mail train back up the coast and there would be nothing to eat on the train. His manager had given him $20 for winning the fight.

Soon after, Dave beat Dick Turpin for the British Empire Middleweight title, then beat Robert Villemain who had beaten La Motta. He also beat Carl "Bobo" Olson, who subsequently became world champion and Henry Brimm, who had fought a draw with Robinson. When Olson won the title after Robinson retirement, he said "This title should have belong to Dave Sands. It would have belong to him had he lived." When he died Dave Sands had fought 104 bouts, winning 60 by knockout and 35 on points. He had earned $48,000 in a career that lasts nearly 10 years. At the time of his death Dave was hauling timber to help supplement the family income. We wept when he died in that car crash in 1952. A local schoolteacher pointed out that few tears had been shed by Australian over the death of King George V1 and the boys in his class had pointed out that enough people in the world could morn for The King; there were only nine million Australians to mourn Dave. He had boxing in his veins as did his five brothers who were all professional fighters but Dave was the best of them all. At the time of his death in 1952 at the age of 26, he held the Australian Middle-weight, light heavy weight and heavy weight titles in a decade career.

The family dynasty boxing connection stretched back to his Grandfather on his mother Mabel Russell's aboriginal mothers side. Bailey Russell had been a noted bare knuckle fighter when boxing was performed on level open ground surrounded by men betting on the sideline. Their father, George Richie was a well known rodeo rider and timber cutter of mixed Aboriginal and of European descent. The brothers fought under the name 'Sands' after 'Snowy' Sands, a local railway guard and boxing fan. Known as 'The fighting Sands', they wore green and gold shorts with a white star. The legend was borne but like so many heroes of peace and war soon forgotten. It took until 1998 for Dave Sands to be induced into the International Boxing Hall of fame. On the corner of Glebe Point road and Parramatta road, Glebe there is a plaque to commemorate Dave Sands and not far away in the Redfern, near a Gym (now a bookshop) were he trained when in Sydney, is a lane way called 'Dave Sands.'

There was another Australian legend prior to Dave Sands who rose to fame and died broke and broken. He too was the a legendary boxer- the famous aboriginal born, Ron Richards, was a family friend of my grand father and often stayed with the family in Grafton when on the skids.

Ron Richards grew up in Ipswich Queensland in an Aboriginal Presbyterian mission, the son of Aboriginal parents Richard Richards, fencer and his aboriginal wife Florence nee Thompson. Ron had a basic education at the local state school but by 14 began timber cutting with his father and became a superb axeman. He was excepted from the Aboriginal Protection Act (1897) and moved around the district as a share cropper. Ron Richards began boxing at Boonah and Ipswich shows and like Dave Sands grandfather, his father was a bare knock fighter too. Ron at age 20 had a year of brilliant fighting around Gympie and preliminary bouts in Brisbane; in 1932 he knocked out English middleweight Joey Simmons. He became state middleweight champion. Queensland's became "crazy" over his counter-punching technique, style and physique. Her earned good money for boxing in those days and invested his earnings into four houses with one for his family. As all offers to fight overseas fell through, his finances dwindled as mismanagement plagued his career and he was exploited. During the 1930s he fought 76 opponent in 142 fights and drew large crowds.

Richards discontent with boxing management was evident as the outcomes of his fights become more unpredictable. Sometimes he outboxed opponents when promoters expected a knockout. Yet he fought hard, although his managers often accepted fights against boxers a stone or more heavier. Gambling damaged his career and his reputation and he was perceived by then a 'temperamental' boxer who sometimes experienced 'unaccountable lapse' in form. After his wife died of tuberculosis in 1937, his career direction and his financial affairs were in chaos. By 1940 Richards was unfit and drank heavily. Uncharacteristically he asked for postponements and broke commitments in boxing and to his family. His second wife Colleen Boyle, an Irish immigrant, tried in vain to manage his finances. By 1945 he was outpointed by men he had previously beaten. After a lucrative career Richards had nothing by 1946. The native affairs branch of the Queensland Department of health and Home Affairs was requested to place him under its jurisdiction when police in Sydney charged him with vagrancy in May 1947. Classified as a 'half caste', he was incarcerated at Woorabinda Aboriginal settlement but was released after three years to look for work in Brisbane. Richards returned to Sydney briefly, was arrested for drunkenness and vagrancy and, under the provision of the 'Queensland Act,' removed to Palm Island Aboriginal reserve where he spent seventeen years. He worked as a carpenter's labourer and managed a single men's home. He returned to Sydney when his daughter sent news of his estranged wife's illness. Richard's died of a heart attack in Sydney on the 14th January 1967. Survived by his daughter, Richards was buried in Rookwood cemetery. The crowd at his Catholic funeral was almost like a boxing hall of fame. In a society which generally excluded Aboriginals, his popularity and boxing skills stood out as a testimony to his greatness.

Grandfather Barney was also friend with Jimmy Sharman senior as was my Dad, many years later, with the Jimmy Sharman junior. Jimmy Sharman senior was a boxing promotor who hailed from Narellan, New South Wales, one of thirteen children who left school at 12 (1899) and initially took a labouring job on a dairy farm, but soon began fighting in boxing tents at annual district shows. At Campbelltown in 1906 he earning eleven pounds ten shillings in a sideshow fight. Cured of farm work he ran away from home and won himself a reputation as a fighter among the shearers at Cowra district before being sent back home by the police. He took a job at Cataract dam and continued fighting in crudely erected rings with makeshift equipment. A southpaw lightweight with a heavy punch, he claimed to have won all but one of his seventy-eight bouts in the four years of his fighting career. In 1912 a five hundred pound a side fight with Jack Carter at Wagga Wagga, about which conflicting accounts are given, boosted his reputation.

Married that same year, Jimmy became a boxing promoter at the Star Theatre Temora before fulfilling a long standing ambition to run his own tent show. The Sharman Troupe took to the roads of the Riverina area and by 1915 was well established at agricultural shows. Jimmy's gravel voiced cry of " Who'll take a glove?" above the crowds that flocked to his boxing troupe tent became his trademark. Boxing troupes, or tent boxing circuses, we're at their prime in the beginning of the 19th Century. An ensemble of professional fighters would follow carnivals across Australia, where boxing tents would be the main stage fo open fights with local competitors accepting a fight for the five pound prize money if they won. Sharman's Troupe would stand on a dais lining up across the stage in front of his tent whilst Jimmy would beat a drum and cry out "A round or two for a pound or two, who'll take a glove?"

There was always a local strong lad who would take on one of Jimmy's boxers and the crowd would pay their two bob to enter his big tent to watch the fight. We kids not having two bob to bless ourselves with would sneak in under the covers at the back of the tent to watch the action. The infamous boxing tent of the Sharman troupe attracted a number of Aboriginal boys that looked rough, mean and 'ready to rumble' but more importantly, they were looking for respect, equality and a bit of dough to put in their pockets. Back at a time when the only contact perceived as equal respect between a white fella and a black fella was in a boxing ring meant that boxing tent gave indigenous people a long shot to make a living. Many of the Aboriginal boxers came from Aboriginal missions and would take to fighting in order earn money as there was little work on offer. It was a time of the white Australia policy and many white Australian's saw the aboriginal as inferior. Jimmy Sharman was not one of those and took pride in the disclipine of his troupe around the eastern coast of Australia.

Jimmy travelled for forty years with troupe, initially by train and by the 1930s by motor truck, visiting up to fifty agricultural shows a year, setting up his tent in side-show alley. He insisted on a tight contract with his boxers, prohibited consumption of alcohol by both performers and spectators, discouraged punch-drunk fighters and opposed colour discrimination. He boasted that many Australian champion

began or ended their career in his tent, including Frank Burn (middleweight champion), Harry Mack (featherweight), Mikey Miller (bantam and featherweight), George Cook (heavyweight), Jack Hassen (lightweight) and triple titleholders Billy Grime and Jackie Green. The touring tent boxing circuses showcased the talent, tricks and physical power of young indigenous men hungry for not only the sport but the prize that came too.These troupes saw champions; Lionel Rose, Douglas Nicholls and Tony Mundine get their start. Jimmy Sharman was lightly built with a weather beaten face by the time he was an old man. He remained fit and alert and continued to train every day until his death at age 78 on 18th November 1965. Jimmy's son Jimmy Sharman 11 had taken over the boxing business a decade before. Jimmy Sharman senior had no doubt met my grand father Barney when he was displaying his skills sheering sheep at the local Grafton show and they became the best of friends.

My Grandfather Barney McPhillips was the first man sighted to sheer a sheep on the North Coast at a show and was a renowned horseman, gold miner and cattle teamster on the New England and Liverpool plains in his prime, until he settled down outside of Grafton to farm sheep. He married a local girl Isabelle Cowan, my grandmother, and raised a family of six sons and one daughter and one of those sons was Eric, my father. Dad disliked his home duties after school working the land. His greatest dislike was having to mind the sheep at night to keep dingoes from attacking and killing the flock. Dad excelled at school, was Dux off Grafton High school in his final year and not long after graduation went on to study engineering. He was also an accomplished pianist and swimming champ whilst still in high school. When my grandfather 'Pop' (Barney) died the homestead and land still stood as an asset in the family inheritance. By that time Dad was running his own successful engineering business and refused to take any monies for his share of the property. He left that inheritance to his brothers and sister to share between them. Dad hated that sheep farm so much that he did not want any part of it nor the residue of moneys gained from it sale on Pop's death. My father was on the foundation committee raising funds for the building of the town swimming pool and was a key donor to the local Surf Life saving club. Despite his passion for the ability to run events to raise funds for the pool and provide personal finance to the Surf Club, to my knowledge he only ever took to swimming once and that was when he swam the flood filled river to help save a friends furniture in the 1950 flood.   Apart from that I never witnesses him swim ever again.

My Grandfather Barney and Grandmother Isabelle helped a lot of people during the war years. Apart from Pop's support for Ron Richards, who stayed with my grandparents when he was down and out and residing in Grafton, they helped German Interns during World War 11. In 1939 the Government regulations required 'illegal aliens' to register and limit their travel to between work and home and within a specified distance from the local post office. They had to obtain permission from authorities to travel further or change residence. Both my Grand parents went to bat for two German school teachers who were living in Grafton at the time. They vouched for the German men and both came to live with Pop and Nana (Isabelle) remained teaching locally and became a part of the family.

Nana cooked, washed and cleaned for the men as she did for her two remaining unmarried sons living at home. The German men spent the rest of their natural life living with my grand parents.

I was relating these events to the psychiatrist in vivid recall as I sat with my eyes closed returning to that time in my life when all seemed lost and unreal to me and my soul was empty. It was the event of the Saturday after John's death that I decided I was no longer me, but a manifested 'Me' and I remained that way until my life become real again and I returned to being renewed 'We" instead of the old Me. I had found through much suffering, heartache, loss, pain of depression and alcoholism that I was powerless and that is when I returned to the 'We that is Me upside down.' This 'We' of a Higher Power than myself I embraced unknowingly through my early childhood but all that changed on the Saturday after my Uncle Johns's death.

The psychiatrists had listened patiently to my story thus far but reminded me of his request to recall the earliest most painful experience of my childhood and asked me not to digress from recalling and recounting that event. I scanned my mind again, thinking of the witnessing of my Uncle Johns death, The drowning of my best friend at age 12, the drowning of my Father and the suicide of my son, and returned to the most painful of memories when my life commenced to change forever. It was at dusk on a cool winters afternoon, one week after my Uncle John had died. I was standing near the front gate no more than five years of age, lost and bewildered, looking vacantly at the flower garden bed beside the fence line. The plants were all but finished with little life to be had in the winter of the afternoon of their life and my discontent. I could not tolerate my sadness any longer and turned to walk in the back yard were I had many an enjoyable time with my Uncle John. It was then and there that I created a new image of who I was and what I had to do to survive. It was a false impression of living in the ego of my imaginary new self. It was the strong inner self will that had got me through the next six decades of my life. It worked to serve me well until my life was completely turned upside down in my late fifties and a few years later I returned to the real me. It was then that I recognised that I was not at all alone in the world, that there was a Higher Power within me and We, the Higher Power and myself became me, living in a new world upside down.

I turned my teary eyes to the psychiatrist who looked at me with intensity and asked a revealing question: "On a scale of one to ten, one being the least painful experience of your life ten the most painful experiences you have shared with me over recent weeks where does this one rate?" He repeated:"Consider the number one as being the least painful on the scale and ten being the most painful. Where now on that scale of pain does that event as a small boy rate with you?" I thought for a moment of the life events I had shared with him from John's death to the drowning of my best friend, to the suicide of my son and many other painful experiences.

I thought of the years of life in rehabilitating the thousands of depressions pills taken, the 23 ECT treatments that I had endured over the past decade before I answered. "I reckon right now it rates about 2." The Psychiatrist was surprised and added "and what about the other nine major traumatic experiences you have shared with me over the past weeks. Where do they now rate?" I thought for a moment and scanned them all before answering: " Well, I think they rate about the same, two." He put a hand to his chin and fiddled with his clip board, reread the notes he had taken down during the course of my recalls and replies: "Doug, there is nothing more I can do for you. Do you have a reasonable amount of money to get you though for the foreseeable future?" I replied in the affirmative. "O.K. then I suggest you travel the world, spend up big and get as much sex as you can possibly muster." With that our time together had ceased. I did as he suggested for a time, travelled a lot, did and lot of walking and had my share of women folk too. The advise he suggested did not really work for me when I came to analyse it.

However, the adventures of the long tramps on the Camino de Santiago in Spain, my hiking adventures in Ireland and New Zealand all served to help me with a lotus flower of creative ideas and a spiritual sense that came to be real. The adventures of my past, present and indeed my future have and will continue to serve the greatest of all that one can only hope for, service to those whom I love. In the depth of my heart, a service to my fellow man were ever possible seems to be the hope of my remaining talents to offer, to give to future generations and reason for living and hoping too. The thought of the happiest times of my life always seem to drift back to story telling times and images of my Grandad.

CHAPTER 2.

THE RACONTEUR

Picture a gaunt prospector, face and body drawn in over the last grain of food, sweat dripping from his weather worn brow, swinging his pick and digging deep into the hard earth with all his might, following a gold seem in the hope of the mother lode. Consider the same man sitting short squat and strong in the saddle driving cattle across the Liverpool plains to a loading dock and collecting his well earned cheque for his trouble. Indeed, think of the same man riding once more in the saddle high, cracking his whip as he rounded up ranging cattle high in the New England Ranges for the next muster.   Picture that and you have my Grandad. That very same man who travelled to sheds, a sundowner sheering sheep in the season for a quid and showing his skills as a sheerer at a local agricultural show whilst his long standing friend Jimmy Sharman, the boxing promoter stood outside his tent nearby beating is drum and chanting : "Who'll pick up a glove?" The very same man who told all and sundry of his life experiences as he danced and sang thorough the night tapping to an Irish jig. The old man who told stories of years gone by neatly woven from his experiences over a hard working life, sitting on his verandah in his dotage, smoking the last of his 'roll me owns' and telling us kids the tales. That man was my 'Pop,' my love , Barney McPhillips.

My Grandfather Barney and Gran Nan purchased a home in South Grafton before the beginning of the Second World War. The home thou small was always crowded with people, mainly the family of Dad's brothers and sister, my cousins as kids and two young German 'enemy aliens' who my grandparents had gone to bat for to deter their internment during the war and who remind with the family for the term of their natural life. The daily routine at my grandparents home, more pertinent during the winter months, was to congregate in the small kitchen were a table with chairs and bench box seat with a lid to store fire wood for the fuel stove stood.t. The two brothers of my dad who lived with my parents all their unmarried lives had the duty to chop and carry wood to the kitchen, store in the woodbox, start the fire going in the stove and await their Mum's presence to prepare breakfast.

Apart from bacon and eggs being the stable morning diet, remainders from the previous evening meal were reheated to a high temperature to ensure that any contamination or food poisoning would be avoided. The old fuel stove was built into a wall with chimney much like a fire place and the plates made of cast iron or steel could be removed for cleaning with a steel gadget that hung on the side of the wall with all other cooking implements. I recalled the stove had a huge iron pot with a tap on it and regular pots of tea were made from the boiling hot water. There was also a host of steel pot and pans that hung nearby the stove. The big pot with the a tap also served to provide hot water for washing up after the meal as there was only one tap as far as I recall and it had only cold running water supplied by an outside tank next to the back door and the chook pen. Pop had thought out the logistics of having the water pump from underground bore to the tank nearest to the door, the chooks nearby benefited also for easy of feeding from the kitchen with pollen mixed from his bee hives and other ingredient from the pantry. The excess pollen collected from the hives was mixed with flour, water and some left over seeds or fruit. It was a good source of muesli meal for us and the chooks, particularly when heated up in winter.

The kitchen stove threw out a lot of heat which was great for all to gathered in winter. However, the Grafton summer heat was stifling so we would all congregate then around the large wooden table in the dining area adjacent to the kitchen where most of the eating, talking and card game playing took place. The early morns were occupied with proposed agendas for each family member for the day, listening to the national news on the ABC and 'Blue Hills' radio programme by Gwen Meredith. The series was a daily 15 minute episode of a   story that revolved around 'The Lawson' farming family and lasted from 1949 to 1976 with a total of 5,795 episodes in all it was the longest running radio series ever. Listening to that program was to me mostly boring. Nana meanwhile busied herself with scrubbing down the kitchen bench and dining room table as well as storing the weekly meat quota in the meat safe which hung above the back door. It had a thin gauze wire on every side to ensure adequate cooling and to keep out the flies. There was also an ice chest for keeping food cool and Nana would keep it topped up with tucker from the garden when not preserving fruit in jars, or making jams. Pop had no other animals to care for than the chooks.

I guess Pop had enough of sheep, dogs, horses and cattle in his farming and droving days to last him a life time. Once Pop sat down to have a smoke on that old verandah in that family homestead, us kids would quickly squat at his feet, eager to hear his latest tale. Pop was the greatest of raconteurs and had plenty of material to call upon to tell his tales to us which he had gathered from his colourful life of long gone occupations and experiences. This was when I became acquainted with my cousins, Peter, Neil and Micheline; Uncle Fred McPhillips and Aunty Ethel's children. Uncle Paddy's brood were Max and Kay and like my other cousin Bernie were teenagers then, so they were passed Pop's story telling but I am sure that would have heard all his yarns more than once when they were young nipples too. I recall the morning when some local kids, who had no doubt heard some of Pop's stories before, turned up to join the McPhillips tribe of all hearing ears and seeing eyes. Pop was the Pied Piper of Hamilton in our eyes and his cheerful nature and quick mind had us mesmerised from the moment he began to tell a tale.

On this particular morning he looked at these two ring-ins with a stern countenance and took his pocket knife from his pocket, opened the blade and said forcefully: "I saw you both taking fruit from my trees without asking my permission, is that right?" The two kids no more than six years or so stood with heads lowered and nodded their heads in unison. Once he had their undivided attention and mine he announced: "If I ever catch you doing that again, I will cut you up into tiny pieces, put you in a sack, tie the top and take you down to the river and drown you." Like those other little boys, we never questioned Pop's logic when it come to such serious matters and his fond regard for his fruit trees.

The lemon trees were his most precious fruit and the means of best medicine, save a brandy or two, for everything that he needed for good health. When Pop had a cold he would cut up a lemon, skin and all, and boil the hell out of it, drink the lot and eat the skin. If he had a cut or a bruise, raw lemon juice cured all and he would insist that within a week his ailments would leave him fully recovered. Some how or other this medical marvel with lemons had always seemed to work for Pop. He closed the open blade of his pocket knife that he had pointed at the 'fruit tree thieves' as we sat at his feet on the verandah.

Once more he returned to another of his many a tale. His colourful tales of his time in the saddle rounding up cattle or sheep and of his droving days, time in the boxing ring, tap dancing and doing an irish jig. I witness his agility on his feet when as a little lad I attended Nana and Pop's 50th wedding anniversary. On the night of celebrations he preformed a tap dance with tap shoes and all to show that he still had the flexibility of a young man. It was a Friday night from memory and my Mum sternly reprimanded me for eating a whole heap of cocktail Frankfurts at the celebration table. It was a Catholic tradition not to eat meat on Fridays as it was mortal sin in her eyes as it was with many Catholics of those times. The Local Bishop was in attendance at the celebrations, as he was a good friend of Pop, and he gave me a dispensation on the spot. It was from that day onward that I got great delight eating a meat pie on Fridays and I continued to did that all through my Catholic upbringing. After all I had a permanent dispensation from a Bishop, so who could top that- so to me it was no longer a sin to eat meat on a Friday.

I did make a supreme sacrifice on Good Friday however, as a reminder of Christ death on the cross for our sins. It was the least I could do for the man who forgave me all my sins. "Kyrie Eleison, Christie Eleison." Lord have mercy, Christ have mercy. Pop and the Bishop enjoyed chats over a brandy or two and a cigar. As far as I know thou, Pop never went to Mass as far as I recall but he and the Bishop were great friends. My favourite yarn of Pops was the one he told of his days looking for water during a drought using a water divider. He had used the divining method with two twigs and it was also know historically as a sacred way to find water or metal under the ground. Divining to this day is employed by those who have 'the gift' to locate ground water, buried metal or ores, gemstones, oil, gravesites and many other objects and materials without the use of scientific apparatus. Divining is considered a pseudoscience and there is no evidence that it is any more effective than random chance has a high probability of winding water in a favourable terrain.

It is more coming know in Australia as 'water divining,' whilst in the USA it is called doodle-bugging, particularly when used in search for petroleum or 'water witching' when searching for underground water. The process involves taking a Y- shaped twig or fork called a diving rod - virtues divine were the subject makes unconscious motions allowing the rods to move involuntary to a specific area where the metal or water is buried.

Divining first come to prominence in Germany in the 16th century, when it was used to attempt to find metals under the ground. As early as 1518 Martin Luther listed dowsing as an act that broke the first commandment as it was considered an occultism.

It was enormously popular in a Germany in the 16th century for deep mining technology and any practitioner who had 'the gift' were in high demand throughout Europe and Elizabethan England. It was use effective in Elizabeth's royal mines for calamine at the time and in silver mines in Wales. It was a happy coincidence that in the admirable life of St.Teresa of Spain that in 1568 she was offered a site for a convent but there was no water supply there. Happily, a Friar Antonio came with twig in hand, stopped at a certain spot, appeared to make the sign of the cross with the twig and in her owns words she said : "Really I cannot be sure if it were the sign he made, at any rate he made some movement with the twig and then said 'Dig just here'; they dug, and lo! a plentiful fount of water gushed forth, excellent for drinking, copious for washing and never ran dry." Theresa having not heard of dowsing considered it a miracle. This, I believe, is the first historical reference to dowsing for water. At any rate, Pop considered he had ' the gift' for finding water and times were desperate on the land in drought back then as it is today.

So I guess he resorted to the art of using two twigs to 'dowse' for water on his land. Well as he recounted his experience, he coloured it with style and irish baloney to keep us little ones sitting at his feet all ears, and told of using the twig rods all day and into darkness in a desperate bid to find water. Pop related to us that he had all but given up hope and as it was too far to late to return to the homestead. He resolved to camp for the night and tied his horse to a nearby tree, rolled out swag and blanket for his bed and lit a fire to cook some tucker he carried in his nap sack. Pop reliving the story, picked up two twigs in the garden and demonstrated how he had both twigs in hand the night he camped, when suddenly they began to turn down toward the fire. This was always a tell tale sign of something laying beneath the surface and how good dowsers could feel the pull on the twigs that set alarm bells going in the head. Pop said: "I decided then and there to put out the fire and dig where I had made it to see what lay below." Pop had a pregnant pause for a moments as good raconteurs often do in telling a tail, then he continued: "To my surprise there appeared a large bolder of pure gold ore."

Then Pop's the baloney of the story reached a new dimension. "I dug and dug and could not reach the bottom of this mountain of gold, so I just cut off a piece as a sample to take to a buyer in the morrow to determine the purity of my find."

By this time our overactive minds were in awe of his find but somehow I suspected that he was just making it up. "How did you know it was Gold Pop; it was dark wasn't it when you found it? You would have had trouble seeing it in the dark once the fire was out right?" I reasoned. I could see the glint in his eye as he rolled another 'roll me own,' cleaned out his cigarette holder with the small blade in his pocket knife he had threatened to cut up those kids with, placed the neatly rolled cigarette in the holder and began to smoke. In a slow but contemplative mood he replied."You doubt your old Pop's word boy?" "Well my boy, let me see what I can do about that." He reached deep in his trouser pocket and pulled out an old rag of a handkerchief, unfolded it and low and behold there was a solid piece of gold right there. "This is that piece I just told you about that I had analysed. It's pure 22 karat and worth a fortune and I own a mountain of the stuff." There was no truth in it of course but he always had his ammunition ready to verify any story he told and I always ended up believing him.

My Nana always cooked every meal at Christmas time and the womenfolk of the family helped preparing the table for Christmas lunch. There was every conceivable meat variety for the lunch and stacks of greens, baked potatoes and pumpkin to be had. The whole family seemed to be seated at that big table; including wives and kids. Copious amounts of food and drink, laughter and tears were had at that table in my childhood. I always loved Nana's Christmas puddings best as they were covered in Brandy sauce and the pudding stuffed with silver coin for us kids. I did my best eat at least three plates full just to get more than my share of those precious zacks (5 cent) and trays (three cent) pieces. After dinner was over, the table cleared and out would come the cards. This is when the menfolk played card games- usually crib with a crib board to keep score. Pop would always sit at the head of the table and all the sons including my Father would be roped into playing the games.

You always knew the games were getting serious when Pop would call out to Nana with authority: "Isabelle, bring the brandy bottle." Pop was the only one who was allowed to drink whilst the games were in play. I was later amused in recalling those table games, with my Dad and Uncles, full grown men at the time, jumping to the beck and call of their old father.

My Grandfather Barney (Pop) was not an alcoholic but as it turns out most of his sons who survived him were. There was exceptions maybe, as my Uncle Pat always gave up alcohol and cigarettes for lent, fasting and abstaining from alcohol before Easter. This was not the habit of a full blown alcoholic who never has that sort of control by their own self will. My Uncle Pat always returned to the drinks and cigarettes as soon as the Easter Christian celebrations were over and he continued this ritual for the remainder of life. Uncle Fred was also an exception to the McPhillips rule of alcoholism too and both Uncle Fred and Uncle Pat built their own freehold pubs when in retired and both became quite wealthy out of the Pub game. The pubs were built out of local timber that they cut themselves from the same forest being of the family name "McPhillips."

The rest of the brothers became full-blown alcoholics and died of the disease. My Uncle Jack was put away in a padded cell when the drinking got the better of him, He too was an exception to the rule as he gave up the drink when Nana died. Mick, another brother never made it to alcoholic stage, as he died in a freak accident saving a timber cutter from a falling tree when in his twenties. He put himself on the line to get the man out of the path of the falling tree and was killed by it in the process. It was my parents custom to spend a week every year at Christmas at my Grandparents home and thus I was the only grand kid out of a cluster of cousins who got the most personal attention from Pop. He devoted much time and patients to be with me and gave of himself to guide and protect me, filling my head with wild stories of old and doing his darnedest to entertain me. I remember one Christmas when I was maybe five or six, when he woke me after midnight on Christmas Day to follow Santa Claus. We crawled around the house in the dark with torch in hand looking for clues as too were he was putting out the Christmas gifts. He would lead me into the lounge and whispered that he could see him near the fire place and convinced me in the dim might of the torch that I could see him too, if I looked hard enough. "Look, there he goes. " he said: "See, he has just put the presents at the front of the fire place." And sure enough the gift for the family were there and at the foot of my parents bed too. "Quick Dougie" Pop called, when he distracted me for moment to look at the Christmas gift, he then whispered : "Look, Santa's heading up the Chimney." and he moved stealth like to the fire place with me following closely behind him, quickly stuck his hand up the chimney and with his hand stuck there exclaimed: " I've got him by his beard."

I was all excited but joy turned to disappointment when Pop said: "Dash, he has got away." he said, as he pulled out his hand and showed me that had grabbed some of Santa's beard. In the moonlight of the night that cotton wool he had in hand looked like the real thing. I was completely taken in and wanted to pocket it but Pop said it was a treasure and had to be keep in safe keeping with that piece of gold he had shown me on a previous occasion. I was completely taken in and believed his stories until I reached an age where reason took precedence over my imagination. It was not until after his death in the cleaning out of his bed side draw that the small gold piece and the cotton wool of Santa's beard were again discovered. Pop died one cool evening in the Grafton district hospital in his early seventies. At the time, it had been declared by the family and the medicos that he had not regained consciousness before he died. I pleaded with my Mum and Nana to allow me to visit his bedside one more time to say good bye. I think I prayed deep in side to my God that he would come back to me. Just for a brief moment he did; open his eyes, turned to me and held out his hand to mine. Pop gave me a great big smile before he lapsed back into unconsciousness and parted from this world. Barney McPhillips died that night in peace after a full life and I, his grandson always believed and swear to this day he returned to me for a moment on that fate filled evening, but nobody ever believed me. Nana held on for a number of year after Pop died but when she too died I did not want to go to her funeral. It had been far too painful for me after attending Pop's Mass and grave side service. I can't recall the words of the Bishop in the Mass at the Cathedral, and I never ever returned to his grave, but his majestic imagination still lives on within me an in a sense his stories have influenced my writings too.

Likewise, I never ever made a visit to Nana's grave either but had a timely reminder every year at cracker night. It was her solemn duty ever year to send me a parcel of fire works for the 4th November annual fire works. A few days before the event a parcel of penny bangers, jumping jacks, throw downs, Catherine wheels and sky rockets would arrive by post from her. On the day of the fireworks the whole neighbourhood would be involved. Us kids would collect anything that was ready to be burned and through it on the backyard or neighbours bonfire. Once the sun went down, the bonfire would be lit and kids would be running everywhere letting off crackers, and sending up skyrockets acting them burst into a star of flame in the night sky.

Whilst there were a few singed heads and eyebrows and the occasional fingers burn from holding crackers a little too long after setting them alight, there never was anyone serious burnt or injured to my knowledge. Although you would occasionally hear on the radio were someone lost and eye or got seriously burnt form a bonfire, somewhere in Australia on that night. It was in truth a seriously dangers activity for un-supervised kids to be playing with fire and what were really explosives and it was ultimately banned in Australia. Bonfire night or Empire night as it was known as in my childhood was celebrated but by the end of the 1970s was a thing of the past. The sale of fireworks was considered illegal by then except for the annual events which are done as huge displays in capital cities throughout Australia every heard on New Years Eve. Empire night ended for me in my childhood the year Nana died. My usual parcel of Crackers did not come and it was a timely reminder for me that she also was never to be again in my life. As for my Grand Dad on Mum's side, he never visited very often. He was born here of French Canadian parentage on his fathers side and Irish and German from my Mum's mother side. Raising thirteen children on his own after my Grandmother Mary died; it must have been as difficult task. He was a big strong man and could have followed in his fathers footsteps as rowing sculler. My great Granddad came to Australia as a sculler representing Canada in competition here against our most famous sculler of the time Henry Searle. He was beaten by Searle , met and married a local irish lass Mary McCormack, managed to stay in Australia and that's how Mum's branch of the family tree came about. Searle was our most famous champion oarsman, born and bred in Grafton and took on all the international rowers in his short but brilliant career. Apart from my great grand-dad, he also beat ever established rower in the world including number one ranked American champion William O' Connor on the Themes in England in 1889. He tragically died of typhoid fever three weeks after his return to Australia.

My Grandfather George Cooper, Couv'ee in French, was of mixed blood; French Canadian, French, Irish and German heritage, was too busy working and raising a large family to take time out to train for rowing competitions but he never lost the admiration for his fathers ability.

I recall a family claim to fame when one of my Uncles, George junior was mixing it up with some local lads in a pub. The boys were attempting to bate him having proclaimed "That French Canadian guy who rowed agains Searle, he couldn't row."

My Uncle George junior, in defence of his Grandad, proceeded to clean up the bar taking on all and sundry - he could fist fight very well and there wasn't a man left standing in that bar except my Uncle 'Tar-brush' George. Grandad Cooper was a strict father with his large family and I guess he had to be. He was also an accomplished poet in his time as was my Aunt Angie, a daughter and my Mum's sister. It is strange how in our DNA life repeats our forefathers talents to some degree. I coxed our school first rowing eight, first four and third four in the five years of high school education and two of my sons, Scott and Sam, were accomplished rowers whilst at school . Both boys were pretty good in a fist fight also. Peter, on the other hand, was more accomplished at being a leader, preferring to let Scott and Sam take the sporting glories. He saw the wisdom in guiding others in their chosen Rugby sport rather than being a heavy participant.

My only other inherit claim to fame consisted of one fight against a pro in my single days. It was a challenge I accepted that I lived to regret. I was unfit at the time, smoked and drank heavily and was not really in a a good space to be entering a boxing ring. The guy I fought was the right weight for age but unbeknown to me, he previously won nine professional fights in England. If I had known that before I stepped into the ring that fight would never have taken place. I, of course, had no real ring experience, brawled a bit in pubs prior to that fight but that was it, apart from what Uncle John had taught me. I managed a draw in that fight bout out of sheer will, but I know who really won the fight that night. I was the one with concussion, black eyes and cut lip. Only a foolish alcoholic or head high tackler of a rugby league player would attempt such a feat. I had swelling all over my face and felt like I had been hit by a truck. After that experience I steered clear of fights but did find myself unwittingly in a pub fight or two over the years more often than not inebriated. I always came off second best. Come to think of it, I never ever won in any way as a drinker. The personality changes that I experienced were always unpredictable and I also suffered alcoholic blackouts and would often not be able to recall what had happened on the previous night. This was long before I came to realise I was powerless over alcohol and life itself and headed to the doors of the AA fellowship.

Ashley Kearns live no more than a stones throw away across the street and we employed ourselves making mischief smoking basket cain for cigarettes and jumping off the side of their two level verandah or watching with inquisitive eyes whilst his teenage sister took a bath. We were still far away from the age of reason but our minds were at the ready racing with the prospects of what lay beyond. My immediate neighbours behind our back yard vegetable patch were a German family of some thirteen kids who like Ashley were just a stones throw away. John was in my primary class at school and Roy, a year behind became a good mate. We both played in the winning North Coast Rugby League team and I use to hang out a lot there infatuated with the size of the family and his little sister Jennie who kissed me a lot.

We boys in our primary years enjoy the fun of billy cart racing with our home made contraptions to fly down the steep hill at the front of our homes, but as soon as we reached a knowing age and saw James Dean on screen, we graduated to playing chicken on our pushbikes. More on that later. One of my mates in my early teens was Glenn Owens. His sister Margaret was in a relationship with a young South African Pro Boxing champ by the name of Dickie Williams. Dick arrived in Australia in 1959 to fight our Australian welterweight champion George Barnes. The fight did not take place until February 1960 but Dick arrived after his last fight in the local arena, Durban in November 1958. He had met an attractive white girl Margaret Owens in his travels and he was keen to marry here. A dark man from South Africa was accepted by the Owen's family much like Ron Richard, the Aboriginal boxer was accepted by my grand parents when I was a child. Dick didn't train much over the year prior to the fight with Barnes. Glen and I use to enjoy being around Dick whilst he took it easy at Margaret's parents place. Any training he did consisted of a run and some sparing practice and we got great delight in running with him when he finally got around to getting ready for the fight. Dick had twenty two fights in his career having won six of those by knockout, three by technical knockout (TKO), six on points and three draws. He had only lost one fight and that was by an "in the game" jab to his ribs resulting in a ring side decision against him for the fight.

However, when it came to that fight against our Australian Champion, Dick was no match for our match fit champion. A black South African 178cm tall, a natural athlete, built more like a middle distant runner, considered himself lucky to have a boxing career in his former life, as the tolerance for the black race was worst than the dark years of our 'stolen generation' Australian in the 1950s and work was not easy to come bye, as it bordered on slave labour. George Barnes was 168cm tall, some 10 cm shorter than Dick, and an orthodox boxer, who in his sixty seven bouts career had won twenty two by knock out, five by TKO losing one by TKO, the rest he either won or lost on points. George had seven hundred and seventeen rounds in his career and boxed for fourteen years before becoming a well known professional referee in the early days of T.V. Dick had one hundred and thirty eight bouts in his six years in the ring. Barnes won that fight in February 1960 in a knock out in the thirteenth round. Dick walked away with a fighters 'purse,' it was enough for him to set up his own painting contract business in Canberra. He had won in his mind as the fight was a monitory goal to start a new career with Margaret, his new bride!

Interestingly, George Barnes, who had grown up in the boxing tents at Temora, when Jimmy Sharman was challenging young hopefuls too 'take up a glove," ended his fighting career with four losses in a row after fighting Dickie Williams. At last count George Barnes was referee matches some where in heaven and Dickie Williams is painting heavenly waiting rooms for the boxers yet to arrive there. This was long before I was married, raise a family, divorced, lost all I cared about including most of my hard earned possessions. This was long before I discovered I could write poetry and sing my own songs and made some reasonable monies writing short stories. Yes, I had inherited the poetic spirit of my old grandad embedded in my DNA on the one hand and the ability to be a raconteur from the other. God bless

them in the spirit world for their contribution to my life and my now chosen path as writer and events promoter. In the dead of night I sometimes feel them close by and hear their whispering imparting more creative thought to me through the thin vail between my remaining life and their world of the spirit. It was the influences of old Barney "Pop," on that verandah in South Grafton when as an impressionable child he told me stories of the bush that finally steered me on the course of being in the bush with my Uncle Fred.

He was a tree feller in the Wild New England Ranges and I loved him a great deal, especially because he drove a bulldozer. He was not my Dads brother Fred but my Mum's sister's husband. He was the one, other than my " Pop" that I could get really close too as he knew like 'Pop' how to give his full attention to a little boys cautious mind. In the far of hills of the New England rangers I went camping out with Uncle Fred when I was only 5 years of age. He was a timber getter and apart from his ability in driving a bull dozer to knock down trees in the forest he was a crack shot with a rifle. He become the New South Wales champion small bore rifle champion when I was in my teens. In my camp out with him he used a 303 short magazine service rifle which he probably got from military service after WW11. It may have been in the first or second night of our campout. We were just about to go to bed when we heard a series of dingo howls nearby. Looking into the bush I could see the bright shining eyes off a pack of dingoes attracted to the smell of the remaining food in the pan. Uncle Fred raised the 303 and fired it in to the air above his head. The crack and echo seems to ring for ages and the dingoes scattered. They returned more than once to howl nearby but Uncle Fred keep the fire up all night and they didn't venture into our tent. My Uncle Fred had taught me to shot and I was only five at the time. Sitting back in bush location one morning he handed me his rifle and I did my best to raise up the barrel and tuck the butt into my shoulder. Uncle drew the bolt back and forth and a long nose bullet entered the chamber from the inventory in the magazine. He had me cock the trigger with my index fingered put his hand under the barrel to raise it at a very large magpie sitting on a high branch in a not too distant tree. He just said. "Hold your breath, aim at the birds chest, pull the butt tight to your shoulder and squeeze the trigger. The jolt to my shoulder was a sudden hit, the noise of the crack from the gun deafening and the bird fell silently to the ground. I felt elated but at the same time like an assassin. The days in the bush were always long, busy and exciting for me.

We always rose from the tent before dawn and Uncle Fred would light the fire, boil the billy and we would commence the day with tea and cold damper he kept in a tin in the tent, tucked away from bush creatures or anythings that come bumping in the night. At sun up we were up on the bulldozer, me seated on his knee all day for safety, whilst he proceeded to push down chosen trees with the blade of the bulldozer. Then later, I would sit on the big blade and watch him cut off all the limbs with an axe.

I sometimes listen for the echo of the axe through the mist of my mind in a silent moment but its no longer there, just the noise of passing cars on a busy city street or the far of sound of a fire engine or ambulance on the way to a nearby hospital were I now live. Like all the rest of the madding crowds of commuters and us side walk cafe coffee drinkers watching the world go by, we have our tales to tell.

Once Uncle Fred had felled and cleared the tree with the axe and cut of its base with a saw, he attached it to the bulldozer and dragged it to a bush track for collection by the truck drivers with trailers who would haul the load off the mountain side to one of the many timber mills that dotted the boundaries of the many little towns along the Mid North coast of New South Wales. Life was simple but physically tough for the working men of the first decade after the second world war. Timber getting employed the vast majority of men among that coastline when I was a boy and the truck drivers were a key part of the industry. When Uncle Fred had secured enough logs for a truck load, we would have a 'smoko' whilst waiting for the first of the trucks. Some bush nuts, a bit more damper and maybe a banana or some bush berries I and another cuppa.

The bulldozer blade was used to lift and push each log into place before the load was tied down. This consisted of a number of heavy chains dragged by hand by the drivers and thrown over the load of logs and tied down each side of the trailer with a metal bracket and bolt arrangement to restrict the movement of logs on the long drive down the mountain side to the main road to the mills. I had attempted this work once in my single days. Out at 5.a.m. and on board the truck, into the forest by 7 am, loaded and unloaded by 10 am and straight to the pub to drink a couple of schooners. In the middle of summer it is no big issue to drink two large beers straight down after such physical activity. The trucks would return to the forest mid afternoon for one more load and my then Uncle Fred would have another great pile of logs laid out on the side of the track for the loading. Night meal by the fire with Uncle Fred usually consisted of cooked fish and some raw vegetable from his veggie garden out the back of his log cabin garden in Nymboida. The township comprised a few timber cabins, a trading post and not much else. It was a small village near the river up their north of Grafton on the coast. The fish we ate at our sitting was caught from that river higher up in the river valley.

The Nymboida river is the longest whitewater river in Australia. These days its a great place for canoeing, rafting and swimming. However, back in uncle Fred's day it was more for fishing, and the river ran about 1300 metres below our camp sight. It was no mean feat to climb down to catch fish in the pond near the river but Uncle Fred always seem to come back with something to eat- Bass, trout or perch fish were the order of the day. Those were the days before the the word 'child abuse' was ever heard of. I always felt safe with my Uncle Fred but fell out of favour with him in my adult years. We had an argument and I lost my cool with him and verbally abused him over a family matter I though he had no business interfering in. By speaking out rashly, the ability to be fair minded was lost on the spot. I was angry with him and when I am angry it is always self centred. I was probably in the wrong when I look back in hindsight, but it is too late when the person you need to make amends too is dead and gone. I hope somewhere in the universe of the spirit that Uncle Fred is listening and can accept my humble apology for my lack of self control on that occasion and to let him know that I was in the wrong.

Those good old days are but distant memories of bush adventure and story telling too. My love of the bush continues as it did back then. My pre teen years were often spent with mates wondering around snake infested swamps, barefooted, foolhardy brave. Faces of my childhood friends come floating back now. Climbing trees with Des to gather yet another speckled egg from a birds nest for our collection, trapping a variety of birds with home made trap for our enjoyment, killing lizards with our pocket knives or equally carving a bow and arrow or making a slingshot shanghai for our arsenal of weapons of mass destruction. We did not see the harm in killing a few frogs, birds, lizards or snakes back then. In this day and age I am appalled at our small child behaviour in that regard. They were certainly times of grand adventure and simplicity. We were free and we felt free and our parents did seem to worry too much about our whereabouts. At weekend we were out and about at dawn and the only instruction was to be home by nightfall.

Discipline when it came was strict and we learn not to rock the boat. We had out household chores to do and the usual extras like mowing the lawn or washing Dad's car. Saturdays mornings once the tasks were completed we were free to roam to the bush, the beach or head of to the pictures. The local movie theatre had Saturday afternoon matinees.

Myself and my mates heading to Mick's Greek cafe for a milk shake to sip on and some Jaffas to role down the aisles to the aboriginal kids in the front row. They were mates we sat with in class, played football with and went bush with too, but we were not allowed to sit with them in respectable public places. We did not see the prejudice and double standards that the community dictated at the time. It was what it was and we learnt not to question because we never ever got a straight answer. All Mum ever worried about in that regard was that I didn't marry a black when I grew up!

The movies were a grand escape from the reality of our existence. Our heroes on the silver screen came from the artificial world of Hollywood and we were in awe. The afternoon in front of the screen was a long one as we got a treat of the weekly series of western good guys versing the bad, a couple of cartoons, advance advert screens of up and coming movies attractions and two full feature movies. The whole experience cost two and six. i.e. two shillings and sixpence or the equivalent of twenty five cents in todays currency not counting inflation. The heroes of the silver screen we mimicked as they epitomised what we thought real men should be. That is until along came James Dean and the streaks of my rebellious youth began to emerge.

So many wild and potentially dangerous living events I some how survived through living in that little village on the Mid North Coast. Many of my childhood friends didn't survive thou and and I have lost them all somehow along the way. Mimicking James Dean in 'Rebel without a Cause,' we lads played 'chicken' on our push-bikes and later in our motor cars. The game of chicken emerged in America and was a form of brinkmanship. It was initially played by choosing a long straight stretch of road with a white line down the middle, like any highway, starting two fast cars towards each other from the opposite direction. As they approached each other at high speed, mutual destruction become more imminent. If one of them swerved, as they passed each other they turned their heads, shouting 'Chicken.' That brief lack of concentration at high speed with the cars almost touching often caused one of the cars to swerve thus declaring the looser and object of contempt. As was played by irresponsible boys, this game was considered decadent and immoral in 1950s America, though only the players were at risk.

In the movie 'Rebel without a Cause' Jim Stark (James Dean) and John 'Plato' Crawford (Sal Mineo) played a game off chicken, racing headlong towards a cliff. The chicken game actors jump out of the cars just before it went over the cliff. The first to jump out was christian 'Chicken.' 'Plato' dies when his coat sleeve gets caught in the door handle of his car and he goes over the cliff,Jim Stark (Dean) jumps out in time and is tagged with ' Chicken.' The troubled teenage youth of James Dean in this movie and in all his performances, made him a hero to look up to for us troubled youth of the 1950s. Tragically Dean died in a car crash driving his racing Porsche which he named the 'Little bastard' and had it painted under the car's emblem. He was killed instantly along with his passenger in Cholame, California September 1955, he was 24. Dean received a posthumous Academy Award nomination and is the only actor ever to receive two posthumous acting nominations. He died before the film was released. Tragically Sal Mineo at age 37, was murdered in the alley behind his apartment block in Hollywood in 1976, and the female actress of the Film, Natalie Wood, age 43, tragically and mysteriously drowned with undetermined facts still surrounding the death, in November 1981.

My risk taking continued right up to into my twenties in cars continued but I was blessed, despite repeated car crashes, survived to tell the tail. Perhaps the riskiest thing I have ever done was back in my late 20s, when I climbed the mast of a Russian ship between Perth and Singapore. We were six days into a cyclone, and a Dutch photographer and I decided to take a photo of the ships bow disappearing into an oncoming wave. If I had not been as drunk as skunk at the time, I probably would not have attempted it. The last big risk I took in my sober senior years was climbing a volcano in New Zealand in 2017 and falling at 1640 metre up. I escaped any serious injury that day but had three falls in all of that mountain. It is the hardest walking with a fullback pack that I have ever done in my life and I have remained shy of returning to another climb like that since. My girth is getting fat already so I guess sit here now I'm thinking it won't be long before I set out on another fool hardy venture. It seems to be in my nature to eat too much sugar foods and then have to go and sweat its out on some come by chance trail. Apart from the boys games, the change to win the heart of a a favoured girl was ever present when we reached an age of our hormones going haywire.

The senior girls were too busy looking at themselves in the mirror, putting on lipstick and painting their nails to be interested in young boys. However, the not yet teenage girls were always keen to have a kiss or two.

My greatest childhood sweetheart was Robyn the bakers daughter. My heart swooned and jumped a beat every time I saw her. I use to write her love notes at school and put them down the tube of her pushbike handlebars when ever the opportunity arose. It became a ritual once she cottoned on to what I was up too. I eventually won her over with a cuddle or two high up on top of the bags of flour her father kept in his bakery storehouse. There were other, too numerous to mention, all were cute at the time, but no one rated as highly as Robyn did in my pure innocence of boyhood ! I did return back to the old primary school some 20 years ago for a fiftieth reunion of those still alive who attended the school during the decade of the 1950s. Those who survived all met in the local RSL club for a get together after checking out our school classes. I had attended from kindergarten to year seven at that school and had some nostalgic recall. The teachers were all Sisters of Mercy back then and they ruled us by constant use of the cain as the weapon for moral discipline and learning spiritual lessons. The place was packed with the old and the not so; a sea of grey headed old folk and a few bald heads like mine there too.

The whole school consisted of three class rooms in all. One for the kids from kindergarten to year four. Years five and six were in the next room, and the senior years seven to intermediate students had the end room. It was a mighty effort for one nun to teach a whole room of kids; three teachers in all teaching a whole school from start until graduation of the Intermediate. The constant canings, the duties of cleaning the toilets every Friday, washing out the ink wells at the end of the day and keeping the school yard clean fell on us boys. I could well have done without all of it as part of my education. The plus side of a religious education of Christian principles and a head down and bum up work approach didn't do me much harm thou, when I look back on it all in retrospect.

The biggest fight of my primary years broke out on a hot summers afternoon whilst playing cricket on midweek sports afternoon. I was in the outer field at the boundary with a steep gully drop directly behind me and was being baited by a young in fielder by the name of George Mulder.   George's father had won the heavyweight 1939 Holland amateur boxing title and was runner up in the competition in 1940. George Mulder senior had nine fights in all during the war years winning one on points and two by TKO. I was not about to get into a big scrap with his son.

George Senior had made his way to Australia in 1955 and was knocked out by Alfie Sands, Dave's brother, in a a professional fight in February that year. Money was on the table for his fight against Richie Sands, another of the 'Fighting Sands' brothers and won that fight by KO in October that same year. He settled in my home town of Macksville, working at the local meat works to raise his young family here. Like so many a migrant families in those early years after WW11 who came to Australia, they stayed. George was roped into another fight five years later against Geoff Kennett a young man half George's age at the time. George lost that fight on points and hung up his gloves after that. Now back to my fight with his son George Junior.

I never did much like playing cricket and always thought it a slow and boring game. On the day in question I had a bumper headache and didn't much feel like playing cricket but one did what the Sister's of No Mercy told us to do back then, no ques-tions asked. I recall that George had stood behind me attempting to move me out of the way and my Irish reached boiling point. He gave me a shove and I turned and push him hard and he lost his footing on the embankment. As he fell over that gully, I took the opportunity to dived on top of him and belted the living daylights out of him. He lay there with broken glasses in hand and bloodied nose as I turned to climb the embankment. Out of nowhere, his friend 'Fighting' Foley was on top of me and pounded me so hard in the face and in the head I didn't know what hit me. The outcome of that fight was my being concussed, delirious for days and con-fined to bed until I fully recovered. Foley came from a large poor family and did not own a pair of shoes, his clothing was hand me downs from elder siblings and he learnt early that life was tough and so was he when it came to dishing out punishment . When I awoke from my delirium a good class mate and fellow football team member was seated beside my bed concerned probably more for the football season ahead than my current sorry state. My friend Roy's words echoed in my ears. "Will you be o.k. for the football season, we need you mate."

I may not have been a grand boxer, but I was not a bad little rugby league player back then. Although I suffered concussion twice more in my primary school football career, I managed to Captain an inter school football season competition that took out the premiership. It was the 5 stone 7 pound B primary Rugby League North Coast football competition. We played all the schools that stretched from Coffs Harbour in the North to as far south as Taree. The competition took on all public and Catholic schools in the various districts and was sponsored and run by the NSW Country Rugby League. One of the hardest matches we played was the kids from Burnt Bridge Aboriginal home, near Kempsey. They were children of the 'stolen generation' and we had to take off our football boots to play them barefooted as they had no football boots nor shoes to wear for that matter. As luck would have it half our team were Aboriginal and they were the back line and us white kids were the 'pigs' (front line). The rules were more open then and there was more open play and our back line was fast. Michael Bryant, was a classic back who later played for Manly Club in the years that Bob Fulton was at his career best. Michael was the first Aboriginal to pass the N.S.W. leaving certificate and later became a school teacher. The other Aboriginal boys were the Mumbler brothers who were quick too. Harry Mumbler and another brother won bursaries to St. John's college Woodlawn, near Lismore, to finish their senior years. Paul Mumbler, a friend and football mate of mine, joined the Public service in the-PMG Department in Sydney when he left school.

Another of the talented players was Garry Williams who became a lawyer in his latter years and to the present day teachers the local Aboriginal language to black kids on the Nambucca and is currently a local radio announcer. The other quick as greased lightning indigenous player was 'Cyclone' Edwards who became a local fisherman at last count. Also Donovans boys were good league players too but their real claim to fame was more when they received their Bronze Medals as members of the local surf lifesavings club and were written up as the Aboriginal squad in the paper. I lost track of them all with the exception of Mick Bryant and Garry Williams of whom I have had the good fortune to meet again in my latter years. It was Michael 'Cactus' Moran who taught most of these boys to swim and surf.. He is credited as founding the 'nippers' surf life savings association which he began with us kids at our favourite beach, Scott's Head.

CHAPTER 3.

THE LEARNING CURVE

Where it acme to rugby league though, it was Par Rankin who taught us the skills and Sister Emanuel who indoctrinate the will to win. Pat Rankin, who at the end of his football career with St. George club was contracted by the local Rugby league to coach the team.

It was common practice in those days, when a footballers career was over in Sydney they usually ended up in a country town, as a player coach. The pay was not too great but they always seemed to score a job with the local council to supplement meagre earnings from the club. It was not like the current day of professional footballers at career end the greats left without any payout and headed bush to find a job. They usually did road work which of course helped with their fitness. Throwing up full garbage bins of rubbish on moving trucks for three days a week, clearing land, painting and doing road work was labour intensive and strengthening. These retired ex Sydney players still had it in them into their thirties to play a level of football in the country that more than matched the locals. They all took on the job of player coach and when that career ended usually found work locally in a business or started their own, happy to stay in the country rather than return to the big smoke.

Pat Rankin went a step further, he wanted to help school kids in his spare time by coaching Rugby league and that's who honed our football skills. I was one of the smallest kids in our team having two talents as a player; I could win the ball more times than not as a hooker and was quick to get to the ball in the dummy half position. Perhaps I should have been a half back but it was the fact that I could win scrums that put me in the hot seat as the hooker. My far too many hits to the head told me in my latter years that I should have been the ball boy or a linesman. Pat picked all three teams for our knockout competition and asked the five stone seven pound team who should be the Captain for the knock out competition. I immediately put up my hand and said "Me, Mr Rankin." Pat with a wiry smiled said "And why you Doug?" I quick as a flash replied. "Well, if we win the competition, my Dad is going to donate a trophy to the school."I got the job and then went home to tell my father that I had been appointed Captain and the Nuns expected him to donate a trophy to the school in the event that we won the competition.

Dad being a mathematician considered the odds to be in his favour, accepted the commitment and to his surprise we won the seasons event. Dad true to his word donated the trophy but I kept it on my mantle piece and nothing more was said about it. My good mates in that team, Kevin, Greg and Roy must have thought me a little shit but they did not say a thing about the trophy or my status as Captain, they had the good sense not to rock the boat.

Kevin was the brother like friend I was born next too in the local hospital and he was the one that drowned when he was at the beach with Greg and I and it was not long after that I was sent off to boarding school. In the Rugby league juniors you had to weigh in before the match to see if you made the weight or were two heavy to play. In my case I played hooker for three grades and I made the weight by taking out the padding on my shorts and filling them with rocks before I stepped on the scales at weigh in. I had one game in open play but got knocked pretty badly in a tackle and only played half that game. I was there to win the ball for all teams and I did that more times than not. I learn to tackle as best as I could around the backside and slipped down the legs hanging on for dear life. I knew that it didn't matter how big the opposition player was he could not run without legs. Mostly, I let most tackles go for the bigger team players who could out gun me in tackling.

Sister Emanuel was our coach when Pat Rankin wasn't there and when we won the final against the toughest match of our tournaments she was there as observer. It was against the local public school and there was as much grudge against a strong opposition as there was Protestant against Catholic. We won that match 3-0 and Sister Emanuel, the assistant coach on the sideline asked us to all on that Saturday grand final to go back to the school for our reward. Apparently one of our players had punched another kid in the opposition team in a scrum and she had spotted it. It was my best mate Kevin and she called him out for unsportsmanlike like tactics. We were all given a lecture and knelt down and we copped six cuts of the cain across both hands for our reward. I was glad I kept that trophy. I guess looking back in hindsight, the older I get the better I thought I was as a player, but in reality I only had those two basic football skills. To many dizzy spells and concussions ruined any chance of me progressing up the ranks when I went into high school as I was at my tallest at age 13 and never grew an inch since, standing only at five foot six and three quarters. Notice how short ass kids like me get our correct height measurement and always seek to be the leaders over men of great stature.

At boarding school we played Rugby Union and I was at my tallest height when I arrived at Joey's, the most famous Rugby football school in the GPS competition. I went o.k. in my first year at boarding school in Rugby but as boys outgrew me in senior years, I slipped down the pecking order. The C grade was the best I reached but played most of my time in the D grade. There were nine grades in all and I was heading more towards the bottom than the top. At the lower grade I could still win the ball in the scrums and got great delight on being first on a loose ball. I had a technique of diving on the ball rolling over it and using my body as a shield to stop the opposing team from getting to the ball. I copped a lot of kicks in the back but never got hurt by the grace of God I now believe.

In senior football I learnt to play dirty when I met a hooker who could outclass me. A punch in the nose or a finger in an eye usually gave me an advantage for the next scrum. It was as simple as releasing one hand from my props shoulder and delivering an upper cut or an eye gouge. This was my logic never dreaming that the opposing hooker might repay me the same way too. It never happened so I was lucky in that regard. Another great character of my youth was a local timber worker. He was an al round sportsman axeman and League player too. Alex 'Slugger' Cooper may have been a distant relative of the family but no correspondence is entered into in that regard. The 'Slugger' as his nickname suggested was pretty good with his fist. More than that, he was a colourful character when I was in my teens and many a story related about him rang true.

Slugger was a local timber getter, and like most of the timber haulers and milk lorries in the area, he always had his truck serviced by Eric McPhillips, the known genius of truck engineers on the mid North Coast. ""Chunder the wonder" Dad was known by his clients and friends alike but I never did find out how he got that name. The trouble was 'Slugger' just kept on working until the truck and its tyres could take no more. He would then limp it into town and it would be in Dad's hands for the next few days for motor overhaul, new bearings, new belts, nuts and bolts and new tyres all round, from cabin to trailer. The bill would always be a big one, due to the fact that 'The Slugger' never had his truck serviced nor tyres replaced until the motor played up and the tyres were bald.

Sluggers philosophy when it came to trucks was a simple belief: "A White truck is like the mighty jeep, it keeps on going from sun up to sun down, it just keeps going and going like clock work." Slugger would make such claims once 'the White' was back on the road but good as his word he always paid his repair bills to Dad, as soon as he got his next timber hauling cheque.

Often local crop grower customers would leave a basket of fruit or a water melon as a token of appreciation for a job well done by my father and his engineers. However Slugger was about, there was no gift left to be had by the family. I once witnessed him pick up a saw from a mechanic's tool box and use it to cut up a water-melon that was left there for the family. Slugger didn't hesitate, he ate the lot in one sitting, then marched across the road to a near by cafe to consume a full bottle of cordial whilst he was waiting for his truck. It was breakfast time and whilst most dignified customers settled for a cup of tea and some toast, the Slugger settled for water melon and cordial! On a visit to the Royal Easter Show in Sydney one year, the tale was told by Slugger to Dad whilst he was filling in time waiting on his truck to be serviced. Apparently he had dressed up in a suit of sorts with a white shirt on and big bright yellow coloured wide tie.

Whilst waiting to attend the Australian Championship wood chop events, he went and purchased an ice cream. Walking towards the arena where the wood chops were held he was confronted by a group of young thugs who began to shove at him. The leader of the pack pushed the ice cream into Sluggers face and the milky cream spread all over his face. Slugger just kept on smiling, eating his ice cream and licking his mouth and lips consuming the messy ingredient. It did not seem to trouble him one bit that these clowns attempting to make fun at his expense. My father later that day related the story to me. Apparently Slugger saw red when the gang leader attempted to whip Sluggers face with his fancy yellow tie. He had said to my Father. "It was like hitting the starter motor on 'the White', it took just one go.." It was reported in the news that the ring leader had dropped like a stone on the spot when Slugger clobbered him and his dingo mates just scattered and ran like all hell from the scene. Slugger was not interested in talking to the cops, he was only interested in getting to the wood chop to see the champions in action.

When the main event was to begin one of the wood chop contestants had hurt himself and could not make it to the block, so the promoters to encourage crowd interest invited any member of the audience to participate as a challenge to the champs. Slugger made his way down from the grandstand, took off his coat and tie, picked up the nearest axe he could find and got on the block against the best of Champions. It was a fast and furious race to see who could chop through a block tree stump the fastest and Slugger left them all still chopping away as he put on his coat and tie and left the Stadium. He had beaten the best but was not looking for any accolades nor money, he just wanted to prove that the was as good as the best of them and he was. Other stories abound of Sluggers encounter with big George, a local hero during a grand final football match between Nambucca Heads and Coffs Harbour. Apparently they stood toe to toe in the midst off the field in the middle of the game and slugged it out. It took quite a while for both men to back down before the referee got the match under control again. Like so many starved for news journalists seeking a god story, the incident made the local paper. The best of stories to my mind was the time Slugger and a mate had been cutting sleepers up in the 'horse shoe;' a nearby mountain cutting were timber getters use to cut and hauling time to a local mill. The weather had turned fowl around ten, so Slugger and his mate settled for a few drinks in the pub. They spent most of the day their propping up the bar and by late afternoon having had their fill, decided to head on home.

Along the Pacific Highway, between Macksville and Nambucca Heads, Slugger and his offsider began to argue over who was the best with a chain saw. Slugger announced that there was only one way to settle the matter, so stopping the truck, proceeded to unloaded the chain saws and handed his mate one. The challenge was to see who could cut down seven guide posted on either side of the Pacific highway. It was decided who ever did this the fastest was to be considered the better man, thus settling the matter. They both agreed and lined up on either side of the road started the chain saws and began to run to the nearest guide post proceeding to cut them down. The guide post were separated some 100 or more meters apart along the highway. Both men full of alcoholic vigour quickly ran the distant in the rain, chain saw in full flight and cut down guide post after guide post until the seven were completely flattened. Slugger won that event and word got around as to what they had done.

The local police went quiet on the subjects as every one loved the Slugger as a larrikin, a timber getter and a good sportsman. It took the department of main roads about six months to replace those guide posts with steel ones. I guess travellers on the highway wondered why there were timber guide post all the way from Sydney to Brisbane but just outside of the township of Macksville there were seven steel posts on both sides of the road!

When Dad sold his truck business, Slugger started his own maintenance and haulage at Urunga township. He had gained the wisdom by then to maintain his own trucks. Another character of my childhood was my cousin Max McPhillips. He once tried to teach me to swim by throwing me in the deep end of the Grafton swimming pool. I kept taking in water in my attempt to survive. Once he realised That I was not going to 'teach myself' the fine art of staying afloat he dragged my water logged body from the water. I reckoned with the amount of chlorine I swallowed that day, I was cured for life from any tummy infections. it was not until my teens before I could swim a length of a swimming pool but I did learn early to dog paddle and catch waves. I mastered the fine art of wave catching quite young in my life, having figured if I missed a wave I could catch the next one that came along. I had little fear of the ocean then and enjoyed the beach and the beach sprints as junior participant in the local surf carnivals. However, it took me until my teen before I qualified for my water safety certificate and could (perhaps) save someone in difficulty in deep water. More than likely it would be my own self that I would need to save thou. Tragically, my best mate drowned when but a boy and my fathers' freak accidental death by drowning even also had me cautious when it came to swimming. Dad was a proficient swimmer but his drowning left me with a healthy respect for swimming in the sea, a river or indeed a swimming pool.

Everyone looks forward to the July Racing carnival in Grafton as punters and bookies alike have done since its inception. The Schaffer House Museum is no exception as they delve into their extensive collection of memorabilia to showcase all things racing. Visitors and locals enjoy the range of displays curated by the Clarence River Historical Society. Items of interest include racing trophies that date back to 1880 including the prestigious Grafton Cup, Clarence River Jockey Club race books that date back to 1096 and members badges to 1923.

There are photos past winners, displays of horse shoes, spurs and stirrups back to 1881 and vintage clothing, possibly worn to the race carnival throughout the museums rooms. On the quirkier front there is the rug worn by Ramoenie Handicap winner for 2007 and 2008, The Jackal. The horse was ridden to victory by champion jockey Robert Thompson on both occasions. There is also the bookmaker set up with the original Max McPhillips tote and stand and his Bookie's bag with a life like image of Max and a punter dressed up ready to hand over some of his cash. My Cousin Max was a local and well known racing identity on the North Coast of New South Wales. Max started his 'career' in racing, when as a school boy at Woodland College, Lismore, he began to run an illegal book making set up which extended to his school holidays in Grafton and came to the notice of the police. This did not deter Max who continued his activity under the nose of the local cops, who for some unknown reason, turned a blind eye to his activity. Max attended Armidale teachers college after leaving school and taught primary school kids in isolated villages, often arriving at school, like the kids on horseback. He kept up his bookie activities on the side and by the time he had advanced in education graduating to teaching High School year twelve students in Mathematics and English. He focused his efforts there on those who were less fortunate. Max never gave up his activities as a bookie and at his career teaching height he took long service lead for three months to get his racing book records in order.

Max was the local bookie, owned or had interest all bookies from Coffs Harbour to the Gold Coast, taking interstate bets on the trots. He was awfully fledged make of money through gaming. Every weekend he announced at the Dogs in Grafton on Saturday night after back to back horse racing meetings during the day. Max made a lot of money from racing and was a millionaire in his own right and also owned a lot of houses as investment properties too. He was a good all round sportsman in his youth and was picked to play for Country verses City in Rugby League in his prime but due to a knee injury he could not play. My cousin was a character that everybody loved and was a hell of a tormenter too. He had some funny sayings like: "That kid is so thick, he needs all his fingers and toes to count to 11." When people turn their back on him he would announce: "They will miss me when I'm gone." He called me once to discuss investing in the stock market with the words: "I think I'll tumble into a few shares, what do you reckon?" Max was always tumbling into something.

Max use to give me a hard time in my early primary school years about girls, until one day I turned on him and told him his tormenting didn't work as I had no issue on that front anymore. Max died young, age 56 form a heart condition which was no doubt the aftermath of his hard work load but more than likely his habit of heavy cigarette smoking. At his funeral there was a guard of honour by the Primary school and High School students he taught and a special one by the Police force. He was A greatly loved larrikin with kind heart.

Max's sister Kay was always favourite of mine as a child and in my early single days in Sydney too. Kay had a close affinity with my father as a teenager and when home form boarding school at St.Mary's in Lismore, stayed with my family frequently and when she was there she was like an old sister. She was always very artistic and created signage for Dads mechanic repair business that stood for years as a mural on the wall in the showroom. One such sign featured a young man standing next to his car , putting on engagement ring on his future wife finger. The caption read: "When you're in love with your car, become engaged to our friendly service." Dad was often travelling with the Macksville Gift professional athletics committee and Kay would tag along with the men. She seem to have a natural ability to make men feel at ease in her company. The story goes that they were all staying at the Gilgandra hotel for their Athletics Gift Carnival. Meeting at breakfast, Kay had asked for a glass of water and remarked to the waitress, that the water had a strange taste. The waitress replied that it was bore water from under the ground and Kay quickly retorted: "Gosh, you sure don't waste much of the pig around here do you." She was always quick and we enjoyed drinking together too. Kay later held a key role in The Engineering Department of the PMG were I work with her for three years. She handled that role without the utmost confidence and ability. The men folk did exactly what they were told to do when Kay gabble a command. On another occasion, the members of the Macksville Gift attended the Gunnedah Gift; Trevor Owens, Glenn's elder brother started the races with a sawn-off shotgun. The gun second barrel was only used when a runner jumped the mark in the race and Trevor would pull the trigger on the second trigger total the runners back to do a restart. It was essential to have a correct start, as not to give advantage to any runners each was running on a handicap and there was a lot of prize money riding on the Gift final.

On this occasion, Trevor and his Dad Jim, who like my father was a founding member of the Gift, were staying together at a Gunnedah hotel with my cousin Kay. Dad related the story on his return home. Apparently it was Sunday morning and people in the street were making their way to church, or going to get the Sunday papers form the nearby news agency. The four intrepid travellers, had breakfast, loaded the Jim's car and were about ready to leave when Kay and Dad come up with an idea to have some fun before leaving town.

What happened next was Dad pretending to act violently which was right out of character for him. He had physically manhandled Kay and made a lot of noice in doing so in the street. Meanwhile Kay acted out an unmerciful scream loud enough to wake the dead and all the patrons of the hotel which also attracted a great deal of attention from the street. The menfolk had all dressed up in Bonny and Clyde like suits with Panama hats turned down at the brim over their foreheads. Kay had mocked up a 1920 like appearances in her dress and hat too. As the morning Church crowd passed by, Dad apparently opened the back door of the car whilst he manhandled Kay, threw her on the back seat and then jumped in after her slamming the door as he did so, calling out " Hit it Left-ie." Jim immediately put his foot flat on the accelerator and the car tyres screamed and burnt rubber on the get away. Trevor pointed the shotgun skyward outside the window as the car pulled out from the curb and let go both barrels. The noise and confusion prompted crowd reaction from the street and people began to run in all directions away from the scene. The incident made the local press and Gunnedah has never been the same on a Sunday morning since that day. That was typical of the McPhillips clan as far back as I can remember.

A couple of other incidents come to mind in my recall. Like the time on new years night when Dad was having a few drinks with a neighbour Ron McNeill and they hatched a plan to trow a New Year party. So Ron and Dad headed off to get a few mates and business men to attend. It was the way they went about it that was intriguing. Firstly, Dad enlisted Trevor Owens, who was already in bed with his new bride Jean. He used some means of convincing Trevor that it was an urgent matter and he quickly dressed and the three headed off to collect Don Aleman from his bed. He was in his panamas and was one of Dads employees, so he did what the boss asked. dad told him not to worry just come quickly as it was an important event.

Don's wife came to the door with puzzlement and watched the men head off in Dad's car. He had already phoned the publican Herb Sanderson to deliver a load of beer to the house ensuring that there was a good whisky for the local parish priest, Brain Murphy to drink.The Catholic rectory was nearby so the priest was the next to be enlisted. By this time, all the players were aware of what was going on. They had enough men to start the party, so thy all headed back home to our house.

Mum was already busy in the kitchen preparing food and left over Christmas pudding and cake for the revellers.The dye was cast and the procedure of capturing the menfolk went on until about one in the morning. It got so that they didn't bother explaining anything to the kidnap victim. They just rang the door bell of the unsuspecting male resident and captured him returning to our home. with another batch of people. I was allowed to stay up throughout the whole proceedings. It was quite amusing to see menfolk huddled about with some in suits, others in pyjamas, some with dressing gowns and others just PJ bottoms, all drinking, laughing, singing by the piano and having a grand time. The party ceased at dawn and somehow or other the menfolk made their way home to face the wife! in mums case she stayed up to empty the ash trays, throw out the empty bottles and clean up the kitchen and bathroom. Dad was already in bed sleeping it all off.

It was not the only fun filled events of my youth that I recall that involved Dad's one-upmanship or scary tactics that he employed to keep people on their toes. Dad hailed from Grafton when he was first married to Mum and worked locally after graduation in engineering. Whilst he had the ability mathematically to achieve any career he liked, he settled for mechanical engineering as a work choice because motor vehicle were becoming more popular as a mode of transport as passenger vehicles after WW11. He first considered becoming a butcher as a career option too. Abattoirs were in their infancy and butcher's had a lucrative career cutting up sheep and cattle for farmers and supplying the local domestic markets too. In his youth, Pop had purchased a property at the five mile mark on the old highway just south of Grafton and Dad, being one of six brothers had his night duties looking after the sheep to keep away dingoes. It meant sleeping out all night by a log fire with a gun to protect the animals. Dad hated the land and took every opportunity to escape it, despite growing up on a rural sheep farm. He learnt how to play the piano and worked after school to earn his two shillings a week to pay off a piano, selling honey and doing odd jobs in Grafton.

It was a five mile journey to and from his teachers house to learn to play efficiently and he did that every day. That instrument I inherited when Dad died and I had learnt to play on it as a child and learnt to write the theory too. I reached intermediate standard on the piano by the time I was sent to boarding school at age 13, I was more than ready then to give the instrument away. It is one decision I always lived to regret, as it would be a handy means of assisting me now to write and record my own songs. The piano was part of the furniture in our home for years. It's top was used as place or photo display and had a secret compartment under the foot pedals which was a prefect place to hide the days takings when I was a retailer. It was a means to an end to help get through those years of expensive private school education. Little loot on the side was insurance in times of financial difficulty. It stayed that way for years until my daughter Emma came on the scene.

One of my fathers best friends at Grafton high school was an Indian snake charmer, Edward Royce Ramsamy who later changed his name to Ram Chandra and took up entertaining for a living in his adult years about the same time Dad went into the mechanic trade. He had no doubt shown my Father a thing or two about the art of catching snakes when they were kids on the land. Ram lived at Woolgoolga, not far from my Grandfather "Pops' sheep stations. Ram had no end of snakes to catch around the family's sheep farm and learnt dangerous tricks with them too. He performed at local and state shows with daring feats and did tireless investigations into milking snakes to develop an antivenin for those who were unfortunate enough to get bitten. Ram moved to Mackay as a young man, where he developed a lifelong obsession with taipans. By the 1940s, he was working with the 'Carnival of Eastern Wonders,' a travelling show that had Ram dicing with death by handling venomous snacks in the dramatically named 'Pit of Death.' Ram used his showmanship to learn as much as he could about snakes. At the time theTaipan was thought to only live in Far North Queensland; but in the 1950s several mysterious deaths following bites by 'brown' snakes had the medical profession perplexed. Ram identified the culprit as being a Taipan. the type that was though until then to be only in far North Queensland. He began milking the taipan for their venom and sending samples to the Commonwealth Serum laboratory to enable them to develop the first antivenin. It was first used on a 10 year old victim Bruce Stringer, saving his life. The following year the antivenin saved Ram's life when he was bitten by a taipan in the "Pit of Death.'

Ram once visited Dad on his way through Macksville on his return from a 'snake show' and I remember him as being of dark skin but different some how to the black kids I had grown ups with. Of course, a snake charmer meant little to me as a child but it seemed to mean a lot to Dad who was excited to see his boyhood friend again. During his lifetime occupation,Ram survived many a snake bite and raise thousands of dollars for the ambulance service in Queensland. He was awarded the Order of Australia for his charity work in 1995. He died in Mackay in 1998 and a year late the Ram Chandra Park was opened in his memory in Mackay, his adopted hometown. He had a unique ability to charm snakes and his talent in that regard has never been matched since. Whilst bitten more than once over a lifetime from deadly snakes he had built up a resistance. Ram was a lovely man who using his charm, friendly smile and gentle nature to win the hearts of Australian's throughout the nation.

Dad joined Clive Sayer's Engineering business in Macksville in 1943 and I was born a year later. He often told of his early exploits as the junior mechanic working for Clive. The one that come to mind as the most interesting was when the whole staff except the junior mechanics were invited to a local business Christmas party. Dad was peeved about it and decided with a one of his mechanic mates to make the party attendees pay for their indiscretion. He took along another mate, Mick Denham as 'cockatoo,'a lookout for his pending prank. All three had made their way to the home of the businessman were the party was in progress.

It was agreed that Mick would jump he back fence and check that there was no one about that could identify the the two young mechanics when they went into prank mode. As fate would have it, Mick jumped the fence and who should be on the other side but a vicious German shepherd guard dog. Mick had primed himself with enough alcohol prior to this endeavour to have no fear of the consequences and immediately dropped to the ground and on all fours advanced towards the approaching growling dog. The two met face to face in a split second and Mick out-growled the savage beast. The dog backed off and Mick kept advancing towards the animal, still on all fours and barking wildly. Eventually the dog headed for its kennel and Mick casted the back and front of the house before returning to the pranksters in readiness to give the all clear. The cars of the mid 1940s were open with wind up windows or canvass see-though side windscreens, so it was not an issue the two young mechanics to set each car up for the prank.

The cars had manual gear stick back then and the handle break was the only other safety feature which had to be let off by metal squeezing a trigger like handle in order to put them in drive mode. The too pranksters wired the metal handed to the battery, so that when the car started the driver would get an electric shock.

After setting each of the cars belonging to the party goers in this fashion, they then returned to the next task. They took the jacks out from each of the cars and put the jack under the axle so that the back wheels were slightly off the ground but undetectable to the naked eye. They had only just completed their endeavour when the first of the car owners returned to his car. He started his motor and attempted to release the hand brake at the same time letting out an almighty scream. He swore and tried then to reverse the car but the wheels just spun and he was stuck. He returned inside to tell his fellow party goers what had happened. In matter of minutes all the drivers were trying to figure out how to get the car moving and many in their own cars fell for the trap of attempting to let the handbrake off after starting the motor. Vehicle wheels were left spinning but the cars remained stationary and had perplexed drivers scratching their heads. It was a cloudy night and primed with alcohol they elected to return in the morning to retrieve their cars. Dad and his two companions sat behind a fence across the road and had trouble containing laughter. Clive Sayer related the story about his car the next day to all and sundry but was none the wiser that it was Dad and his fellow employee that had done the ghastly deeds.

Another incident I recall as a young teenager on holidays, whenI managed to travel with Dad and a group of athletes to the Gift at Dorrigo. There was always a load of prize money to be won at these Gift carnivals as they were professional events. Dad with Trevor Owens and his sidekick shotgun ventured up the Waterfall Way for the events in the company of local athletes. We travelled in Dad's utility which he usually used for carrying truck parts or defunct engines to the local tip. We left home before sunup and in the back of the ute; a number of hopeful sprinters who had trained under Paul Lawson, a skilled rugby league football who later proved to be a grand coach of professional running due to his own skill in the sport. As we crossed the low bridge below the Dorrigo mountain Trevor encourage by Dad put the shotgun out the window, pointed it skyward as he traditionally had done for starting races and let go both barrels. The half asleep runners in the back almost shit themselves. Both Trevor and Dad could not stop laughing.

Paul Lawson, a painter by trade hailed from Canberra originally and had played A Grade Canberra Australian Rules switching to Group 8 Rugby League with the Canberra Raiders. He came to Macksville to play for the local side after an illustrious football career playing first grade for Canterbury Bankstown. Venturing north to the bush playing for Inverell and Kempsey, finally settling in Macksville with his wife to raise a family. Like many a keen league player chasing prize money, Paul ran in the Macksville Gift coming in second. He also ran a second in the Graduation race and won the 130 yards Novice handicap in 1958. He competed at many Gift carnivals and had a 2nd place at Dorrigo and ran second in the Gift at Grafton the same year Paul held evening training sessions after work each week at the local Macksville show-ground. The hopefuls who lay cramped and huddled together in the back of Dad's ute that early cold morning were Bede Clarke, who had competed at Macksville in the 1957 and ran third in the Consolation event. Paul had him primed to win at The Dorrigo Gift and Bede should have been seated up front as passenger with Dad, to be comfortable for the race. Bebe being a gentleman elected to be in the back with the rest of the runners. He won the Dorrigo Gift hands down and collected the first prize money with no doubt a bonus for his trainer. I ran in the mile event that Dorrigo Gift in a personal best effort of sixth position.

I was no athlete but I did love the travelling to other towns, being involved in the athletic action despite my lack of skill. Paul did try to teach me a thing or two but encouraged me more with fitness than speed. Paul went on to train local athlete winners at the Macksville Gift; Jim Downs, Malcolm McIlwain and Darren Smith. Paul later trained Bede Clarke, after our back of the ute experience who won the Dorrigo Gift, went on to win the Commonwealth Sprint Championship in Canberra and played Rugby league for the Macksville side and Kempsey too. My good mate Ashley Kearns showed a lot of promise and ran second in the Novice handicap and whilst at school had won the sprint for age North Coast School Boys Athletic Championship. Ash remained a good friend and later I was the best man at his wedding but our contacted dwindled in our mutual married years. He had joint the Police force up North and died at a relatively young age. He was a Sargent of the Police at the Gold Coast at the time and was my best 'Chicken game' competitor when we first gained our driving license. I have many a fond memory of our childhood friendship.

Paul lawson's training of runner Jim Down had him rated as one of the most naturally talented athletes to come from our district. He was a noted Rugby League player and a member of the 1963 Macksville team which was considered the best team ever to play for our town.That side defeated all teams they played and won the Harry Gillett Memorial Trophy for night cup football, The Caltex competition and the Southern Leagues Zone Premiership. In Sydney they defeated the previously unbeaten Bankstown United and finished the season by defeating Coffs Harbour to take out the Group 2 Championship. Jim was also a member of the Macksville-Scotts Head SLSA junior boat crew that won the Branch title. He was a good swimmer and beach sprinter.

I managed to be in the relay team that unofficial won the four man junior team relay in the finals at the Taree Old Bar Surf carnival, but we were disqualified. I had jumped the mark in taking the baton as the third leg runner. The rest of the team were not impressed that I had let down the side and I felt like crap that I had been too keen to play my part in the team effectively. A 25 meter dash I could do o.k. but anything beyond that up to a mile I was hopeless. I did excel at great speed over longer distances thou and I guess I am still like that. Perhaps that is why I have walked the 800 plus kilometres of the Camino three times or maybe I am just a glutton for punishment as an adventurer. The Macksville Gift Professional Athletic Club was the first NSW Gift carnival to run professional foot racing for prize money.

In my research for writing on the subject of the Club I found this opening statement in the inaugural 1953 Gift programme's opening paragraph: "The year 1953…will dwell in the memories of all Australians   for all time. It is the year Queen Elizabeth 11 was crowned, the year the Korean War ended and the election of war hero Dwight D. Eisenhower to the position off President of the United States. In the field, we lost the cricket to England for the first time in 20 years. America entered the international Rugby league, and just as the year 1878 lives in memory as the introduction of the Stawell Gift in Victoria, 1953 will live as the year of the introduction of the Macksville Gift in New South Wales."   Then, with the success of the Macksville Gift in the ensuing six years the following opening statement on the programme. "Perhaps of all the six years passed in the interim this current year is quite the most momentous, for it marks a period of interchange of visits between leaders.

Our Queen and Prince Philip visited Canada and the U.S.A. The British Prime Minister MacMillian has seen both President Eisenhower and Soviet Prime Minister Khrushchev in their countries, and now Prime Minister Khrushchev has visited Britain and U.S.A.The programme continued: "The avowed objectives of all these visitors and visits is the preservation of world peace and the end of the 'Cold War.' This year of 1959 may go down in history as the year of the peacemakers and the world of these leaders acclaimed for all time. With the majority of people in the world, we hope fervently for these achievements, which, amongst other things, will allow us all to concentrate our minds and activities on the best things in life- including good sportsmanship- and promote the ideals which will take us Ever Onward!"

I for the life of me wonder why Dad mixed memories of Queen, Prime Minister's, and Presidents, the Korean War aftermaths and the Cold War as an introductory programmes for a professional athletic event, but he did. Perhaps it was his duties as a young mechanic or energy plane spotting duties during WW11 that set him off. Or maybe it was the Korean War when he released one of his mechanics for military service, or perhaps it was the fact that he was a patriot and a real socialist at heart. His belief became even more staunch when Bob Hawke headed up the Unions and Don Dustan was elected Premier of South Australia. Despite being a relatively large employer in a small business one would think he would have been in support of The Country Party or the Liberals, but he was 'dyed in the wool' left of the political spectrum. Dad was a strong believer in unionism, a businessman of extra ordinary ability, it seemed out of character, his labor persuasion.

Dad also put his money were his mouth was as a generous philanthropist and a man of action. At any rate he was a grand promoter of sport and a great supporter of athletics, surf and golf clubs, being patron of all three. He attended regular monthly meetings of the local Labor Party and had me attend as the youngest member at 16 years of age during my holiday vocation. I reckon Dad would have turned over in his grave, when I became the town delegate for the Country Party in my years in business on the New England Tablelands and later helped form a State branch of the Liberal Party, being its first Secretary. Up until that time I had always voted Labor in the state elections as the local member got things done more often than not when another party was elected. These days it is more about the collective party and not about what sitting members can or can't do, but don't get me started.

CHAPTER 4.

EVER ONWARD

Eric McPhillips, the businessman who never took a day off work, the school boy champion swimmer who was patron of the surf club but never went to the beach. The Golf Club patron who never played golf and the charitable donor to all the local religions who never went to Church really proved himself as a successful business and first Secretary foundation member of the Macksville Gift Committee, from its humble beginnings. Dad saw life as a glass half full and lived the" Ever Onward" motto. The   Athletic Club still carries the motto " Ever Onward," owes much to my fathers brilliance and enthusiasm for its success as it does to its other founders. Not only does the annual event promote local charities, it has made the town a tourist attraction too.

Macksville is situated 500 kilometres North of Sydney on the Mid North Coast of New South Wales. The picturesque country-side has the beautiful Nambucca river flowing through the township and out to sea at Nambucca Heads thirteen kilometres east. The township boasts a town population of 7000 according to the sign post as you enter town. The reality according to 2016 census is a population of 2,785 but it swell to double at holiday time and when Macksville hosts "The Gift." In 1953 when the first Macksville Gift was run the town had a population of around 1200 people. Although only a small town by completing standards, it was a prosperous, economic vital, growing township with unmistakable community pride.

The town boundaries in the 1950s there were three timber mills and an abattoirs that employed 100 men, a family owned small goods factory, a butter factory and a cordial factory.The town had its own hospital and plans were underway for a new more modern hospital too. A High school had been established near the location of the newly planned hospital to cater for the needs of secondary high school children's education in the district. There was already a Catholic high school to intermediate standard which had a primary school and a local non-denominational public primary nearby. The community boasted a healthy acceptance of God with established Churches and adjoining rectories for Catholic, Methodist, Church of England and Presbyterian Church's scattering the landscape. Dairy and beef cattle, timber getting, banana plantations, professional fishing and small good crops of beans, tomatoes, peas, cucumbers, maize and watermelons supported the town's economy to the greater extent. However, Macksville at the time still had that small town mentality and needed a new spirit of innovation injected into it to turn it into a thriving metropolis.That miracle came in the shape of a money man with a vision. The Manager of the English,Scottish and Australian Bank at the time was Athol Dane. Athol was transferred from Victoria and was reared in a house situated next door to the Central Park, Stawell, the home of the oldest and most famous professional footrace, the Stawell Gift. Athol was well aware of how a popular event could become beneficial to a town. He made an effort to convince all manner of organisations in Macksville to endeavour to organise such an event, but could not get any interest from the locals at the time. Although not a Catholic himself, in a desperate move to get a "Gift" established in town, he approached the local Assistant Parish Priest. Father Russell Redford, apart from his priestly duties, had been charged with the responsibility of raising funds necessary to build a Catholic Church at Nambucca Heads which like Macksville had a growing Catholic community with a town population of around 1500. The two townships combined held the bulk of the district population of 7000 people.

Bowraville, had some 500 in their community with a large aboriginal settlement as well. Bowraville already had a Catholic Church and primary school and Mercy Nuns as did Macksville. The Sunday Church services for Macksville, Nambucca Heads and Bowraville and the Aboriginal settlement at Bellwood were all held by the Macksville Parish Priest, with outlying areas having a monthly service in their local hall. Athol Dane, having exhausted his efforts with other district organisation, convinced Father Redford that a professional foot racing carnival would be a good fund raiser. However, Father felt that he didn't have the time or the know-how to organise such an event himself. The Priest mentioned the idea to Monsignor Bartlett of Rozelle (Sydney) on a visit and the Mons; said that in his opinion Macksville already had the ideal man to organise the event, This man was Keith Eyles. Keith was employed a Macksville's Abattoirs and was heavily involved in Rugby League and League referring. In 1946 he officiated at a North Coast match against a touring Great Britain side. In 1948 he referred the Country vs City Match. Keith turned to coaching Macksville's League team leading the team to a premiership win.

By 1953 he was one of the most respected referees on the Mid North Coast. Upon being approached by Father Redford, Keith said he needed a week to deliberate as to whether or not he should take the task on organising a foot racing carnival. After a week of heavy thought, Keith accepted the challenge stating first that he would give away the Rugby League responsibilities for a time to devote his energies for a period of time to the "Gift." Keith had some conditions that Father Redford must agree too, including: 1.That he alone would hand pick his first committee. 2. He would accept suggestions but would have the final say on what would be done and where. 3. He wanted to know how much money Father wanted him to make from the "Gift."

Keith had a final requirement too: He stressed that Father Redford must understand that he liked the citizens of Macksville, and believed that they liked him in return, and while Father's aim was to raise money it was Keith's aim to organise the "Gift" in such a way that Macksville had a lasting legacy from him. That is to say that he would raise what he could from the "Gift" but it must be done in a fair way so that all Macksville would benefit. On a handshake Father Redford agreed to all conditions saying that Keith should raise as much money as he could from the event initially to help fund a new Church at Nambucca Heads and then funds could be distributed however a Gift committee decided. After due diligence Keith set a funds target of 500 pound ($1,000) profit for the first meeting. This figure would equate to around $27,000 in todays value. Even through the " Gift" was to raise funds for the Church, Keith wanted the event to be non-sectarian and non-parochial, as he wanted the whole town to be a part of it. Keith's idea was to have a Committee of people not only from Macksville but also from the entire district and beyond. He set about selecting a few local people with the idea that they could expand the Committee themselves.

The first ones chosen were Bernie Laverty, a local taxi driver and later Shire President, Eric Mcphillips, innovative engineer and Don Allman, a smart man of administrative skills. Keith chose himself to be Secretary and asked Clem Partridge, a well known Catholic committeeman to be President. The new committee also decided that there would be a Ladies Committee to raise funds leading up to the"Gift" by selling memberships Tickets, assisting with food, etc at house parties to organising and providing food on the day of the " Gift" Carnival.

Evelyn, my mother was a member of First Ladies Gift Committee and worked tirelessly for many years assisting with fund raising, food preparation and late night 'cuppas' and food for the committee meetings at our home. Mum gave Dad wonderful support with his Gift Carnival activities travelling many thousands of kilometres throughout the East Coast of Australia. Home was always open for drink at any time to any wayward traveller who had athletics in their veins. House parties in the 1950s were commonplace as a means to raise funds for various organisations. The Catholic Church house parties did not allow the sale of beer. However, Keith and his Committee wished to sell alcohol at the 'First Gift' house party. Father Redford agreed that beer could be sold on the night. The Publican at Macksville's Nambucca Hotel, Herb Sanderson, who when told of the "Gift" house party been allowed to have beer sales offered to donate a keg of beer. The Committee insisted they pay for it and Herb agreed to sell it to them at cost. Herb was well known to all and well liked but swore like a trooper and embellished his speech with very colourful adjectives in conversation. Father Redford had never met Herb and knew nothing of his manner of speech. At the first house party Herb arrived with the keg of beer and some two dozen mates to support the party. Keith quietly told the Priest that Herb was a vital link in the Gift fund raising plan, but was known to use colourful language. He asked the Priest not to take offence at anything he said. When introduced to one another, Father Redford shook Herb's hand and said "How are you going you old bastard." Father Redford and Herb were great mates from that moment and ever Friday for the priest remaining time in Macksville he had a free fish dinner at Herb's pub.

The marketing of the Gift to raise more 'prize money' for the first professional footrace race included a printed shield to wear proudly on the day of the Gift. The wearer paid one pound ($2) which entitled the member free entry to the show ground for the race carnival.The Ladies committee went from door to door throughout the district to sell those shields. At the Sunday Masses Father Redford and his new found friend Herb Sanderson addressed the congregation at Taylors Arm, Nambucca Heads and Macksville. Father addressed the congregations about supporting the gift instead of his normal sermon. At the conclusion of the Mass, the Ladies Committee sold membership shields to the people who had not already become members.

To boost sales a gold membership card was introduced for a five pound fee ($10) and this entitled the member not only to free entry into the carnival, but free meals in a restaurant, morning, afternoon tea and lunch, and free beer at the bar. The bar area at the Gift for Gold members was fenced off and waiters introduced to serve them. The Committee was not afraid that the members would drink their fill and they would loose on the bar takings. At eight pence (seven cents) a 'middie,' they would have to consume 150 middies in the day to equal their gold membership price. As time got closer to Gift day advertising became intense and 2KM (now 2MC/FM) came to an agreement with the Committee to advertise the Gift, free of cost, every hour on the hour for one week leading up to the big day by announcing-"It is now 10 o'clock and one hour closer to the Macksville Gift" and so on. Another novel form of advertising was having a boat moored in the middle of the river west of the Macksville Bridge, with a large banner, that simply said, "GIFT." People travelling through Macksville would enquire what it meant and thus they learnt of the coming event. To bring the crowds to the first Gift special trains had been arranged to run from Kempsey, with buses from Dorrigo and Coffs Harbour. To boost the crowd all other sporting events in the district were cancelled for the running of the Gift. Runners had been recruited far and wide from the fastest of Rugby League footballers along the North Coast to compete in heats on the day and be selected as one of the seven finalist to compete for the grand prize money.

The seventy five pound purse was more than most footballers had for a basic wage that year. In order that all runners got off their mark with an even start, a special gate was designed by Dad and built with the help of his employee and fellow Gift Committee member, Kelly Gossip at the garage. 'The Gate' proved popular with the runners and time keepers and was believed to be the only one of its kind in New south Wales. The starting gate, it is claimed, was a " gimmick" to gain publicity. It was only used for the first Gift, as from 1954 onwards all races were handicapped. Getting the gate from Eric McPhillips garage to the show ground, some two kilometres away, proved quite a challenge. It was a very big contraption and quite cumbersome. A International big red truck sold by Dad to a local was enlisted to load the gate onto and transport to the show ground. Once loaded the gate proved to be a problem; it was far too long for the truck trailer. Not to be deterred the innovative menfolk of the town agreed to walk behind the truck and hold up the gate with lumps of timber. This proved to be quite an arduous task, as only after short distances, breaks had to be taken to rub shoulders and hands to ease the pain of their burden. A further problem was that due to load limits and traffic laws being enforce, this transportation took place in the wee small hours to avoid detection. When the load reached the overhead rail line nearing the show ground it was discovered that it was too high and would not fit under the railway bridge. Once again the ingenuity of Dad and his helpers came to the fore. They let air out of the truck tyres which lowered the load height and the procession was allowed to continue. As the sun came up on the horizon the gate was in place at the starting mark off the track. A final inspection of the well manicured grass track surface and the runners lanes, all white wash painted by hand in preparation, was completed for the big race of the day. It was the 19th of September 1953 my ninth birthday and the day of the first of the Macksville Gift Carnival.

A clear spring morning with no rain in sight, a beautiful blue sky and lots of sunshine. All workers arrived at the show ground early to ensure nothing could prevent the running of the first Macksville Gift running smoothly. Childrens races began right on time at 10.a.m. and it also marked the first of prize money events, the running of what was called the Five Mile marathon. At the first Macksville Gift Keith Eyles " called" the races from start to finish, advising all the listeners over public address system the order in which the runners were placed throughout the events. By the 'calling" of the races this way, the spectators became involved in the event. The manner of "calling" much like a horse race, was the first for any sporting event and added to the excitement as spectators become more involved. This manner of calling is common place these days in sport. Macksville was the first club to introduce runners by advising the public of where a competitor was rated in form and a short history of his athletic achievement.

A semaphore board much like those for cricket or a football match was arranged so that the spectators knew when the winners and place getters were as early as five seconds after each race.   Apart from the fine food and cool refreshments, there was one other notable attraction at the first Macksville Gift. One amazing James Patrick O' Grady, affectionally known as 'Saus', was not a member of the Committee at the time even though he had assisted in many ways getting everything ready for the big day. As he had no specific job on the day he offered to organise a knock -em-down attraction. He had arranged to make up several blocks of wood, painted them different colours and set them in place on a plank inside a tent he had borrowed for the day. He acquired several tennis balls and a rope barrier. The idea was for contestants to pay one shilling (10 cents) and endeavour to knock all the blocks of the plank by hurling the ball at them. If a contestant was successful he was to be paid ten shillings ($1). Saus was given strict instructions not to loose money and some Committee member was appointed to enquire ever so often during the day how it was going and Suas always announce that "he was making money." No matter how many times a contestant tried, he could never knock down the last block. Saus made money for the Church fund raising that day, but no one knows to this day why the last block could not be knocked off the plank! Perhaps it had been nailed down or perhaps God was on " Saus's side. The profit target of five hundred pounds was set that year was well and truely bettered when cheque for six hundred and eighty pounds ($1360) was handed over to the Nambucca Heads Catholic Church Building Fund.

On the Sunday after the Gift the committee presented a silver tray engraved: "To Keith and Dot Eyles, In Appreciation from the Committee of 1st Macksville Gift, 1953." although not a committee member themselves, Herb Sanderson proprietor off the Nambucca Hotel at Macksville and Jack Kingston from the Victoria Hotel in Nambucca Heads were in attendance. The second year of the Gift began on the 1st October 1953 when officers were elected. The position of General Secretary was taken up by Eric McPhillips who was considered by all to be 'a meticulous and thorough man' for the job. Keith Eyles was unanimously elected the President by the committee. Dad held the Secretarial position for the next decade as the Macksville Gift carnival grew to be the biggest professional athletic event on the stage calendar, eventually running the Australian professional racing championship attracting professional runners from all over the country and as far afield as the island of Jamaica in Dads time as General Secretary.

The McPhillips clan had always been involved in sport when I was a child. My cousins Errol and Leo, sons of Uncle Barney and another Auntry Ethel were well known bicycle velodrome racing champions. The brothers were nicknamed respectively 'Vitamins and Tablets' in their teens' by my cousin Max, because of the amount substances they consumed. The bike riding competition throughout the world has always been in controversy over drug taking, but back then it was an accepted practice for fit athletes to build strength for up and coming events and was not seen as giving any bike rider an unfair advantage.

Max would have had a fair inkling as to the benefits of performance enhancing drugs with involvement in the 'Sport of Kings'- horse racing and the family involvement with greyhounds. My Uncle Paddy, Max' and Kay's father had made his money out of the timber game when he had a fleet of log trucks. His real fortune came when he received a pile of listed shares when Tooth's took over Grafton Gold top brewery Uncle Pat had a major share holding. Once cashed up he retired from the hauling timber business to take up full time greyhound training and racing at age fifty. The next decade my uncle raced his dogs and made lots more money. Ever year Uncle Pat purchased a new Chevrolet and took out the back seat, creating a screen between back and front so his racing dogs could travel in comfort to race meetings. I had the pleasure of walking the dogs with him early one morning on a visit there on school holidays. I watched as Uncle Pat fed his dogs a stimulant he had imported from Russia. It no doubt helped their performance too.

By the time he reached age 60 Uncle Pat had done with the dogs and spent his dotage as a proprietor in his own freehold pub which he built out of timber on the town boundary. It was on the Glen Innes road, next door to the sale yards and near a planned battery manufacturing business which reportedly was to be a big employer. The weekly cattle sales covered his cost with drinkers lined his pub bar, and the motel like accomodation units on roadside attracted many an overnight traveller heading up to the New England Tableland. It was the same route old briny, his father and my granddad road on horseback to deliver mail between Glen Innes and Grafton back in the 1920s. Uncle Pat's pub was up the road from the Five Mile hotel owned by Dot Willett, who later became Mrs Dot McPhillips when Max and Kay had grown up. Dot was also on the board of the AHA hotels association and had been a publican all her life. Uncle Pat had raised Kay and Max with the help for his sister in law Aunty Madge, as wife and mother Ed died young with kidney disorder. Uncle Fred, another of Dad's brothers in the timber industry followed his elder brother Paddy's venture into the pub game and built his own freehold Pub at Half Way Creek near Woolgoolga, like Uncle pat cutting his won timber to build it. Uncle Fred and Aunt Ethel were great tennis players and they had their own tennis court, so the children, cousins Peter, Neil and Michelle, became very good players.

Neil was picked to play at White City courts in Sydney, in the selection for Australian tennis playing representatives. Unfortunately he injured his arm with what is commonly known as tennis elbow and could not compete. He missed his opportunity but didn't seem to mind too much. The fame came from a different direction, as Mark Taylor the cricketer was a regular visitor to the family and eventually

married one of the McPhillips' offspring. He more than once represented Australia in cricket and was the Captain for a time. My Dad's sibling, Aunty Elsie married Vince Brotherstone, of a well known Grafton race horse breeding family. Their son Bernie, my cousin, moved to Sydney, working as a taxi driver initially and later on the waterfront in his youth. Bernie, known affectionally in the family as "Flaps' was given the nickname once again my cousin Max because of the size of his ears. He never seemed to mind his nickname either. Bernie always dressed with the latest fashions, was considered a bit of a dandy.

When he marriage he returned to Grafton was a top golfing identity. My Fathers Uncle, Dick McPhillips, by the time I was sent to boarding school, owned two shoes store in George Street Sydney. Dick commenced his career shining shoes for daily commuters in George Street during the depression gaining enough money to commence a shoe repair business at 509 George Street opposite Central Station. It was at the time, particularly in the 1950s, the hub of the commercial centre of Sydney, the main local, intra and interstate rail head for commuters. It was also the terminal head for tramway from all point of the compass and the main bus link too.

Naturally, a network of major Department stores stood nearby, with Mark Foleys and Co; Anthony Hordern and Grace Brothers being the predominant ones. The McPhillips shoe repair business was always the height of activity for commuters and in a short space of time Dick Mcphillips made enough money to start a second shoe store business; a two story store located in the QVB building. He grew the business by importing Packard shoes and carried all the best known brands too. Uncle Dick was a well known millionaire by the time I arrive on the scene as a school boy at St. Joseph's College, Hunters Hill. He was also a well respected patron Rugby League supporter of the then Newtown Football Club and advertised frequently in the newspapers as patron and seller of what become known as "Dick's kickers."

In my first year at Boarding school, I got permission from the Headmaster to go to the city to buy a new pair of school shoes. Dad had given me the money to buy them when I was at home on school holidays and insisted that I buy them from Uncle Dick. Upon arrival at the store, Uncle Dick greeted me and called all his staff from both floors down to meet me. He announce to his twelve staff members: "This is Doug, he is Eric's boy from Macksville, remember I told you about him." The staff feigned interested and in unison replied: "Yes, Mr.McPhillips." After the staff had all gone back to their respective duties and Uncle Dick had dispensed with formalities, called son (another) Bernie aside and advised him that I was to fitted with a good wearing school shoe. He advised Bernie to give me the usual family discount. I got 10% off the retail price and I realised then why Uncle Dick was a millionaire.

A good friend of Dick, Norm Brooks, provided him with leather for his shoe repair business at 509 George Street. Norm Brook's junior told me some years later that his Dad had special pricing for customers he didn't like or from whom he sort to make additional income. He would say in front of the customer to a staff member " Give him the special STB discount." Norm Brooks junior told me the customer always thought he was getting a special deal when it fact he wasn't; the STD stood for "Sting The Bastard." Uncle Dick's give 'the family discount' on what was already an inflated price was not far removed from the Brook's one. In my youthful days in Sydney I ran into my Uncle Dick at an illegal gambling Casino in Kings Cross one Friday evening. He was playing cards for big dollars and I was playing Roulette. I enjoyed the clubs service of free alcoholic drinks to the gambler at the wheel and being served by a good looking young women with low cut dress and child bearing hips whilst at the table was healthy bonus. I called in the next day to the QBV store to visit Uncle Dick to see how he had made out playing cards the night before. He told me with little concern that he did not finish the night well, for he had 'dropped a thousand' on the cards. The business was thriving and a loss of that magnitude did not even put a dent in his financial assets. To most punters back then a thousand pounds ($2,000) would have been a small fortune, but for Dick it was pocket money. The field of creative arts ran in the family too, with Dicks son Bobby becoming the Head teacher at the Arts Department of Meadowbank TAFE. Uncle Reg, a younger brother, who travelled around Australia as a Commercial artist, became involved with Athletics and did sign writing for the Macksville Gift ,was later employed by Caltex Oil Company in the USA for his artistic skills. He never did come back to Australia. My son Samuel seemed to have inherited these family genes, as he too has chosen a career in commercial art and has achieved a lot of commercial success as a freelance consultant.

In 1954 the Gift committee commissioned a Blazer for any member who wanted one. They were maroon in colour with a winged running shoe embedded onto the coat itself with NSWAL above the shoe and beneath it in white the words "Ever Onward Macksville Gift.,"embossed with the title of the wearer. Early in the year the Macksville Gift Committee received an invitation from the Stawell Athletic Club to attend the richest and largest professional Athletics meeting in the world. The invitation received by Secretary Eric McPhillips was for six members to attend the Stawell Gift over the coming Easter holiday weekend. That year Stawell was worth one thousand, one hundred and fifty pounds ($2,300). On route to Stawell Eric and Keith called on the NSW Athletic league and spoke about Macksville becoming registered with that body. Upon their return from Stawell Keith Eyles wrote a detailed report to his Committee, which showed the Stawell Club in a most favourable light. The organisation of the Stawell gift was the best and most professional ever witnessed by any delegation.

The excitement of the final had no apparent equal. The hospitality extended had to be witnessed to be believed and the extremely experienced men at Stawell courteously and cheerfully answered every questions and query put forward. The Macksville delegation came away from Stawell better equip and ready to organise future carnivals and felt the journey there was worthwhile. Good Friday in 1954 saw the men from Macksville strolling around Central Park Stawell, observing all that what was going on. Dad in his wanderings had tripped over an object of the tracks and this gave him an idea. In preparation for the 1953 Gift, the lane markers had clogged up the Convert School marker, the Primary school marker and the High school marker. In desperation they used a watering can to finish marking the lanes about midday on the day of the event. Dad quickly sensed that this could not happen again, which would have cost twenty pounds ($40) to make. A workable non clogging marker, a rather expensive option for the time when you consider the basic wage back then was about two pounds ($4 per week).The object Dad had tripped over that left white paint on his clothing was the Stawell lane marker. It consisted of a a handle, 2 wheels, a belt and a washing up dish. Total cost about seven and six (75 cents). This marker could never clog up, would mark lanes that rain would not wash out and would mark grounds in minutes, so Dad made one. That alone was a gain for the Committee when Dad duplicated the design, built one on his return home.

During the next decade Dad, along with three other executives was awarded life membership to the NSW Athletic League. The League and the Macksville Gift committee agreed to hold the 1954 Macksville Gift Carnival on Monday the 4th October with all arrangements progressing well and all athletic clubs throughout NSW had been advised of the incoming, first registered Macksville Gift, as being on that date. In Sydney, a public holiday was a permanent fixture on the first Monday in October. In NSW country, if such a luxury was to be enjoyed, application had to be made to the local Council.It was usually a matter of course that the local holiday would be approved without a fuss. Before putting request before the Council, Keith Eyles approached the Chambers of Commerce in Nambucca Heads, Bowraville and Macksville. He also spoke to the Abattoirs as well as local shop keepers inviting their support and due to the previous years success of the First Macksville Gift every one approached agreed that a holiday on 4th October would benefit the whole of the Nambucca Valley.

In July the Dad wrote to Nambucca Shire Council seeking formal approval for Monday 4th October 1954 to be a public holiday throughout the Shire. Almost in the return mail the answer from Council was a resounding "NO." This totally unexpected reply really threw a spanner in the works. Chambers of Commerce were approached, protest meeting held and resolutions carried which asked Council to reconsider its "no holiday" decision. The Shire President and his fellow Councillors were informed and there was a change of heart. Not all Councillors were in agreement but it was generally agreed that the majority would go for it at the next meeting. However, the next bombshell to hit the Nambucca Shire Councillors was in the form of a letter from the NSW Chief Secretary's Department. Unbeknown to the majority of Councillors, the Gift Committee through their own initiative had contacted the Chief Secretary's Department, and they had written to Dad advising him a public holiday would be gazetted for the Nambucca Shire on October 4- the Six Hour Day. Copy of the letter together with a brief note he sent to the Shire Council office. Gazetting of the holiday, and the manner in which it was done caused a furore among Shire Councillors and heated discussed took place at the next Shire meeting.

Still, the holiday had been granted so the Gift Committee were able to continue with preparations for the next carnival as planned. It may well be asked "Was the Macksville Gift Committee responsible for the Six Hour Day (Labour day) holiday becoming a permanent holiday for the whole of NSW?" The Gift final in 1954 was sensational. It was the first ever professional handicap final in NSW Athletics and would go down in history initially as a non event. With the finalists on their mark ready for the race, there was a movement by one or two of the runners an instant before the starter's gun went off. The starter pulled the trigger to fire the second barrel to halt the runners for a rerun, but the cartridge did not explode. The runners, completed the 110 yard course in 10.6 seconds with Aisbett first, Schneider second and Bickley third. In the re-run Schneider was first Aisbett second and Bickley again came third.   The journey was again 10.6 seconds and only one inch (2.5cm) separated the places. A machine, used at foot racing in Stawell since 1947 was developed by Clarrie Draper and his "Draper Machine" had been proved proved accurate to 1-16th of an inch (around 1.5mm) over many years in race finals. It was the catalyst to proving who won that race in the end.

The Draper machine was second to none in determining the winner and it was clearly John Schneider. He was 23 at the time. As a St. Joseph's schoolboy, John establishes a G.P.S. 100 yards (91.44 metres) record for the under sixteen year age. It was the first time he had a pair of spikes and he reckoned he "Flew." Whilst still at school he was a member of the Australian junior 4 x 100 relay team. In 1949 when competing at the annual St. Patrick's Day event at the Sydney Show ground, John won the blue ribbon sprint double, the Cardinals Cup 100 yards and the 220 yards Championship. During that year John was the only St.Joseph's boy to gain selection in the Associated Schools First Fifteen Rugby Union team. He owed much of his running ability to Brother Stephen at St. Josephs College. He said also that he had been trained by Jim Carlton who was the only white man to run in the 1928 Olympic sprint final and later joined the Priesthood. When John won at Macksville he was living on the family farm at Krambuck. In his latter years he returns to the farm and lived there for his remaining years. I was present at that Gift Carnival in 1954, a 10 year old boy who did not know it then, that I too was destined to be sent like John to St. Joseph's College for my secondary school education.I would live to encounter Brother Stephen methods of fitness, the Marist moral, the riggers of Rugby football and running.

The 1954 Gift came and went as a resounding success, as did the Gifts that followed and the mantra of what the "Gift" had achieved, every since Athol Dane, first planted the seed of the idea in the head of Father Redford, to provide a "Gift" programme to help establish the necessary funds to build a New Catholic Church. During Dad's time as a founding member of the Gift, the Committee had help fund the building of the Church, an Iron Lung for the hospital and an Olympic Pool in Macksville and continues today to aid many projects for the benefit of the community. The necessary ingredient to make the Macksville

Gift successful and still running today consistence of a Community spirit to be united in a common cause. This is has always been the case with the running of this programme of athletics. The ingredients for success was (is) the forming of a committee. So without a sufficient number of committee members such an event would not take place. Committed people have to be prepared to work on the Gift day as timekeepers, judges, check starters, colour boy controllers, gate keepers, canteen and bar workers and the list goes on. Macksville has been lucky in this regard as it has always had willing workers to help on Gift day. The efforts of that first Committee to bolster up sponsorship has continued to this day. Since the tireless efforts of those pioneers the sponsorship monies have continued to flow in.

When the Gift started in 1953 there were four banks in town and now there is only two, but in their place are large Credit Unions. There is no longer an Abattoir, Cordial manufacturer, butter factory or small-goods manufacturer. However, there are forty five small businesses that function in the manufacturing industry in a relatively new industrial estate. The Abattoir use to employ 100 people. Now there is a Motor Manufacturing Industry that employs 114 employees. The town as it has done for many years boast a district co-operative of town folk as members help boost agriculture in the district. In my Dad's business he use to service log trucks that hauled timber from the bush to the many sawmills that dotted the coastline but that's all changed. The cafes bars and restaurants have not gone, just the old owners replaced by new ones with different ideas to attract customers.The two pubs still stand as does the religions. C of E, Catholic, Presbyterian, Methodist and the Salvation Army. The Gift bolstered community generosity of spirit which help keep this small township afloat. The Gift committee in dad's time were instrumental in funding the building of a Catholic Church, swimming pool and an iron lung for the then new hospital.

CHAPTER 5.

DAD AND HIS MEN

Christmas Eve, when not travelling to Grafton to my Grandparents for a few days, usually resulted in a pre- Christmas get together with the immediate family or may well have include the neighbours for a light dinner, the first taste of a "Mum baked' Christmas Cake and a few drinks before getting ready for the Midnight Mass celebration at

our Catholic Church on the hill, a five minute walk from our little home. It was the only Christian service that Dad attended. He was roped into it at my insistence, having had my indoctrination from the Sisters of (no) Mercy: "Get your Father to Christmas Mass." It was also Dad's birthday, which the Nuns used in their advantage on their method of Christian evangelism: "Your Father was born on Christ's birthday, so reminds him of that, and encourage him to come to Mass on Jesus's birthday day."

This particular year was an exception to the rule, as Dad had knocked off work earlier than usual to purchase Mum's Christmas present. It was a kitchen dining table and chairs set, which he purchased from John Smith, the local furniture store. The table and chair set took pride of place in the kitchen area. I always wondered why he bothered, as we already had a hardly ever used dining room with a beautiful polished cedar table and matching chairs built in with red velvet cushions. Dad had also purchased that dining room set from John Smith on another Christmas Eve in the not so distant past.

Dad had not yet troubled John Smith on Christmas Day, to open up his store especially for him to do his Christmas shopping. That lot had traditionally fallen upon Norm Poole, who owned the local white-goods store. He would phone Norm around 9.a.m. on Christmas Day and drag him away from his family to open up his showroom, so Dad could browse at his leisure to purchase Mum's Christmas gift which was usually for the house. Norm never showed any sign of annoyance at this activity, as Dad would usually buy at least one item from him, which Norm then had the dubious task of delivering to our place that day, in the hope that he could join his family for Christmas lunch. He made a pile of money from my Dad on the day of the Lord's birth every year. Dad had purchase from Norm Poole and Sons, a new freezer, washing machine, refrigerator, record player, radiogram with a magic eye for tuning and a host fancy other goods.

Norm Poole must have breath a sigh of relief in some ways when Dad turned his Christmas day activities to John Smith's furniture store. Dad had softened John up for the future by uncharacteristically purchasing Mum's kitchen table and chairs on Christmas Eve. John like Norm prior to him was now in Dad's purchasing trap loop for the coming Christmas days until I went off to boarding school at age 12.

Over the years from John Smith he purchased two large crystal chandeliers, one for the lounge room and the other over the dining room table, a fancy bar cabinet, a new glass top to protect the cedar wood table, a camphor laurel timber bedroom suite and matching dressing table and a large clothing cupboard, curtains and blinds on all windows and a single clothing cabinet for his own use. This was followed by a three seater lounge with matching single chairs and the list went on and on every year. John Smith too must have breath a sigh of relief when he no longer had to deliver furniture to Dad on Christmas Day, but he like Norm Poole made a lot of retail sales from one customer every Christmas whilst this procedure took place.   The home I lived in with my parents for the next 8 years prior to being shipped off to boarding school was small. It was designed by Dad and finished in 1950; a two bedroom, one bathroom fibreboard cottage, with living room, kitchen come dining room and a sun room for visitors with built in bed in the wall. The sunroom bed was much like a sleeper on a train which was the order of the day for long distant travellers first class and overnight to Sydney. The sunroom comprised a sitting room with a library of books and magazines and an ideal place to have a private meeting or time for private meditation. It was a small home full of stuff that I considered unnecessary. The rest of the home Mum was adorned with holy pictures and statues of the Madonna and Saints. I sometimes felt that I lived in a Church, for there was so many relics, even in my bedroom.   There was no way this little women's soul was going to Satan but she sometimes made my soul hell on earth. Her flights of fancy was full of eccentricities which usually resulted in new shoes or clothing for herself. Dad giving her much in jewellery, silk sheets and bed attire. Her passion thou was to go to Edna Stride's clothing tailor business and have dresses made in the material of her choice. This for some time became a once a fortnight event. First for the selection of material and the return to try on the new garment before Dad paid the bill. He was more than content to shower her with Gifts as long as he could be free to do his own thing.

I think he preferred to be at work then be at home with her, as Mum had the unhappy knack of nagging him and in his absence it was always me who copped it. Dad had in his wisdom built the laundry below the sunroom off the house. It was fitted with a clothing 'shoot' under a storage cupboard to the laundry for easy transport to the laundry basket below. It served a two fold purpose for me. Sometimes I would climb in and let myself fall down too a pole of dirty linen left there for Mum to wash. It was hidden from view at the end of the built-in bedhead, matched by a storage cupboard at the other end of the bed. A shoot exit in the laundry with a cupboard to catch the clothing and a door that appeared like any other cupboard from the outside. I also used it, sometimes with a mates, to climb up into the house when there was no-one home to raid the fridge, play the radio-gram or just hang out there with my mates. It also served as a means of quick escape from a house crazed cleaner who nagged me about 'cleanliness being next to godliness,'as I slaved to her instruction. Similarly, once the the mission with mates was completed, we simply dropped down the show again and made our escape. Neither Mum or Dad ever found out about the secret endeavours via the "shoot." In the back yard below the staircase to the back door was a shower room, a breeze way for drying clothing and a toilet. This shower and toilet building sat underneath two large water tanks for household supply, as there was no town water or sewerage for homes back then. The toilet was of the pan type and the lavatory man came once a week to replace the full one with a new empty. As time progressed, the toilet gradually made its way into the bathroom and when water and sewerage was connected we had two toilets, one outside where the pan use to be and the bathroom one. So for a small house where there was a bath with over head shower and the outside shower as well as having toilets was pretty much unheard of in our township back in the late 1950s when these conveniences were introduced.

The Christmas Eve that Dad purchased the kitchen table and chairs, one James Patrick O' Grady came calling to the back door. Patrick, as formally mentioned, was affectionally known as "Sausage," occasionally worked in the slaughter room at the Abattoir and made home made sausages for the family and the Catholic fund raisers from his meat allocation from the kill.

Patrick O' Grady continued with his unofficial Macksville Gift duties as a loyal and longest standing servant of carnival. "Saus" carried out most of the chores including groundsman, track pre-parer, cleaner, semaphore operator, builder, painter, and of course knock-em-down side showman. 'Saus' O' Grady is probably best remembered for two major incidents that happened when I was still living at home as a child. The first of those was the pig kill and clean incident. Dad had employed the 'Saus' to travel to Sydney by train with him on many occasion to collect British cars off the ships at the docks and drive them up the coast to be cleaned and renewed for display and sale in the garage showroom for po-tential purchasers. Eric McPhillips Motor Business held the agency for Standard Cars, Rover, Triumph and International Trucks, trac-tors and farm equipment for the term of my youth and into many of my years into adulthood. It was historically a thriving motor vehicle dealership in the 1950s and 60s in a thriving country town. So Saus, when not working for the meat-works or doing the also ran jobs for the Gifts, was employed by Eric McPhillips.

On this particular Christmas Eve, Dad had employed "Saus" to go bush and find a wild pig, kill it and prepare the meat for storage in a new freezer ice chest that Dad had also purchased for home use, from Norm Poole of course, on some past Christmas day whim. Patrick the hunter, set out in that early dawn Christmas Eve on that fate filled day with his 303 rifle with the express purpose to find a wild pig, kill and cure it for our a family. Dad was so busy getting customers cars roadworthy for the Christmas break he had almost forgotten about 'Sausage and the pig.'

It was around nine o' clock at night when Patrick, drunk as a skunk, appeared at our back door, with a dead pig over his shoul-der, dripping blood from it forehead where the 303 bullet had pen-etrated. The 'Saus' proceeded to our kitchen, where he promptly dumped it on the new Christmas gift-the kitchen dining table. Mum almost had a fit and ordered him and the Pig and all out of the house. Dad, Patrick, dead pig and I proceeded to the shed out back were Dad set up a table, washed it down and the well primed slaughter man Patrick commenced to carve up the beast with his butcher knives. He occasionally stopped to drink another beer whilst he related the events of the day that lead up to his late arrival at our home. In his eagerness to complete the task, he ran the butchers carving knife over his arm cutting it deeply. Without so much as a pause, Patrick O' Grady competed the task of carv-ing up the pig, took the Ute and drove home drunk to his family home, leaving Dad to store the meat in the freezer. It was around

10.30 p.m. when we all headed to bed for a brief nap before getting up again around 11.30 to get ready for the Midnight Mass celebration, as most local Catholics seem to do in preference to the next morning service. The Church was packet when we arrived and who should be seated with his family, dressed in suit shirt and tie, sober as a judge, with a bandage on his arm; none other than Patrick O' Grady. How he managed to drive home drunk and come to the Mass celebration stone cold sober an hour and a half later was some kind of miracle. Perhaps it was because he was Irish for the Irish have amazing skill drunk or sober as I have come to learn over my lifetime.

I guess " Saus" with his belief in the power of God had asked in his Irish way for a miracle to get him sober quickly that Christmas eve and he got it. He later related how he had found the wild pig early on Christmas eve morning and with one shot between the eyes had completed his initial task for our family. Returning to town around midday, he parked the utility behind the pub with pig and gun in the back, and headed to the bar intending to have a beer before completing the deed of carving up the pig.the Being the Irishman that he was, the Christmas cheer with fellow drinkers went on until early evening, when suddenly Patrick had the presence of mind to complete his duty, so that's when he headed for our home to carve up the beast. Nothing more was said by Mum or Dad about the pig incident. We feasted on the pig meat for the next six months as the main meal on Sunday dinner. I sometimes wonder how Dad, in his wisdom, allowed Sausage to drive that Ute home that night. Perhaps Dad was more in his cups too and reasoned that the 'Saus' would be o.k. driving. Perhaps he knew that God looks after, widows, orphans and drunks with special blessings. Besides, Dad like Patrick O' Grady came from good Irish stock and two much blood in their alcoholic system was an unquestionable reality.

Howard and Sons, Pyrotechnics has been for decades the fireworks company which has helped celebrate the opening of the Sydney Harbour Bridge, numerous Royal visits and the many New Year's Eve celebrations that Sydney has become famous for. It was another innovation of Dad's that the Macksville Gift should be celebrated with a fireworks display that would be memorable. So, with me tagging along back there in 1953, we made our way to the manufacturers warehouse in Sydney.

Dad ordered the same rockets that the Howard family made for Sydney's New Years celebration. The rockets were massive and like any large rocket, required a specially built launch pad to send them skyward. Dad returned home with the largest order of Fireworks imaginable for the first night carnival.

The Gift final at night was always highlighted by a spectacular Fireworks display. Ever since the Gift programme contained night events, our friend 'Saus' O'Grady had fired all types of rockets towards the heavens. He had enjoyed that activity as he had stated that it brought enjoyment to thousand of spectators and competitors over the years. So, one night at the show ground before the Gift carnival, Dad told him to place all the firework under the race winners dais, as the local radio station had predicted rain. Dad deduced that the dais was the closes proximity from where 'Saus' would be firing the rockets. Saus suggested to Dad that somewhere safer should be located for the hideaway. Dad insisted that under the dais would be safest so under the dais they went. What followed later was a spectacle the likes of which had never been seen at Macksville before or since. The very first rocket that Suas lit, instead of going skyward, slithered across the grass under the dais and into the centre of the cache of fireworks. Sparks flew into the air then roman candles, whizzers, stars and all manner of rockets went in every direction. Dad, as it was witnessed, was jumping up and down on one spot calling him a "bloody idiot" with fireworks of all colours whizzing around him. Some of the displays went over the Bowraville Macksville roadway and above the cattle in Morgan's nearby farm. Saus reckoned those cows were so surprised they did not let their milk down for the next six weeks.

Travelling with Dad to and from Gift carnivals was always fun. One year heading north to Grafton for the Gift Carnival, we crossed a new bridge on the Pacific Highway, just North of Coffs Harbour. Mick Denham was Dads' pillion passenger on that day and as usual I was in the back with the local team of gift athletic participants. The bridge was high above a river and as we crossed over, a worker was making his way, half way across, on an outside rail without any protection. He was balancing on a pipe as he walked and carried a long steel rod on his shoulder. Mick, wound his window down as we passed and at the top of his voice cried out: " Drop that!" It startled the worker so much, he lost his balance and fell, steel rod and all into the river below. Luckily the river was not flowing fast and he managed to swim to shore. Once we could see he was safe, minus the steel rod, we hightailed it out of there and back on the road to Grafton.

Whilst my father was at work more often than not, we had not the opportunity for a father/son time, except when I had the pleasure of his company on long journeys to and from Sydney. Those journeys of a business nature involved picking up of a new car or truck and driving it back to Macksville to add to the inventory of motor vehicles for sales in Dad's business. To transport a vehicle from the docks of Sydney and up the coast was quite an ordeal. All Dad's new car purchases come on board ship from the U.K. The ships were not designed for motor vehicle transport and cars were chained to the deck and coated in tar to protect them from the elements of exposure and scratching of the car body paint. Upon arrival from England the cars would be lowered to the dock and once the paper work was complete they were handed over. It was not an initially long process to get the vehicle mobile for Dad simply applied chemical onto the windows to melt off the tar, then he would clean them with methylated spirits with some old news paper. The next step was too tie trade plates to the back and front of the vehicle to cover the legal requirements of driving an unregistered vehicle on the Highway, then start the motor and hit the road. The next few days we're the difficult parts of the exercise. If the "Saus" was travelling with Dad and they had two vehicles to travel North in, it was common practice for them to stop at every pub along the route for a beer or two. In those days there was no breathalyser or for that matter Police on the highway, so motor vehicle drivers pretty much determined their own rules when it come to sobriety. Dad never drank when he travelled with me, so it was business as usual as we travelled North on the old sometimes dirt and occasional gravelled road known today as the M2 expressway, but back in the early 50s it was called the Pacific Highway. It's was not much of a highway really and we on more than one occasion came across a fatality.   The road followed the old route taken by early settlers with horse and buggy and in the thirties during the depression years, swagmen heading North took the route looking for work in the bush. On route the route between Sydney and Brisbane, there were twelve river crossings. Each of these locations, was an excuse for the drivers to stop for a break, purchase a bottle of oysters from the roadside oyster farmer and polish them off with a bottle of beer recently purchase at the last hotel out of Sydney exit at Hornsby.

By the time I came on the scene the Hawkesbury River bridge (1945) had been built, so the need to stop disappeared, but the oyster farmers stalls remained. We always had a breather there for a feed of oysters after climbing the steep hill out of Sydney, and down to the river crossing. The old highway snaked its way to Belmont and across a ridge were we could see the smoked filled uniformed black layers of soot from domestic coal fires, smoke-stacks of industry, steam rail trains in the city below us. Newcastle was the city black as the coal in which it was built on.

The By-pass was at the Hexham River Ferry, another rest stop with blanket to wrap around our shoulders in the winter and picnic basket of fruit or whatever could be to eat whilst we rested. The highway then turned sharply westward through Stroud and turn North once more to Hawkes Nest, across the river from Tea Gardens. There was a small car ferry on the Hawkes Nest side, with a house for the ferry driver on the far shore near Tea Gardens. Across the road from the ferry driver was a Pub, purpose built to accomodate the traveller with a few beers, a belly full of food and a bed for the night before venturing on the next day. It was the practice of the ferry driver to check how many cars were arriving on the far shore and only come across to transport the vehicles when he was assured of full load. This benefited the publican, be-cause the ferry driver quit early evening and did not do a return trip across the river until early the next morning. So a lot of pubs sprung up at ferry stops on the old highway north.

I dare say the ferry drivers were in cahoots with the publicans in the delay in the number of times the ferries crossed the rivers to transport cars and passengers too distant shores. It was not un-common to be held up by old semi trailers going up hills and not being able to pass them because of the narrowness of the road. At some point the driver of the trucks would stop off the road for a rest and we would get underway again. Apart from the ferry cross-ing at Karuah, the highway went eastward again, there was anoth-er at Dawson river near Taree, still another another at Coopernook Lansdowne River, Blackman's Ferry across the Hastings River near Port Macquarie and one at the Macleay River at Kempsey. The rest were creek crossing north which had small timber constructed bridges built mainly for stock crossings that served there purpose for a number of years, made a lot of noise when crossing, due to wear and tear of the timber planks from increasing traffic use. The wooded bridges designed to be just above the creek come high tide level worked effectively except in flood which was another ex-cuse to take a bypass to the nearest pub location.

The journey to Macksville without mishaps took around 24 hours, allowing for the frequent stops and pub stopovers. There were a further half a dozen ferries north from Macksville to the Queensland boarder with equal crossing delays. Once the vehicle arrived at the McPhillip's showroom, a team of Dad's employees stripped off the tar around the body of the vehicle with a cutting compound of Kitten No.2; were they then cleared away any remaining surface blemish and finish off with a buffing machine of the Kitten No.1 polish. The job complete, the new vehicle with the 'run in' odometer reading from Sydney clearly shown as testament to its roadworthiness, was driven to the local Court of Petty Sessions Clerk to register. The car was then proudly displayed in the new car showroom window for sale. The whole ordeal from ship dock to showroom took the better part of a week to complete. Dad was always full of creative ideas for his engineering business, the Macksville gift, sales and marketing of cars, trucks, tractors and farm implements. Dad's enthusiasm was infectious, particularly when he was in full flight, there were no boundaries that could not be climbed over, burrowed under or bypassed. At one Gift Carnival he thought it would be a good idea to 'open' the event with some notable dignity officiating. He could think of no one better to ask than the then Prime Minister, Bob Menzies and set about to invite him to the District for this purpose. He received a reply from the leaders office stating that whilst the P.M. was honoured in being asked to perform the duty of "opening" the Gift, earlier commitments prevented him from accepting the invitation. This reply also contained an offer to have some other dignitary from the Prime Minister's Office come instead. Dad's reply to this " knock back" was that as the Prime Minister could not come he would choose someone else to perform the duty and would not be taking suggestions from any outside source, including the Prime Ministers's Department.

On another occasion, Dad got it in his head to phone the PM for a Sunday afternoon chat. Whilst on a recent visits to the USA he had a meal with the head of International Harvester Company Wally Westercott. Wally had been in charge of International Harvester in Australia before being promoted to the top job back the U.S.A. Dad had got to know Wally on his many visits to purchased trucks from the company in Sydney during the early 50s. Wally Westercott, during his tenure in Australia become good friends with Bob Menzies, the newly elected PM. Phoning the PM's after hours message bank at the time, he was advised by his service personnel that the PM was staying at the Wentworth Hotel in

Sydney. Dad quickly hung up and dialled the hotel reception and was advise that the PM was at a private function in the main auditorium. I was seated near Dad when he responded over the phone: "So go get him." To my great surprise Mr. Menzies took the phone call. Dad said: "Mr. Prime Minister, this is Eric McPhillips at Macksville, (pause) I've just returned from the USA on business and enjoyed the pleasure of the company of a good friend of yours- Wally Westercott and he has ask me to pass on his regards." Well, the PM was delighted and raved on to Dad like he was also a long lost friend. Dad told me later that he could not stop the PM from talking and that the phone call cost him a small fortune. It always amazed me that he had this dogmatic charisma with politicians of the opposite persuasion to his own labor faith. An employer as a strong supporter of the left dealt more with the right of the political spectrum effectively in his working life. Perhaps it was because the Liberals were in power more often than Labor back then; well at least federally. Another idea of Dad's was to arrange a cavalcade of trucks to parade through our town to a display area at the local show ground at the local annual show. He managed to convince trucking companies around the nation to be in attendance to display all current makes and models of trucks, cars and farm equipment and it all went off without a hitch.

Eric Mc Phillips was considered a mechanical genius when it came to trucks and he particularly enjoyed working on diesel motors too. All his mechanics also got much enjoyment working on trucks, but they usually had to lift the engines of its mounts with a chain driven block and tackle pulley system and put the engine on a bench to do repairs and servicing. Whilst physically strong Dad was very small in stature and could sit within the cabin next to the engine of any truck, thus saving time and money to do his work.

He gained quite a reputation with major trucking companies and internationally too. Whilst Dad had a full International truck and machinery dealership, he serviced the bulk of other makes and models. The White Company of Cleveland USA sent a new large hauling truck out from the States to test it for Australian conditions by sending it around Australia. The vehicle broke down just south of Newcastle and nobody, not even their local agents mechanics knew how to fix it. Someone from International Harvester Company here in Australia advised White USA Head Office that if any one could get it going, fine tuned and running like clockwork again it was Eric McPhillips.

Dad got a call from their Chief of staff for White trucks in USA asking if he could see to it to get their broken down new truck roadworthy again.With one of his skilled mechanics, Geoff Grace, they made their way to the broken down vehicle. Together they had the machine back on the road in next to no time. Dad got a tidy some of money for his efforts sharing the proceeds with his employee Geoff for his contribution to their joint engineering master feat. Dad, apart from his mechanical genius was always known to be an innovator. He designed and built the wrought iron gate and fences around our home and numerous objects in timber, including a 'smoko' stand, light stand and side table for the home in his limited spare time. Another of his grandiose ideas was to build truck trailers.

Dad registered a trade name and included employees in the project. There was Charlie, Robert, Eric, Max, and Tom, including Colin .The first letter of each of the participants names in the project spelt out a brand name CREMATIC. So the brand became 'Crematic Constructions' which was proudly displayed on the back of the first trailer : "Built at Eric McPhillips Pty Ltd Macksville by Crematic Constructions." The trailer builder team soon found that the demand and competition to build was less worthwhile than servicing vehicles which was much more lucrative. So the initial enthusiasm for the business model soon faded into the background and they stopped building trailers unless they were requested to do so by hauling contractors.

Ever since the first Wirth Circus and Zoo came to town in the early 50s there have been street parades in Macksville. The Circus was the first that I remember, followed by a car rally bush orientation course, the 1953 Coronation of Queen Elizabeth Parade, Dad's Cavalcade of trucks, the Redex trial and the military parade through the streets of town with the casket of much loved local VC recipient, war hero and Pick-a-Box quiz expert, Frank Partridge. In more recent times it was the parade through town for local born Australian Cricketer test batsman Philip Hughes, who's died when hit in the head by a cricket ball during a domestic match in 2014.

It was billed as the greatest the Show on Earth' for us kids of the 1950's. It was not the actual climax of the event itself that made it all worthwhile but the manner in which it was introduced and the lead up to the show itself. I think Wirth's Circus may have been the first that I saw back in the early 50s but they always arrived by road and were not as exciting to me as the first Aston's Circus, as it arrive by rail and not by road transport.The month before the one night stand, a Circus promotor would arrive with a poster for the front window of the showroom in Dad's garage. He located all the best traffic flow spots in town and provided two free tickets to the show with date and time of the ' big night under the big top' on the poster. This resulted in a free ticket for me and my neighbour mate Ashley of my later 'chicken game' fame.

We both looked forward to the day of the Circus. In those days most Circus equipment, entertainers and animals arrived by road, visiting every major location on the Pacific Highway route between Sydney and Brisbane. However, Aston Circus took it a step further and elected to do it all by rail on their own special train. We look forward to its pending visit by train with great excitement as I recall. The train arrived early on the Saturday of the event and Ashley & I who lived close to the railway station were on the platform as the long train with full head of steam and much hooting of the steam engines horn as it arrived. Troops of entertainers and workers were already dressed for the show it seemed, alighted quickly from the passenger carriages and began to disconnect each carriage, placing some on a side rail where animals were lions, tigers, laughing hyenas, monkeys, birds, horses and elephants were housed. We watched with fascination as inner fancy gypsy like painted carriages, with the animal manager were transported to the ground with the help of elephants, who were the main slaves of their master doing the heavy work of towing the large cages on wheels and lining them up on a dirt road on the far side of the platform.

Once unloaded, the passenger train was moved to another line, with only sleeping quarters still in tact. The last item to be unloaded was Mr. Ashton's Golden Rolls Royce, to follow up the rear of the pending parade. By lunch time Saturday, at the height of local in town trading hours, the parade through Macksville began with Ring Master out front, closely followed by brass band and and the consent sound of a bass drum. We knew the route the Circus parade would take, and made our way to the footpath outside my Dad's garage to watch the passing parade. The Ring Master with a swirling baton lead the way followed by a well rehearsed band of players and entertainers.. Clowns, jugglers, ladies standing astride well groomed horses, men either riding or leading horses, a lion tamer cracking a whip, trapeze artists, acrobats doing cartwheels along the road and elephants towing two long trailers of zoo animals and Mr.Ashton in his Rolls at the rear.

CHAPTER 6.

FAIR GAME AND FOWL DEEDS

The whole task of erecting the Circus tent from reception entry to the main arena covering the size of two football fields in width and depth took possibly one hour from start to finish. Meanwhile the wagon trains of animals were displayed on either side of the entry for ease of moving in and out of the main arena during the performances. The lighting was subdued throughout, with the bench decker seated audience mainly a shadowed reflection from the central lights. It was not designed as an effect as much as the local council restrictions on how much power the Circus took from the town's grid on that evening. I recall after the introduction by the Ring Master, there were performing clowns, jugglers and men, women and monkeys doing all sorts of amazing manoeuvres on horse back. This was followed by the fast erection of a large lattice work globe in which to motor bike riders began to manoeuvre around and over one another at high speeds. It was called the 'Globe of Death,' but the riders were so proficiently skilled that the act went off without a hitch. Whilst this act was underway, the erection of a large metal enclosure and the carriage carrying the lions were set up centre stage.

The act of the Globe of Death completed, attention was drawn to the Lion tamer, who prodded the beast from their cage and into the metal enclosure continuing to crack his whip as the lions growled loudly performing well rehearsed tricks under his com-mand. The act climaxed with one of his assistance putting their head into the lions open mouth and out agin before the angry beast closed its jaw. The final act of the night was always the trapeze which had the tight rope artist swigging high above the big top with a small net below for safety. This act included the women performers doing a threesome swing and jump to a platform on the opposite end of the tent big top. The final act usually consisted of the male leader of the trapeze swinging from one end of the arena to the other getting as much height on the swing as was possible and attempting to do a triple somersault to the arms of a catcher hanging upside down on a swing at the other end of the tent.The spectacle over the Circus ended and the Big Top come down for another year. The crew, entertainers, animals and equip-ment were soon gone from town and on to the train the next day for another nights performance in some expectant town further north.

Perhaps the most memorable Circus night I ever lived was that night. My friend Ashley was picked from the audience to ride a fast pony around the arena with a belt tided to a rope around his waist and hitch to the ceiling. As he started his ride, the clowns pulled the rope and Ash went flying around and around the tent above our heads, but not before a clown had pulled down his shorts as he was hauled into the air. Ash had no underpants on that night and totally exposed his private parts to the amusement of the crowd, Ashley's repeated attempted to reach his pants hanging below his knees was to no avail. The crowd roared with laughter as he went around and around that tent enclosure, but to my red faced friend it was no laughing matter. I saw the funny side to it all but was likewise embarrassed for my good friend too. Nothing more was said about that night and to his dying day I assume he never thought much about it either.

The rally trial that followed as an orientation bush bash was the next parade of cars throughout the township before the rally began. One of Dad's employees, Bob Ellicott owned an old pillion passenger car. I don't remember the make or model but Bob kept it immaculately maintained. The pillion passenger seat, outside the main cabin was like a boot lid that opened up with leather lounge chair comfort seat. Another mate Phil Morrison and I had the joy of riding in the back whilst Bob and his navigator did they're best to win the race. Cryptic clues were set up for each stage of the race and at critical places the car had to stop for recording time taken and gather refreshments for the next leg. At the end of the race, the winners were announce on a point score basis. I can't recall if we got a place in that race or not. I just remember it was fun bouncing around dirt roads in the bush in the back of that car in that race.

In June of 1952 Her Royal Highness Princess Elizabeth was on a Safari in Kenya, on route to Australia, when she received news of her Father King George's death. She made haste back to England and as a 25 year old young women was coronated. By the time she arrived in Australia in 1954 she was the Queen of England and the British Empire. We at St.Patrick's Macksville Primary School boarded an all night train to Lismore just to get a glimpse of the Queen and Duke of Edinburgh as they quickly passed by in an open vehicle. Every attendee at the ceremony was given a cardboard periscope with a bottom top mirror to view above the heads of those who were taller that stood in front of us. Our little twin township of Macksville in 1953 went into overdrive with a huge parade of colourful floats and marching band to celebrate the crowning of our Queen. Dad had made a huge crown replicating the one worn at her coronation and it adorned a carbon copy of the his garage business which seem to float on air above the roadway. It was actually built over one of his new international trucks and taken out of display for the day to be used in the parade. It was June 1953 and no sooner was the parade over, then preparation for the building of the starting gates for the first Macksville Gift began.

One of the efforts to raise funds for the running of the Gift carnival in 1953 was when the Redex trail came through Macksville. It was an around Australia car race and was promoted by popular radio personality Jack Davey who was a competitor in the race. The first leg of the race was Sydney to Brisbane and one of the pit stops was Eric McPhillips's garage at Macksville. It was the first place for petrol and quick service on the Pacific highway as the cars entered town. As the cars were to come right through the middle of town in the middle of winter the most senior executive of the Macksville Gift Committee, who happened to be a Senior Meat Inspector, suggested the Ladies Committee make soup to sell to the drivers and crew as the cars checked in at the pit stop, it would be a boost to fund raising. One ladies objected to it :"We can't cook soup in a garage, it's against the law." The Good Samaritan lady who supplied the soul was married to the Inspector and the law was successfully bypassed. It was an all night vigil and I was a proud participant in the proceedings of the night. It was raining cats and dogs as each car pulled in, and as quick as a flash, oils were topped up and tyres changed, whilst coffee, tea, fresh bread rolls and soup were served. Then just as quickly the rally car was on its way again.

Every hour on the hour Dad stopped to call the local radio station at Kempsey advising the announcer of details of cars and their progress as they entered and left the Garage. The takings sky rocketed, Dad made moneys for both the Gift and the garage and a lot of good-will from the rally organisers in Sydney and the media for his efforts. It was win win all around, and McPhillip' Garage was now known via radio from Sydney to Brisbane. The Redex trial drivers competed around the country through rain, sleet, dust storms, sunshine and shadow. The controversy over the importance of the race raged for months after the event.

The trail had set out to test the reliability of competing cars under all types of conditions Australia had to offer. It certainly did that. The 1953 Redex resulted in modifications for the 1954 trail and more improvements were made on vehicles from that experience too. These trails then helped in improve the durability of cars being made for Australian conditions. The trails were also set out to test the skill of drivers and navigators and they certainly achieved that too and learnt a lot themselves as a consequence.

There were a couple of significant incidents that centred around the geographic location of Eric McPhillip's Garage that involved me in my younger years and caused some bother to Dad and his staff as a consequence. The whitewashing of the family Vista law mower was not one those for I had not reached the age of reason when I figured the lawn mower needed a new paint job. No, the first major event was when I was about three years of age. Dad had taken me to work at the garage with him to give Mum a break and to escape her constant nagging. I had a little Teddy Bear at the time and always carried it around as my friend. On this occasion I had wondered off when Dad was distracted with a client. My Father had installed four different company brands of fuel pumps at the time and had bulldozed a deep well at the side of the garage to sink an even larger fuel tank there. The Well hole was about 5 metres or so deep and my curiosity got the better of me when I went to investigate. Peering over the side to see what was down the hole I lost the grip on my little bear and it fell to the bottom of the well. Being an adventurous spirit I began climbing down a side wall of the hole to rescue my friend and fell to the bottom. Lucky for me the bottom was loose clay and it cushioned my fall. I had landed on my head and was a little dazed but remember calling out for Dad to come to the rescue. He turned up not long after and with one of his employees climbed down the hole and passed me up to waiting arms at the surface. I was rushed off to Dr. Pope's surgery and after a complete examination he declared that I would be ok. I recall that I had to rest up overnight and felt sick but didn't throw up, so I must have had minor head injury due to the softness of the mud base at the bottom of the hole. It was the first of many concussion to follow. Further hits in the head over my teens and young adult years were mainly due to contact sport, and getting into fist fights, but they later morphed into depressive episodes.

The next error of my ways was when I went working in the car service area of the garage for Dad in my teens during school holidays. A visiting salesman had been advised by one of his clients to take his car for service to Dad the next time he came to Macksville, Apparently the vehicle owner was having difficulty getting an adequate service completed in his City location and held on for service until he got to Macksville. Dad had me run about as dogsbody to the mechanics in his workshop. It was a matter of handing out spanners, hammers and odds and ends like a nurse does for a doctor in the operating theatre.

The event that ended my prospects of ever working with Dad in the garage was the day I was asked to move the travelling salesman's car to the front off the driveway after it had been serviced and repaired. At that time I was to young to get a drivers licence but was given the task to start the car, drive it out on the main highway for about 5 metres, turn under the awning next to the petrol pumps and park it in this traditional age old spot for serviced cars until the owner turned up to collect it.

It was not the first time I had cared out such a task and had learnt to drive quite early for Dad. He had insisted he take me out to the local show ground in my pre teen years and I learnt to drive a blitz wagon. You know those WW11 heavy duty military carrying vehicles, well It was impossible to change gear without a double shuffling like a drummers feet movement in tune with the music or in this case the motor. Once I had mastered that feat, Dad went to the trouble one weekend to pull down a gear box and show me how everything worked in unison and how important it was not to crunch gears changing them. I was a master of the wheel for truck, car and tractor driving well before I ever went for my driving licence at age 16 years and 10 months. But for now back to my parking of the travelling salesman car and the consequences that followed. I remember it had a column gear change and a hand break next to the drivers seat. It was a new novel idea that meant the driver for additional safety had to press a button at the top of the break when pulling the break handle. It was an extra precaution which meant the button had to be held in when the break was released. I had no problem doing this and pulled the handle as tight as I though was adequate, took the keys out of the ignition and returned to the workshop with the keys in my pocket. I had not moved but two steps into the workshop when I notice all the mechanics exiting the building towards the highway at hurricane speed. Dad was attempting to be in hot pursuit but keep falling over the mobile tray he had been laying on under the vehicle he was then servicing. I began to laugh at the comedy that I witnessed before me. That is until I happened to to look at what all the fuss was about. The vehicle that I thought was safely parked was in fact travelling slowly down the highway backwards, gaining momentum as it travelled. I had left the gear shift in neutral and the hand brake was not enough to hold the car in a stationary position on a slightly tilted uphill driveway. I propelled my legs at maximum speed, towards the car as it increased its speed towards an unknown destination. Everything seems to be in slow motion and a fellow crossing the road hesitated as I passed him bye he exclaimed in a sort of a daze: "That cars got no driver."

I was first to the car and attempted to jump in and apply the breaks but to no avail. Fate had it that I kept getting knocked out of the way by the opened car door. I had tried to use the steering wheel as leverage in my attempt to jump on board; it was a bad mistake. The car changed it pace direction backwards into a nearby parked car. It just so happened that Dad's panel beaters had only just repaired that car from another workshop mishap and parked it outside his place of employment in what was thought a safe location. The car belonged to a telephone technician at the exchange opposite. He had parked it near Dad's second hand car lot next door to the exchange a week before. A runaway vehicle on Dads lot 'without a driver' coasted on the highway and smack bam into this guy's car. Well here it was nice and shiny after being repaired for free naturally by Dad's panel beaters and who should come along but me with another runaway car smack bam again into that car. The outcome was extensive damage to both cars and more 'no fee for repairs' to both cars by Dad and his men. Dad's dark and stormy look was enough for me to cringe on the spot. It was somewhat a relief for me when he just said with clenched teeth "Go home."   Every now and again such incidents of the forces of my nature dropped in on me. Another such incident was at Jack Hughes' home. Terry, the son was a friend of mine as was his sister Robyn who was in the same class as me all through Primary school. The parents were away on business at a time when all us kids got up to mischief. Robyn had organised a party of young boys and girls for indoor fun which included games with prizes usually resulting in hugs and kisses. Some of the boys had not reached that knowing age where the hormones ran wild within but I was not one of those.

The fun at the Hughes home stared when I began to chase Judy Lord, a fellow class mate through the house to give her a kiss. She was playing hard to get and I was gaining on her as she entered the lounge room. As fate would have it , she closed the two beautifully large plate glass doors on me and without a change in my stride, I went straight through them without so much as a scratch. The doors did not fair so well thou as they smashed to smithereens all over the lounge room floor. That was the end of the 'hugs and kisses party' and all including me left after doing our best to clean up the mess.

I have no idea to this day what Robyn or Terry told their parents but nothing more was ever said about that mishap either. My last recall of time with Terry was when I was on summer vacation from boarding school in my mid teens and instead of heading to the beach with some friends, decided to try my flippers in the new Olympic size swimming pool. It had been built with the help of funds from the Macksville Gift Carnival and I reckoned I owed it to Dad's efforts to at least have a dip there. I was never much of a swimmer despite being in the Surf Life Saving Club ' nippers' in my pre teens. My claim to fame was beach sprints and I had passed water safety standards in my first year at boarding school and had a certificate to prove it, but my swimming skills lacked speed and technique and for that matter distance. Terry like always was in the pool doing training laps. I quickly put the flippers on my feet and dived in the water. As Terry returned for the next lap I put my flippers into action and got in pace with him. I keep up his pace and increased mine beginning to pull away a little from him about 50 metres from the finish. Terry was sucked in and increased his pace, we swam neck are neck to the end of a 100 meter dash and reached the pool edge end at the same time. Terry was completely taken in and surprised by my ability to give him a run for his money; intrigued that I had managed to keep up wit him considering that I was never sighted before at the pool and was not know to n be a competitive swimmer. It was not long before I come clean about the flippers on my feet and he laughed out loudly with relief that he was still the champ and that he was.

It would be remiss off me not to mention some events and equipment fraught with danger that we kids never thought twice about in putting into action. Terrys Hughes was a good case in point as he had developed a Viking like very large catapult in his back yard to fire chook eggs from the family hen house into nearing front yards.

The goal was in reality to see who could use this sling shot to shoot across the neighbourhood roofs to the football field beyond.The field was hidden from view by a very high fence, so we could achieve our aim without drawing attention from the neighbours or any one who happened to be in the target area. After many mishaps and a broken neighbourhood window or splatting mess on passing cars, we finally achieved our aim. Its small wonder we did not do more harm, but the contraption was soon dismantled after we had our share of fun with it. The Hughes property and surrounds did not need to attract further attention after my previous glass door shattering incident.

In the case of Greg, Kevin, Morris and myself, it was often our summer bare foot stomping inhabits in the swamp lands close to town searching for birds eggs in trees and emu eggs on the ground that was really fraught with danger. The Swamps were infested with every creature know to man, not the least of all poisonous snakes. On one occasion in the heat of a summer tramp with Morris and his gun "Old Betsy" carved in the butt in honour of Davy Crockett of Alamo fame, we foursome adventurers made our way around a large swam in search of more birds eggs. I had once proceeded to cut up Mums fox fur cape to make a Davy Crockett hat but was caught in the act, so bush bashing for birds eggs with his Morris's 'Old Betsy' was the next best thing to having a Crockett fur skinned cap, particularly when he let me shoot it.

Morris having the weapon of mass destruction had the honour of the lead and stepped over a mound on the ground near the swamp. I followed planting a bare foot on the mound as I passed over it. As it turned out, the mound was alarmingly a black snake curled up asleep and I had disturbed his slumber by stepping on it. The snake shot out behind me directly at Kevin who sped at the rate of knots in a drastic retreat closely followed by Greg. I had looked down when the snake moved under my foot and saw over my shoulder its path of trajectory towards my friend. Changing its mind the snake slid into the swamp and we thought that was the last of it and continued on our merry way. It was not to be so as the snake doubled back on us in the swamping waters and we spent most of the rest of that day avoiding it. Like some not so nice people, they are not called 'snakes in the grass' for nothing. On another occasion, Kevin and I were on a stay over at Greg's home at the edge of town. The family had a farm up country but they also had a rather large back yard and paddock next door for chooks and egg production. This of course was an added attraction to red belly black snakes as they not only injected poison in the chooks but killed and ate them when the opportunity arose.They also gluttonously consumed their eggs too and Rupert Fleming, Greg's Dad, had a pet hatred for snakes because of their culling of his livelihood inventory. It was because of this hatred he had an array of snake catching gadgetry in his back shed. A shot gun for killing with a rifle was too quick for Rupert for he wanted to inflict as much pain as possible on the creature before its spirit departed for ever into snake hell.

It was on this auspicious occasion that we boys found ourselves picking red berries off the tree near the back verandah of the family homestead. Our mutual attire of cotton T-shirt, shorts and bare feet was our usual summer wardrobe, as it was on this day. At some point in the midst of our feast, someone cried " Snake" and all but I bolted to the verandah nearby. I thought Greg was up to his usual tricks of scaring somebody, so I ignored the warning until I heard Rupert Flemings' voice from behind me: "Don't move Doug." He continued speaking quietly without alarm. "There is a large black snake advancing towards your left foot, so don't move an inch." There was no way I was going to do that, I was frozen to the spot with fear. Glancing down without so much as the slightest movement of my head, I watched as the snake went around my bare feet left and then right before it began its journey up the back yard hill with Mr.Fleming in hot pursuit. The snake made it to its entry hole near the back fence and began to disappear into a hole in the ground. As quick as a flash, Rupert had hooked its tail with a wire and began to haul it out belting the living daylights out of it with a leather strap in his free hand. By the time the six foot (near 2 metre) agent of Satan was at the surface it spirit had departed. That snake would never again tempt another Eve or Adam to eat the forbidden fruit from the tree of knowledge much less little boys eating berries from a nearby tree. I think sin died that day a second time, as Christ had already died for that purpose some 2000 years beforehand.

So many events of my childhood all seem to come to a head in my final year at home. I recall now the fun I had climbing trees to rob the nests of a birds for another speckled egg with my mates. The shoe box full of those shell treasures hidden in the shed out the back of the family home, hidden from the view of my father who frowned on such activity. The silk worm farm I had created also hidden from view of prying eyes.

Mum didn't seem to mind my ill-gotten goods being proudly showed off to mates when we compared our natural treasures from time to time. She was also aware of the catapult I had hidden under the house and retrieved when I went bush with my mate Des to kill a crow or two. We boys had clone 'Bowie knives' which was our little secret to go on a killing spree in the bush. Other than snakes and lizards, black crows were our deadly enemy. They would swoop down from anywhere, peck you on the head and move on. We took great delight in taking specked eggs from their nest and killing them with stones in our slingshots when the opportunity arose. I think Mum was more akin to me in my hobby collecting or killing things nature provided. Dad was quite the opposite in that regard, he didn't like anything that involved capturing, killing or caging what was born free in the natural environment. I think at heart he was a greenie.

Large green bull frogs were a plenty in the swamps, domestic tank water and a hazard at night when walking barefooted to the outside loo. The feel of a cry from the frog once stepped upon in the dark was worse than the actual sensation of the slimy creature under ones feet. If I wasn't half asleep heading to the loo, I was more than awake in the dark heading back to bed mindful of the prospects of stepping on another of those freaks of nature. You don't see them around much anymore and now I regret our unthinking nature when we disposed of them unmercifully back then. Mum's idea of putting them out of their misery, if found in the vicinity of the loo or the outside shower, was to throw a petrol soaked rag over their body and set it alight- a fried frog is not a pretty sight. Of course, it was probably no worse than my mate Glenn , who would demonstrate a perfect method of disposal by shoving a cigarette in the frogs mouth and lighting up. The frog would continue to do the drawback with the smoke but could not exhale, the result was an exploding mess of smoke and frog everywhere. Mum, to her credit drew the line at that method. They were beautiful looking creatures for us kids but we were advise to stop collecting them and feeding them insects as their piddle caused worts on your fingers. When those disgusting skin blemishes from the frogs appeared on my fingers, Mum would enlist the local chemist, a master of crunching up ingredient to cure all ills, created a liquid that once applied had the effect of burning away the dreaded worts and was akin to shoving ones fingers into battery acid but it worked.

The last of my boyhood ended in the summer off 1957. It was the last time I played cowboys and Indians with Morris and our outfit. It was to be also the last year of a fight with a boy of my class under the school house were I learnt to play dirty tactics to get the upper hand on someone physically stronger but lacked my tenacity to win and my killer instinct. I felt guilty about that for a long time after the bout. It was the year T.V. had come to our home from a signal at the first North Coast channel at Lismore some hundreds of miles North. Dad had Norm Poole make a special trip once more on Christmas Day and that was the year the Saturday movie track to the theatre with friends died its natural death. We had our fair share of feature films, an untold quantity of cartoons and episodes of serials that played each week and that we just couldn't wait to return to the theatre to see what happened next. It was the end of rolling those orange coated chocolate Jaffa balls down the theatre stairway to the aboriginal kids in the front rows. The end of the making of a cylinders of Vincents APC headache powers into a cigarette, lighting the end in the dark theatre and blowing the lighted end, scaring the living daylight out of the kids seated in front with a flame of phosphorus igniting overhead. It was also the end of my fantail collection I kept hidden

from view of Mum and ate my way at night to the dentist for the inevitable filling of decayed tooth or tooth extract as a consequence.

It was the last year of games with Des, Glenn, Trevor or Nick who like me were being wizzed off to boarding school in the New Year too. No more killing lizards, boiling frogs or blowing them up with cigarette smoke, no more collecting birds eggs, climbing trees to rob nests for our collection. No more using a shot gun with my cousin Robert with barrel in the water to create and explosion of rising dead fish on the surface. My parents no doubt wondered how I was so good at catching fish. I hardly ever caught one with a hook, the borrowed shotgun always did the trick much easier. It was no more corkwood cutting for the gain of a pound or two (two to four dollars). My father put pay to my corkwood cutting with Des despite the money we made. He never stopped me being with him but he didn't like Des. They were too much alike and Des could hold his own with a smart arse answer or 'extreme' show of disrespect when the mood was chosen.

Des and I had our implements for killing and stabbing anything that moved in the bush. Our favoured tool was our replica Bowie knives and in the case of corkwood cutting, his dad's machete which we extracted from his weapons of mass destruction he kept in his shed. I remember Dad's key manager, Kelly Gossip upon hear a scolding I was getting from Dad on unlawful gained goods for our adventures stating to me: "Little boys who are not fools should never play with sharp tools." It is amazing how sayings come back from time to time. A couple of rhyming quotes come to mind other than that one. Ron McNeill was our local journalist on the Nambucca District News. These days its a part of the Murdock Empire but back then it was a typical local rag.

Ron was our next door neighbour who was a regular evening visitor to our home. After the evening meal Dad and Ron would get together over a few beers and pick words at random from the Webster Dictionary. The game was easy as each in turn had to speak fro three minutes about the chosen word using it repeatedly in every sentence spoken. The looser was the one who could not make the time distance as they played this for hours getting more inebriated with the telling and less and less coherent. I had a little autography book at the time and use to ask all and sundry to write in it something of value. Ron came up with this one: "Owen Moore went out one day, Owen more than he could pay, Owen Moore came back that day, Owen more." He didn't sign it Ron McNeill he signs it Owen Moore. Another that has rung true for me over the years is one from my Mum who had a sixth sense about most things of the heart. "Love many, trust few, always paddle your own canoe." It has taken some hard lessons in life to see the wisdom in those words, but they are ever present now.

There was to be no more tricks like Des and I played when we were flush with cash from our corkwood sales. Tricks like one we had played when we tied a piece of fishing line to a ten bob note, leaving it on the highway in the middle of the road. We ran the attached line across the road and hid behind a tree. The trick was to wait for a car to stop and the driver alight to collect the money. As soon a the unknowing driver left the vehicle to pick up the money, we would quickly pull the string and retrieve the note; watch the driver scratch his head, get back in is car and move on. It worked for a half a dozen times until we struck a driver with a clue. He didn't go for the note, he just chased after us.

We ran and hid in the bush, watched him collect the note, cutting the fishing line with his pocket knife and with a smile towards us he just waved and drove on. Thus ended our mischief making for the time being. Otherwise it was pelting stones at passing cars hubcaps with our catapults in a bid to see who would be first to create a dent by hitting a hubcap. It inevitably resulted in a chase by the driver on foot, as we ran off once our act of having achieved our moving target goal was 'Fait Accompli.' There was only one incident that caused me much pain attending the Saturday afternoon 'flicks.' As we graduated with age, we moved higher up the theatre arena to the back seats, away from the mass audience. The louts who were more knowing than innocent us pre-teen kids seem to win the girl of choice and ended up kissing and cuddling in the back row. There they made all kinds of weird noises with their passionate activity. We of less knowledge and a sense of 'goodness' remained engrossed in the movie. On this occasion, a girl called Sandra of dubious morality with big boobs was making out with a boy directly behind me. I turned to request they both keep quiet and got an eye full of what I later learned to be foreplay. The not so moral Sandra was taken aback that I dared view her exciting 'hot spot' reacting with a mass of profanities, telling me to "turn my gaudy F**k head around and watch the film." I had not turned for more than one second when she clobbered me over the head with the heel of her shoe. It was like an explosion going off and I suffered the afternoon away with a stinking headache. It was always an object lesson to this very day: "Mind your own business."

The two bob it cost to get to the movie always allowed me to budget my choice of sweet for later. Sometimes I settled for chocolate coated ice cream at interval. A ice-cream in cone cost a zack (five cents) back then and these days at the movies it cost six dollars for one, which proves that inflation has skyrocketed since the 1950s. Eating that delicacy in the dark during a movie always resulted in chocolate melting down the front of my shirt. So when Fantails came into vogue they became my choice of lollies to purchase and chew at the pictures. They were a chocolate coated toffee that stuck in your teeth or the roof of your mouth and it usually resulted in a trip to the dentist as an aftermath. The lollies were so named and came in a weird triangular shaped box individually wrapped with a paper profile of the movie star of the days written in small print. Impossible to read in the darkness of a picture theatre, my habit was to save some of mine and take them home.

I would hide under my sheets with torch light during the night happily trying to pry my mouth open when the toffee got stuck in my teeth, as I chewed away and read the prized wrapper advancing my next trip to the dentist. I didn't mind going to the dentist really; in point of fact I actually enjoyed it.

Jimmy Black was our family dentist and was a very skilled magician too. He kept me amused with his amazing tricks with cards, disappearing eggs and a light show on his surgery ceiling whilst inflecting pain in an extract of tooth or replacing a filling as a result of the fantail toffee glue and sugar coating. I wanted to stay in his good books too because he had a gorgeous brown eyed girl as his daughter and I was smitten at the time. She also liked football and I sometimes retreated to a local park to play 'force em back.' I didn't realise it at the time but our game proved to be a mild form of Australian Rules.

My Fantail ventures added to my dental decay but not quite as savagely as the toffee for they not only removed fillings when one attempted to dislodge the sweet glue but sometimes resulted in a tooth being broken. I never liked having the needle to ease the pain when at the dentist, preferring to accept the short term discomfort of the drill for the cleaning and filing of a cavity or the yanking out of a bad tooth. It was better in my opinion than putting up with a numb mouth for hours afterward. I knew I had the whole dentist thing licked when I awoke one morning with teeth aching from far too many nights of sugar kick from eating lollies and headed for the dentist. I never let on to my parents that I was suffering. I made my way to Mr. Black's surgery requesting his help with an exclamation: "Its the same ones that you filed Mr. Black." The kindly dentist concluded that I needed two immediate extractions and I agree if he promised not to inflict a needle in my gums. We agreed on a handshake and he proceeded to extract the two offending teeth. I went home with the bill, a knowing smile and proud as punch for I was seven years of age as I recall and had beaten pain.

The end of October 1957 was the first year of a three day festival of the Macksville Gift Carnival which saw the township decked out in bunting and festooned lightning to brighten up the lead up to the big race on the Monday event evening. Luminescent signs were arranged by the Pacific Highway to catch the eye off passing traffic through town. Shops keepers in a community spirit decked out their window displays in keeping with the festival. A new Gift Queen competition was organised to further raise money for the Catholic Church, who had agreed that it was the last year monies would be donate for it cause. A new Gift giving scheme had been introduced by the Church that year and it was no longer legitimate to accept the Macksville Gift donation.

The three days of festivities included a business float procession through the main street, a street party, the crowning of the Gift Queen, special golf, bowls, tennis and basketball tournaments were held, and a bike and car observation trail. The usual dance the night before the climax of the athletic meeting was held at the show ground on the Monday night. It was a weekend of fun and sport activity never before seen, nor maybe never will be again. A large crowd had payed their entry to see the running of the most colourful in the nations professional athletic event which took place in a darkened arena brilliantly alighted by rockets and fire crackers unequalled except maybe New Years eve night on Sydney Harbour. The rolling of the drums faded at the show-ground that night as did my remaining childhood and better memories of that little country town.

Friday the 1st of November rolled in, as it was all Saints Day, a solemn reminder in the Church calendar of the 'Faith of our Father's Holy Faith' and a day of tragedy for me and my friends. In the minds of three little mates Kevin, Greg and myself, it was an escape day to the beach were the year six girls were having a supervised beach party. No boys were allowed but we had decided to gate crash it anyway. We had lied to our respective parents that we were invited and made our way on foot to Bellwood Beach, some 12 km away. It was our chance to chase after our favoured girl. Much of the activity on the beach involved girl games so we decided to wade across the river tributary at low tide to go birds nesting on the nearby island between the river the mainland beach. Time had passed when we returned to the rivers edge the tide was come in and some swimming was needed to make it back to the beach. It required wading out touching bottom for as far as we could stay upright before we began to swim. I watched and waited until Greg stood up near the distant shore, calculated the swimming back as about the length of a pool and realised I could make it. I began my journey and without much effort made it to the beach. Glancing back for a moment I noticed Kevin was sitting on his haunches starring into the water. I thought no more about it and like Greg made my way to join in the softball game the girls were playing.

An hour must have passed before we came to the realisation that Kevin was missing. Retracing our steps we were advise by a lady on the beach that she saw Kevin dive into the water just after we crossed but she did not see him come up again. She had thought no more about it, absent-mindedly returning to reading her book. After an hour or more searching, with all on the beach in the search party, we made our way to the nearby Aboriginal settlement and enlisted the help of a local fisherman to row his boat to the location on the river were Kevin was last sighted. It seemed like forever that we stood their waiting for the fisherman to appear above the water surface. When he surfaced, he carried in his arms the body of my best friend Kevin.

The Church was packed with mourners of family and friends and Greg and I served as altar boys for the Black Mass the next day when we buried him. It was All Souls Day and something died once again inside me as it had done when my Uncle John parted the earth in that very same decade. We had been born next each other, almost lived at each others house, sat in the same class all the way through primary, played junior Rugby League in the same team, went birds nesting together and generally got up to all the mischief that little boys do as they explore life and all it has to offer. Kevin's mother could not look at me after that sad day. Overtime when I passed her by in the street or at Church tears would well up in her eyes. it was not long after his death that the Clegg family, Kevin's parents and siblings left Macksville for good. It was not far behind them either, destined for boarding school and the loss of my childhood innocence.

Initially I was destined for Woodland College in Lismore as was my close friends Des Chapman, Glen Owens and Nick Byres. My fate was sealed not to be sent to that famous old Marist Fathers school where my cousin Max has been schooled, won the prestigious Blue ribbon which was the ultimate accolade for a student there. Des Chapman had a brother who had attended the school so he was given no choice but to follow family tradition. Des was super bright and achieved top marks academically at Woodland as well as excelling in sport, in particular high jump, parallel bar and vaulting horse as a Gymnast. He graduated with honours but elected to follow in his Dad's footsteps becoming a partner in his fathers building business of George Chapman and son. Des once married settled in Campbelltown and I hasten to add that there would not be many houses in the older side of that city that don't have a nail or three hammered in by my good friend of my childhood..

CHAPTER 7.

BOARDING SCHOOL

My mate Glenn Owens was destined for Woodland to follow in the footsteps of elder brothers Trevor and Brian. Both brothers graduated with a coveted school Blue Ribbon under their belt and loads of trophies from sports proudly displayed on the family mantlepiece. Glenn had loads to live up to. Glenn ultimately achieved fourfold in the sporting filed in a bid to outrank his siblings. He later repeated the Leaving Certificate at Macksville High and died some years after when working as a security guard in Manly. Nick Byres was another story, he had no real connection with the College but his father Harry believed, like my dad, that boarding school away from local temptations would be a good learning curve instead of being with mate at the local Macksville High. Nick had other ideas and after less than one term at Woodland, snuck out of the dormitory one night, made it to the local railway station and walked the line south all that night and half the next day home to Macksville. Harry, his Dad, acknowledged Nick's doggedness in completing such a long journey on foot with all his worldly possession in toe, allowed him to go to the local High School where he topped the State in most subjects on his graduation. I lost track of him after a beer one evening decades ago but from what I recall he was a very successful academic.

It was decided by my parents, with the influence of my adopted Uncle Phil, that I be sent to St. Joseph's College Hunters Hill. Phil Garvin in-laws lived across the road from our family home. It was my sworn duty by my parents, when I was old enough to start the lawnmower, to do their lawns after I mowed our own. It was not just start the mower and go exercise, it meant filling a small can with 95 percent petrol to 5% oil and it had to be two stroke oil. The small tank of the Victa mower once filled required the fuel tap turned to the 'on' position before attempting to start the thing. The walk behind and push machine featured a pulling mechanism designed to turn the crank shaft to start the engine. It sometimes took a lot of repeated effort to rewind the rope around the drive shaft mechanism before the stubborn machine eventually started. That was if the needle to the fuel didn't get stuck and flood the motor. Then it was a a matter of turning off the fuel line and working like a slave pulling the cord and rewinding to dry start the thing before attempting a restart with fuel on again.

I soon found a neat trick to overcome the problem of flooding the motor, I simply pick a nearby rock and gave the needle housing a good hard belt and it worked every time. Anyhow, Uncle Phil used to bring his family up from Sydney every Christmas holidays and took over the mowing of the lawns and stayed a few weeks extra to fix up any issues that could not be done by Pa or Nan, his in-laws. Pa Sutton was not long for this world, and was on a military disability pension due to being shot in WW1. He had a bullet still lodged near his heart in one lung and it was left too long to chance an operation. So in the latter years of his life he was mostly bedridden. It was during Phil's stays that he convinced my Dad that being sent to Joeys would be the best for me from a discipline, education and getting to now the city prospective. He deduced that boarding at Woodlawn where I would be with my childhood mates was a waste of time and money. Uncle Phil's view was that I may as well go to the local High school as to go to Woodlawn College in Lismore. Phil made a promise to my parents that he and Aunt Peg (nee Sutton) his good wife would look after me during my time away from home. Phil and Peg Garvin honoured their promise, attending all my Rugby football matches and rowing events during my school boy days. More importantly, they took me into their home as one of their own and on many of my monthly good behaviour days out from school, I ventured to their home at Bondi using it as a base whilst spending many an hour at Bondi beach.

I managed to attend Aunt Peg's funeral a decade ago and Uncle Phils in 2018. Aunt Peg like so many women of that era had never worked outside the home. She raised two children and was a loving wife to Phil. He had spend his working life with the Australian Taxation Office and was on the Board of Review. He died just before his 98th birthday and apparently had to call his son in law Ian to his bedside, whispering in his ear his final words before departing: "I still owe the Tax Office seventy eight dollars." Son Phil junior attended Joeys which was inevitable considering Phil's generosity to the school and old boys. I had been a close part of the family unit in my formative years at Joeys and am mindful still of the way Uncle Phil always found time to come and see me at school. It was something that my own Dad rarely ever did in my five years as a boarder.

A catastrophic event took place in my Dad's business the night of New Year's Eve 1957 that I thought at the time would put to rest any thought of my attending boarding school after the annual school holidays. On the stoke of midnight, when the still awake populous were singing in the New Year with the traditional "Auld Lang Syne" and the townships roared with the sound of firecrackers, drums beating and sky filled with skyrockets. Simultaneously at that time three explosion occurred unnoticed in three different town locations. The safes in the local Greek cafe, Reid's milk bar and McPhillips' garage were all blasted open with gelignite.

It was reported later that both food outlets had a substantial amount of cash in New years eve takings. In my Father's case the robbers got away with not only a weeks takings but a substantial cash reserve of monies belonging to the Macksville Gift destined to be donated to the Catholic Church as final gesture to the Church before the future programme would run for the community at large. Dad had no time to spare during the week leading up to the New Year with cars and trucks to service and repairs he had promised to do before closing up shop for a New Year break. He believed his own takings and that of the Gifts donation was safe as a bank in his Chubb safe.

The safe key entry had an embossed cover emblem proudly boasting "Fire proof, burglar proof and explosive proof." Dad had no reason to believe otherwise and felt it 'safe' to leave all the cash monies until after the New Year break was over in which he intended to bank the next day the Commercial Bank was opened in the New Year. Between the three outlets robbers the burglary mass quite a cash haul in their robbery, but it was to be short lived for them. On file with police were their modus operandi and they left clues. The gelignite was set in each safe by the same expert. He knew exactly how much to use to blow the safety catch. Normally such an explosion would set off another safety lock but he was an expert at his 'trade.' The arm of the second locking devises wavered but the safe cracking expert knew exactly the amount of gelignite to use to ensure that it would not activate. The Police knew there was only three safecrackers in Australia capable of completing that task and the one who did it left a vital clue which nailed him.

The Police were waiting on the doorstep for him at his Vaucluse Mansion in Sydney when he returned with the stolen loot. So unfortunately I was still destined for boarding school much to my regret. Mervin "Merv" King was the townships local constabulary for Macksville and surrounds. It was he who, on New Years day, after the business owners had discovered their safes had been robbed reported their loss to the Policemen. Merv sprung into action questioning each business owner and with their help identified a photo of the offending safe cracker. He had frequented each business on his reconnoissance mission to gain the necessary insight into his targeted victims within 24 hours of completing his mission.

Merv King was also a great stalwart of the Macksville Gift Carnival running his own 'horse racing' event to help bolster funds for the Macksville Gift. The race was run on a turf like layout on a large table at the police station. Each horse was lined up at the start and a wheel like contraption with magnetic engineering caused the horse to move forward at different paces. It was a fair race because the magnet would activate at different stages of the race propelling one or another horse in a stop start fashion to towards the finish line. A lot of bets were made by gamblers shelling out hard earned cash to bet, knowing the proceeds were for the Gift.

It was Sargent King who once handcuffed me as a small boy to a neighbours backyard cloths-line leaving me out of harms way whilst a party was taking place inside the house. He later emerged with my Father, undid the cuffs and both of them proceeded to escort me to the Police station cell, locking me up for a time. it was Dad's way with the good Sargents approval of teaching me a lesson that 'crime doesn't pay.' I must say, even though I was but a little nipper, their experiment didn't faze me none, I was use to being incarcerated by my mother in a play pen from an early age. Besides I hadn't committed a crime and knew they would be back to let me out sooner or later. It was Merv King who granted me my drivers licence within days of my turning seventeen. I had driven to the Police station on the edge of the town boundary, just arriving in time for Sergeant King to do his rounds of the town. On his command of 'you can drive me to town,' I became the designated driver for the cop. Merv had me stop and restart outside the Commonwealth Bank, the Post Office, the produce store and various locations that he needed to call to complete his daily chores. On my return to the Police station, before leaving the car he announced that he had best ask me some questions.

I had breezed through with flying colours but the final question had me stumped. It related to recognising obvious signals when driving at night in a built up area. The good Sergeant gave me a saving hint: "Gee, those street light up ahead are bright at night." That was the hint and the third piece of the puzzle. "When driving in a built up area at night, make sure your lights are on low beam.." I answered. Sergeant King stamped his seal of approval. Now as a fully fledged driver, I was licensed now to play 'chicken' in a car instead of on my pushbike.

In the movie 'Rebel without a cause' James Dean and Sal Mineo played a game of 'chicken', racing their cars headlong towards a cliff. In the chicken game the drivers had to stay driving their car and either stop short or jump at the last minute before it went over the cliff. The first to jump was tagged 'Chicken' and as it happened the Mineo character dies when his shirt sleeve got caught in the door handle and he goes over the cliff. Dean's character was tagged 'Chicken.' In reality the troubled youth of James Dean and his film made him a hero to us troubled youth of the 1950s. It is worth repeating he tragically died in a car crash driving his Porsche and was killed instantly along with his passenger in Cholame, California September 1955 age 24. Sal Mineo was murdered in an alley behind his apartment in Hollywood 1976; he was aged 37. The third actor of the 'Rebel with a Cause' film, Natalie Wood, age 43, tragically and mysteriously drowned with undetermined facts still surrounding her death in November 1981.

With the "Rebel without a Cause' movie still in our veins we headed in our cars outside the town boundary to an airstrip built for a proposed resort that failed to materialise. The flat straight dirt strip for landing aircraft was ideal for our game. My neighbourhood friend Ash, of circus fame, volunteered like me to be the first to attempt our planned game of Chicken. The rule was to hurtle down the dirt strip runway at breakneck speed, do a U turn with foot flat out on the accelerator, then a sharp right turn along a narrow dirt road adjacent to the river, challenging each other for the lead. To the entry of town was a tributary of the river with a bridge crossing for one car at time passage. To make the challenge even more interesting, not more than 50 metres from the end of the bridge was the Police Station were months before I had been granted my licence.

So on this foolhardy venture, Ash and I drove neck a neck in our respective cars towards the bridge crossing. Whoever hit the bridge first would win the race. The looser would have to either concede by slowing down, allowing the other car to cross first or end up in the river. Our cars were almost touching side by side as at once stage I had the lead and then Ash made it close to me neck a neck to the bridge. I had the inside running and just focused on making the crossing as I was determined to win. Ash did concede about 10 metres from the bridge and came to a stop at the bank of the river as I crossed over, quickly braking so as not to be exceed the speed limit passed the police station. It was not so many years after that my good mate left town and went to the Police academy.

Ash phone me once when we had lost contact for a while, tracked me down through police records when I moved to Sydney. Obviously he deduced that I would hold some kind of Police record for the most speeding fines. He was looking at my driving record at the time and asked if I was interested in what he had uncovered. I replied that I preferred not to know as obviously there was a long list of fines over the years. The last time I caught up with my childhood friend was at the 50th Anniversary of our old Primary school. Ash was then a Police Sergeant up Grafton way. It was not many moons later that I got notice of his death after a heart attack. Despite being a good sportsman and sprinter in his youth, he continued to smoke heavily which was the ultimate cause of his early demise. Come to think of it, I lost contact with most of my childhood friends due to my years at boarding school.

Whilst I did return home after graduation and joined the local Commonwealth Bank for the first year after my leaving, most of my childhood mates had moved on. Roy, my football buddy was married and a fully fledged Baker in Coffs Harbour. Greg Fleming and his brother Brian had joined the Police force and were stationed in Sydney. Morris Allan was floating around the country side with his new bride doing music gigs at country town club and the rest I had no idea of their whereabouts. Russel Street who was my turntable buddy when on wet days we stay inside pretending we were radio announcers. Russell is just that and has been for years as a News reporter for T.V. and radio stations. Des Chapman at last count was still building houses out Campbeltown way. Brian Casey was not about when I returned from boarding school. He was busy for many years cutting roadways for new links to the New England Tablelands. Our paths crossed when he was living and working up at Walcha, back when I owned a business there. I lost sight of him too, at least until I attended his Dad's funeral a couple of decades ago. Garry Williams, another football buddy ceased practicing Law in Sydney and went walk about up in Alice Springs for a while, returning with a new bride to teach the local aboriginal language on the Nambucca and also become an announcer for the local Aboriginal radio station. Mick Bryant was another aboriginal friend in Primary and was the first Aboriginal to pass the New South Wales Leaving Certificate. He played football for the Manly side for a number of years before returning to the North Coast as a school teacher. All those old faces and memories of youth are now faded.

My first day at Joeys was a rude awakening to regimentation and physical cruelty of a boarding school. There were many grand moments over the years of my five years there and the punishment I took of which some was warranted but much of it was not. As a new kid on the block so to speak we 'hay seeds' from the bush started first year a day earlier back to school than the city kids. It was to get to feel your way around the place to settle in quickly to the routine. I made it a habit at the beginning of each term to turn up to school a day ahead for the term of my imprisonment, of which I will explain my reasoning later in this chapter. On my early arrival Mum had helped me unpack my clothing and laundry need into my little locker after we had found my dormitory and bed allocate number on the entry wall. Once done, Mum continued her crying 'act' off mixed emotion. Part of her pain I figured from the loss of her son to a group of so called religious men. Partly too that she would have no kid to vent her frustrations out on during my school term and an opportunity to put on a good show for Uncle Phil and Aunty Peg, who kindly drove me to the school. Aunty Peg spent much time pacifying Mum even before I arrived at the school. Still my Uncle Hep, who was married to Mum's sister Angie, once stated "The Cooper women were born with their bladder far too close to their tear ducts and that was why they cried so much." Considering Mum's five sisters all seem to cry a lot, I concluded that there was some truth in my Uncle's deduction.

Once I had freed myself from the clutches of Mum, gave Aunty Peg a kiss and shook hands with Uncle Phil and my Dad, I was free to roam the school until the evening dinner bell was rung and all the new year seven boys would assemble in the refectory for our first taste of a bulk cooked meal. I took a peak out at the window at a relatively new swimming pool near a large grassed area at the front of the school. I quickly changed out of my new uniform, donned a pair of shorts and T Shirt and headed out of the main building running bare footed across the grasses area to the pool. It was a novelty for me as we only had the beach and the rivers to swim in back home. The pool would no doubt be a novelty to many of the boys as at that time there were only three know Olympic size pools in Sydney.

The North Sydney Public pool, the Balmain pool were Olympic Champion Dawn Frazer trained and our school pool which the New South Wales diving team used because of its high and low diving boards. The two Konrad's, John and Elsa, both Olympic Champs also trained in our school pool when not in their training facility at the North Sydney public pool. Anyhow, I was running hell for leather across the turf when suddenly I was stopped by the resident Priest, Father Con Duffy. The Priest had his own private living quarters at the school and I was later to learn he live like the Elite, with his selection of red wine and evening meal deliver and serviced by a chief from kitchen staff. It was the priest policy to select a final year student to dine with him at least once before departing on graduation. I did get that privilege imposed upon me in my final year too. This day thou, it was my first time meeting the priest, which was no privilege. The goodly Father greeted me with a friendly smile which soon turned to a sneer. Where are you from son?" I answered his litany of questions that followed, anxious now to get to the pool. Before I knew it he lit upon me like a wild hound dog, grabbed me by both ears and twisted them all the while lifting me off the ground. The pain was excruciating for an instant and seemed like an eternity. "Welcome to St. Joseph's College" he said through clenched teeth, "we don't run around here bare footed." he said "and we certainly don't take short cuts across the grassland." He put me down just as quickly as he had lifted me up: " Go on then, go for your swim." I had a new goal now as all I wanted to do was get in the pool to cool off my ears. I did my lonely self a stay in that pool for as long as I can remember before drying off, heading for the shower to get changed for my 'official welcome' over dinner.I was quick to learn that boarding school was to be no picnic.

The first thing one finds difficult to adjust too is the complete surrender of freedom and the complete cut-off of contact with the outside world. Sure we had the opportunity of an occasional visit from friends or family on a Sunday afternoon and the audience of the public at GPS Sports activity but is was always under sur veillance and ordered discipline to all aspects of College life. The Marist Brothers order was a French one with common men of rudiment ability to educate young boys teaching them to be independent, strong, brave committed to rise above mediocrity with noble vision, to appreciate the things that are worthwhile, to choose what is right, despise the petty, shun all selfishness, be pure and happy, docile yet courageous, devoting everything to God above all things.

The one bright note in all of that was great acceptance and fellowship of boys and old boys alike. Whilst there were Elite snobs who came from privileged classes that the school was a great leveller. We all learnt to see each other as being no better or no worse than the next person. Joeys's to this day is a member of the GPS school system based on British Elite school principles. The Marist brothers however would have none of that! We were privileged to have the education we got and life time of friendship and assistance no matter what station in life we held in the future life. I off course didn't buy it all and knew that in the real world there is a pecking order and thus I weaved my way through the College education system and survived to tell this tale.

It would be remiss of me not to explain a little about the Brotherhood of Marist and its founder to give you, the reader, an insight into the philosophy to which I was educated.The Founding Father of the Order, Marcellin Champagnat was born in Marlhes, in the Loire valley in France in 1789 and died 51 years later in 1840 at a place called Our Lady of the Hermitage, in the valley of Gier about thirty kilometres from the place of his birth. He trained and worked as a parish priest and founder in this region throughout his lifetime. He never did anything that usually accompanies greatness, he had no credentials but himself. He lived in a region of materially poor, educationally ignorant and moral low ebb: for the French Revolution and Napoleonic Wars had taken its toll on all of such districts in France at the time. Marcellin, with great opposition, founded an Order of Brothers intent on alleviating the misery of the poor and needy for both near and far flung places. The authorities considered him mad, incapable of such work, lacking sufficient brains and destitute of sufficient resources.

But when he died in 1840, some 320 or so men had already chosen to follow his lead. Within 20 years this number had expanded to over 2000, so that today there are more than 7000 brothers teaching over 500,000 students throughout the world. For the Australian Marist and particularly St. Joseph's College the link with the Founders spirit has been quite close. Br. Francois, who was the Order's first Superior-General and a close personal friend of the founder died as late as 1881, the year in which St.Joseph's College was founded. So we realise that the brothers who came here from Europe and carved the College Chapel, living quarters and first class rooms by hand from the sandstones of Woolwich Point, in the late 19th century. Many of Champagne's first brothers, who personally had known him for his spirit and charisma, applied his methodology from the day the first stone was laid at Joeys. We boys who were educated by his design for living, be that by a more modern template of the founder followed the characteristics of his simplistic indoctrinated from the very first lesson. We learn early to have no pretence, learnt to show compassion to the less fortunate, to be open minded, to have a devotion to the Virgin Mary and to trust in God. The attitude of gratitude was instilled in us, to learn to never give up despite what life may dish out. That despite disappointment we can fight on, stick to all things, not lie down. We had to study hard and train hard no matter what we were attempting. If we make a mistake and when we're in trouble, we can get over it, not give up, bear no grudges, and strive on. This is what Champagne taught and this is how he lived and how the Marist who taught us tried to instil and it worked!

It would be breaking the anonymity of the people herein involved if I were to use their names let alone the circumstances that will hitherto unfold here. Therefore, to protect the sacred right of each of the Marist brothers with whom for better or for worst I had contact as my teacher or tormentor during my years at the College, I have chosen to use their nick name or Nom de Plume. Likewise the students who appear throughout these pages, names are changed to protect the innocent but in some cases they are not as these still remain in my heart as special friends who don't need such a mask in my telling here. So firstly let me introduce the Marist brother players. For us students , we always used an abbreviation when addressing a brother. It was either Br (pronounced Bra) when we wanted attention or "Yes Bra," when being chastised or given job a to do. Enter the Head Master, we shall call him 'Omar' for he truely was our Leader of eloquent speech, flourishing; a Sheik in dark habit. Next came my first

Dormitory Master Br.Geronimo. He was a fiery warrior when the mood struck him. Built much like the Apache himself, he was a great guy when in vacant or pensive mood and the energy on the charge when not. Then there was Br. Rock because he was solid of sterner stuff, tough as Magnetite with the ability to smooth out any blemishes in our character. He was a hard one but equally a fair man too. Pat the Rat I encountered on many occasion. This brother looked like a little rat, had a squeaky voice and could be very cruel. He always got the cheese instead of us kids. A great teacher of Geography through my senior years, grand coach of Rugby and admired for his cricket coaching ability. Perhaps more painful in my case, sending me for six when he belted me across the bum with his his bat.

The next player of the brotherhood was Bulwark for he was certainly a hard one to come up against. He was a dormitory master in my senior years and the Head of the Airforce cadets when I was in his unit. A big man, strong, forthright and commanding attention for what ever reason. He never seemed to fit in the mood of a Marist, kept to himself a lot but was passable as a teacher. Br, Charlie Marx was also dorm master in my second year at school. He taught me chemistry and was instrumental in introducing me to be a Coxswain in rowing. He also coached junior crews too, so I had a lot to do with him in my first two years of school. A "Charlie" was the nickname given to anyone who didn't tub, that is take a shower. The room he had in the dormitory was always untidy and he some times smelt sweaty too. He was perhaps the happiest and fairest man of the brothers. However, he elected to leave the brotherhood after five years before taking final vows, returning to his practice as a suburban Chemist. Then there was 'Mop Top' because of his large crop of hair. I was given the handle of "six way mop" at one stage because I had a head of long hair that seem to go in six different direction according to winds of chance. Mop Top was the Master of Disclipine in my first year but he had no idea about that. He was possibly the easiest to get around but under his punishment regime the place for a while become like a scene from the movie 'blackboard jungle.' Unfortunately he was replaced by a mean bugger who shall remain just that "mean bugger.'

He did however change the dress sense from mufti-day dress of leather jacket or a Canadian in the winter, Presley pink shirt with collar turned up, black stovepipe pants and iridescent coloured socks. It returned to more conservative school uniform on all occasions. A suit with school tie always and well polished shoes otherwise a belting.

Whispering Death was a very old brother who taught me Intermediate maths and without his diligence I may never have passed the subject in the final examination. Then there was Lead Lids, he would always paraphrase his opening sentence in Science lessons with 'there there.' His eyes would close or appear too close whenever he spoke his words of wisdom as he twiddled his thumbs together in expiation when some thick h kid like me didn't get the Science. Never a problem teacher nor a harsh word did I hear him utter from his lips, he was all about science. Another was Br. Claudius, like 'I, Claudius' the Roman Emperor. He had a funny way of teaching and made us laugh a lot in his chemical experiments. We managed to blow up more test tubes with explosive chemical under his tutelage than learn the formula of his creations.

Claudius had a bird avery at the back of the kitchen area with all types of ground and flying species. Sometimes I had the privilege of helping him feed the birds. More importantly, I got time to play with the school mascot, "Lassie" the collie dog. Many times in my loneliness I retreated to that animal who became my school counsellor. We never had a human one when I was at school. There are other characters which I shall introduce in this rendition of memory rambling. They can wait until they come as players in their own scenes. The first week at College came and went and I managed to team up with some new country kids from the mid north coast. We all came from timber towns stretching from Taree to Coffs Harbour, so I felt quite at home with them. Except for one boy from the city, my name sake another 'Fergie,' I kept free of the rabble of city brats. Doug " Fergie' has remained friends for the term of our school days.

CHAPTER 8.

TRUE GRIT

I never got homesick except maybe in class one day in my first week,I happened to look out the door towards a photograph hanging on a hallway wall. It was a country scene of some large pine trees, reminded me of the one Des Chapman and I use to climb at his grandparents place. They lived just up the hill from our family home. The distance photo of those pines on the school hallway wall were a recall of memory of the ones I could see from the verandah at home. Tears welled up in my eyes when I recalled and I had a lump in my throat, a funny feeling in my gut, but I didn't cry. The feeling lasted the rest of the day but by the next morning I had resigned myself to my fate at my new home away from home. My bedroom so to speak was a dormitory full of boys mainly from the country but some even from overseas. We out numbered the city boys four to one. I thanked God for that as most of them were little shits. The dormitory life consisted of a wire frame base beds much like you see on country fence gates. The bed had a steel framed head with cross bar which was an ideal place to hang ones towel after showering or to dry sports socks and football gear. They were the only items we had to wash, the rest of our dirty cloths were placed in our personal laundry bag which had name and laundry number sown on the bag. All our clothing had that number and mine coincidentally was the same number as Uncle Dick's shop number in George Street city oppose Central railway.

Over the five years I lived in that building the dormitories varied from ones who had worn out old mattresses to one near the roof which leaked like a sieve above my bed. I had to move the bed aside and place buckets around in order to stay dry in bed and not slip on the wet timber floor when going to the toilet in the dark of the midnight hour. The regimentation of lights out in the dormitory by nine thirty in the evening and into bed, rise to the clap of a Marist hand at six; make the bed, take a quick shower and dressing for Mass at seven, then breakfast at eight, class at nine until twelve noon followed by lunch.This daily routine was engrained in the brain and like robots we went about the place without question. There was a break for an hour to relax over a meal and catch up with friends then back to school work until three in the afternoon.

Sport always loomed high on the agenda from three thirty until five thirty, then it was an evening meal at six and back to study at seven until nine in the evening. It was straight to the dormitory after that to hand wash sports gear and socks. Fortunately metal cross bars at bedhead were ideal cloths lines. Sometimes one or two boys would have a challenge as to how long they could wear their dirty socks without washing them. It was their policy to hang the socks at the end of their bed at night like they had been washed and the stink soon got objections from the masses of boys calling for them to yield their filthy game challenge. Ultimately the resident brother in charge the dormitory would force them to wash or cane them into submission. It was the only time I was in agreement with the brothers on the matter of 'sparing the rod and spoiling the child.' Fridays and weekends the routine changed somewhat.

Friday was military cadets day, so we dressed in military uniform and were required to clean and polish our boots, whiten our webbing and gators and look the part throughout the day. After school we put on our military hat and supposedly assumed a military mental attitude for the rest of the day, until meal time. This involved marching to the beat of a routine, like troops who were being prepared for some future battle. We troops had to stand to attention for hours on end, learn the drill of slope arms, stand at ease and stand easy. A General Salute was also a matter of course for pending passing out parades were the Governor General would turn up at our 'military day' inspect the troops and make a long and boring speech. The boring speech that followed usually resulted with two or more cadets passing out on parade from heat exhaustion whilst suffering the verbosity onslaught.

The idea of doing our cadetship never appealed to me from the first time I donned a military uniform. My maverick spirit just could not accept the brand that we were meant to live by during those cadet days. I guess I was somewhat of a conscientious objector before I ever had heard the phrase. The idea that a fellow classmate who were normally good blokes could become right bastard just because they wore an Officer's uniform I always revolted against. This resulted in being singled out for special punishment as a consequence. The punishment I took on as a matter of discipline was of a 'non military style' for which I accepted with an attitude of gratitude   and which baffled the sadist who inflicted it. What he and his superior 'militant' brother consider formally legitimate I used to my advantage.

Always a Marist brother had the highest ranking on the day and wore full military regalia outranking his senior student Warrant Officers who wore a special peaked cap and military lapels. The Officer could and did usually inflict more punishment than his Brother Superior had knowledge of. NCO Bunt, more insightfully chiselled in my brain as " Bunt the C**T, " may have been granted a military rule book to teach through a pain process disabusing the notion that life's fair. To shock one into the reality that one had to knuckle down and buckle up as a team if the occasion arose that someone somewhere knowingly or unknown started a future war. The idea was that we, with military indoctrination, would be on the ready and maybe survive the onslaught.

At any rate Bunt selected this wayward cadet for punishment for minor mistakes of which I always felt sure the mastermind always had a personal agenda to inflict pain. He could not do this during the normal routine of school life, except maybe on the Rugby field without a good canning for his ghastly deeds. My punishment usually consisted of a drill; like being loaded with a dozen 303 rifles across my arms and being made to duck walk back and forth across a football oval. This punishment I accepted as a great way to strengthen my back and legs for the coming football season. The weight on my arms prove effective in flick passing the ball in a Rugby match. The ball seem to feel as light as a feather after my military fitness punishment. Whilst I did not have the outward appearance of muscle growth, I had extra strength from the punishment. The other more common punishment was to stand at attention holding my rifle by the barrel at arms length without flinching or moving in any way. The punishment normally lasted about three minutes if you could keep the rifle still. Nine times out of ten, the arm would go into a pain spasm and the rifle would move just enough to have to repeat the drill process all over again.

The better part of the Cadet life was going off to a military base for two weeks to learn the ropes from the military in a military atmosphere. We did many a long route march in the middle of the night, ran through jungle like conditions with rifle always at the ready. Whilst our school had a rifle range to practice on, we had more opportunities with live ammunition at the base. Part of our experience also included being tied in like cargo on Hercules aircraft and taken on test flights and climbing all over fighter aircraft in the hangers after being given the privilege of watching the air acrobatic team put on a show. We usually travelled by train to military camps which was a time for unravelling a toilet role or two, holding one end and letting the bulk of the role go out the window of the speeding train. The new Master of Discipline happened to be on the last leg of our speeding train. He was stationed two carriages back and when I let go the role out the window it was perfect timing.

The C.E.O. brother just happened to stick his head out the window at that moment to cop the full force of the toilet role in the face. I quickly shot my head back in the carriage and escape without recognition. He did come looking for the culprit but I looked innocently at him as if I knew nothing about it. Otherwise it would have been six of the best on each hand with his cane on my return back to school after holidays. The RAAF Base was at Queanbeyan on the New South Wales side of the boarder near Canberra was the training location for the Sabre Jet Fighter Squadron as well as the troop carrying Hercules aircraft. We also had the experience of taking a jet flight and experiencing the pull of gravity on the body riding in a non pressurised aircraft. Our routine at the Base, when not assisting in the cleaning of aircraft and our .303 rifles and equipment was military drills, long route marches around the base and getting to know and understand the routine of airforce personnel. The best part of the military base was the food. After living in a boarding school and eating what was back then very basic, the food the soldiers ate in their refectories was to us five star. It was a real pleasure to eat like half starved refugees at a banquet. Breakfast, lunch and dinner was always a treat and you could go back as many times as you liked for more.

It was better than my Mum's home cooking, as back then the family Sunday lunch was the best meal of the week which usually consists of three basic vegetable and a lamb roast with gravy, bake chicken or an occasion roast duck. A resident priest in full military uniform said the morning mass on Sunday, so any boy who volunteered to attend that mass and take communion was awarded a sleep in and late breakfast with the fighter squadron. I jumped at that opportunity as it meant missing a routine foot march around the base carried out in the middle of the night full equipped with pack and rifle. I never saw no sense in that but a sadistic NCO thought otherwise. Once the majority of the boys went off on their drill, a mate and myself who had time to kill before Sunday mass headed for the shower recess and proceeded to block the drainage system and turned on all the showers, getting great delight flooding the place out.

Thinking back, we were just two little bored shits. I never bothered to confess that to the priest that morning, piously attending Mass and then running to the mess for the banquet breakfast brunch with the jet fighter squadron. A fellow class mate and I were the same two cadets later reported as attempting to cross the Queanbeyan river Weir against the force of the stream overflow. We both made it to the middle of the torrent of water. We both got swept over the edge of the Weir surfacing downstream at the rate of knots. Fortunately a branch protruding into the river was the lifesaver and I made it to the river bank to find my friend laying their exhausted from the experience. We made it back to base as undetected half drowned rats. Thankfully that there was no roll call in out absence. We were later singled out for KP-kitchen duty being under suspicion of being up to something. Whilst the rest of the cadet troops were attending to their uniforms for the next parade we scored kitchen working gear that were military issue. I had to roll up the legs and sleeves to wear mine. They were tagged 'EL' meaning extra large when I should off had a 'S' for small size. The only consolation was they hung down a long way in the crutch as it gave me the mistaken impression that I had a new status among my contemporaries as a 'long dick.' We were slowly learning to be a crack team of cleaners in the huge officers mess. It meant cleaning an enormous quality of kitchen utensils, scrub and metal stainless steel table tops which seemed longer than a bowling alley and just as wide. We did our duty and thank God it was the once only for me in that camp detail.

Our Airforce Cadets unit attending that camp but never once fired a rifle. That did come later at our school rifle range and at future camps. Between study of aircraft recognition (Plane spotting) in the unlikely event that an enemy aircraft attempted to invade our school. Back at Joeys we did get to mess around a bit with military weaponry. A group of us cadets under a junior officers supervision managed to get mortar duty which included firing a dummy bomb from the mortar. Our practice session was on the same oval at the back of the school that I had my past military discipline inflicted. We set the sights on the intended target, a drum near the furthest boundary fence. The oval being raised above a side street with a line of colonial type houses along its perimeter, we had a greater chance of hitting the target or at worst the fence behind it. The fence was made largely of blocks of sandstone that could take the impact of an A-Bomb, so we figured if we missed the target we would not do to much damage to the fence with a blank mortar shell. Due to the weight of the projectile encased in steel, one cadet had the duty of holding the mortar gun whist the others duty was to set the fire in the hole so to speak. We were pretty confident but just to make sure we set the the target range a hundred metres higher than the target. Our intention was for the bomb to rocket upwards instead of outward and try to hit the target with a downward motion. The supervisor knew little about mortars and we- nothing! On ignition the rocket bomb flew up and away over the fence and appeared to be heading for the house opposite. The women of the house had taken her young children out to play on the front lawn precisely at the time the bomb headed downward from the sky above. It buried deep in the front lawn centimetres from the two children. Watching that bomb hurtling down towards those kids seemed like an eternity. We rescued the bomb unnoticed by the mother inside and quickly returned the mortar to our armoury. In our setting of the mortar sights we failed to allow for the fact that the oval height had been raised 20 meters with top soil when being prepared for football season. We had miscalculated the trajectory. This was not uncommon for us teenager students and despite our appearance of maturity we're still in our formative years.

We had been given a choice to join the schools Air Force cadets or opt for the Army cadet unit. Our Air Force camps were tame in comparison to those cadets who attended the Army Camp. The same fate we experienced did not apply to the Army Base camp up in Singleton which was happening for our Army cadet unit whilst we were at Fairbairne Airbase.

Joe Fazio and Michael Farrell were two of the schools sporting heroes and Cadet Officers who were on a reconnaissance mission playing war games with a cadet troop when fate took a turn for the worst. Singleton was one of the many training bases where new recruits were sent to before being shipped out into war zones for battle. On this particular mission these two young men happened upon a live bomb and it exploded when Michael pick it up- .He died in the ambulance on the way to hospital reportedly saying the " Hail Mary."

Joe, was badly wounded having four lots of shrapnel imbedded in his back but survived after a long recovery, returning to school half way through the next term. It was that same Joe Fazio who rowed as stroke for our schools in our winning first four and eight during his last two years at Joeys. After leaving school Joe had an illustrious business and sporting career. He rowed in champion crews in Sydney and Melbourne and was the number three man and later won a silver medal at the 1968 Mexico Olympics when

Australia run second to Germany. Joe's rowing career was almost cut short by that bomb accident as a school boy which resulted in him having four vertebrae being fuzed. It is remarkable that he was able to row, let alone win an Olympic silver medal. He was a well liked, tough boy, possessing great strength and skill as a successful and respected oarsman. He continued rowing in winning crews for the next decade. Joe's working life was dominated by his time in senior positions with Qantas aviation. He also had many business interests later and one perhaps best known to rowers was the development of a high quality rowing shield. Many a successful crew has been recognised with such shields. He died in 2011 after a long period suffering dementia being tended by his wife and children.

I was indoctrinated into the summer rowing season in my fist term at Joeys being relegated to the fifty four as Coxswain. Usually new boys learnt to row and cox in the tub fours for a year. These heavy wooden boats were much wider and slower in the water than a rowing shell. However, I had but a week or maybe two in a tub, when the Cox of the fifth scull took ill and I became the replacement. The fifty four was a back up crew for the fourth four.

The first four men crews and Eight rowed in the GPS rowing competitions comprising eight of the nine Sydney GPS schools, Sydney Grammar, The Kings School, Newington, Sydney Boys High, The Scots College, our school St Joseph's,Scots College and our Catholic arch rival on the Lane Cove river, the Jesuit school, St. Ignatius College. There was (is) one more GPS school, The Armidale School. All bar Armidale participated in the GPS Rowing on weekly Sydney Harbour Regattas. The Regattas pitted the best of club oarsmen in Sydney Clubs scattered around the harbour foreshores and included a flotilla of Associated non GPS private schools. The two final races of the year were the river view Gold Cup two weeks before the biggest regatta even for the GPS schoolboys: the Head of the River at Penrith. In our training we often passed a rowing crew from Cranbrook school. We always stopped rowing to cry out: "If you can't get a girl get a Cranbrook boy," I don't know historically reason for when that started. Perhaps it had similar origin y to our primary school chant at the local public school: "Catholics, Catholics, ring the bell whilst the Protectants go to hell."

All the GPS schools pitted themselves against each other in the winter season in Rugby with Armidale playing some matches but not any as a part fo the GPS competition because of the distance of its country location. Armidale alway attended the GPS athletic competition and seem to excel in that area of their participation. In my second year at Joeys I had graduated to the third four and join a ragged crew of misfits. We argued and chastised each other in training on the a water and back in the school yard. Hated would be a mild word for our distraint for one another at various intervals during our rowing training. However when it came to racing we seem to fuze as one unit with a burning desire to win at all cost. Our rowing crew won every preseason race against GPS schools and Club crews. Returning after the Christmas break we followed up with the same success rate and won the Riverview Gold Cup too .Our misfortune came in the 'GPS Head of the River.'

The Warragamba Dam ceased the water flow into the Nepean river a week before the race. This always resulted in the crew in the centre lanes still getting some river flow whilst outside lanes got nothing but dead plankton to row in. If one managed to draw one of those lanes it meant an unacceptable handicap. we of course drew lane eight and lanes four and five were the fast flowing ones. Another handicap was rowing in fresh water. We had only two weeks of training on the river prior to the big race. We were race fit for salt water regattas but the extra burden of lane draw and fresh water rowing made the going much more tougher than usual. We had a mishap just before the race was about to start. One of our crew members broke the slide on the seat and at the last few minutes before the start we borrowed a boat. It meant that powerhouse of the boat, the number two and three crew members had to swap seats due to the boat rigging and row on opposite sides, being stroke side oarsman on bow side and visa versa. There was no time to make any boat adjustments with minutes to go before the start of the race. Being a powerful crew over

1000 metres we took the lead early but were soon challenged by Riverview College whom we had clearly beaten in their Gold Cup two weeks earlier. Despite the fact that Riverview had a middle lane we rowed neck-a-neck to the finish line and they beat us by a a nose at the finish. Despite being a fighting lot, it was the best crew of the season by far.

In our training camp on the Nepean a week before the Head of the River Regatta we rowed an unofficial race record against Olympians and came in a credible third which had us in the running for possible Olympic contention. It was not to be because it was not official but we had proved our worth. This was the same year that Joe Fazio stroked the first four to victory in the GPS Regatta.

In my third year I was the Coxswain for the first four and we had a credible season of wins but nothing like the experience of that third four the year before. By the time I reached fourth year High school, I was the Coxswain for the Ist Eight and knew my fair share about rowing by that stage. I could discern when a member of the crew was not pulling his weight, shooting his slide with his legs resulting in an out of body alignment and less power pull through the water. It was my duty to ensure in a race or training, we kept perfect timing with a stop watch and managed to steer a straight course in racing.

I had honed the German techniques of training rowers and applied those principles to the oarsman in the eight . We started the season on a winning streak but after Christmas holidays we had passed our peak and our wins became few and far between. Brother JB for short, was the coach of the eight and he was a hard task master. He worked on the principles of fear very effectively and more than once I copped a backhander or the cain from him as did so many of my fellow rowers and students. JB would give me the instructions which usually included a distance fitness row at high rating up to Ryde bridge and back followed by weight train at weekends and a dispensation Sundays, but we still had to attend the 7.a.m. daily Mass. The rowers would do their weights at night during school week and I likewise attended. Back then I could press my body weight on a stand and squat repeated exercise. Brother coachers back then were not so much rowing coaches but fitness trainers.

Joeys seamed to do o.k. as the Coach Joe (another name for a brother) ensured the boys were the fittest of crews on the river. Everything changed the day BJ introduced a speaker system throughout the boat linked back to the Cox and the school speed boat were he controlled and administered instructions from distant locations on the Parramatta river. This meant that we we seemed to be under surveillance even when his speed boat was nowhere to be seen. On return from Christmas holidays we had a different attitude to our training. The introduction of a speaker system in the boat and two way communication with the Cox allowed BJ more freedom to keep an eye on other crews leaving me with instructions to follow a set plan one fine Saturday. As it happened there were no regattas to attend, so we headed off to a Cove near the Nestle's factory in 'Hen and Chicken' Bay and adjourned to a club bar for a few beers. We calculate the time and headed back to the boat, just in time to see BJ seated in the bow of the speed boat with a junior boy steering full throttle towards Ryde bridge. We were hidden from view in the Cove when he passed us and we knew we had to high tail it out of there and concoct a story to satisfy his mind that all was in order. We had only just hit our straps back on the Parramatta river, when the speaker on the two way sprung into action. We elected not to answer and I switched off the mouth piece. Once we were in range of Ryde Bridge, I switched the mike back on, to hear BJ's raging voice calling "Where are you Cox?"

My immediate lie flowed from my lips like honey fortified by the beer. "Heading back from Ryde bridge Brother, rating 36." This meant that we were doing racing mode of 36 strokes of the oar per minute. I somehow defused it all when the speed boat pulled up along side us. "Where were you?" JB said again. Another quickly lie. "you passes us near the bridge Brother, you were looking towards the shore at that moment." He had no defence for that as this was sometimes his habit. We completed our training session after that with BJ pushing the boys harder than usual, suspecting fowl play still. We got back from the rowing session in the dark. At least we didn't get caned.   Our rowing shed was an old timber building that house five rowing shells and our only speed boat. The tub fours were keep in Tarban Creek on moorings as we didn't have room for them in the shed. We had a full time caretaker who lived like a hermit in wooden cottage next door to the shed. Bernie was a part of the place, natures gentleman and an alcoholic. His job was to ensure everything was in place in and outside the shed when we all vacated the premise. The old school tidal pool was behind Bernie's cottage and next door to the main shed. It was always full of green slime but it didn't seem to bother us much, we just swam through it for a length or two and headed for a cold shower over a dirty old bath tub on the floor above the pool. It was almost winter as we lined up for the cold shower when BJ appeared at the entry.

Senior boys, Holden and Lynch had, unknown to the rest of us taken the speed boat for a midnight spin on some wild escapade, returning it to the boat shed and quietly retreated back to bed before dawn. They were both young senior 18 year old boys, strong and fit and were drying themselves off as JB approached. We were all told to stand in our own nakedness along the shed wall parameter. I remember Peach was still standing ringing wet when JB bellowed and eyeballed each one of us.

Peach turned off the shower and stood ice cold still as did the rest of the rowing team in that room. He still had a semi erection and I admired its size, making a mental note to masturbate more often in the hope that I could develop one similar. Peach's erection soon subsided when JB commenced his punishment on those two strong lads. He caned them over and over until their bodies began to convulse. Eyes cast down afraid to look up, we all stood in fear that we would be next. Both boys didn't cry but their bodies were acting independent of their head. They both admitted that they had taken the speed boat for a spin. JB recommenced his punishment, Holden and Lynch were a complete mess. JB only stopped thrashing them when he got far too exhausted to continue. The Brother's eyes were wild and his mouth seem to shape into a kind of sneer, drooling saliva like Lawrence of Arabia when he slaughtered the retreating Turks. JB was a strong man who could bring down that cain so hard that it would seem like the pain would never end. The memory of that punishment is engrained in my memory bank forever.

When Irishman are crazy they are really crazy. I only coped it once from JB, apart from a back handed over the head with close knuckle fist. He gave me a canning across my buttocks for talking after night study on another occasion. It was nothing like those two rowers coped but it was painful enough. Later our illustrious Br. Head Master limited BJ's action wit the cain when he broke a students wrist in his application to inflict more pain. The Head, Omar, was a bit like calling the pot black, he too welded the cain with great power but he was not a patch on BJ's unique ability and possibly sexually frustrated actions of extreme cruelty. In my time at school rowing was considered a summer sport and the then Head Master, Omar, didn't much like boys leaving school grounds to attend training and rowing in weekend regattas. He has the view that he could keep an eagle eye on the 'prisoners' within the school bounds much better than second hand reports form outside the school. In part he was right for the wearisome of us got up to a lot of mischief which required much discipline. Omar too had a mean streak when it came to rowers.

When I coxed the eight in 61, we were on the water by 5.30.am. each day for train. It meant that, if JB had us on the water longer than usual then we it was a very quick cold shower, dressed in school gear and a run up the hill to make the 7 am mass with the rest of the school. As Cox, I had the added duty of washing down the boat as it come off the water, drying it off with a cloth and applying graphite on the leather bind where the oar met the rollick so all the oars were at the ready for the next training session in the afternoon. On this occasion we all had to move in double quick time and despite our best effort arrived at the schools after mass had started. The crew elected to hide in the down stairs toilet area rather than draw attention to our late arrival. I consider it best to run to the Chapel on the first floor entry being only five minutes late. As I passed Omar's office, he was standing at the door and he called me back and questioned the reason for my lateness. He had me kneel and gave me six of the best on each hand to ensure there would never be a repeat of that performance. I managed to make it a habit to be late just to spite him and always got past his door without further detection.

One of my earliest disciplines was attendance at music lessons and Choir practice. It was an added extra subject, the first at the insistence of my Mum and Dad, the second by Br. Vessel who picked me out to join the Choir because of what he perceived as being" In good voice." Mr. Radford came to the school once a week to teach elocution. He no doubt-passed on my vocal abilities to the Vessel.

The family on Dad's side were musical with Uncle Jack playing the violin, Dad the piano and Pop the tap dancer. I learnt under sufferance to play the piano from the age of six, hated the practice but under sufferance persevered reaching Intermediate standard within the two years of commencement. I also learnt how to write music theory drummed into me by a nun at the Convent. it was my duty to be at the Convent early Saturday mornings for a time to receive a very disciplined instruction when I much preferred to be out in the bush having fun with my mates. I breathed a sigh of relief when this ceased in my first year at boarding school.

The piano teacher at Joey's come once a week for my lessons. We had a music room for night practice away from the main building. It was an old wooden building possibly built by the founding Brothers, of acoustics it had none. The piano players were unsupervised, so not much practice was had. As for the once a week tuition from Master 'He knows best,' well that ceased soon enough. The room with the piano he taught me in was built for meditation as it was down stairs under the chapel. It had great acoustics but a bum teacher. Every time I played a wrong note 'he who knows best' would either hit me over the knuckle with a little stick or insist I climb out the window, jump the one floor to the ground, below, race around the building and back to the piano. My music skills did not advance much but I was extra fit come football season. Eventually I lied to my parents that I had extra school studies to complete and could no longer fit the music in. They some how accepted the lie and I felt a sigh of relief. The second musical feat I managed to escape was the choir. I enjoy the singing but hated the practice.

Br. Vessel had a brilliant ear for music. He use to walk up and down in front of us Choir boys listening to the crowded harmony as we sang a rehearsed song or hymn at his bequest. On this particular morning we were in in the great Chapel with organ in full swing, as we did our practice for a coming High Mass. As usual Vessel was walking back and forth with his hand to one ear listening intently. He suddenly ceased the singing, turned to me and said: "Mc Phillips, Coxing or Choir?" My immediate response was "Coxing Brother."A one word response from Vessel was "Out." I departed immediately with a sense of freedom. Both decision of giving up singing and piano I lived to regret. The constant yelling at the rowers meant I had to gargle some concoction from the school infirmary to retain my voice. I still love piano music, in particular the classics. All that yelling at rowers in my youth ruined my vocal cords as did my daily habit of cigarette smoking for a decade or two.

Now that I sing my own songs and work with professions when studio recording, I wish in hindsight that I had more discipline and continued both musical practices as a young teenage. Afterthought: At a recording session on my first album I had difficulty staying in tune with the music and my lung capacity on some end notes meant rerecording. I apologised to the band for my lack of ability back then to stay in tune. Paul, the lead guitars quipped back at me. "Doug, musicians have a saying that singers can't find the key and when they do they don't know when to come in." Now that I have written and recorded two albums of my pwn songs I have developed some discipline in my efforts. However, without the advances of digital recording I would be stuffed as a would be musician.

At the side entrance to the main ground floor of the historic school building was a large bell with a gong that used to be rung every time there was a change in class. Boys would move from room to room for the lectures much like at a University campus when the gong was rung at the end of each period. Somehow, some individual got the idea to ring the hell out of the bell at midnight and vanish before being discovered. Whoever was ringing it did so for a whole term and got away with it all.

The Shield was our Dorm; Master and head of our cadet unit too. It was a habit of his to go around the dormitory after lights out and spring a bed check by flashing his very large torch light at the head of each sleeping student. As our dormitory was directly above the side entry three floors below we were always woken at midnight by the bell ringing. This got the better of 'the Shield' and he made his way to the balcony stairs with torch in hand intent on catching the bell ringing culprit. Peering over the balcony, he noticed a figure standing perfectly still in the shadow against the wall of the stair case. Without haste, he lined up his torch and dropped it like a missile towards the victim below. It was the Headmaster, Omar the rock of ages. It was he who copped the full force of the large torch on his head and he dropped like a stone. He too was hoping to catch the bell ringing culprit by standing near the staircase. It could not have happened to a nicer victim. Somehow I felt vindicated for my unfounded punishment for being late for Mass.

In the basement of the main building of the College is the walled foundations of the building. It housed the main kitchen and storage facility for the 500 boarders and staff of the school. It was affectionally know then as 'Carrot Canyon.' A door opposite the kitchen in the bowels of the building, a bunker like room with multitude of mottled green Bakelite covered tables and wooden benches awaited the herd of elephant feet of young boys rushing ing for a table position to eat their daily bread. This one was our year seven refectory and it was always supervised by Br. 'Importance of being Ernest'

There in that refectory we ate our fair share of Sanatarium 'Wheat-bix' or lumpy bulk cooked rolled oats which were moist on the outside and full of dried flour in the centre. In the winter months we ate copious amounts of those oats, drank fresh cows milk, fresh bread and jam for breakfast. A good supply of bulky beef or chicken for lunch with three veg including copious quantities of mash potato was the order of the day. The evening meal was usually a light one but sometimes included mince stew and 'Sandy Joe' with bulk custard for desert. Sandy Joe was a mix of plum pudding mixed with sand. We came to look forward to the heavy tack and the custard was always hot. Our butter supply was limited and was cut in eight equal shares by the head of the table at each meal. We use to save our share in a jar under the table and add salt and water to preserve it for Thursday night desert which was always a half brick of ice cream between the tables of eight. Like the butter we cut it into eight squares and traded our butter for an extra helping to boys who preferred the butter to the bulk ice cream.

Our tea pot was a big one like my Grandmother used and included tea with boiling water mixed with copious quantities of bromide salt to reduce our libido and create the minor effect of sedation.The quantity was increased at night meal to slow us down a bit before bedtime. We use to get the best of IXL jams at our dinner table. They were supplied by a tubby kid we called 'Peach-jam' on account of the fact that his father owned the IXL jam company and he kept us in constant supply. Henry Jones IXL brand was a prime manufacturer of jams, conserves and sauce in our College years. He later sold the business to a USA conglomerate known as SPC. His son Henry junior or 'Peach- jam' was a good bloke and intelligent. He had a unique ability to read weather patterns and predict coming changes.

You might say he had an eye for it, as one eye was brown and the other green. The green eye was half green and half brown and the iris would begin to turn brown whenever the weather was about to change. At least that is what "Peach- Jam' would have us believe. Like the long-range weather forecaster of the same heritage Indigo Henry ' peach- jam' Jones became quite famous in our school but like his name sake most sceptics considered his predictions guess-economic.

'Peach Jam' seemed to be right more often than not when it came to the predicted weather ahead and would blame his green brown eye being out of whack if he got it wrong. He may well have had the power of changing the colour of his eye by his own willed thought patterns. Of that we didn't know, but I do know the rock group INXS got the idea for their brand from an IXL jam advert on TV long after Henry Jones senior and junior were out of their own business jams. The tables were served from a side smaller kitchen than the main one which served the boys and staff on level one in two seperate refectories lifted manually by a dumbwaiter. Our servants of starving rats were men of dubious means who were recruited from the rejects of Matthew Talbot Hostel in Kings Cross. Mainly newly sobered lost souls with good hearts who got food, clothing and shelter in a building owned by the College across the road in a side street, to cater or us at meal time, wash the kitchen plates and utensils and wipe down the tables with contaminated stinking cloths. Food hygiene was not considered and strangely no one seem to go down with terminal food poisoning.   It was normal proceedings for the boys to be making a before Br. 'Importance of being Ernest' rang a bell which instilled silence like alight switch being turned off. He would then proceed to say the 'Grace before meals' whilst we were already moving various eats as close as possible to our plates to jump in first on the food.

Our conversions then went back to a rabbled chorus as we ate. Importance of being Ernest' would sit up high on a bench at the end of the Refectory to check out the scene and maybe consider who should get singled out for punishment later. On this particular morning that was not hard to ascertain. Morocco, a devotee of the latest crazy of bodge clothing with high collar turned up and hair greased back with California Poppy had just finished putting away his comb when Borland, another crazy kid from the west reached over Morocco's plate and pinched his table spoon. They hated each others guts and were always in conflict from the day they arrive. Unfortunately we were obliged to include them both on our table of eight, Morocco, short but stocky, leaned over the table and bloodied Borland's nose. The reaction was electric and they both immediate stood up toe to toe across the table and began to belting the hell out of each other. Importance of being Ernest eyed the situation and calmly rang the bell in front of him. The place fell silent but the two crazies were by now out in the middle of the refectory floor still in a fully fledged boxing match. Importance rang his bell once again and with a stern but slightly louder than usual voice cried out. "If you want to behave like animals go outside and fight."

The two angry contestants exited and Important of Being Ernest resumed his steel like gaze and we return to eating. We had ten minutes to go to the end of the meal and as soon as the good brother rung the bell for "Grace after meal,"we hightailed it outside to watch the fight. We were in the make shift ring outside the entry to Carrot Canyon, watching the two animals still going blow for blow with cut eyes, bloodied noses and cut lips, but there was no give in either of them. It was a fight to the death but they both eventually ran out of steam at the precise moment Importance of being Ernest appeared on the scene. He walked up to the 'boxers' like a good referee would and instead of declaring the winner said:

"Had Enough?" Before they had the right of reply he grabbed them both by the head and in one mighty crack of their heads together said:"That's it. There will be no more fighting." Both animals were like beaten beef and docile as kittens. I reckon their heads hurt more from Ernest's hammer like head crack than the 20 minutes or so of hand to hand combat they had inflicted on each other..

Carrot Canyon's main kitchen had huge refrigeration units stocked with food and as the chosen Coxswain I was elected to go steal more food from those cold storage units to feed the hunger strong oarsman in my charge. It was a simple matter of entry into the main passage where we boys in first year herded to our nearby refractory to fill our bellies. However, exiting stage left and entry to the kitchen rooms was strictly forbidden. I figured the best time to do that was early in the morning before breakfast assembly and just after senior rowers returned for breakfast. Thus, I had less chance of being detected when the kitchen staff were busy preparing the bulk of their meals for the whole of the schools hungry mouths. it was easier than I thought.

I just watched the movement of each kitchen staff member do ing their duties and weaved my way from behind every building foundation pillar until I got to the required food item. Copious quantities of fresh milk, bread and beef jerky was supplied to those growing bodies. I always had a cockatoo on the look out for the unexpected. More so I needed a helper with the quantity of food I had to carry to the teeming starving multitude. The senior rowers always respected me for my due diligence in attention to cater for their tummy needs. At heart I consider my actions as not sinful but rather helping the starving herd. It was to my young mind a good thing and besides it gave me an adrenaline rush in carrying out the task. I also drew an analogy to justify my actions. I figured I got punished more often than not for not being in the wrong than when I was in the wrong.

Morocco didn't last as he got the boot from the school before the end of the third term. We never did get to the bottom of what he had done but it must have been pretty bad. The only other case of someone being banned from school was a temporary thing for one of our school heroes. Dicko who was rowing in our GPS eight and a star footballer for the First XV, was given the boot for one year. He was allowed to join his fellow team members after school for the remainder of rowing season and football seasons. Dicko completed fourth year high school at St. Pius College Chatswood and returned to Joeys the next year to star in his final year and completed his leaving certificate with the SJC crest on his academic record and no no space left on his honour blazer for this sporting achievements. I too received and honour blazer in 1961 for Coxing the College Eight but it was the only pocket I had sown on my jacket.

Another claim to fame for Dicko was an incident with his fellow Rugby XV mate " Pat the Lawyer." They were both in their final year and on school holidays. Dicko's Father owned a well known funeral business and to keep the boys occupied over the holidays employed them both as grave diggers. Apparently they were sent out to the Eastern Suburbs Cemetery to dig a grave. It was a hot day and once they consider that had dug the hole to specifications headed to a nearby pub to reward themselves with a beer or two. On the day of the funeral it rained and the funeral service was a disaster. In their enthusiasm to get the job done and get to the pub the two intrepid grave diggers had not dug the hole deep nor wide enough. To make matters worse the hole was half full of water. The coffin got stuck half way due to the narrowness of the hole but the funeral went ahead anyway. The grieving offspring were advise that the coffin would be lowered once the rain stopped and the water pumped out. The professionalism and dignity of the Funeral Parlour made for acceptance by the clientele.

Dicko's Dad was furious with the boys and promptly sent them to the graveside as soon as it stopped raining to extract the coffin, dig the hole wider, lower the coffin in and fill in the hole. Surprisingly when the Funeral Director arrived at the scene some hours later, the grave was filled and covered with dirt. Both the now retired grave diggers sat chatting waiting his verdict. He was pleased with their effort and took them for a number of beers before discharging them.

Unbeknown to the Funeral Director, the water had subsided and the clay in the hole seemed soft, so the two now wise men of grave digging simply used their own body weight to jump up and down on the coffin until it was far enough under the ground to disappear from the surface. Dicko in his wisdom had also figured that he and his mate would not have a lot of top soil work required to do to fill in the hole. Those of us in the know are aware of the fact that out at Eastern Suburbs Cemetery is a grave that holds the remains of some poor soul that is only three feet down instead of the mandatory six foot under! Lesson learnt, Dicko would pursue a career in sales and service well away from his father's funeral parlour business. Dicko's mate Pat leant a lesson from that experience too and pursued a career as lawyer when he left school.

CHAPTER 9.

NORTH COASTERS

Over at our main sports fields about ten minutes as the crow flies, we had five football fields. A part of the area below the main field was a small sheep farm. Br. Importance of being Ernest use to tend the sheep and in my first year enlisted some of us country boys to help with the drenching and crutching.

The idea was that we would make like a circular fence around the sheep and move in closer until one of the more experienced country kids would bring the sheep down and help complete the task of the ' dip or crutch.' I was only ever enlisted to help once after my apparent appearance of cowardliness. It was when a rather large Ram decided to ram me.The wool bound warrior had charged directly at me as I held on to my fellow sheep herders, I made like a gate, let go of one of my fellow students hand and the charger passed me by. Ernest somewhat sarcastically remarked: "….and here I was thinking you as a country boy McPhillips." My response enlisted a further smile from the Brother. "My Grandad was the sheep and cattle man, I just like to tell bush stories Brother."

My claim to fame as a country boy was as a 'North Coaster.' There were a number of us who travelled too and from school at the beginning and end of each term on the North Coast mail. A lot of our clan came from the Hastings district. We rode the second class carriages which were divided into opposing bench railway green tanned leather seats wide enough to hold four boys bums with some latitude for spreading out. Above each seat was a wire rack for luggage and on the dark wooden walls, hung old photos of bush scenes depicting railway activity or the unveiling of a new train. Each compartment had a metal foot warmer which was great in the winter when the floor would get ice cold. Placing ones socked feet on the gas filled metal cylinder guaranteed warmth and the residue of chilblains in the not too distant future. We also had a large container of water and a glass on a shelf attached to one wall just in case of an urge to drink might overtake us. I can't remember any of us ever drinking that water. We preferred to buy a tea bag and hot water with some 'railway biscuits' at major stopping point along the way. It gave us enough time to stretch our legs, go to the platform toilet and get some fresh air away from the soot spewing from the coal fired engines that pulled the train to its next destination.

The journey from Central station took about twelve hours to my home town platform at Macksville. Most of my fellow Intrepid travellers had alighted by the time the train reached Taree. Heading home on the night train was always an adventurer. We didn't sleep much and would close the sliding carriage doors and bind the doorhandles with school ties so as not to be disturbed by the night guard. Once he had punched our ticket we were pretty much left to our own devises. That is unless there was a complaint from another nearby passenger or we got up to some mischief. As a delaying tactic, if the guard appeared and tried to open the double carriage doors, they appeared to be stuck when in fact that were tied down. Securing the doors like that gave us time to dispense with our cigarettes out the window and clear the smoke before undoing the doors.

The train snaked its way north were at each major stop the majority of the Joey's rabble jumping off. Newcastle. We always lost one or two around Foster with most of the clan alighting at Taree. Names like Gus Skullard who was Captain and Hooker of the First XV Rugby team left the train. Gus's family were well known in the pub game as was my family as publicans on the North Coast. I often wondered back then what it would be like to live in a pub. I did try it in my youth for a while but the drink got the better of me and I had to find some place further away from the bar to survive. Others alight at Taree, Phil Basel whose Dad was a local journalist for the Manning Daily. Phil had a stunning sister Lena whom we all had the hots for. So naturally Phil could pretty much get us to do his bidding, our motives being more from our loins than our heart.

Leonard Fenning was another North Coast mate who alighted at Taree. Charles, his Dad was a well known in the timber and cattle game. Leonard later became possibly the single largest Timber Mill and Cattle man in the North. Peter Noble got off at Kempsey, Peter Simmons, Paul Joseph got off at Macksville. Peter's family being Assyrian were naturally in the rag trade and Paul family all graduated as Chemist. Lew his Dad was our local Compound pharmacists. Peter and Paul were older than me so the last three years it was just me that stepped onto the platform then. David Mulhearn was the last to alight about a half hour further North at Ulong were his Dad owned a timber mill. We both became good friends at school as did Len Fenning with David because of their affinity with timber.

I later in life crossed paths and worked on the Walcha township business committee together were we renewed our friendship. Leonard in his latter years still is in the timber game running the largest totally computerised timber Mill in Victoria. Our exploits, apart from smoking and the odd drink on our journey homeward included playing 'spot what tree is that' for each power pole we passed. The idea was to pick a tree type and see how many poles were made from that tree over an allotted distance along the side of the track. Each power pole had an identification stamp denoting its tree source. TT was tallow wood, PP was pinewood, GG was grey gum and so on. This amused us long enough until we got bored and then we would come up with a song or two and sing along until the wee small hours.

Chris Lean, came from around Kramback, the same area that John Schneider of Joeys and Macksville Gift athletics fame came from. I recall one year returning from school at the end of the term, we shared a compartment with five other boys. Somebody asked for a drink of water and Chris reached up grabbed the bottle and glass and just as he was about to poor it, as quick as a flash throw the bottle out the window. As luck would have it, the train was passing a railway siding at that precise moment and the bottle shattered all over the concrete platform. The Guard in the next carriage happened to be leaning out the window at the time and caught the action. Chris grabbed his suitcase and quickly made his way up the train into the next carriage with the train guard in hot persuit. Chris was due to alight at the next station so before the guard could grab him, opened the carriage door and jumped from the moving train. The suitcase burst open on the platform with all his worldly possessions flying everywhere and Chris rolling over and over on the platform. The last sighting of Chris Lean was a he left the platform running with cloths sticking out that suitcase, he never did return to Joey's at the start of the next term.

David Mulhearn and I made a pact to return back to school the morning before we were due back. We caught the night train arriving in Central at dawn. We had a game plan and the days activities in the city worked out well in advance. Making our way by bus to the College, we first checked out from a list on the notice board our allotted dormitories for the next term. The idea was that we would firstly test each bed to find the most comfortable. Next we helped each other to pick the best location in the Dormitory. It was simply a matter of moving the best sprung wire bed frame and mattress near the window and doing a swap. This was closely followed by unpacking our bags in our lockers, taking a shower and getting dressed into some casual gear to catch a bus back to the city. We would start the day with a big breakfast followed by a morning film show. After the movie, we usually made our way to the State theatre for ice-cream and popcorn whilst we watched the latest newsreels. The State film clips ran on a non stop basis, so you could enter the theatre at any time and watch until the same news came around for the second time. It was then off to buy a newspaper to see what other film were on that we could watch. By the end of the day we retired back to school to greet our fellow inmates and cat up on holiday stories. I always went to bed after that day of activity with a roaring headache and flaked. This mad movie day activity continued for the rest of our time at Joey;'s together.

David Mulheran had great difficulty settling into one particular class. It was a personality class with the Br. Jack of all Trades. He taught us mathematics for our leaving year was also a rowing coach so I had a bit to do with him outside class. David, on the other hand had a fall out and Br. Jack refused to teach him but allowed him to attend his class. By the time mid year came around we had a pile of homework to do each night. Math, English,Modern history, Ancient history, Geography and Economics if you weren't doing a language left us with overload for evening homework. Our class had a meeting one evening and mutually agreed that we would skip doing our Math's homework to fit all the rest of our assignments in for the next days assessments. When Br. Jack of all Trades asked a couple of us to answer questions relating to the previous nights assignment, the retorted was " We didn't do it Brother." Br. Jack then requested those of us who hadn't done our home work to stand up. The whole class except Mulheran got to their feet. Jack taking the metal edge of is ruler began systematically to crack each of us over the knuckles for our failure of adherence to to his orders. When he came to muller, he was till seated. Br. Jack asked him if he had completed his homework.David's answer duplicating ours and Br. Jack ordered him to stand and take his punishment. Mulhearn replied that he was not in the goodly brothers class anymore so couldn't be punished. Br. Jack replied: "you are now back" and proceeded to bash him across the knuckles too.

Both Mulhearn and I failed mathematics in the leaving Certificate. The General mathematics paper had changed to a two hour examination with the first 32 questions being multiple choice. It took me 30 minutes to complete the multiple choice and I left the exam room not bothering to do the rest of the paper. The multiple choice represented 32% of the marking. As it happened I scored all questions right, a 100% mark. So if I had stayed and attempted the whole thing I may well have had a fluke pass. The strange nature of career events throughout my lifetime has always been mathematically centred. I pursued a banking career, worked in engineering which involved mathematic statistics, worked with actuaries in insurance and later ran my own businesses all interrelated with mathematics. In Mulhearn's case, he drew a perfect replica of a D9 bulldozer during that exam and had he have been marked on that drawing he would have scored 100%. David in his career at one stage owned nine D9 bulldozers which he used to employ drivers to cut through the jungles of New Guinea to open up new territories for both the Government and private enterprise there. Both David and Len used their timber talents in volunteering to complete unpaid task for the catholic Church. David built a timber Church at Ulong and Leonard a new primary school at Walcha. The indoctrination of the Marist was well founded in those two men's hearts.

In my Intermediate year I was still not applying myself readily to evening study. One nights study class, Doug Ferguson and yours truely decided to unravel a golf ball after we broke open the casing. The third year high school had three classes for night study, all divided by partitions. The First level comprised the Honours student who studied Sciences and language. The Second level, those of mathematical persuasion and us in Level three were more devoted to History, Geography, English and the Arts. On this particular night study class, Ferguson and I were bored and commenced to run the rubber entails of the ball around the class passing on a length of it to the next student. The rubber band spread student by student right through the three class levels. Pat the Rat from his lofty height over-looking all classes had spotted the rubber strip unravelling and tracked it back to my desk seated next to 'Fergo' now caught in the act of letting out more rubber slack. Pat the Rat ordered us to go to the front of the class and touch our toes. The Rat, the immortal cricket coach, returned with a cricket bat and headed down the back of the room got up a mean pace and hit us each in turn for a six. Neither Ferguson not I could sit on on the cheeks of our ass for a week.

By the time I had reached fourth year I had given up physics but retained chemistry. I was pretty good at chemical formula and was not too bad in Math's algebra, but of the rest of Math and Science I just didn't have the head for. I use to get in the high 80s for Chemistry and 30s in Science. So naturally when I got to L. C year I switched to Economics which was the first year it was introduced as a Leaving Certificate subject. I was still not applying myself too well at class, preferring to skip Economics and Ancient history classes in favour of disappearing to the library to read of historic adventurers.If and when I got caught, I gave the impression that I was busy in study. To be fair, our Economics and Ancient history Master was one and the same person but not not the best teacher. We called him Colossus because

of his sizeable tails of historic sexual exploits of known leaders we studied. Brother's name gradually changed to "Spunky,' the nickname back then of someone who spoke frequently of penis complex and erections. My marks in Geography were of A grade standard having topped the class in the half yearly trials. This already assured me of 10 marks in the final paper. My modern history papers were used by the teacher for honours students research so I had no problem in that quarter. Wool classing was still a Leaving Certificate final subject as was music. They were the last two examinations before Ancient history exam eleven days later. So I read the whole syllabus with in the 11 days, concocted some algebraic formula mixed with history dates and got myself a pass.

The contact with my fellow students after leaving school extended to almost ever town I had occasion to be later appointed too.I am thankful for those contacts which often came at times when life had handed me a lemon. My old comrades of school years some how helped me to turn bitter lemons of life into lemonade. Some of my fellow students exploits after leaving schoolmate still make me laugh. Bob Barrett from Brewarrina was a case in point. Bob was nugget like hard guy from that wild west town of mining and inland stream fishing. Desert sand country with most days as hot as the fires of hell and cold as Siberia at night. Bob, after leaving school, managed to drum up enough money to buy a local bloody house of a pub. Apparently when a fight broke out in the Brewarrina pub, Bob was always in the midst of it all, throwing the trouble makers out the door. On one occasion Bob was busy trying to keep the local drunks fortified with ale when a brewery truck arrived and loaded as much beer as the pub storeroom could take.

Bob, surveying the situation, jumped into the drivers seat and backed the truck at great speed into the rear wall of the pub. The wall collapsed from the impact leaving a gaping hole in the pub. Bob reportedly jumped out of the truck, pointed to the hole in the wall and retorted: "Stack it all in there." Apparently he returned to the bar shouting that he had solved a storage logistics problem, he felt vindicated.

It would be remiss of me not to mention one of the night competition events that used to on occasions take place with betting odds taken on a likely winner. Boys would line strip naked, in the dead of night with erect penis in hand and race each other around the school parameter, dart in and out between stone pillars at the base of the Chapel. The game rule was that the first into bed fully dressed in their PJs after the naked race would be declare the winner. This activity ceased the night one of the boys slipped on wet concrete and skidded right into a stone pillar with penis still in hand. It was a bloody mess and he spent the next week being treated in the Infirmary by Br. 'The Dog.' At the time of the mishap to make matters worse one of the boys had in his wisdom of the missile crash ent to the emergency medical cabinet and returned to pour a quantity of antiseptic liquid on the wound of the warrior's tool. The scream could be heard far away like someone had just strangled a cat.

In conclusion, we were taught at school to live by the Golden rule of do unto others and be compassionate, independent and free. The lessons therein took more than my school years to learn that rule and that life is not about Doug at all. My holidays ended abruptly as Dad insisted with some interoperation to employ me until my Leaving certificate results come out in the press. I did not enjoy working in the garage doing menial tasks and returning home at night looking like I had fallen into a vat of grease. I was relieved to receive my results closely followed by a letter from the Commonwealth Bank congratulating me and offering me a start at the local branch for two pounds above the basic wage of a banker officer. The exams results ensured I would be accepted for the next intake for teachers college if I so wished to pursue that option. Dad was jubilant that I had passed in his opinion with a fine mark for the likes of me. He drove me to the Bowling Club at Nambucca Heads to join his mates in a drinking celebration. I on the other hand had designs to be a Dental Mechanic and was dis appointed some what with the prospects that I had not made the grade. After our drinking session and Dad's continued praise of my 'second rate' results, I took the opportunity to plead my case for sending me back to school, promising I would do even better next time. I had not studied much and knew I could have done a lot better if I had been a little more diligent with my efforts instead of skipping classes in favour of the library. Dad's would have none of it advising me to take the bank job as I had my chance and it was now time to settle down to a career. I was not on the same wave length as my father and figured he wasn't being far sighted enough but knowing it was his money that afforded me the education I re-signed myself to banking. I had in my final year at school did some volunteer work for the local dental mechanic. In that time I learned a lot about the chemical compounds for filling teeth and use of 18 caret gold for fillings. I also learned how to take the moulds for the making of false teeth relishing the activity. So dentistry was my real career choice but my failure to study hard ended that career path. As it tuned out Dad actually did me a favour in the long run. The three and a half years with the Commonwealth bank helped me mathematically. I rose from the ranks of a junior to Savings Bank Examiner before I moved on. My initial job in the bank as a junior meant that I had to handle the writing up of the small ledge accounts for each and every transaction of the customers of the day.

At the end of the week all these transactions were recalibrated for the Big Book, the General Ledger or total record system over-riding all. We were still using fountain pens back then and these LSD (an acronym for pounds, shillings and pence) transactions had to be entered into a Genera Ledger with a neat hand and no mistakes were tolerated. This system worked perfectly except for the fact that the junior ran from the withdraw shoot when a bell rang, collect a passbook with withdrawal slip dropped in by a wait-ing customer.

At the same time the teller dealing with the cash would leave a completed and stamped deposit slip for recording of this transac-tion too. My job was to find the customer ledger page from a smaller duplicate of the 'Big Book' enter the transaction, plus or minus on both the customer passbook and our bank record, tally both and return the book to the teller who completed the task with cash back to the customer, passbook stamped and initialled topped off with a friendly smile. The transaction completed the customer was satisfied with proof of a plus or minus entry in the account with bank stamp seal verification in his passbook.

One of the tricks played on new recruits to banking is to send them off to another competitor and request their Big book for examination by our Bank. I was sent up to the then local Rural bank to complete this task. On arrival I was met at the counter by a new female recruit who like me had just started in the bank. She promptly completed my request by handing over the large weighty book. I wound my way back through the busy streets of Macksville on that Monday morn promptly dropping the large book with thud on the customer counter. My then first boss, Paul Petersen, after being advise by fellow staff member came flustering at the rate of knots from his office to the counter. He quickly picked up the phone advising the Rural Bank Manager of the predicament.

So it came to pass that I returned to the Rural bank with their Big Book closely followed by a security guard and our branch Accountant. The Joke had backfired on all and sundry in our branch and no one every tried to take 'the Mickey' out on me again in my short but illustrious banking career. That one year after leaving school was eventful. We of the banking staff as well as every shop keeper in town stood at attention as the military parade funeral march of local war hero Frank Partridge passed us by. A horse drawn gun carriage with coffin sitting on the wide barrel slowly passes to the sound of a drum beat. The large contingent of military dignitaries WW11with foot soldiers marched by on their way to the local cemetery for the burial ceremony with other local War veterans tagging along. Many veterans   recalled Frank Partridge marching on the annual Anzac Day march not unlike the march on this day. Frank won the Victoria Cross in the dying days of the Pacific war. Badly wounded, he snatched a Bren gun from a dead gunner and challenged the enemy to come out and fight before storming their bunker and killing Japanese with grenade and knife. He was 21, the youngest and only military man to win the VC. Frank was lionised and went to London in 1946 to attend the ' Victory March' and returned again for the 1953   coronation of Queen Elizabeth11. Frank always returned to his father's dirt-floor farm house outside Bowraville where he read the Encyclopaedia Britannica by kerosene lamp and honed his extraordinarily retentive memory.

In 1962, Frank starred on a television quiz show , Pick- a- Box, compered by the American Bob Dyer. Already grey-hired, Frank's dry somewhat haunted manner strangely counterpointed his know-all wiz rival Barry Jones. They both became awkward early TV celebrities.

Frank Partridge died two year later in a car smash at Bellingen. Shocked, Australia mourned for man caught between heroism and celebrity. He left a new bride and a three moths old son Lachlan Partridge who still refuses to sell the VC of the father he never knew. At the little township of Bowraville a tenderly cared museum honours the town's most famous son, Frank partridge VC and in the middle of the main street where bullock teams once dragged cedar logs as the Anzacs fought in Gallipoli, a polished trachyte column bears 45 names of the local men who fell in the Great War. My remaining year in Macksville had me involved in long distant running in various Gift events around country New South Wales. The Marist Brothers indoctrination had me attending St. Vincent de Paul activity with local Catholic businessmen.

Before the first quarter of 1964 was over, I was already on my way to my first transfer post for the Commonwealth Bank at Inverell on the New England Tablelands. As a stranger in town I soon got to know the local youth putsch. My background growing up Catholic gave me a 'heads up' to join the Catholic Youth Club. Little to do with being Catholic, it comprised young men and women over 18 who joined in weekly social activities. Most of our Club met regularly at a weekly dance in the Inverell town hall or those of us who owned car made our way to Glenn Innes to a local pub dance. It was an around 50 kilometres trip and a great way to get cuddle on the way too and from the dance. Our weekend activities, when not racing cars was to pay a 'chicken like' game with unsuspecting drivers. We would meet at a service station just outside the limits of town and choose a car that had external door handles. When the driver pulled up for petrol, one 'pillion passenger ' would attach the right hand to the left hand front passenger door handle. When the driver took off heading townward, the 'rider' learned out with the grip arm bent and knees leaning against the body of the vehicle. As the car picked up speed the rider began to straighten the grip arm leaning further and further outward. Once the rider was in danger of loosing grip, the idea was to lean back in and knock on the passenger window with face appearing there. Apart from scaring the driver, it always resulted in a sudden stop. Nobody got hurt but it was dangerous fun.

In the winter months I managed to get a run in Second Grade with the local Rugby Union team. They were fun trips playing rugby in various townships on the New England. As usual when the game finished we would adjourn to the bar. The habit of indulging in too much heavy drinking sessions was the norm for socialising and a daily after work pastime for us bankers.

I had not realised it then but alcoholism already had its grip on me from the moment I took my first sip of beer. My infatuation for a quiet dark eyed beauty in the course of my daily banking routine made it hard to concentrate on my daily duties quite a lot in my year in Inverell. Desire became obsession and ultimately a progressive realisation of a worthwhile pre determined goal. So for a time Pricilla in passion was my constant companion and with her many an evening was spent fogging up the windows of my car. As for my driving, it was reckless at the best of times. On a trip to the movies at Delungra one evening in her Dad's car we were in passionate embrace as I sped along a dirt road to paradise. In my enthusiasm to complete more than one task at a time, I had inadvertently taken my eyes off the road and missed an approaching bridge. We flew through the air ending squarely in the middle of a dry creek bed. Fortunately the country was in drought and the creek was as dry so.Pricilla and I maintained our passion without so much as a fibrillation of a heartbeat. Deed done we drove along the creek bed to find a way out and back on the road again. Usually it was my small two seated sports car that was not conducive to passionate embraces we need up in, thus ended our regular embrace with sore backs. It gave me some joy to take her Dad's car for a spin. Besides it had a column gear change in contrast to the awkwardness of the gear stick in my little sports car.

There was only one other incident in Priscilla's affair that put pay to me using the family car was a weekend on the Gold Coast. Somewhere in our crossing into Queensland, we drove along the beachfront and pulled over onto the edge of the beach to celebrate our arrival. Oblivious to the fact that the car was slowly sinking into the sand as we sank into the rhythm method. Unable to open the doors, I climbed out of the window and enlisted the help of some young surfer types. The boys were out on a late night drinking spree and in good humour helped me lift the car back to a stable surface. All the while Pricilla sat starry eyed in a kind of haze watching the proceedings unfold. Our relationship came to a rather abrupt end not long after I was transferred to the Commonwealth Bank Coffs Harbour. I was still on the road to rack and ruin, driving like a love sick maniac too and from Inverell at weekends for a while. Around about the time I put my car into a spin on the journey west and took out a guide post. I notice in the rear vision mirror in my haste, the guide post flying through the air as I struggled to keep the car on the road. Dirt roads in drought can be a God send for a young driver as the loose gravel save the car from flipping. I never missed a beat, hammering that machine towards in finity. The romance died the day a mates mother gave me the Inverell times to read. Pricilla's photo appeared larger than life with her new husband. It was her wedding day not three weeks after we had separated. It appears she had been two timing me all along. That girl had an insatiable appetite for lust.

In the third years of my short lived banking career whilst still in Coffs, I had save up a small fortune of some three thousand pounds. I noticed on a lunch break that a business premise on the entry corner to the shopping centre was up for sale. It belonged to a local engineering business who was seeking cash flow for the business and would be in agreement to lease the business back as tenants for a keen purchaser. I had the money to buy the building but not the experience. So, on a mission of due diligence I approached my boss, the CTB Bank Manager. When seeking the best person for advise back then, it was taken as fact that the Bank Manager had the goods when it came to money matters and the Priest had it for sin. In hindsight, my experience proved to me that they both lacked credibility in most instances. The Boss bankers advise: "Leave your money accumulating interest in your savings accounts Doug, Coff's Harbour will never go ahead." How wrong that advise turned out to be.

It was the 14th February 1966, the day decimal currency was introduced to the public. We had a busy week exchanging monies for our customers to the new currency and explaining the workings of the conversion. I had driven the one hour journey on the first Saturday morning of a new economic means of exchange to my home town. I fled into the Nambucca hotel. Dad like a flash had captured the currency change opportunity. Hanging above the bar on a neat chain was a white board conversion chart with the old currency value on the left column and the new decimal currency on the other. Dad had overnight built and designed this for the benefit of the drinking public. The black print on white paint hardwood had been completed with the precision of carpenter, sign writer and marketing entrepreneur. The sign also promoted Dad's business. "This information supplied by Eric McPhillips Pty.Ltd;" The sign hung over the bar for many along days ahead, until the pub was eventually purchased by a new owner and it was no longer relevant.

CHAPTER 10.

WORKING FOR THE MAN

On my return trip to Coffs Harbour, I passed a 'land for sale' sign. It was for a new subdivision at nearby Valla Beach, about eight clicks north of Nambucca Heads. I made my way to the Real Estate Agent, next door to the only business in Valla Beach at the time. A general store for emergency supplies, milk bar, post office and estate agency all rolled into one. The sign in the window showed the land priced in the old currency at five hundred pound per block. Considering I had three thousand pound saved I could have easily purchased six blocks. I made my way to the beach front to view the small estate of eight blocks. However, by the time I reached the outskirts of Coffs, I had changed my mind. The next weekend I made my way to Kempsey to sink the bulk of my hard earned savings into a previous owner 62 EK Holden. My father had come along to inspect my pending purchased, gave it the once over approval before I parted with my money. I was in my element, after all it had a column gear change and it would suit my carnal desires.   My final year with the Bank was Liverpool in Sydney. It was the fourth biggest brace of the Commonwealth Bank and had staff union issues from the day of my arrival. In that year the Union visited the Bank Premises on eighty occasions with employer em-ployee issues. A pig of a man who shall remain nameless to allow his soul to remain at peace, was the bane of every young staff member at the time. In my case, he followed me like a shadow whilst at work, in my lunch hour and sometimes before work.

By the time I resigned off on my services to banking, I was a sleepless nervous wreck. The banks secret service man stood in the shadows whilst I ate my lunch, adjourned to the bar for a beer or attempted to escape into the arms of another lover. I was ap-pointed 'Teller One ' in a series of eight tellers in that branch. Liv-erpool was a growth suburb but still had the appeal of something out of the wild west at the time. It was near the end of the train line for city commuters, had a large working class population of city office workers, Italian market gardeners, small retail business, car dealers and a one of the first large retail shopping centres in Syd-.ney. The township had a consistent bus and train service and was a stones throw from Bankstown airport. The suburb grew west-ward with a housing and farms from as far way as Macquarie Field. There was also a new housing commission estate at Cabra matta for the not so rich dependent upon shopping in Liverpool. Nearby Heathrow housed a large Army base of which we were responsible to service for all things money related. That apart from our Friday night duty as bankers to visit the new migrant hostel at Heathrow which was mainly filled with"Ten pound Pom" arrivals. It was always Friday night fever for us. The job was to collect the pay from those tin hut dwellers and stamp their Commonwealth Bank passbooks as proof of their diligent saving, return to the bank around nine p.m. and locked the loot into the safe. The musicians at the migrant camp were often practicing on our arrival there. The young English lads, the 'Easybeats,' belting out "Friday on my mind," as we counted their parents meagre savings. At my height of achievement in banking I graduated from the job of Teller 1 to Savings Bank Examiner.

The last post was trumpeting out my banking death note. It was no mean feat for a seemingly average student who scraped through intermediate maths to reach such dizzy heights of banking but I had switched off from my banking career prospects. I felt like I was going to crack but had not realise at the time, my 'SS shadow' and Management had grand plans for me up the ladder in the CTB banking system. I was doing good job for them but was possibly far too young to take on the responsibly I found myself in, shackled with an extremely busy banking environment. I had decided to take a break and on my return from holidays tendered my resignation.

The big boss pleaded good reason for me to stay on and suggested another holiday but I had already made up my mind. I did not have a clue what I wanted to do, I just wanted out of the restrictions of white collar work and the artificial greetings of Mr, Sir and Madam. I applied applied to Qantas to join the fight steward training with visions of international travel in the back of my mind. The first interview I breezed through and was called back a week later to attend a final selection. In front of me sat three men who plied me with questions relating to current affairs, international events and finally a question on two articles I had read in the daily press that day that had caught my attention. As luck would have it I had read the headlines and the feature cartoon on the way to the interview. I passed with flying colours and was immediately sent to the Qantas GP for a once over.

The only block to my career prospects was my height. The minimum height for flight stewards back then was 5' 7" and I was 5'6.5" barefooted. Fortunately I didn't have to take off my shoes for the examination and my boots had a least a half inch heel, so I made it. There was a fortnight's gap before I would get the confirmation of acceptance and joining date, so I had to find something to do in the meantime. I was in a new romantic relationship and having some fun in drinking sprees with a couple of my banking mates, but needed some cash flow to get by with food, clothing and shelter in the meantime. I was living in a boarding house at Mount Druitt at the time and had used my payout from the bank to pay a couple of weeks rent in advance but apart from some petrol monies I had zilch.

On visit to my Cousin Kay at the engineering section of RK radio, I was offered a job there due mainly to her influence, as an Exempt Technicians Assistant. I threw in the Qantas opportunity when I got acceptance confirmation and opted to stay with this new part time job. The Engineering section was a part of the then PMG but the job was pretty cool. Whilst my initial intention was to stay for the two weeks before joining Qantas, all that changed when I met the Head of Engineering, John Day. He took a shining to me and offered me a permanent post as his designated full-time driver and chief cook and bottle washer so to speak. I fact my initial duty was to build him an Engineering library. He had enquired if I had any idea how to do that. My immediate reply was "Yes, Mr. Day,' although I did not have a clue, I accepted the challenge. Once he had headed back to his office, I went looking for the best person to give me the right advise within the Engineering works. I was soon pointed in the direction of the Senior Technician with the most clues. He quickly pulled out a file and a binder and explained the A to Z procedure for recording a filing all matters relating too engineering. He even produce a wooden cabinet with shelving which he said I could use to house the new library which i figured would do the job just fine.

Armed with this information and a template of filing procedure and a leather bound file, I set to work. The money resources to achieve my task was no issue. it was after all the Public Service and funds were released within 24 hours thanks to my cousin Kay's connections. I had the whole engineering library documented in neat files much like our CTB savings bank files. In hindsight I had unknowingly duplicated the CTB system. John Day was genuinely impressed and a reward he gave me a PMG Utility as my vehicle to use on and off the job.

My duties changed from administration to be on call for any just in time delivery work that took the man's fancy or was considered essential to the needs of the department.   One day I would be attending duties at the ABC Television Station with technician at Gore Hill in St. Leonards. The next I was on my way with him to Moruya to check out the Australian broadcasting commission tower with the John Day, the boss himself. On another I would be climbing a T.V. tower with a technician to check out some problem with the signal. Back then the PMG, which later became Telstra, was responsible for all technical equipment for radio, T.V. cable and phone lines. Our area was focused on TV as it was our responsibility in and expanding network in that decade of the 1960s. It was not only TV Stations and towers had to be completed and maintained but booster stations for country areas was also our responsibility. I was in what was called the fourth division of the public service.

In the then PMG in employed technicians who were responsible for TV equipment, radio and telephone exchanges, the linesman and techs who maintained the on street equipment and the Primary Works Department for underground cable. In my time in the PMG I graduated to work in all those areas.   Under John Day's tutelage I took the role ad title of Acting Senior Technician when and Seniors Tech took his annual four weeks leave. Officially the PMG would not have allowed an unqualified person to do that gig, but I had The Man as my connection. It was another of those straight forward roles,

recording all the statistics for the Country TV powers of Little Brother Mountain, Big Brother mountain and one other up on the North Coast. The daily task of signal recording and graphing same was a bit laborious but I completed the task without a hitch. The admin then sent in my high duty payment sheet kindly endorsed by John Day and my pay rapidly increased.

It was at this time I was asked to assist a newly appointed Russian engineer and trainee was on loan from NSW University for practical experience in the field. As for the practicality of the intended engineering task, things didn't go exactly as intended. Alex the Russian engineer was to all intent and purpose an accident waiting to happen. Once appointed to the PMG and our department he decided to go for his driving licence. Alex had attempted it multiple times and failed repeatedly. It got to the stage that the Police were afraid to ride with him because he was too erratic and a danger to himself and the travelling public.

Alex finally obtained his licence by bribing a cop at the Redfern police station. He had purchased a new VW beetle and was travelling on his merry way from Redfern Police Station back to our city as a first day licence holder. He never made it out of Redfern. One hundred yards up the road from the Police station he lost control of the car, wiping out three telephone boxes in the process. Those little red telephone boxes stood on the main route for where pedestrian flow was at peak. The phones hung from the back of the box with a coin slot attachment for payment of the call. Redfern had three of them side by side and were not far from the Redfern railway station. They were bright red and could be seen from a long distance on ground and for that matter from out space too. It was unusual to find an empty one and people wishing to make a call usually had to line up and wait for an empty cubical. God must have been on the side of the telephone users as on this rear occasion the three phone boxes we empty just at the moment Alex came beetling along. He didn't slow for a fraction of a second and neatly took out the three boxes and totally wrote off his beetle. The police were on the scene in matter of minutes and Alex lost his licence on the spot. The PMG covered up the incident but Redfern remained without three public telephone conveniences from that day forward.

Alex the Russian, David the trainee engineer and a clueless tech's assistant, namely me, left Mascot on a plane bound for Dubbo loaded with technical equipment for field work. We were to do area strength measurements for Television in the Pilliga Scrub, somewhere between Narrabri and Coonabarabran on one one bright mid summer Saturday morn. We arrived at Dubbo airport Avis car hire counter to arrange a car for a week hire to complete our assigned tasks.The paper work was duly completed by Alex and the receptionist requested Alex's drivers licence. He turned to me and in a semi demanding tone requested my drivers licence, making some excuse that he left his at home back in Sydney. I found myself taking responsibility for the car hire and the driving of same. I had been taught never to question a boss's reasons for a work duty. However, I did question Alex after we left the counter although he had the authority over me, I was taken aback by the fact that I ended up with the vehicle responsibility as well as driving duty. It was then that Alex came clean about his loss of licence. It was no more than than five minutes into the trip into town that Alex insisted on driving. I never realised then that how dangerous that decision would become within the next 24 hours.

The journey was no more than ten minutes into town and the streets of Dubbo were deserted except for one young teenage girl wandering along the main street. I asked Alex to stop, winding down my window I asked the young women for the location of the hotel we had booked for the night. She replied , pointing in the general direction. "Well you take a f**ken left at the next corner, then take the next on the f**ken right and its on the next f**ken corner." I thanked her for here explicit clarity of direction and we journeyed onward. Once we had booked in and dropped our gear in our rooms we headed for the bar. Thus began our week of continuous drinking, driving across country, setting up equipment, climbing a t.v. tower and flirting with danger in a small aircraft.

The morning after the night before we left the Dubbo hotel early on a mission to get to Coonabarabran T.V. tower before the local studios began the early morning programme. Alex was behind the wheel in our Avis Ford Falcon rent. The RTA had recently completed a duel expressway raised about ten metres above the flood plain and surrounding landscape. David the trainee Engineer and I were had both fallen asleep as soon the car gained some speed on the long straight stretch of road, due in part to our heavy drinking session the night

before. Alex seems to be coping o.k.behind the wheel even thou he downed copious quantities of vodka the evening before whilst we matched him drink for drink with beers. There was a sudden bump in the vehicle which caused me to wake up fully alert to the situation. Alex was driving with his foot hard on the accelerator, head down trying to tune in the radio. He had inadvertently turned the steering wheel without realising he had done so; too intent on his need to hear a radio broadcast.

The impact of hitting the edge of the road had woken me; undeterred Alex from his radio tuning activity was heading straight for a guide post. I threw myself to drivers side grabbing and turning the wheel as I did so. The vehicle spun sideways narrowly missing the guide post and head at full speed down the expressway. Alex now alter to the situation clutch the steering with both hands in a vice like grip and hung on. The tyres suddenly gained a temporary grip on the road and I was catapulted like an arrow half way out the passenger door window. I grabbed both inside supports and with my upper body being forced toward the road surface yelled at Alex to let go the wheel. I was trusting the vehicle would right itself by sheer momentum but it was not to be as Alex's hands were glued solid to the steering.

The back rear passenger side tyre was almost off its rim and I prayed it would not blow. Just as suddenly the vehicle gained road traction and the sped across the double lane highway with me still yelling at Alex to let go the steering well. The immediate effect was to send me flying back into to the passenger seat. It was to no avail, the vicelike hold of the big Russian remained tight on the steering with a right hand lock grip. The vehicle left the road still doing top speed as Alex not only held the steering tight but his right foot was hard upon the accelerator. The Falcon went airborne across a barbed wire fence, as livestock and cowering crows scattered and the car headed up a slight slope and lodged between two trees.

David in the back seat had bounced around the cabin. Alex sat in a daze with hands still vice like on the steering wheel. It was a time before seat belts became mandatory in all vehicles so 'knuckling down and buckling up" was not an option. Miraculously no one was injured. We quickly assessed the situation and realised that apart from slight damage below the door line of the car, all was fine and dandy. The mud caked below the door base was our saving grace. The recent rain and soft paddock had cushioned our flight and rough landing. All that remained was to get across the paddock and upon to the expressway again.

After calling Alex "A bloody idiot" a number of times, David and I took charge of the situation. Alex busied himself taking photos of the car lodged between the two trees. We manage to push the car over a slight slope and as luck would have it the areas was a stoney and there was a break in the fence. The vehicle started without a hitch and with me now insisting, I took over driving duties, consciously aware that the vehicle was hired in my name.

We made it to the TV equipment technicians office just in time for our allotted appointment. Alex made an agreement with the T.V. studio to show test patterns to replace normal programs for three minute intervals at agreed time slots during the next week of programmes. It was our intention to drive within a 200 km radius of the T.V. tower and signal to do some area strength measurements with our on board equipment at the precise time the test pattens appeared on screen. We were to test the signal and recording our findings back to PMG RK radio for their decision as too a booster station or a further T.V. tower to be installed, based on he findings of our measurements.

Once we had breakfast and a couple of beers at the local pub we set off for our first lot of experiments about 50 km from Coonabarabran township. We completed four experiments within a 50 Km circumference around the tower and all in all did some 300 km by nightfall retuning to the pub for a late dinner and adjourned to the bar for a further drinking spree. The pub allowed us to drink on beyond their 10.O'clock closing. By 11.p.m. we had made our way to bed and I was out cold after a belly full of beer with rum chasers. Alex returned to his room with a bottle of vodka!

The very next morning we headed out early a little worse for wear as we had arranged for the first test pattern of the day to be at 8.am on the dot for three minutes. We set our plan to do four tests on the day at a circumference of 100 km each apart from the T.V. tower. The equipment took about ten minutes to set up, three minutes of recording the signal and ten to pack up and head to the next location. We repeating the same experiment equidistant from the tower at all points of the compass. The process worked well despite the heat of the day and the pests of little flies. We were making great progress and had three more days of testing to complete our work. Surprising with my young driver skills on the dirt roads, but ever mindful of a current T.V. road safety advert "Young drivers are most skilled, but they are also the most killed," I play it safe into corners and only

gunned the car on the straight. We were safely back in the bar by late afternoon for another   drinking session. The Publican arranged for the pub to provide our dinner there and drinks flowed until closing time. Around closing time I was well in my cups as was David. Alex a little unsteady of hand had tied a handkerchief around his neck so he could hold the glass without shaking whilst drinking another vodka. We staggered from the bar with a a repeat sleep pattern. We all slept in and didn't get too breakfast until 8.am. The pub had just cracked their line of kegs and were testing the beer, so we helped them with the test.

Outside the pub Alex insisted on taking a photo of us drinking underneath the town monument and town clock. The clock struck 9 and we had already missed the first test pattern at the nearby TV Tower. The publican obliged us with a photo on Alex's camera, drinking a beer with the hands of the clock proving proof the time of our morning reviver. Our next point if the compass reading was 150 km away at 11 o'clock. So we hightailed it into the Pilliga Scrub with time to spare and set up the equipment covered again with annoying little flies. They were in our eyes, our nose and ears and nearly drove us mad. I made up my mind right then and there to apply for a permanent appointment in the Third Division of the Public Service to further my career. I concluded I was too educated to sit on a metal box in the middle of nowhere doing what seemed useless work experiments. Besides I was not qualified and was only a temporary employee and didn't want to pursue a technical career. I could see myself climbing the administrative ladder supporting University educated academics or some such.

Meanwhile, we still had two more experiments to do before dark at the appointed times with the TV station, so we set forth in the scrub to the North West for the two rendezvous as planned. We had already recorded that the first experiment of the day had failed. Another night of drinking was taking its toll on us but keen to get the job finished we were up bright and early before the heat of the day got the better of us and more importantly to beat the flies. We had now to do the 200 km circumference four experiments at all points of the compass. It was a long trip to the first sight for the test and we manage to get a weak signal for about a minute of the three on the test pattern. It was then that Alex came up with a bright idea. Well on paper it seemed that way but in reality it proved costly to the PMG and a failure. Alex had the notion that if we hired a pilot and a plane we could rig up an antenna on the aircraft wing. In so doing send a signal to the equipment on the ground at the base of the TV tower and use a range finder from there to gauge the distance of the plane to the tower. Thus, the measurements could being recorded without any further need for field experiments. So We set off to Dubbo to hire what we needed. We contracted a pilot who's working for a crop dusting company and got an agreement to use the companies Piper Comanche aircraft for our purposes. 'Dangerous Dan' the pilot, we late rfound out, had been grounded by Qantas for a year for low flying over a private beach as a dare and wiped out a fence scaring hell out of a farmers cattle herd. The farmer phoned Civil Aviation with an official complaint and our illustrious Pilot was caught red handed. He had landed the commercial plane neatly at Mascot on a training flight but the barbed wire and a fence post wrapped around one wing gave him away. So to fill in the year grounded from his Qantas training he accepted a job as a crop duster at Dubbo. Alex the crazy Russian Engineer enlisted the help of 'Dangerous Dan' to drill a hole in the top of the right wing off the aircraft and feed a connection back into the plane for the unproven experiment.

David and I headed to town in search of a Range Finder and as luck would have it we found a disposal store and hired an old army one, using Alex's expense account credit card to pay. On our return to the aircraft Alex was waiting for us. It was all set up for the Pilot to fly outwards from the TV tower at Coonabarabran mountain top. The Pilot was instructed to turn on the equipment at a pre-determined time and fly in circle patterns outward from the tower, increase the distance with signals from the ground and a mud map drawn by Alex with appropriate distance for the flight pattern included. We felt pleased with the Alex's plan of action for the next morning and were back in the bar a little earlier than planned to take up where we left off our drinking session from the night before. Early the next morning, despite hangovers, we were up on the mountain top twigged the equipment linking with the nearby TV signal getting first class reception. Now, it remained a simple matter to meter a corresponding signal from the aircraft to the ground equipment. David and I had the dubious duty to climb the tower with the range finder and quote the distance the aircraft was circling its way around the tower, advising Alex who recorded the signal strength below. My job was to support David a couple of rungs below him, yelling the Range Finders reading

to Alex. I was relieved that I had only to climb half way up that skeleton of steel, hanging in the wind on that man made structure in the sky above the mountain top. The flight pattern and signals worked ok for the nearest experiment but the communication broke down between the pilot and Alex for the distant circles, so we had to abandon day 1 of the experiments. We adjourned to the bar mapping out a plan for the next day.

It was agreed for David to go up in the plane with the Pilot the next day and gauge the distance from the plane to the tower, in-crease that distance at pre arrange times with the aid of binoculars and Range Finder, advising the Dangerous Dan of his next move. My job was to assist Alex with the equipment on the ground and signal the plane to move out further from the tower for the next round of test pattern signals. It meant that David had to the car trip to Dubbo and back to the disposal store for hire of strong binocu-lars for our next level of experiments. Our usual drinking session continued as we mapped out the next days activity. We were all up bright and early as David drove Alex and I up the mountain to the stored equipment and headed off to Dubbo for his assigned task. He was to return back to us after returning to Dubbo airport with "Dangerous Dan" at the controls of the Piper.

All seemed to work ok for some of the closer experiments but as soon as we attempted to do the distant ones we lost the plane signal. It proved a frustrating day and as Dangerous Dan was running short of fuel the plane turned back and he tipped the wing to let us know he was on his way home. Alex via a telephone to the airport spoke to Dan on his return to base and suggest the boosting of the battery charge on the PMG apparatus as it was apparent that the gear was low on signal and was showing a red light. It was just a matter of putting the battery on an overnight battery system to get full charge strength for the planned   signal. We agreed with Alex that he should return to Dubbo in the morning to ensure all was ready for the last try at completing the desired test results.

David and I had a weeks worth of signal experience, we were appointed by Alex to take over the duty of recording the metered signals below the tower the next day. The plan was for Alex to drive to Dubbo to fly back to the tower with 'Dangerous Dan' to complete the tasks ahead. I mused to myself which was the greater risk, Alex driving the car on the expressway he had lost control on or the riding with the Maverick grounded Qantas pilot flying around the country skies. Little did I know then, the tide would turn and I was out to be

plunged into that danger zone. We were awake bright and early after another night of drinking. David met me at breakfast, he like me was keen to have the morning cooked breakfast of bacon, eggs and bake beans on toast with copious amounts of tea to get our body back in shape. Alex appeared at the doorway looking worse for wear. He had been vomiting convulsively throughout the night and was in no shape for the drive to Dubbo, let alone flying with 'Dangerous Dan.' So it was agreed that I would take the wheel and drive to Dubbo to be the pillion passenger on the plane for the final days duties. Alex had figured that he would be all right to do the ground work up on the mountain top and he gave me some final instructions as to what to check on the plane. I had a list to ensure the antenna was in tact on the wing, the wiring inside the plane was connect to the antenna ,the signal equipment and the battery were at full charge. Armed with these instructions, I dropped off my follow drinking companions at the top the mountain and headed for Dubbo. Dan was waiting for me and seemed a little annoyed but patiently awaited as I checked and rechecked all the list of items as instructed by Alex before we taxied out for take off. The ride was smooth and strangely peaceful as we flew high above the clouds.

The little cockpit was tightly designed but comfortable with plenty of leg room, much like that of a racing car. Ten minutes into the flight I broke the silence by asking Dan how the steering control worked. He said "if you want to go up you just do this." A sudden surge of the pit of my stomach being in my mouth hit me as Dangerous Dan pulled back on the joystick and the plane rose steeply upward. Then before I knew it Dan called out above the now labouring motor," If you want to go down you do this." He quickly pushed the joystick forward and the little plane plunged into an equally steep nose dive. I had bile in my mouth but not the anger kind. No, quite au contraire- the greenish kind of muck, but it subsided as I swallowed hard. We dropped for what seemed an eternity before Dan eased back on the controls and we levelled out some 500 metres above the surface of the green landscape below. I settled into the quiet zone again as did Dan and made a mental note not to ask questions to this crazy Pilot. Yes, Dan was aptly name 'Dangerous.' As we approached our destination a storm was brewing and the cloud cover was thick. We hardly see the mountain top let alone the T.V tower. Dan turned the aircraft closer to the tower and we could see it like a shadow in the mist. There was no way we would be doing any experiments that day. Dan with my approval turned the aircraft back towards Dubbo. High above the clouds now, I settled back content to be heading for terra-firma.

Half way through the return flight Dan enquired: "We have a full tank of fuel on board and the PMG ha stop pay for it anyway, so do you mind if we have a little fun now?" I said " Sure" and dam replied:" I will show you what we are not allowed to do under aviation rules as a pilot." He pointed to a black cloud ahead in the distance and headed the aircraft in that direction. "We are not allowed to fly deliberately into unknown territory beyond our designated flight plan." Dan headed deep into the cloud and we suddenly went from daylight to darkness like a train in a tunnel. Daylight appeared soon enough and we were back on course again. We were back into a pleasant sunlit day as we rode in silence towards Dubbo airport. I thought that was the end of Dan's idea of fun until we flew above a large country estate. I remarked how beautiful the property looked from our birds eye view in the sky. Dan's "Where?" was answered by my signal outside my pillion passenger window, I pointed downward. it was what dan had been waiting for: "Lets have a look" he said. Dan leaned the joystick to the right and forward and the plane began too shudder and make an eerie sound as we dived like a fighter plane of war ready to mix it with the Bloody Red Baron of Germany.

The rooftop of the homestead was fast approaching as we headed towards ground zero. At the last second Dan pulled back on the joystick and turned the plane left as it roared its way back skyward. That was not the end of it, Dan had danger in his eyes now. He quickly retorted "Brace yourself," turning the plane upside down as we climbed and did a belly roll back upright. I was relieved to see the Dubbo airport below. Dan grounded the aircraft and I alighted a little unsteady on my feet. My face must have looked as green as the pastures of Ireland. Dan had a stupid grin on his face as I fought back the desire to throw up. Back in control mode and in the airport hanger with Dan, I said my goodbye as I grabbed his hand for a final handshake." We had some fun didn't we?"was his final parting words. I was feeling better and now raise a grin, said "Yeah and good luck with getting your suspension lifted with Qantas." I never did catch his surname but every time I board a Qantas flight and hear the Captain say" Good Morning, this is Captain Dan……" I wonder if its him and say a quite prayer that the plane doesn't go into a belly roll in flight or head towards earth in a nosedive.

Back in Coonabarabran we collected our bags and headed for Dubbo again. A hot shower, a few beers and a good nights sleep was what I longed for now. Alex was still sick as was David and they both lay on their respective beds in the hope of recovery. I was feeling grand and visited their motel room. Alex in his wisdom had kindly swapped his room with me and moved into a twin share room with David. I looked at them both in their misery remarking: " You guys are weak." Famous last words as I headed for the motel swimming pool to do a couple of laps and cool off again before bedtime. On arrival at Mascot mid Saturday afternoon I said goodbyes to my intrepid travelling companions. I was keen to catch up with my then girlfriend and head out to Parramatta Golf club for a night of drinking and dancing.

Esther the beautiful blue eyed blond greeted me with a passionate embrace. I felt like Omar Sharif embracing Julie Christie in the movie " Dr. Zhivago." Such feelings didn't last long as I began to drink my first and only schooner at the Parramatta Golf Club that night. Feeling an attack of vomiting coming on I rushed to the toilet and did just that. I emerged some minutes later in a confuse state, with storm loss of coordinations and difficulty breathing. I handed my car keys to Esther and she began to drive me back to her home near Bankstown. The journey was slow as I needed to stop frequently to throw up.

By the time we reach Burwood I had asked her to stop at a pub and I headed for the bar, downing a Port wine and Brandy mix in an attempt settle my stomach. It was to no avail and Esther headed the car towards the nearest hospital at Summer hill and the Emergency ward. A nights stay in hospital, intravenous feeding off a Saline solution and some drug to settle my stomach did the trick. The night sheet at the end of the bed read 'Alcoholic poisoning.' It was no wonder after a long trail of heavy boozing for a week. I should've seen it coming and taken this event as a final warning sigh but a lifetime ahead of alcoholism, awaited me in the future. Who can foresee, I was young and considered myself bullet proof.

Monday morning had Alex, David and myself on the red carpet to give our report on the designated assignment we had endeavour lured to complete. Alex had two neat files ready to present his case to the PMG Engineering Department regarding the area strengths measurements outcome and the other file for the Divisional Clerk's stamp of approval of the excessive expenditure on our given assignment for the previous weeks activity. Alex file showed not only the area surveyed for the experiments but the record of every experiment that had a positive result and the ones that didn't. He even included the one we failed to attend when we slept in. It was filed as a failed experiment which should have been recorded as 'N/A,' not attended! He justified the recording of one only successful experiment at the furtherest distance from the tower and recorded the aeroplane idea as abandoned because of storm interference. When it came to the overblown costings of our journey into the wilderness, Alex had neat columns of figures right down to the last drink.He backed this all up with the photographs of the car incident with photographs of the car lodged between two trees, the undercarriage damage done to the Avis hire car, shots of us all drinking at the clock tower at 9 o'clock in the morning, night shots of us drunk in the bar with strategic placed files of statistics off the bar to give the impression we were still working and not just on the booze. The aeroplane hire was backed up by photos of preparing the equipment for installation including the antenna on the wing, the signal system in the plane, equipment under the tower for recording signals and a couple of photos of David and I up the tower.

CHAPTER 11.

ANOTHER RUNG UP THE LADDER

Morrie, the Divisional Clerk listened to Alex's explanation with a serious look and a steel gaze. When Alex at last ran out of wind, Morrie took the file and a smile spread across his dial: "Best we forget about this file and expenses, we will find another way to write it all off." he said. And with that he took all the photos and put them in his top draw and shot the file of Alex's hard work in recording costs into the waste paper bin under his desk. It would not be the last time that I experienced money wastage by the Engineering Departments of the P.M.G.

The Monday week after our return from the bush everything had returned to normal routine. I took the opportunity after John Day had returned to his office from a field trip. He was away when I was deep in the boozing week with my-intrepid travellers at Coonabarabran and had not yet heard of our 'activities' of work failures and fun times. I announce to him my intention to complete the Public Service examination for entry into the 3rd Division of the Public Service. John was very understanding even thou its would be the end of our association at RK Radio and me being his right hand man. My job as a lowly temporary 4th Division Tech's Assistant and personal dogs body for John Day was coming to and end. He was most understanding and invited me to join him at lunch up the road, on the corner of Pitt and Park street were the Water Board had an in-house restaurant   on the second floor. Once we had eaten our lunch I joined John to ride the lift up top the top floor. It turns out his father was the head of the Water Board at the time and he just wanted to introduce me to him. On the way down the lift he explained. "When you are accepted into the 3rd Division of the public service you will have a choice as to which branch of the service you wish to work. Should you choose the Water Board, Dad will be a good contact for you. So I figured I not only had a mentor in the 4th Division in John Day but another with his Dad in the 3rd Division of the then Water Board too.

The then PMG is possibly the best example of the order of workings. The 4th Division comprises all the exempt personnel like me, clerical assistants not clerks, linesman, exempt staff being non permanent, permanent technicians and their assistants, senior technicians, line inspectors and linesman who worked in the pits for laying wiring for telephones and coaxial cable for long distance connections.

The third division comprised engineers, clerks who had different rankings up the ladder from clerk class 1 to clerk class 9. The 2nd Division comprised those immediately under the Post Master General from technical to administrative. The Post Master General himself being a 1st Division Public Servant. The same pecking order applied to the Post Office from 4th Division Postman to Post Office staff and in turn up the ladder to the Post Master General. Every Department of the Public Service has the same levels of order. The Taxation Commissioner, The Attorney General, and every other head of a Government organisation are 1st Division Public servants with those below them in their various roles according to their duty being 2nd Division to 4th Division. The Prime Minister and State Premiers are all in the 1st Division of Pubic servants and those Departments below them rank from 2nd division to 4th Division. I was to find myself not needing to sit for the Public Service entry examination due to my connections with John Day and my cousin Kay's level three influence within the PMG and the fact that I had the Leaving Certificate. John and Kay had go busy with the necessaries to see my entry on a well planned red carpet. I was told then by Kay to high tail it down to the third floor of the GPO armed with my Leaving certificate results, a letter of referral from John Day and one from administration dutifully signed by Kay McPhillips. It took but a week to get a reply that I had 'passed' the entry examination and to be at Customs House at Circular Quay the following Monday at 9.AM.for the allocation of my 3rd Division position. The letter did not stipulate which branch of the Public Service that I would be assigned.

Come Monday morning I arrived at Customs House met by a guide. There were a lot of graduates off the entry exam standing with with me in the foyer. We were ushered into a large room and asked to be seated. It was like sitting in church waiting for the priest to arrive for the Mass celebration. The duly appointed Public Service spokesman appeared, introduced himself giving all those present a welcome congratulations on acceptance to the Public service. It was much like a Papal blessing followed by communion as he launched into his duties. He briefly explained that there were plenty of jobs to select from any department within the Public Service. He then commenced with the offers, encouraging his own department first:"Who wants join Customs" he said. A show of hands and then he took down the names. So it followed with Tax Office, Water Board, PMG and so on.

I had not thought about where I might wish to go, but with my intermediate only Maths pass, I figured it could not be the Tax Office. Instead I opted to stay with the PMG when I raised my hand and my name was then recorded. Once the names were all recorded we were given a short toilet break returning then to out seats. The duly appointments clerical spokesman raise this head from lectern and began to call out our names . When it come to me he said "Douglas McPhillips, PMG, 2 Primary Works Department, Homebush."I was boarding   with a Yugoslavian family in Croydon at the times travelling too and from Homebush my new Class 1 clerical duties above the Homebush post office was a piece of cake as was the job. The Master of the house were I was a lodger was Boris of Serbian birthright and his good wife had been off Royal Macedonian bloodline.

They were kind people and their four bedroom house with three boarders joined together for evening meals proved to be one big happy family. We often discussed how the dutiful wife and cook's family wealth and power went to her male siblings on the death of her father leaving her and her financially poor husband to migrated to

Australia. Without the stories around the family dinner table, I would never have known of the Yugoslavia communist state under Prime Minister Tito; the six republics of Serbia, Croatia, Bosnia and Herzegovina, Macedonia and Montenegro, as well as two provinces of Kosovo and Vojvod combining under the one Federal People's Republic to become known as Yugoslavia. Considering that family fed us and charged minimum boarding cost we three intrepid lodgers whereon a good wicket and learnt a great deal of their history. We learnt of the Austro-Hungarian post World War 1 hostilities between these Kingdoms which was quelled when Tito came to power. He was the embodiment of what a good Dictator should be, keeping a tight reign on ethnic tensions between the different races of peoples. This was in the late 1960s, so the pending racial wars of independence for the various republic seats that followed Tito's death decades later was not news.

Boris, who although not educated like his 'royal' wife, warned of tensions and a bloody future for Yugoslavia. Interestingly, most of what he predicted came to pass as much blood was shed in the fight for independence of the various wars between races. It took until 2006 for independence to reign for all of the former Yugoslavia regions to be declared independent of one another, for NATO troops to return home and for the UN, EU and USA to recognise the peace that followed a bloodY mess.

My daily duties as a clerk in my first official indoctrination to the 3rd Division of the Public Service, was the responsibility of all mechanical aids used by the PMG lineman working on the laying of 'Niggerville.' It was a contemptuous term for the possible ethnicity of the pending population to reside there. The suburbs official name being Blacktown. My duties apart from recording the logistical locations of tractors, trailers, plant and equipment right down to portable toilets, included the pay run once a fortnight. The duties of keeping the official registered number of all inventory checked and verified every fortnight ensured nothing went astray and could be easily located and moved to another destination at a moments notice.

The linemen were of white descent comprising many immigrants as well as white native born Australians. I can't recall evert seeing a native Aboriginal out in the field in the PMG back then. Coming from a country town and growing up with Aboriginal boys as primary school class mates and football buddies I could not recall ever questioning the colour of their skin, even in those days of the White Australia Policy. As far back as the 1800s the majority of white Australians shared attitudes towards people of different races that by todays standards were openly racist. Criticisms of non-white groups were based on the idea that they were less advanced morally and intellectually as white man. Australia had focused particularly on people of Asian descent but this applied equally to all non whites, including our own indigenous population who were considered a 'dying race.' All that change somewhat with immigrants from England and Europe after WW11. Lost souls looking for a new home and way of life. However, even they suffered the slings and arrows of locally born Australian attitudes, being calling 'Dago' or 'Spik' as a matter of course. My duties on the fortnightly payday was to meet the Mayne Nickless 'Money mover' van with three other PMG employees to collect the loot and arrange it for distribution to the linesman at their particular work locations. The monies were signed over to 'Shorty' the Paymaster; an old grey-haired Senior Clerk who proceeded to haul the load up a two level stair case with the help of us fellow assignees. It was always a daylight early start and once we had loot spread across a large table on the top floor of the Homebush Post Office, we counted it all from large notes too lesser denominations, sorting the coin in a similar fashion. Once we had ascertained that all moneys were there and checked with the payslips, we were each assisted a task in preparing the pay-packets for for linesman.

Linesman requested various ways in which they were to receive their wages. Some requested two envelopes, one with the pay slip and cash included in one and another with the overtime and cash for same included in another envelope. Others still would request a certain sum to be put in a third envelope to payoff their bookie or a mistress. Those that chose to spend their overtime on themselves with gambling or drinking sessions or asked for a 'secret fund' envelope could go home with the real wage to their respective wives and hand over what appeared to be their total wage. It was not in our brief to make a judgement but simply to do as ask.This way we kept the linesman happy and the Unions at bay.

A typical pay day would see us on route in a PMG sedan, with a large battered briefcase of all the pays packets in alphabetical order on the back seat. My job was to ride shotgun next to the Paymaster

with a six shooter in my jacket pocket. In the passenger front seat, our front line security guard carried a shotgun on the floor in front of him. The driver was unarmed but at full alert being at the wheel. The drill was to drive up beside group of linesman on the job, wind down my passenger window and began to dish out the pay packets. The linesman would identify who he was, I would callout his name and "Shorty, the Paymaster' would hand over the required number of envelopes to me to give to the wage earner . The then next in line would appear at the window and the procedure would be repeated.

By about 10.am. we would have dispensed with at least half the case of cash pay envelopes. It would be then considered to be our morning tea break. We simply drive to the nearest pub or Club, parked the car and locked it with the suit case left on the back seat. We never worried about the money as it wasn't ours and we figured it was insured anyway. We were soon seated at the bar knocking back a few bars with our six shooters hidden and the shot gun down the trouser leg of our front seater security man. Whilst he should have been on workers compensation, he preferred light duties and riding shotgun for us as opposed to being off work. In truth he did not want the embarrassment of filing a P500 form, although it was the official preliminary form necessary to apply for Workers Comp; in the PMG at the time. It was my duty to get this form completed to assess his case but he just would not fill it out. When considering the circumstance of his accident, I could hardly blame him. The accident that ensued which should have resulted in time out for him was both personally painful, equally embarrassing and if one has a warped sense of humour somewhat funny. Our Lineman whose name shall remain secret to protect his right of anonymity; so as not to cause him any anxiety, was carrying out his daily duties on a given day. Together with another employee, they lifted a manhole lid with the intent of climbing down into the pit to work on a faulty telephone cable. It had been raining at the time and the heavy manhole cover slipped through his hands he lifted it. This was a bad omen as one corner of the steel lid cut through his pants slicing his old fellow from top to tip. Our unfortunate hero fell to his knees screaming as blood sprayed every witch-way. The fellow worker put down the other end of the steel pit cover he had been holding and ran to a nearby work van extracting a bottle of disinfectant and some bandage from the medical kit. He returned to the scene of personal agony and proceeded to pour the disinfectant on the treasured body part of our suffering soul. The tortured victim screamed in agony in disbelief at his misfortune. The caring attention of his fellow working was observed by passers bye as he wrapped the not so small but now dysfunctional weapon with a copious quantity of bandage, winding it around again and again, so that our victim would appear to have a very large precious gift to be later unwrapped by an enquiring nurse. So the P500 waa never completed and that is why he was riding shotgun on our pay run. To all intent and purpose it looked like he had a stiff leg as he hobbled to the bar I was never quite sure if it was the recovering personal missile that caused his stiffness or the shotgun down his trouser leg. In my case and 'Shorty the Paymaster,' we must have appeared like two gun toting comical underworld characters from a kids comic book. Our only other gun toting duty was ever second Thursday we had to adjourn to the rooftop of the GPO in Martin Place for pistol practice. Our duty was to fire six rounds of ammunition with our hand guns at a target.

The accuracy of our shooting was never question or checked. It was a simple matter of firing the gun as rapidly as possible to get off the six shots, handing the gun back to the duty officer in for safe keeping until next pay day and taking off to a nearby bar for a few beers before returning back to work. It must be said that like my school day Marist Brother teachers, I have created nom de plumes for each of the following characters in my happenings of my future career to protect the innocent and not break any of my fellow associates anonymity. Whilst the following fact herein played down are true , some licence is given for my recall accuracy for now that I am old there is always the possibility that my recall is more coloured by my imagination that the workings of my current day linear conscious mind. So, now read on and weep for those of us who with the darkness of former deceit hid the light that every man carries in the depth of his heart.

An opportunity came up a year later through the Government Gazette, for a Class 2/3 Clerical promotion with 2 Primary Works stationed at the Carlton Centre in Elizabeth Street city. My duties there and the aftermath of those times still effects telecommunications and city transport to this day. Ron 'the Willing' was my Divisional Clerk and I was his dubious 2IC. Ron usually swanned his way into the office around 9.30 a.m. already 30 minutes late for work. This was his daily habit and mine was not much better. You could always hear him as he entered the nearby corridor singing he as he entered his very own tune: "The working class can kiss my ass, I've got a bosses job at last." Ron, not knowing what was on the agenda for the day always enquired " And what have we as priority for today sunshine?" Our first offical duty together was to proof read a forced retirement package sent from Staff and Industrial for our sigh off on a very generous payout for not so old employee on the grounds of ill health. The intended recipient had been a long term employee of the PMG, a Divisional Clerk in the Engineering Section and a dyed in the wool alcoholic. Joe, whose surname shall remain nameless has long ago passed.

At the time of Joe's pending payout he was in the depth of alcoholism and was in noway capable of doing his job. Well at least that what I was given to understand. Not that it matters much in the case of most Divisional Clerks in the Engineering section of the then PMG and for that matter this newly appointed second in charge or as abbreviated 2IC. I had read his personnel file given to me on the quiet by a spy from Staff and Industrial to help me with my decision making. Joe's daily journey to the city on his way to work was on the Manly ferry and fortunately or unfortunately for him, it meant passing the 'Ship Inn' public bar. Joe never made it pass that bar without first sinking copious amounts of amber fluid to tardy him up for the given tasks ahead. Whilst his work a day world was limited it coincidentally proved to be the same for for me in the long run with my then PMG career. However, at the initial appointment time I was a conscious worker and not a conscientious objector as was later to be the case with the progressive killing machine of the Vietnam War still in play.

I had perused Joe's file and in my then industrious mind found it difficult, having given due diligence to the payout for a still suffering alcoholic, decided that would not counter sign Ron's signature on the document for the approval of the payout.

It was not long after that the document reappeared at my desk and black biro was handed to me. I looked up and there hanging over my shoulder was my Divisional Clerk, the Chief Engineer of 2 Primary Works and a Key Personnel Officer from Staff and industrial. Ron began to speak: "Doug, you have to counter sign this document. Joe was a Changi prisoner of war who escaped the Japanese after much suffering. He spent fourteen days on a barge in Pacific Ocean in his escape, without food or water and was lucky to make it too allied territory and survive. Without the likes of Joe, neither you nor I would have a job; we too would be slaves to the Japanese, so sign the bloody document." I thought off my Toyota car, the radio I owned and the many Japanese products in my possession including the biro in my hand, thinking of the fact that I was a slave to the Japanese anyway and wondered who really had won WW11. I signed away my life on that document and my small reality of noble morals. The task completed all the witnesses to my signature on that retirement package document returned to their dubious tasks and Ron invited me to join him at the New South Wales Leagues Club across the road for a few beers to celebrate Joe's new found fortune.

Well, as it was 10.30 am. and morning tea break I felt well justified to slip away from my apparent duties. It did't take me long to bury the red tape deed I had just completed. Maybe it was the third or was it the fifty beer the I realise I had sold my soul to the devil and Ron had me hooked into more fowl deeds. So as it turned out my future dubious document counter signing approvals were necessary to keep the Government fund allocations rolling, the PMG Engineering work flowing for further job creations, future budget allocations and the topping up of employees wages too. The usual morning greeting from Ron as he entered the premises continued; "What on the agenda today sunshine?" I quickly spelt out the details of the plans and documents for a new Coaxial cable up George street and further Coaxial cable across the Harbour for the much needed telephone line for increasing a commercial developing North Sydney.

The typical daily activity was for Ron to adjourn to the bar at the NSW Leagues Club for a few beers on his own with instructions for me to join him after about an hour, having answered a constant ringing of phones. I eventually escaped handing over my duties to the new clerical assistant to keep the ball rolling. What I didn't know, it was as simple as to write out a list of unanswered enquiries for Ron to complete on his return to the office later in the afternoon.

Most of the time he was on the blower, head down and bum up for the remainder of the day, completing outstanding orders for the Engineers. whilst i didi the most of paperwork. Our usual I morning time together meant that I had to leave my desks and head to the leagues club to join Ron. Turning up with files of pending Engineering jobs to be perused over copious amounts of alcoholic beverage, we would ascertain how much overtime moneys each tasks should be allocated for the Engineering Department, Staff and Industrial, right down to the Technicians and linesmen carrying out their relevant duties, and

of course their Clerks and Clerical Assistants. So it was that the first of these files of urgency awaited by the Engineers assigned fo the task for completion being diligently read and proofed for approval on this fine morning for drinking, by my Divisional Clerk and his industrious assistant and fellow drinking mate, 2IC me.

It took us two weeks of cross checking our figures over copious quantities of alcoholic beverage in the Leagues Club to justify the overtime and give our seal of approval. The Head Engineer, Norbert the Quirky one, was anxiously at my desk day in and day out waiting for our approval stamp and document signatures. Although Engineers were University qualified but were answerable to the Administrative staff for all matters, much like the Prime Minister is mostly answerable to the Prime Ministers Department. We approved 28 hours of overtime for the administration duties of all and sundry for the telephone Coaxial cable to be laid from Circular Quay along George street to Broadway. The administration could easily have been done in normal working hours but that would have interfered with good drinking time. So the overtime was approved so that very little was done during the daylight hours. I never felt right about that first Coax cable approval and use to go back to the office at night and attempt to do the overtime work. I was the only one in the building after-hours, no one did any overtime and the admin was drawn out and anatomised over the life of the job. I soon realised that my efforts were futile and somewhat dangerous being in a Commonwealth building without approval after lock up time. So like every other employee I said naught and accepted the 28 hours overtime without complaint or completion.

To be fair however, we did have extra duties that caused us sometimes to stay back after-hours without extra pay to sort things out. This more often than not was when, either the Water Board or the Electricity Commission would call our Office enquiring if we had laid any cable down George Street or some other city local lately. This was the time when no Government Department liaised with another.

They simply went ahead with their plans to lay water pipes, electricity and coaxial phone cables without consulting each other and with limited Union influence. The relevant departments never worry too much about sticking to a plan, they just completed their work in an appointed time to justify their extra pay and got on with the next job.

CHAPTER 12.

WILD ONES

It is interesting to note that when the recent tram rail was in progress for completion up George Street there were many delays by the contracted Spanish company's completion of the project. The State Government had no plans to verify a gas pipe being broken nor telephone cable or electricity wire cut in the pathway of rail line being laid. I shrugged my shoulders when mishaps happened but would protest my I innocence of all charges. My job was to approve plans, it was the Engineers duty to see the plans were followed to the letter and plans filed fro future reference by other Government and other authorities before any future project be approved be either the PMG, Water Authority or Electricity Commission. As those plans could not be found anywhere with the aforesaid authorities, then my signature of countersigning approvals was safe somewhere in the archives, perhaps in the bowls of the GPO basement. State Government could plead their innocence having not been informed of what lay beneath the surface of the proposed tramway. It is no small wonder that the project took so long to complete and cost blow out continued to occur every time a hole hit what was considered a foreign object.

We do not have the history for ancient European artefacts to be considered when digging into the grounds for European essential services and infrastructure, but we certainly create our own delays without plan or favour in the underground tangled web of tunnels under the centre of our city and under the harbour for that matter. The laying of Coaxial cable for both phone and radio frequency was a large undertaking and continuous work across the waters from a barge on the western side of the Harbour Bridge to the bottom of the harbour and across to North joining up within pits by linesman on both sides to existing services. There was not much and administration paperwork for us. It was a simple exercise of a supervising Engineer on the barge guiding the bargeman on the roll out of the cable from a huge timber reel. The thick round shape of the twisted pair was not Ethernet cable but more likely copper with thousands of strands encased in rubber side by side, making it some 10-15 cm in diameter.

As well as rubber and plastic encasement it was also encased in lead, so the cable itself weighted a Tonne and had to be winched in to place at each end for connection. Whilst it was used mainly for link to satellite antenna facilities it was also the main electric cable for business connections well before wifi cam into being.   The yellow cable played along side this Coaxial cable also encased in lead and laid under the harbour for telephone connections. If there was a major black out on any of the cable networks the Powers- that- be didn't fix it, they simply laid another cable. So the then the link from North to Eastern Suburbs Harbour tunnel was built the divers found a spaghetti like network of coaxial lead encased pipeline crisscrossing each other. There was no way they could fathom (play on the word) the live cable from the dysfunctional. Once the concrete roadway and the tunnel was completed, the telecommunications Networks were checked. So if anything didn't work, they reverted back to the old method of sinking another cable and reconnecting it.

Another problem arose cony tenuously for a long time on the Northside. Often when a new copper filled pipeline was connected throughout the North Sydney area, a major blackout would occur. This was not poor workmanship but rather persons unknown simply climbing down one street length of pipe and undoing the connection and doing likewise a street away. The disconnected cable was rollout back up on a reel, loaded on truck and driven away. Fortunes were made during those times of cutting away the cable cover to gain of a large quantity of copper and lead covering. The problem was solved with the introduction of surveillance cameras.

Once in cyclonic storm the whole of the Mid and Far North Coast of New South Wales was out of commission. Radio was the only thing that was reporting the devastation. I was genuinely worried about my parents in that little town of Macksville. For a full morning I tried repeatedly to contact my parents by phone but it was no use. I attempted to contact the various telephone exchanges along the coast in the hope of contact. Lindsay, our 2IC Engineer 'suggested I come with him in the lunch hour and he would do his best to assist me.

I found myself climbing a staircase to a single room in Sussex street City. Seated at two screens, of what looked liked computers before they were publicly known, sat a couple of technicals. Lindsay pointed me in the direction of a door and advised me to pick up the red phone in the room when it rang. There was nothing else in the room except a small desk a chair and the red phone.

Duly instructed, I waited for the phone to ring and heard one of the techs in the next room talking to Perth telephone exchange. The singing on the wire was a faint sound in the background as the connection went via Adelaide to Melbourne and Brisbane Exchanges and the signal snaked its way through various small exchange connections to my Dad's home phone line. The phone rang at the other end and Dad answered. He could hardly believe his ears. "How the blue blazes did you get through?" he enquired. I said something like "luck I guess." I was relieved to hear his voice confirming that the cyclone was easing but apart from my call there had been no communication anywhere. I quickly wished him and Mum the best, mindful of the cost and privilege I had been granted. As we left that upstairs room in Sussex street, Engineer Lindsay advised me that the call just did not happen and the red phone did not exist. I was never to reveal the hidden red phone which was, I was later given to understand, a direct link to the PM. This was over five decades ago, so I feel in this modern day of Wifi and satellite communication, social media and the like, that the secret I was then sworn to matters little any more.

In the days when not drinking at the NSW Leagues Club with Ron, I often made it down the lift to the basement of the Carlton centre bar at basement level. My assistant junior clerks Barrys was always in support, the Carlton centre Mariner Bar had a disco like atmosphere and a modern bar with pretty young barmaid with low cut blouses showing a plentiful supply of bosom. It attracted the best of young men and women after work and the odd alcoholic ones like me during the day. Not only did we relax over a drink or two but we also got our quick fix of sexual delight. Returning to the office after no more than a twenty minute break at the bar, a file in hand giving the impressing that we were calling on anther department in the building for work purposes was never questioned. I don't know why we bothered with the file really as no-one really cared what we did or didn't do in-between contract signings. Before Barry came on the scene, Kevin the teacher filled the job as my junior clerk. He was a teacher from Queensland in Sydney for regular dialysis treatment for his recent

kidney transplant. On leave from teaching in Queensland, he was given the job at the PMG as it was close to the hospital for his treatment. Kevin would go down in history as the first successful kidney transplant in Australia. Outside of work we struck up good friendship and regularly met for creative pursuits like making film on super 8mm and he composing music or using a cover song to align with my script and film. At one time we had another Ron on relief as our Divisional Clerk whilst Ron "The Willing' was on annual leave. Whilst in attendance he was assigned a duty for administration. It was a glitch in a plan costing and he strolled over to my desk requesting my attention to the matter. I explained that as i was busy writing lyrics for a song, to pass it on to Kevin. He likewise rejected the request explaining he too was busy composing a musical score. Ron, puffing on his pipe, calmly smoking on his pipe remarked: "Worse things happen at sea. In our own time, Kevin and I attended to the matter and all was back to normal again for drinking and leisure pursuit times at work.

Apart form the Carlton Centre Marina's basement bar and the NSW Leagues Club over the road in Elizabeth, we had another regular lunch time drinking hole. It was in nearby Angel Place and was commonly known as the Marble bar. There was another one whose real branding did have a Marble bar, but it was not a patch on ours. The bar was a long L shaped with a thick dark marble top. Entering from the street, it was a quick right turn into room full of lunch time drinkers. Occasionally I got sick of the crowds and retreated with a mate from Staff and Industrial to a bar in George Street. IT had found memories for me, as upstairs on level one was where I first got laid. I digress. It was on one occasion at that bar that my Staff and Industrial Department friend advised me that I was being spied upon for my excessive drinking.

I did not believe my friend, so he offered to show me my file one evening when no one was about. After work when the Carlton Centre was empty we made our way to the third floor of the Staff and Industrial Department for our illegal entry investigation. My drinking companion had a key to the office premises, so it was no bother to enter as in those days it was before surveillance cameras were introduced for security purposes. My good friend of that department pointed to a filing cabinet and instructed me to find my staff detail folder.

I read with great interest every detail of my working and private life since joining the P.M.G. Most of it was a glowingly positive report that was all in my favour. However, in the midst of line of text a hiccup was glaring back at me in red ink "Drinks." There was no other detail but I was now a marked man. A notation of my drinking exploits in my Commonwealth bank days was there, but no mention of my drinking week with Alex the Russian Engineer nor Dangerous Dan the pilot and the aircraft experiment. Morrie, the former Divisional Clerk for Head Engineer for John Day had certainly done a good job in hiding that one away.

Another of the characters of my time with Primary works was Wing Fat, a Singaporean Chinese engineer. Wing Fat was contracted for three years to the PMG telephone division and in that short time he totally revolutionised the network. He was a genius but the three year visa soon run out and our Engineering Department with the help of is on administration arranged a Commonwealth grant for a Masters Degree Course at NSW University. The powers that be needed him to attended the course for but it meant another three year working Visa for Wing Fat. Between Wing Fat's exploits at winning over many a top Sydney model to join him in bed to complete his congenial sexual desires, he completed a lot of work for the PMG. I doubt if he ever attended the University other than to put in an appearance for attendance from time to time.

Wing Fat kept a little black book which was filled with the phone numbers and addresses of a host of very beautiful looking women. He was short and slim, not attractive, but a charm that could win over anyone. It was Buddha like spirit that he had us all in his tangled web of deception and fun. On one one occasion he asked me to join him one night on a mission. It was around midnight as we crawled on our stomach's passed the custom security office guard station on a Harbour peer. Wing Fat had arrange to meet an illegal ship entering the harbour under cover of darkness. At the appointed hour the small ship docked at the end of the pier and we climbed on board. It was my understanding that we were there to pick up some bottles of illegal spirits. I drank myself into oblivion whilst Wing Fat disappeared for a time to supposed talk to the captain.

After some hours with warm spirited bellies we crawled once more past the customs security as the ship we had been in sailed away out of the Harbour once more. I didn't know it then but Wing Fat had arranged for the importation of a quantity of Opium. It all came to light when I was invited to a party at his Vaucluse apartment. Upon arrival a Chinese doorman stood at the door with quantities of free Opium to smoke. Inside Wing Fat's den of iniquity Porn films flicked on the walls whilst half naked dances moved with rhythmical drum beat and ear piercing sounds took over my head. I refused the Opium, the drink and the atmosphere. It was nice of Wing Fat to consider me in his party invitation, but it was just not my scene. I just did like crowded drug scenes. Somehow I always suspected Wing Fat had an alternate intention in befriending me. He had tried more than once to rope me into his tangled web of illegal activities but the teachings of the Marist had some how at least keep such temptations at bay. Back then I owned a little white Triumph herald with a leather black hardtop. I use to park it all day at Police Headquarters with the cops cars which back then were all their cars were white. so it was not as if I was an innocent but I drew the line in the sand of my moral code and conscious that i could live with. I parked my car in police HQ for over a year before being approach one day by a diligent Police Inspector with a "Hey Son, you can't park here, this for Police cars only." I feigned ignorance explaining that I had been parking there for an eternity   without any police complaint. I was duly reprimanded and told never to park there again. It was not long after that the parking lot was granted a security guard. It was a sense of pride myself that I had been instrumental in creating a job for a deserving soul. Now parking became more difficult for me on work days, so I approach the chief engineer who approval my park in the PMG vehicle storage lot depot at Woolloomooloo. When Wing Fat got the word that I had scored free parking in the PMG depot, he asked me to arrange to store his car there too. He said he did not want to rock the boat with the Department Head to grant him permission. I, smelt a rat and soon found the reason for his sly move in getting me to help transport the car to the PMG depot with him. Firstly, the vehicle had never been registered or insured whilst in his possession for the past three years.

It was a worn out piece of junk that was hardly drivable but Wing Fat continued to drive it from Vaucluse to Woolloomooloo during the week. He always parked it in a different locations every day but irrespective of his selected hideaways he still managed to cop a parking fine every day. Wing Fat had never ever paid any of his parking fines whist in Australia. The old car was well known to Chinese students over the years as it was always handed over to the next male student on his   arrival in Australia. It was simply a matter of telling the student where to find the car and were the keys were hidden and It was considered a 'not my responsibility' gift from the last university graduate returning to their native homeland or who may have overstayed their visa and had to leave post haste. When Wing Fat and I arrived to pick up the mobile reck in his latest hideaway, there were stacks of unpaid parking tickets under the windscreen wipers including one for that day and a recent defect notice to say it was being towed away within the next 24 hours. Win Fat cleared all the fines and dumped them in a nearby garbage bin then removed the tow away notice sticker from the windscreen.

He did not have a licence but insisted I do the talking at the PMG depot to get the car locked away and hidden from view. Once our mutual assignment was completed we walked back to the Domain car park which was only a stones throw away from the PMG depot. The Domain car park with a a mobile walkway that ran from the bottom of Woolloomooloo to nearby Hyde park street exit was a shortcut to Elizabeth Street and quick on foot commute to our office in the Carlton Centre. I realise back then that it was a better location for me than the previous location with the police cars at their headquarters. Likewise it was a safe logistic arrangement for Wing Fat to take shelter 'the car." It was but a short drive to and from his Vaucluse pad. Wing Fat as an unlicensed driver behind the wheel of an unroadworthy reck of a car with a stack of parking fines to his credit, riding on a wing and a prayer. Like every thing else in his life, Wing Fat was our chance taking telecommunications genius, gamble, possible drug pusher, ladies man and a now endorsed reckless driver without any peripheral vision to speak of. Another of my duties was looking after all the telephone administration for the Eastern Suburbs telephone exchanges and line staff working working in the pit points between home and the nearest exchange connections.

The Eastern Suburbs had a number of different types of telephone networks in operation for best performance trials. We had the latest in PABX, German technology and the old 'click and clack' systems, which the technicians in the exchanges did not agree upon.The new systems had fewer breakdowns and were much easier to resurrect and restore presto but it was never a major issue but i guess they had to have something to complain about. In my travels I got to know all the telephone Exchange codes for ease of access to the buildings, I memorised them in my head so this knowledge become very useful in my next career move. 'Tiny' the clerical assistant to the Line Inspector was stationed at Coogee Beach line depot and was quite a character. He took sick leave at one stage and was off for a coupe of weeks. I telephone him on his return to obtain a medical certificate for his GP to ensure his time off was   taken from his accumulated sick leave accumulation and not his holiday allocation.

I enquired as to the cause of his illness and he replied : "piles for peers; haemorrhoids for aristocratic assholes." He had a lot of funny saying and often left me in stitches with his antics. Part of my duties included visiting all the line depots with the line inspector whose job it as too insured the men were doing their assigned duties. This way I got to see first hand why we paid the men the extra allowance they received. Their benefits included workers compensation, accumulative sick leave for each year of service, holiday pay with a 17.5% leave loading negotiated by the unions. Apparently they had concluded an employee would spend more money on holidays than normally. There was also a training levy for new starters and superannuation long before Paul Keating as treasure made it compulsory. Again this was to benefit me in my next career move. Like the technicians in the exchange, I leant the why's and wear-fore of in the field work. To be fair I had a good handle on it from my early career on pay duty for the linesman on the Blacktown route.

My next career move came unexpectedly as good opportunities often do. A work mate from my days in the Commonwealth Bank days was now an AMP representative and he turned up in my office one day to sell me an AMP Whole of life insurance policy. Stan the man had been a work colleague, drinking mate and go to the races together buddy. In hindsight my association with him although short-lived did not do me a great deal of good,.

My first boss Mr. Petersen (every male in the bank in those days was addresses as Mister.) Well Paul Petersen was my first mentor and he affectionately game me a nick name "McGuarder." I guess he considered me his key support staff member. Mc or Mac in Irish means "Son of support' so the handle made some sense I guess. Anyhow Stan the man was the 2IC of the first branch I worked in for the CTB Bank and was an engaging personality and consciousness bank officer, youth worker and fun to be around mate after hours.

It was not until we both went our seperate ways in career moves and did not catch up for year later that things had changed, He was like me a raging alcoholic, gambler and good time Charlie. I was already on the path to nowhere when I caught up with him and we were just not good company for each other. Just an example or two to verify this comment. One evening we hit the booze pretty heavy. It was pre seat belt days and I lost control of my prized 62 EK Holden at high speed rounding a corner on River Road Lane Cove. The car suddenly went into a sideways slide and I was catapulted into the lap of Stan in the passenger seat next to me. He in a half drunken stupor caught by surprise remarked: "What are you doing over here McGuarder, you should be driving." The car still travelling down the road sideways suddenly righted itself and I was back behind the wheel, shaken but not stirred so to speak.

I found immediate sobriety and we travelled on out mere way once more. On another occasion, Stan the man had heard a certain poker machine in a bar in Kings Cross was dropping jackpots due to a malfunction in its workings. It was around midnight that we stumbled to the bar, we had sixty dollars between us, so we cashed it in for twenty cent pieces and proceeded to play the machine. We lost the lot within the hour and having no money left hitch a ride to my flat on the Northside to crash for a few hours. On other occasions we would drink ourselves sober by dawn at an early opener then head to the golf course for a round before work at nine. Other blunders included frequenting speak easy like underworld bars and meeting the lowest of the low for drinks and a late night feed. It was a time of wine, women and song which usually ended on a bad note.

Stan had already made his bad boy connections and was heading for even greater downward spiral activities. By the time I caught up with him again, I was in a full time relationship, living a 9 to 5 lifestyle, staying out of the lime light and other than my exploits on the grog I had found some semblance of stability. As fate would have it Stan caught up with me after a half a decade and arranged an appointment to discuss the benefits of investing in my future. Stan the man, the then insurance salesman suggested I would be good at selling insurances too and offered to introduce me to his Manager. Stan's later exploits surrounding his elicit activities prompts me to herein hide the surname out of respect for his family. So, out of pure curiosity I agreed to meet his AMP Manager and went to North Sydney to be interviewed by the amiable John Duncan. John had been an ex Army man and heavy weight champion of Boxing for the military. I liked him from the very first meeting, so before I had time enough to think, I had signed up to represent AMP as an agent. It was the benefits that astounded me; whilst it was a commission based job and there was no guarantee of future employment, John offered me a guarantee of six months income almost equal to my then salary plus generous commission based upon each sale, a low rate of interest finance on a new car, a free medical benefits package and after a qualifying period a low interest rate housing loan.

The AMP had industry respected two weeks initiation training school to learn the basic selling skills required to do the job, a marketing strategy of obtaining leads of prospective clientele and a telephone technique to get appointments. So I suddenly found excitement in what appeared to be a no loose situation.

It was only a matter of weeks before I found myself completing the basic training, being supplied with my own office, telephone, brief case and all the product details and application forms necessary to make sales. John Duncan in his wisdom suggested that I return to my old haunts in the public service and focus on familiar territory to make my mark as a representative of the then well respected AMP Society. My motivation to succeed was at an all time high as I prepared a visual to aid me in my presentations to PMG workers and my fellow comrades in the office I had worked for the previous half decade. My motivation was epitomised by putting into action in a small way the ideas I learnt from beefing up on the life of Ben Feldman. I viewed a film of typical day in the life of a man still considered to be the most successful salesman in the life insurance business that ever lived. Feldman was a pudgy well dressed man in a gabardine overcoat of winters day in New York City. He was extremely shy, spoke in a slow drawl and had a lisp. Ben worked as an agent for New York life operating for his office building in his home town Liverpool, an hours journey from the heart fo New York. Ben had grown up in the slums as a poor kid scratch out a living as a $10 a week butter and eggs salesman to become one of the most prolific salesman in history. As early as 1979 he had sold more life insurance than anyone in history. He sold like insurance policy with total face value of $1.5 billion for New York Life from 1942 to his death in 1993.

Ben Feldman sold an average of three million dollars worth of Life insurance every day for the rest of his life and never had a day without a sale. There was an exception to the rule when he took three days off at Christmas to spend the time in a far away mountain retreat fishing on a lake with an old hermit friend who live there. Ben was well planned, employed a fleet of staff and had no qualms in working fourteen hours a day, seven days a week. Money flowed for Ben but his motivation was people and his loving wife had attested to that. When a cheque appeared in the mail box at home one day for $15,000 his wife asks him what she should do with it . He replied" Do what you like with it, just don't give to me because I will only spend it." The lessons he taught by example, I later applied in my own business success that didn't come from an insurance career incidentally. Ben's line "work hard. think gig, listen well" rings true more than ever now as I write these lines in my getting of wisdom. "No one ever dies with too much money" he would say. "moneys funny." he would say. "I don't sell money, I sell time, time is money."

In my naked rawness but enthusiasm I took some gems from Ben's methodology of selling and created my own visual aid. Producing a lifetime graph of values for two policies I preferred to sell, I set about my life insurance selling career for the next three years. I highlight the values in 10 year intervals from age 21 to 65, intent on showing the values of a policy of saving for a home, kids education, repayment of mortgage, an emergency fund for the once expected and a generous amount of retirement allowing for inflation. To top it all off I had in the front of a visual overlapping each other a series of $100 dollar notes. The notes ones at the fronton the visual were real whilst those appearing in the background were just photocopies. My opening line upon opening my visual was '"This is what I've come to talk to you about. Money. It comes in bundles of a hundred, how many do you want?" I would then proceed to sell the sizzle not the steak. My track always led to the Relax first, then disturb second and finally relive with the solution. If I got any objections, I always turned back to the money page and asked: "What is it you don't understand?"My life was made easy with calls to my old haunts in the eastern suburbs. I first started with the technicians in the exchanges. As I knew all the door codes to get into the exchanges and the technicians on a person basis who worked them, then selling insurance was a breeze. Likewise I had an ace in the hole with the linesman too. Norm, the line iInspector for the the eastern suburbs use to drive me around and introduce me to any linesman I had not yet met. He also advising me of which linesman had just got married, had a baby or lost a family member recently. I had no problem getting an average of three sales per week but unlike Ben Feldman, I did't look far ahead to the future. Sure I had my own life insurance policies, so in that regard I did practice what I preached. In truth I had not set any clear goals and did not see the need despite preaching financial goal concepts to others.

Stan the Man and his brother Mick were both in Insurance with AMP during my first year in the business, but their lives in that regard were short lived. Mick as an elder brother had a gambling problem with the horses too. In those times you could borrow a lot of money from finance companies without security to back it. However, the interest rate was prohibitive and neither of them could keep up the required payments to meet their commitments. We were all still on the minimum wage guarantee from AMP and managed to pay our rent and have enough left over for the booze. Stan always spent more than he earned due to his gambling obsession and the finance company was now gunning for both brothers to meet the ever increase loan value over-dues. The problem waa accelerated as they borrowed even more un-secured loans against one company to meet payments with another. Stan had convinced his ageing widowed mother to put the family home up for security on a further loan agreement, trusting that the and Mick would make an appropriate amount of sales to cover the deal. The method in the brotherhood madness was short lived and it soon looked like the ruthless finance company would foreclose take their mum's home. In the panic that followed there seemed to be no way out but to steal. Stan had canvassed a branch of the CTB the week before. It was on of those out of the way small branches and it entered Stans' troubled mind to devise a plan to rob it.

After showing the game plan to his despairing brother Mick, he convinced him that this was the solution to save their mother's home. Not having an alternative Mick agreed. Stan not having a car of his own caught a train to Wynyard Station, made his way up to Martin Place and stole a car for the purpose of use during the robbery. Mick was waiting for his return at a duly appointed designated location on the north-side of the harbour. They headed up the back streets and through the Lane Cover Park to a nearby little shopping centre. It had a one of a kind CTB bank Branch that could have easily passed for a sub-agency. San had cased it and realised it handled a host of local customers who saved more than they spent, so he knew from his banking days it would carry a lot of cash.

It was five minutes to closing time when the two highway robbers entered the banks premises. The teller was busy tallying up the final count for the day to balance the books. Likewise the junior staff member had one of those coin counting contraptions and was in the background making a lot of noise shaking the thing . The manager was in his office with his door opened clearly visible behind his desk

talking to a customer seated opposite. Mick the elder of the two brothers, headed straight for the managers Office with Stan in hot pursuit, calling out as he jumped the counter: "Drop to the floor, this is a hold up." Both brothers had masked faces. Well not quite masks, in point of fact handkerchiefs in bandanna folded above the nose and tied behind the neck in a knot. Stan had a tyre lever wrapped in a cloth giving the appearance of a gun. Mick on the other hand was waving a machete he had punched the day before at a disposal store.

The manager and chatting customer quickly obeyed the command and hit the deck, as did the teller and junior staff member. Mick watched Stan from the Managers Office door as he unloaded the cash from the tellers box. It was a minute to the closing hour when a little old lady marched in and straight to the tellers counter with her passport. She handed it across the counter with a pile of cash and requested to make a deposit.

Stan meanwhile had dropped his mask down but still left the sunglasses on. In point of fact, he had taken them from my car the day before and I had wondered where I had lost them just were I had left them. Stan took the money from the little old lady who seemed half blind anyway. He entered the transaction deposit in her savings account passbook, stamped it with a seal of approval, then as a would be teller wish her a pleasant afternoon and watched her depart.

It was standard practice for a teller to have a gun under the counter with one bullet in the chamber. We were taught back then to shoot first and ask questions later. Regular pistol practice with the Police being the order of the day, Stan thought it wise to run with the gun and the loot in hand. The bank changed its the policy some time later when robberies became more frequent and the bank managed secure adequate insurance to cover the cash anyway. Guns became a thing of the past, as did the need for so much cash with the use of bank cheques, telegraphic transfers and finally computer transactions. The use of credit cards and security guards outside bank premises gave more assurance and the need for a a gun-toting teller faded.

The risk of hold ups lessened as white collar on line crime and internal embezzlement increased. Mick turned to look for Stan and realising he had already left the premises, gave a last minute instruction to the Manager and staff to keep their heads down and stay put. he car had been parked some 500 meters from the little village centre and Mick covered the distance in world record time. He caught up to stand as he turned the vehicle around facing the back entry to Lane Cove national Park. They had pulled off a daring delight robbery with nothing but a tyre lever, knife, two handkerchiefs and some sun glasses. Stan dropped Mick with the loot at a pre conceived hiding place and return over the Harbour Bridge, parked the car exactly when he had stolen it from. He had hot wired it to start it in the first place, so he simply reverse the procedure, attached the wires under the dash, locked the car with its window button on and headed for Wynyard to board the train North. The unsuspecting car owner who had been on a long shop ping spree did not ever know that her car had been used in a daring daylight bank robbery. The two newly qualified bank thieves returned to making appointment phone calls at the AMP North Sydney office for the rest of the afternoon. On the same evening as their robbery under arms Stan, Mick a mutual friend and I met in the city for a bite to eat before heading off to the movies.

Stan had picked a newly released film he thought we would all like; "Butch Cassidy and the Sundance Kid" was his choice. I recalled the last scene in the movie as Butch and Sundance were surrounded in a room in a Mexican standoff and about to die, after robbing nearby Bolivian bank, Butch had convinced Sundance that he had a great

idea if they survived this ordeal. " We will go to Australia." said Sundance. "Australia." quirked Sundance: "it's probably just like Bolivia." No way."replied Butch:"The beaches are grand, the women are beautiful and the banks are easy to rob." The dialogue by the about to die bank robbers was muffled by Stan and Mick in a roar of laughter. I just didn't think the dialogue was so hilarious. Well at that time I did not know the reasons behind their nervous outburst. I was informed by Stan later over a couple of beers in a nearby pub of their bank robbery and how much loot they had acquired as a result. On the following three days they each deposited cash at different bank and transferred the necessary funds to the finance company for the release hold over has over their mother's house.

Stan had been a good mate since my Commonwealth Bank early career days, had introduced me to my AMP agency opportunity and was then my flatmate and more often than not drinking buddy too. It was the day after the robbery that my conscious got the better of me and I made my way to Miller street North Sydney in my lunch break to the back lane of the police station with the intent to dob in my mate so that I could have clear conscious. Sitting in the gutter at the rear of the police station, I released I could not do it and felt all alone with no friend to share the burden on that troubled me. As it happened Peter the irishman, a AMP agent who was busy recruiting 'candidates' for Scientology in his spare time, sided up to me as I sat contemplating my next move. He enquired as to my state of mind and what was worrying me. Before I had time to answer Peter blurted out: "Your not worried about Stan and Mick holding up the Commonwealth Bank are you?"

CHAPTER 13.

A NEW DIRECTION

it was a relief to find the two brothers had told half the staff in AMP and were in that very hour, on their way to Cardinal Gilroy at St.Mary's Cathedral to confess their 'sin' to the priest. The Cardinal in his wisdom apparently advised them to give themselves up appealing to the mercy of the courts as first offenders.I got a phone call from elder brother John who happened to be in Sydney for a conference and he asked me to join him for lunch. We meet in the city and he outlined what had happened when the 'men of goodwill' handed themselves into the police and what had taken place when he visited them in a holding cell at long Bay jail to await their trial.The circumstances of the need to save the Mother's home, the fact that they were first offenders and their contrition to the judge that they would not 'sin' again stood them in good stead.

They were released on a good behaviour bond with the proviso that they repaid the CTB bank thirty dollars per week until their debt was extinguished. Mick went straight from then on but Stan keep up the way of life of a criminal. He got himself a job with Chubb safe learning how the fail safe locking device worked from the inside out thus paving the way for a would be safe cracker to make his mark. Instead Stan the man took to holding up banks again and when it became too hot for him in New South Wales he headed to Queensland to pursue even bigger bank jobs for a coupe of years. Just ahead of the law he ended up in Victoria were he made a lucrative living as an underworld bank robber. He was caught in action on a bank job but escaped with a great deal of cash. He apparently believed he was unlikely to be captured. However the Police had other ideas and were waiting for him at his living quarters in Melbourne. Stan spent the next twelve years in jail and was advised on release if he crossed an interstate boarder he would be taken immediately back to prison. I never heard from him again except a whisper from another of my bank colleagues who advise me that he had run into Stan the man in a Melbourne street. He was working for a local charity and attending to the aged and kids in the street. Stan had admitted that he did the occasional bag snatching in the street to keep his hand in. I trust the good in him finally outweighed the bad. That is if he is still alive and kicking. I remember two favourite sayings of his when we worked in banking ad insurance; " I use to be conceited but now I am perfect." and the other "Alcohol doesn't affect me affect me affect me." On both counts the conceit and the alcohol won.

At the end of my first year in the insurance business I decided to take break and headed to Europe on a three months holiday.. It meant sailing from Perth to Singapore and catching a charter flight to London. It was the cheap way to travel, so I set out for Perth to commence my journey from there.. A slow pace larger version of a country town I enjoyed my three days in that fair city frequenting the local bars and drinking different brews. Basically just strolling around enjoining the freedom of a life of leisure before catching a Russian ship bound for Singapore.

It was a small passenger ship with a total of three hundred living souls on board including crew members. A mass of steel from top to bottom. Stepping on board was like entering the Soviet Union. Romantic paintings of lush forests hung at the entry to the stairs as I made my way down two levels on a solid steel staircase along a corridor to my cabin door. It was the one closest to the bow on starboard side. Like the solid step door entry of alight cabins, the inside was not dissimilar; draped in 1970s style orange, matching the rust of the hull. No fancy appearance just raw steel coated with some anti corrosive dull yellowish paint to keep the floating mass safe from the elements of the ocean. The ships appearance reminded me of the harsh realism of a Russian capitalist with the zeal for no thrills economic growth of the Motherland versus the soft sweat smelling fancy artificiality of cruise ships of a Western Democracy's consumerism. It was a time of sex, drugs, rock n roll and magical free thinking bliss of what would prove to be more time wasting and misuse of precious resources. A time of misguided almost novel false beliefs that proved to be ultimately to our western values detriment.

Observing the three swinging hammocks and steel welded wall cabinet in my cabin, I noted that the other two bunks already had been tagged by fellow passengers. I duplicated their habit tossing a clothing bag on the hammock and my remaining personal possession next to the only tiny porthole with a screw latch to allow in some air from outside the ship. Making my way back along the corridor of cell accomodation, the sense of a lost silent world entered my spirit, except for the sound of the engine churning, the vessel felt lost in slumber. Listened to The ships passengers busy in their cabins I cast my fate to the four winds of chance and the a Russian crew of almost militant persuasion and made my way up the steel stairs again intent on heading for the bar.

At top open deck I opened a heavy steel door and ventured out into the fresh air. I observed a small front timber floored balcony and rail at the bow and steering quarters with an observation deck. Enough room to relax and take in the fresh sea air in calm seas. Towards the bow deck was a sold timber ladder attached to a steel pole mast to the Crow's Nest for distant observation.

The Captains cabin accessible from below deck sat towards the stern. At the stern was a square swimming pool painted blue and left empty. Apparently, the crew filled it up after a couple of days into the journey with fresh sea water. It was once more emptied before entry to the Port of Singapore. An easy way of keeping the pool clean and thus save on pool chemicals. taking it all in I returned to check out the rest of the ship. I had made my way along three levels of corridors and steel doors above the engine room. The crew of Russians slept on the lower deck near a meeting room stacked with chairs. Nearby a small library with a writing desk and many books on Russia which I also noted were all in the English. I flicked through a few of the mainly Russians authors generally know to western readers. No doubt these had been shipped in to cater for western taste, I climbed back up the steel staircase entering the first level kitchen on Port side and checkout the menu. The meal menu was in Japanese, Russian and English. Kaska porridge, bread, butter and ham sandwich, boiled egg and cottage cheese was the order of the day. A Russian salad being provided with the evening meal as an additional bonus to the daily diet. I later learned that Russian Caviar, a red sturgeon fish was available with every meal and was in plentiful supply. The Russian barmen later advised that the ship was on loan to Fairways for a short term assignment from Perth to Singapore route and would soon return to its main task of ferrying passengers from Tokyo to Vladivostok to join the the Trans Siberian rail link to Moscow, a distance of some 9,258 kilometres. I did come to check it out years later, and the old rusty hull was still holding up on that perilous crossing for the remainder of the 20th century. As fate would have it the ship was certainly going to have to prove its metal of 'Russian built ' on this our voyage to the Orient. I found the bar and made friendship with the two young men from Perth I was destined to share my cabin with. We were joined by Aart a Dutch photographer on his way back home to Holland after completing a photo shoot assignment In Western Australia. These three intrepid travellers were to play a vital role in my journey on board and later on in London and Europe. Ian had just finished a contract with the Department of Environmental planning and his sidekick Peter, both teacher and musician was taking long service leave after 5 years teaching. Aart joined us frequently at the bar when trying to sleep in his cabin proved difficult. Drinking Russian Vodka and copious amounts of Russian beer was the order of the day for us intrepid adventurers. Our cabin being not big enough to a swing a cat, the bar became our floating home so to speak. In truth it was our only refuge in the pending cyclonic weather that lay ahead.

We were only a day out to see on our voyage when an initial warning announced over the intercom by the Captain indicating we were shortly destined for some rough weather ahead. It proved to be a lot worse than the Russian captain had initially indicated. After the evening meal my new found friends and I headed for the cabin to unpack our gear, take a shower before flaking in our hammocks. The ship rocked me to sleep as the ocean waves tilted bow to stern repeatedly throughout the night. In the early hours of the morn the ships movement had changed dramatically. Another announcement by the ship's Captain was fair warning to the violence of the cruel sea ahead. The message from the Australian coastguard had given the coordinates to the Captain to steer a course away from the pending cyclone. Unfortunately the Ships captain had mis-understood the advise and headed straight ahead towards the centre of a major cyclone. We were already being tossed around the cabin and made our way up to kitchen. We did our best to hold on to porridge, plate and spoon and get the binding food down the gullet before once more adjourning to the bar. it was the only place on board were we had seats and rails to hold on too as the sea angrily took revenge on the hardy Russian hull.

The next couple of days and nights we spent the time between bar and kitchen, as it was impossible to sleep in the cabin. The ship's bow rose high like a mountain that seem to take forever to climb. Equally this action was repeated in reverse as the ship nosed dived down the steep wave on the others side. We did our best to hold on to the bar and kitchen bench during that violent cyclone. The ship would repeat this process twice straight into the wave and on the third wave, it hit the side of the ship causing it to broadside. The impact of this third wave had the ship shuddering and creaking like it was about to crack wide open. We tolerated this for three days with nothing to do but eat, drink and hold on to whatever kept us upright. Occasionally I headed for the cabin and wedged myself into the hammock catching a short moments of sleep before it got to much and I headed back to the bar.

Early on the fourth morning Aart the Dutch photographer come up with a bright idea over drinks. He had decided to unlock the main side hatch and attempt to climb to Crows Nest intent on taking a photograph of the ships bow as it went down the valley of a wave. I had just enough drink in me to develop dutch courage and I agreed to go with him. We made our weaving way to the large steel door that was securely locked as part of the Captain's instruction to crew to 'batten down the hatches.' It took all our strength to unwind the wheel lock to one the steel door and make our way outside. Aart and I ,with some difficult against the cyclonic wind and rain, managed to close the fridge like steel door and wind it locked from the outside. No sooner had we completed this task and the ship began to climb another wave. Hanging on for dear life we were almost wash overboard a number of times as made our way to wards the bow hanging on hand over hand, up the slop of the deck, holding on to the guard rail. Aart had the added burden of his camera in a water-proof case slung around his neck as he lead the way with me in hot pursuit. We made it to the main mask and began our steep climb at an angle, like climbing a ladder laying against a wall. Aart was two rungs ahead of me and made it to the Crows Nest quickly taking his camera from the case to prepare for the downward motion of the ship. At this point all we could see was the mountainous wave on the rising sea above us. Aart was well prepared and I, stone cold sober now, hung on to the mask and rail as my life depended upon it. I was too wet and cold to be scared and just focused on the front of the bow as it made the crest of the wave pausing briefly at the top before heading almost nose first downward towards the trough below.

It was like riding the big dipper at a fun parlour, but in truth it was no fun. Holding on for grim death, I watched as the bow of the boat disappeared into the approaching next wave. The nose of the ship to the mast began to vanish in a volume of water and I held on tight taking an almighty impact from the volume of water up the mask. The wave subsided as the ship slowly began to tilt towards the stern. We both made our quick escape down the ladder and on the tilting deck repeated our hand over hand return to the steel door. It seem to take more effort to open the hatch this time but we finally opened it, stepped inside and spun the hatch lock closed just as the ship began to shudder sideways and the third wave hit.

It was a matter of luck that we had made it out on deck when a new sequence of waves began. We had managed purely by luck to start our on deck ship cyclonic expedition in the right wave sequence, otherwise we would have been washed overboard on the third wave impact and the shear volume of water along the ship hull and deck. The journey back to the bar was our best recourse and I downed a whisky followed by a vodka before heading to the showers. Contemplating the goal to climb that mast in the cyclone, as agreed to with Aart, I had to acknowledge to myself that I would never had the courage or fool hardy notion to complete such a task sober.

The little ship hit the eye of the storm on the fourth day and we came into smooth sailing for a day. It was pleasant on desk and we sunbaked and swam in the pool which had been left three quarters full from the cyclonic experience. For the first time on the journey we met many of the passengers who had not left their cabins for the whole four days. In conversation we were informed that most has suffered sea sickness for the majority of the journey. A buffet lunch on deck supplied by the Russian chef made for new conversations and some sing a long. In the evening we were entertained by the ships crew and danced the night away. I finally crashed in my cabin with my fellow room mates and slept like a baby in the calm sea. Two more days and night followed before we finally made our way out of the cyclonic conditions and a smooth sea again. We were but a day away from Singapore and longing for terra firma.

As part of our charter flight package we were granted a top notch resort style hotel in Singapore to stay in. Wing Fat from my old PMG days was now working for Singapore Telecom so I gave him a call on the chance that he would join us for a meal. As it turns out he did the organising but it would prove to be more than just dinner together. I was called to the foyer on my room intercom and Wing Fat answered:. "Come and join me now" he said: "and bring some friends if you like." I called Ian and Peter and the three of us headed for the hotel foyer. As the lift door opened I was greeted by Wing Fat with a warm smile surrounded by what I thought were bodyguards. It turned out to be the Chief of the Singapore Police and an entourage of policeman. Wing Fat was still up to his old tricks and called in a Police favour. We three intrepid travellers lost three days in Singapore before boarding our flight to London. It is now a haze of flashes of memory best forgotten, all under police escort.

We, like royalty at the end of the Police organised tour were escorted ceremoniously to our next leg of our journey to Europe. I can still see the smiling Win Fat and the Chief of Police giving us a fond farewell wave and a knowing smile as we boarded our flight. That was the last I recall of Wing Fat. I have since made it a policy over time when landing in Singapore, not to contact Wing Fat nor to his local activities of Wing Fat, nor to contact him. There are vague but unreliable memory of what had happened in those three days in Singapore in 1971 and that is possibly a good thing. It was a strange flight that charter; a one-off experience in a small airplane filled to the brim with cheap ticket holders. Some lucky souls had seats and others simply lay on the floor because there was no spare ones.

The charter company got every cent in the dollar out of its cargo of misfits, hippies and atlas eaters. We were onboard a Douglas Decoda DC 3 heading for Bahrain International Airport on Muharraq Island, adjacent to the capital Manama. The plane was fitted out without sleeping birth to accomodate twenty one seated passengers and we must have had at least thirty on board. I counted nine bodies I had to step over to get to the toilet at the rear of the plane. That was the only inconvenience apart from the low level flight due to the plane being unpressurised; it could not be flown at high altitude. The little windows along the aircraft could be opened a little for fresh air, but not for long. The low wing mono twin engines roared into the fuselage, putting pay to the idea of leaving the windows open. We touched down at Bahrain at the time of another Gulf War. It was good to get out of the plane to stretch our legs whilst waiting for refuelling and fumigation of the aircraft. It was summertime desert hot on the landing strip and I was keen to depart the planes inferno and head to the terminal. I noted that when the fumigation team of Indian workers entered the plane they were followed by a hive of small flies. I prayed that the Indian's spraying the inside of the fuselage would kill the majority of the pests they attracted as they entered the plane.

The airport was alive with fully armed soldiers who stood on roof top hangers and the main passenger terminal with rifles at the ready trained upon us. Word was out from the West that a terrorist group were targeting airports to take control, so the local troops backed by US finance were on high alert. No stone was left unturned and we had military bodyguards nearby at all times in the airport. I was dry as above and settled for an Indian vendor with an ice chest around his waist and supporting rope hanging from his neck.

I purchased a Coca Cola and he quickly lifted the cap with a bottle opener brushing his hand across the open bottle as he handed it to me. I was so thirsty, I let it pass and downed the drink in great gulps. A big mistake, as it turns out the contaminated bottle opener had caused me to be infected by a fatal cholera bacteria which entered my gut and soon began to take effect on my small intestine.

Realising I had made no plans for the future, I made my way from the airport with Ian and Peter, joining them in an Earl's Court private accomodation B & B., unloaded my gear and we headed for the nearest bar for a beer. It was the typical English dark brew and I started to throw up after the first couple. I blamed the beer but in point of fact I had a touch of cholera. I ate sparingly for the next twenty four hours before boarding a ferry across the channel to Amsterdam in Holland.The night journey was the pits as I lay in the passage way between the inner bar and the outer deck on rough crossing hoping someone would kick me overboard and I would depart this mortal coil drowning at sea; relieved of the vomiting and the dreaded cholera diarrhoea. We reached the port at Amsterdam at dawn and as soon as I made it ashore I contacted Aart, the Dutch photographer who had promised us three new found friends a place to stay on our arrival at Amsterdam. Both Peter and Ian had considered staying in the city at a hostel but agreed to come along with me after Aart had given me directions to his father's home.

We caught a bus to Halfwegg, a medieval little village half way between Amsterdam and the Hague and followed Aart's directions along the main canal of Harrlemmertrekvaart; the oldest of the canals of Holland.The bridge across the canal with a small Medieval Castle like walkway was all that the little township had to offer. All I desired was a bed and a room I could call my own. Aart had already left for a photoshoot job on the other side of the country and his Father who spoke limited English reluctantly gave me a room alone. For Peter and Ian he arranged two beds in another small room. Because of our host uninviting attitude, they had made up their minds to stay one night only. By the next morning I was running a fever and bed ridden. I had no choice but to stay in bed all the next day. Both my friends were pleased to leave the house and I could see the relief on the Father's face as they hit the road again. Ian promised me he would return as soon as he found a place to stay near Amsterdam and take me with them then to share the accomodation. My unpleasant host brought me some chicken broth around midday and as I ate he gruffly requested in broken English for me to move on too. My condition had not improved when early the next day Ian returned to let me know he had found an attic flat a little closer to Amsterdam and it had three beds, so we had our digs for the next week. The old dutchman gave me a friendly handshake, but I gathered by his manner that he was more than glad to rid his home off a sick young man, much less a foreigner. I gladly move in with my intrepid travellers and upon arrival flaked and slept fitfully for the next twenty four hours. There was no shower facilities in our accomodation and no toilet nor tap for a drink of water, so we made our way to the Turkish bath about ten minutes up the road. The barman supplied us with clean towels, and use of the pool and bathroom facilities before we returned for refreshments at his bar. I couldn't stomach any food but a small cup of Turkish coffee which sustained me for our bus ride into Amsterdam. I was thankful for the summer heat and left Peter and Ian for their exploration of the city.

I found myself a good location to rest and recuperate, lying down on the warm concrete for the majority of the day, just watching the world float by. Nightfall came and I caught up with the boys for a snack at a bar and drug smoke house. Upon entry I was invited to sit down cross legged with a group of American hippies whilst they passed around a bong in large pipe. I took more than my fill each time the pipe was passed to me. I was as high as a kite when I made my way to the bar for a drink; it was like walking on air in slow motion. I felt nothing but peace and a sense that all will be well. I don't recall returning to the attic at our temporary premises, but apparently I flaked for three days. Peter and Ian had woken me long enough to get some water and bread in my system. They even went to the trouble of purchasing a bed pan and toilet paper in the event that I may need to get up to use the facilities during the night. I don't recall much at all but woke up after what seemed an eternity feeling a bit drained but over the virus and reenergise to some degree.

At the end of the week we found a youth hostel dormitory facility in Amsterdam. It was a large room of double bunks and was always full of mainly young students from the USA. Nearby was a large oval complex which housed some half million young drug smokers and heavy drug users. About every half hour an ambulance would go roaring by taking some poor soul to the hospital emergency having overdosed. Hash in particular was in plentiful supply. It was legal to carry up to a kilo of the stuff without the authorities breathing down your neck. Smoke houses were on every second corner.

At night it cost a gilder (about 80 cents in todays AU dollar) enter to a smoke house, to listen to groovy music and smoke until getting high. There were no tables or chairs in the places, just an empty room with piped music and the haze of smoke house hanging, bodies all around the floor and the occasional little child crying for his now stoned mother lost in oblivion nearby. I quickly recovered from the after-effect of cholera and the desire to take any more hash.

My drinking habits had not subsided and I was still smoking a pack and a half of cigarettes a day, so in that sense I was still an addict. I didn't have travel far to get the sense of a way of life gone wrong. In the bunk opposite me was a young American student in his last year of a pharmaceutical degree. He had taken a gap year to travel the world but never got much further than Amsterdam or Paris. His daily habit was making chess pieces and a stone chess board. On completion of his creation he caught the train to Paris, sold the lot for cash then returning to Amsterdam. His life had become an endless cycle of hash smoking, making another Chess set then running out of cash returning to Paris selling his creation, returning to Amsterdam to smoke more dope. I repeatedly made my way to a bar which were always full of gay men drinking and looking to pick up another mark. The men young and old kissed openly in the street and held hands. It was a shock for a true believer in male to female relationships being the norm, but I was there for the beer and fascinated by the Avant Garde creative types and their crazy world. Female one night stands were easy to be had anywhere in Amsterdam, especially among the hippie set. The high risk factor of contracting a venereal type disease was always a hazard. Every building along the main canal was a red light district. Prostitutes hung outside the doors at street level and on balconies above or used large truck mirror reflecting inside their room for the voyeuristic eye on the street below.

I visited a Catholic Church for a change of pace only to encounter a Priest without collar and note that the Dutch had turned their back on the Vatican and even had their own version of the true Church's Catechism. We lived cheaply on Dutch beer, bar snacks and our nightly main meals at the city soup kitchen. It was simply a line up at a back street eat house to be issued with a bowl and spoon. It cost one guilder (AU 80c) to have the large bowl filled to the brim with thick pea and bean soup and a small quantity of pork on the bone or a pigs trotter. One morning I watched in amazement as a red Mustang entered the main square with three very tall and seeming fit young Negros stepping out.

They moved their way in rhythm along the street called out to clogged feet: "Do you what to buy some shit man." By then I had my fill of Amsterdam and decided to hit the road again. I sat with Ian and Peter studying a map of the Rhine River villages on route and agreed to meet them in Bacharach two weeks from the day. We had enjoyed our time together but now was time for me to take stock and be content to be with myself in solitude. I look back and waved a last good bye to the now fading figures behind me, tightened the straps on my back pack and settled for a long walk to the German boarder.

The days that followed tramping my way through Holland and across the boarder had me averaging 20 kilometres a day with a light load on my back. Most of what I carried was light summer clothing for I had left the bulk of my world possessions in storage at the Port of Amsterdam for two months for safe keeping. I carried one change of clothing, a light jacket and the barest of essentials for my survival. It was in the midst of a dry hot summer so I never even had a raincoat. As for food and shelter, I was relying on my remaining savings and the youth hostel system to guide and care if I got into difficulty. I had no real plan at that time for the future, content to make my way with an eye on what may be over the next hill. In truth I was a lost soul having left behind a broken relationship once more back home in Australia. At the time I was but two weeks of the altar and marriage when my bride to be's mother tried to put pressure on me to fit her template for living and not my own. My intended bride backed her mothers wishes. I needed this time out to clear my head, take stock and consider my future direction in life. The long walk from Amsterdam to Arnhem took five days of relatively easy walking. It was safe on the road so I tramped on making my way to Bonn.

The first familiar sign that came into view was the Australian flag at full mask outside the Australian Embassy. I had made it my policy to collect Embassy stamps in my passport. As it turns out later, the Dutch Embassy stamp proved a blessing when I finally return to the Netherlands some two months later to collect my stored luggage. The Ambassador of Australia of the Department of Foreign Affairs invited me into his Embassy office of polished mahogany timber desk, chair and charred timber wall panels. The fittings likewise reeked of left overs from the Nazi regime possibly stolen from some jewish nobleman during WW 11. He invited me to sit in the chair opposite and began to ply me with questions about home. He informed me the newspapers from Australia were usually a week or two behind current events by the time they received them and was interested in a laymen's view of the political goings on in Canberra. The only news I had was that William McMahon replaced John Gordon as Prime Minister in a 33: 33 ballot on a motion of no confidence in John Gorton as Prime Minister. A gallant John Gorton, as chairman, gave his casting vote against the motion, effectively voting himself out of office. He stood for and won the Deputy Party leader roll. We discussed Liberal politics and the rise of the soon to be Prime Minister Gough Whitlam in the Labor Party. The Ambassador as to be expected of a high ranking public servant was a keen cricket fan. Although I wasn't, he was keen to get my opinion on the potential of the idea of one day cricket, the first of which was a one day exhibition match between Australia and England in January. The test match had been called off due to extreme wet weather in Melbourne and an exhibition was held to appease the fans and recover some of the MCG financial loss as a result. After much discussion on Cricket we turned to Rugby Union of which I had played for over a decade and followed with passion. I left the Embassy with an Australian Embassy stamp in my passport and a small Australian flag which I later sowed on my backpack to show the world this long haired and bearded hippie lout was a proud Australian.

I tramped the day away and flagged a lift to the outskirts of Cologne late afternoon. After checking in at a local information centre for the cheapest place to stay, I headed for a youth hostel a few kilometres along the Rhine River front and bedded down for a week to tour the city. It had been a training camp site for Hitler youth during the war and was now run by a graduate of that time. The blue eyed blond man of Arian race greeted me like a new recruit and i was ushered to my room. I stayed there a few days, checking out all the tourist haunts. On my last day in Cologne I made my way to the Cathedral in a pensive mood. It was at the back of the Cathedral, gazing into the ever flowing Rhine River that I hatched a plan for my future life that would set me on the road to Corporate success and later much success in my own business.

CHAPTER 14.

SIGHTSEEING IN OLD WORLDS

I mapped out the plan, wrote down the goal of being appointed as a Sales Manager for the largest Insurance company in Australia, determined to put my plan into action on my return to Australia. I was no longer in vacant or pensive mood as I packed my planned notes written on loose leaf sheets and placed them into a page I was up too in a motivational book I was reading. Content with my lot, I returned to the youth hostel, packed the rest of my then world goods and made my way to the river once more to continue my adventure in Europe. Riding the Rhine river by ferry, I set foot on land at many an ancient village for a break and continued down-stream to my intended next place of call, Koblenz.

The youth hostel stood high on a hill that was almost a mountain overlooking the Koblenz village and the Rhine. It was an ancient Castle during the era of Kingdoms and Knights of reknown. During WW11 it housed Nazi Generals and their elite associates. After the war It made sense to turn it into a youth hostel, as the revenue from the visiting tourist and accommodated youth allowed first class maintenance of this ancient structure to continue. I made my way through the busy streets to the base of the steep climb to the now converted Castle of a place of abode for back packing wanderers of the world. The track was a series of winding pathways with wooden stairs on each corner of the track taking the climber up yet another level. It had been a hot dry morning climb and I was relieved to pay my accomodation fee and find a cell like room and a bunk bed to lay my weary head.

I had not been asleep for more than a few minutes when I was awoken by the sound of two motor bikes entering the courtyard outside my window. I made my way to the bathroom and had a shower, shaved and a got into my only alternate clothing. Returning to my room, I was met bu two American bikers dressed in leather who were unpacking their bags for a night of shared acco-modation. The room had three bunks and we lay there for a time side by side discussing the ways of our world. Once the American's had time for a rest they invited me to join them at a restaurant in another village about half an hour ride. I took pride of place as a pillion passenger on one of the two brand new BMW motorbikes and we set off into a tunnel entry to the courtyard. The Nazi military had built an expressway lane which wound down inside the mountain in ever decreasing circles. It was an exciting ride around the bends in the tunnel and we finally emerged after around 10 minutes onto an Autobahn. My American pilot gunned the big BMW bike at breakneck speed as I swayed with him in time on each bend in the road, exhilarated but please to be heading to bar for a pre dinner drink.

It was over a few drinks that the young riders told me the reason for their journey to Germany. The two bikes were the first of BMWs 1000cc series bikes German built. They had decided to travel to Europe to purchase one each and ride around Europe before returning with their toys to the USA. It was then and there I learnt that neither rider and more than the two weeks experience riding a motor bike. I noted that I was riding with the guy with the least skills and the greater risk taker. He already had a tear in his jacket from a spill at high speed a couple of days before arriving at Koblenz. We had a grand time drinks and eating together and as the drinks continued it gave my learner rider further dutch courage for our ride back to Klobenz and though the mountain. It was much like the quelled fear in my stomach as I climbed the mast in the cyclone on that Russian ship on my way to Singapore just a couple weeks beforehand. This time it was farewell to the Americans wishing them a safe journey. I said a quiet prayer to St. Jude, patron of travellers as I figured they would need it before they finished their tour of Germany.

I looked back along the road to see them both flying along the Autobahn without a care in the world it seemed. I caught the next ferry downstream for my stay at another Castle mountain retreat in Bacharach. I was twenty four hours ahead of the appointed time to meet up again with Ian and Peter, so I figured I would explore round the place whilst awaiting their arrival at the Castle the next morning.

The scenic youth hostel Castle sitting on a hilltop, looking over the township was not unlike Koblenz; a small town exulting charm and much wine. Other Castles dotted the landscape below; overlooking the river, the Castle and township of half timber buildings and cobblestone street. The hillsides opposite were full of vineyards and charm. Much of the wine growing grapes whereon that hillside on the adjacent riverbank.. I climber up a path around 160 metres above the river to Burg Stahleck; the 12th century Castle then used to protect the town and collect tolls from the traders passing by on the river. Once fortified by a partial moat it had recently been replaced by a small bridge and the Castle itself reopened to the public as a hostel.

The view below from the courtyard was breathtaking. I was kicking soccer ball around the courtyard with other guests when Ian and Peter appeared at the entry gate. We spent the rest of the day on another ferry ride to the ruins of Rheinfels Castle at St.-Goar, then on too Marksburg Castle, still in pristine condition from its first day of being built near 10 centuries before. We sampled many a glass of the fine wines of the region before finally moving on downstream, finally once more on foot, we made our way to Mainz, Mannheim and on too Heidelberg. The small town of Heidelberg resonated to me as it was the birthplace of Hermann Hess , the prolific author who had written many a book that germinated in his mind as he walked the streets of his hometown. The first book of Hess that I had ever read was " beneath the wheel' which describes boyhood scenes of which I was then walking and the tragic ending in the book of the boy's suicide. I was not to realise it at the time, why Hess like the boy in the story ultimately committed suicide. My visit to that little town and the sad story of Hess's creation and the taking of his own life held some deeper meaning to me. It was not until some 42 years later that I walked the streets of the township once more. This time I too had reached that point of no return and was reminded of the affinity il had with that German village and Herman Hess 42 years earlier when I was last there. My own life had turned upside down through death and desolation. It had not been quite a decade before that I had lost the will to live after divorce, loss of my economic security and to a much greater wound to my heart, the suicide of my second eldest son.

We made our way to Munich to enjoy the delight of the beer halls. It was one long beer-fest and exploration of that city. Ian and Peter went on to check out the tour of the Jewish concentration camps during the nazi regime. I had no interest in the misery of such things back then, preferring to explore the Architecture of Hitler's preoccupation. Whilst the buildings I view from the mind of a failed artist held some cold hard classical discipline towards mediocrity, they also stood like gravestones as a stark reminder to the millions who died under the quest for a Arian race. If it were not for architect Speer's killer combination of ideal that resinated with Hitler's ideal, the building forms from the crazed mind of the dictator would never have been built. As I walked the streets of Munich back then, I tried to extract some good from all the evil that the madman had inflicted on our world at the time.

The architectural apology for the work of Speer who brought Hitler's sketched visions to reality by redesigning and rebuilding Berlin, Linz and Munich and other great cities as a stage setting for 1000 years of murderous pomposity. Under the Nazi regime, apart from the cold gravestone cityscapes emerged to some degree into reality, Hitler was instrumental in bring in a vision that came to reality, a peoples car, a rail system that was and still is second to none and the Autobahn originally designed for military logistics, later proved to be stroke of genius for modern day road transport in Germany. Whilst I was left feeling cold by Albert Speer's hard form of architecture in completing a vision of his traditionalist employer, the wannabe artist Adolf Hitler who had walked the street of Vienna in his youth, making a modest income selling his postcard sketches. Hitler would be remembered more for his techniques of obliteration than his construction of sketches that Speer modelled for him. I took some solace listening to Peter and Ian relating their grim sightings at the Jewish concentration camp tour on the outskirts of the city back in the youth hostel that evening. I was glad I had filled in the day looking at Munich buildings and visiting a libraries looking for more works of Herman Hess the author, in preference to the autobiographical struggles of Hitler's Mien Kampf.

It would be within the next decade that I would come in contact with Albert Speer's junior architect and be taken in by the skills of a German who knew not only how to design buildings but to physically build himself. There is an old saying "architects design buildings that builders can't build," this was not the case with Otto Hermann. Otto was the third architect of Albert Speer whose job it was to build the visions of Adolf Hitler and rebuild the cities destroyed by allied bombings. Speer's young assistant architect was no less taken in by the might and power of the dictator in fulfilling his architectural vision. Speer once quoted on reflection of of his part in the war: 'One cannot recognise the devil when he has a hand on your shoulder.' Speer apart from his architectural ability was the minister of armaments and war production. As a close ally of Adolf Hitler he was convicted of war crimes at the Nuremberg trails and sentenced to 20 years. He died of a stroke in London England in 1981.

Otto Hermann escaped to Australia, after the war. Otto became well known for his involvement with the Boy Scouts and designed and built the monument for Scouting that still stands near the scout camp at Mt. Keira, Wollongong. He later moved with his wife, daughter and son in law to Walcha on the New England Tablelands.

In true Architectural style he built a double brick home on a large block of land overlooking the township. He was a brilliant architect and builder too. It was just eight years after my return from my trek through Germany that I purchased and grew a Newsagency business and General store at Walcha. Together with my young family we moved into our first new home; the abode designed and built by Otto Hermann for his family about the time I was travelling through his native Germany in early 1972. We celebrated over dinner his sale of the family home to me. Otto showed me many photo's of himself, Speer and Hitler and told me many inside stories of the mind of Adolf Hitler. The only kink in the armour of Otto was the day after his family move out of their home and we moved in, he knocked on our door to collect his toothbrush. We were still unpacking and had not yet cleaned out the bathroom cupboard. The toothbrush was still neatly placed were as he had left it. He was typical of the type who held on too anything of personal value and no doubt on that day it was his toothbrush.

Ian, Peter and I started out the next day on the main Autobahn to Austria. Ian was keen to visit the Spanish riding school to watch a performance of classical dressage trains of Lipizzaner horses. Peter, being musician, had heard that John Mayall was performing in Vienna. Their wants took priority over my vision to visit the places frequented by Mozart, Beethoven and the haunts of Sigmund Freud youth and the libraries to delve into his philosophy on sex and evolution. It was a sixty kilometre walk to the boarder, so we walked until dusk and had a rest stop at a small pub off the beaten track for a beer, some smoked ham that hung over the bar and bread rolls. It was a cheap way to fill our stomachs on our then limited financial resources before we took to the road again.

After copious quantities of alcohol and argument broke out between Peter and yours truely. Considering we were on our way to Vienna and John Mayall was playing there, we had been debating who was the greatest guitarist player and group was of the past decade. Eric Clapton had recently kicked off a five nights residency in Japan and John Mayall having wrapped up his own tour gigs was invited to join Clapton on stage. There was no argument that the Yardbirds won both our applause but Peter had it in his head that the best guitarist of the decade was Jimmy Page with a toss up between Eric Clapton and Jeff Beck as close seconds. Peter knew his guitar players much better than me, but I stuck to my belief that Clapton was the best having been weened on John Mayall from an earlier ago.We both had enough alcohol to fuel our respective egos and tempers. Peter landed a punch neatly on my chin knocking me off the bar stool. As I fell, I grabbed him by his shoulder length hair with my left and bringing him down with me, punching him again and again in the face as we fell. We both ended on the floor in an all out brawl until the fight was stopped by a middle aged german who said in well commanded english: "Stop fighting immediately. We germans who fought for Hitler's cause and lost have the scars to prove it. Don't fight." He dropped his trousers to display a long thick scar from the hip to his ankle. "This is all that I gained from fighting a so called just cause." he said. "This is all that fighting for Hitler did for me." He pulled up his pants and returned to his beer. Peter and I looked at each other and laughed: "I was wrong" he said. I, ever so quickly replied " No, you win mate. Sorry about your black eye." He just smiled and said: "let me shout another round."

It was near midnight. The cold wind blew and sleet fell on us three wanderers off the road. We tramped on towards the Austrian boarder and around two a.m. we had to stop and rest as we were cold and exhausted. Making out way off the beaten path well into the black forest, we collected broken branches, twigs and dead leaves from under trees then set to work building a bomb fire.The flames grew high and the heat was intense but at a comfortable distance from the flames we were warm once more. We had settled for a clearing in the forest and by the grace of God never set one branch of a tree alight there. We slept until dawn and extinguished the remains of the burning embers. Making our way back to the road we walked for another hour or two. We come across a sign pointing to a guest house some 3 kilometres into the forest. We arrived at an old house with large entry to a room were we met the proprietor. It was a one room guest house with a big kingsize bed but we didn't care. We three all climbed under the warm covers and sleep like new born babies until the next morning. We had walked the 400 odd kilometres to Vienna in just three weeks averaging near 30 kilometres a day. John Mayall had left Vienna much to Peters disappointment so we settled for the historic sights. We walked along the Danube river, visited the architectural sights of The Hofburg; seat of the Habsburg- the official residence of every Austrian ruler since 1275. The sprawling complex of Gothic, Renaissance, Baroque and Rococo architectural movements fulfilled my wandering heart with delight. We checked out the Imperial apartment, the silver collection and the Imperial Chapel, took a bus ride to the Schoenbrunn Place to view even more splendid architecture. Wandering the streets we enjoyed Viennese coffee, cake and pasties at historic coffee houses. The final highlight of our Vienna excursion was to visit the Spanish Riding school which fulfilled Ian's objective to see the horses in training there. So three weary young adventurers boarded the night train to Salzburg and caught up on sleep as we had little money left between us for ac-comodation. We had taken a detour to Salzburg as much as to get free accomodation for the trip on the train as to do some sightsee-ing of the city. After a wander through the city and a visit to the Mozart museum we set about planning our journey to Italy. I so wanted to visit Antonioni's film locations, hopefully to meet the man himself and hand him a recent script I had written for his consideration.

Sitting at a Salzburg coffee house contemplating our next move as a cheap way to Rome, I hatched up a plan. Dragging my two friends along we entered the main office of a German film compa-ny based in Salzburg. Boldly bypassing the secretary, I marched right into the Studio CEO main boardroom with my two not so sure companions lagging behind. As it happened he was there alone so I took the opportunity to introduce ourselves as a film crew from Australia looking for potential locations for a series. Germany had gone 'Skippy' crazy and when I said we had worked on some of the filming, we got the royal treatment adjourned to his office. On the wall behind his desk were fitting posters of mainly famous German films and pride of place a blown up A1 size poster of Skippy, the Bush Kangaroo. The outcome was a road trip for me to the Italian boarder and a train ride for my partners in crime. We set a date and time to meet at the Trevi Fountain of 'three coins in a fountain' film fame in Rome in a weeks time.

I was waiting outside the Salzburg's General Post bright and early. I had not been waiting for more than a few minutes when a late model BMW two seater sports car arrived. The friendly middle aged German owner greeted me with a strong hand shake, loaded my backpacking in the boot and we were on our way speeding down an autobahn. I had apologised for my lack of my limited German but he was not fazed at all. Ollie the sports car owner ex-plained that he had not spoken English for some eight years and this journey together would be good practice for him. He was keen to know why I had ventured so far from home and intended to find out as much as he could from me about Australia playing me with questions on politics, the environment, the film industry, single women and employment opportunities. I did my best to answer as a young not so experienced man of the world would do. He seem to be satisfied with that but got greatly excited over my offering when we stopped for coffee break after a couple of hours. I had quite a variety of coins from my travels and offered them to my host. I had small cash reserve of Australia coins and explained the detail of each animal on the coins. The Commonwealth shield held up by an Emu and a Kangaroo brought him much excitement. Then turning over each coin I showed him a Platypus, a Possum, Echidna, Frill neck Lizard and the Lyrebird on the reverse of each coin describing each of their mammal or marsupial qualities. Ollie was fascinated and even more excited when I offered him the coins as a gift.

By the time he dropped me off on a side road towards Northern Italy Ollie was a true Australian convert and had a new mission in life to get down under. I was not so excited about my Italian quest now as Ollie the sports car driver who was up on the latest in films had informed me that Michelangelo Antonioni was filming in China and would be over there for the better part of three months. I had soon made it to a new express road on foot and cadged a lift very quickly. it was an old Italian businessman on route to Rome. He was driving an old Ferrari and introduced himself as Enzo. It dawned on me later that he may well have been linked to the founder Enzo Ferrari. When we reached the last of the Autobahn he set off at breakneck speed towards Italy. Enzo assured me that the faster he drove the less tollway he would pay at the end of the highway. He was dangerous to be with, lacked concentration and drove that machine like a maniac. I breathed a sigh of relief when I stepped from the car. Ollie said his goodbye returning to his car tp speed on his way to a the world record.

On a lonely rode high in the Austrian Alps near the Yugoslavia boarder I stood at dusk hoping and praying that I would not be left without a lift to the Italian border. I was somewhere near the village of Villach, a traffic junction to the Slavic states and Italy. I had no map and no real idea of distance being still high up in the mountains of what it appeared at the time a not too often traffic route. I looked back along the road and could see far in the distance the Autobahn crossing over the bridge were I had alighted from Enzo's Ferrari. To the right the road ran in a straight line to infinity. I took stock of my predicament, standing on a relatively flat plateau road overlooking a field stood an old wooden barn. On its entrance side I could make out a tractor looking the worst for wear.

My side on view from my distant vantage point revealed a stack of hay piled up against the rear wall of the barn. Nightfall was fast approaching, I was hungry and cold and fearful of being mugged or even worse, being raped by wild men of the hills. I figured once it was dark, just incase I was being watched, I would make my way to the hay stack and make it my warm bed for the night. The two things I wished for then was a box of matches to light a fire and a knife to protect me against the wilds of nature and man. I had almost given up hope when I heard the sweet sound of a truck motor labouring under the burden of climbing this Alpine mountain road.

The truck came into view and I flagged it down as it passed me by. My heart sank as the driver changed gear to ease the labouring motor now that he had made it to level ground. He must have had a change of heart as he suddenly stopped, put his arm out the window waving it and beckoning me to come on board. I breathed a sign of relief as I climbed into the passenger seat. Spiro was taking a truck load of foodstuff from Austria to the Italian fruit markets in Florence. He had but a couple of words he could speak in English and I likewise had a limited splattering of Italian from the back of my guide book. Sign language and the odd bit of joking and laughter made for a peasant journey through the white marble cliff face of mountain. I recall now that I thought maybe it was one of the roads that the artist and sculptor Michelangelo had cut through the mountain pass. Perhaps he had chosen some of those marble blocks he used to release the soul of his creations that I could see on the approaching range. My mind jerked back to reality as Spiro once more changed gears and the motor began to purr again. Spiro, after some of our silence on the lonely road, turned and smiled making some gesture and statement about his truck. I didn't get it for a time so he repeated: "Piano, Piano, piano." I got it, the purr of the engine was music to his ears and I got the feeling this Italian man had a beautiful heart and was content with his lot. The hour was getting late when we stopped at a small truck stop for a bite to eat and coffee. We stayed a little longer than intended drinking a wine or two after our snack and conversing in our sign language of the beauty of my country down under and the country we were now travelling in. Spiro like the german CEO was a fan of the Australian series " Skippy, the bush Kangaroo."

So in my wild erratic fancy I promised him i would send him a stuffed kangaroo and koala bear for his little bambinos. He was delighted and wrote down his address in my travel guide which in my future adventures I somehow lost. My intentions were honourable at the time but my guilt didn't last long as I recall. I was awoken by Spiro at the Italian boarder. The wine had taken effect and I had been asleep for at least an hour.

The boarder security check Spiro's papers but they would not let me cross the boarder. It was midnight when I said goodbye to my new found Italian friend and watched as he passed through boarder control with disappointed written all over his face. The boarder guard took me into his office and checked me up and down. I must have looked like a real bum; unkept beard with shoulder length hair, ragged clothing and a dirty back pack. Why indeed would he allow me into his country. The tall regimented boarder guard spoke reasonable English, examined my passport, looked me up and down once more and said "We in Italy don't like young men with long hair, particularly young Australians." I look up at the photo behind him on the wall. It was a portrait photo of Amintore Fanfani 32nd Prime Minister of Italy, head of a left wing faction of Christian democracy with a head as bald as a badger. I responded with a retort: "I can see why."

The guard told me to come back in the morning and I asked him where I could find accomodation. He pointed the way back on he road "You will find a refuge about a kilometre back," and turned to return inside his office. It was after one o'clock in the morning when I knocked on the door of the inn. The Proprietor quickly opens the door and ushered me to my room. I paid him the required tariff for a few hours respite. Luckily I had changed some German Marks into Lira the previous day. I woke in the dawning light, got dressed, did my toiletries and was back on the road at sunup. Un-be-known to me Spiro had convinced the boarder guard to let me through. To my surprise he was waiting for me on the Italian side of the boarder. I was a little disheartened to say goodbye to my new found Italian friend but promised I would be in touch and send him the prized stuffed toys for his children. I watched as the old truck made its way down another highway and I turned to a nearby village to catch a train to Venice. My motivation to visit this water bound city was inspired much more by the quote "See Venice and die," than the beauty of its creation. Meaning of course, that after such of life peak of experience, there's nothing left to do but die, and die happily. I was of course still in my youthful curiosity and still too young to have experience, taste and test the bitter sweet meaning that life held for me, much less be ready for death. I did however know the pain of longing; longing for love, for creative outlet and the need for economic success.

CHAPTER 15.

LESSONS FROM MY LIFE

My train ride was a reminder of the template of train riding that the poet Herbert Nehrlich had parallels his life with great train journeys across the Americas, Europe, Australia and South Africa. In the poem, when his life was spent and there was no other place to go, the poets character considers that Venice be the final place to visit, the ultimate experience before death therein.

I was a romantic at heart and was not conscious then of the great creative output I would experience in my latter years after much pain and tragedy. I now recall my experience there in my youth and my later return to Venice not yet a decade ago. My poetic heart was not taken back then as Venice being a good place to die and still isn't. Like all men I still want to live a productive life but find that despite my outlet in creative writing of books, songs and poems; my reality now is more about other souls and my association with them and their lives of quite desperation than my own selfish motives for living.

The train reached the Venice station on the mainland early afternoon. I made my way across the square to a waiting gondola for my journey to a hostel I had discovered at the railway information desk. The gondola parked in the canal at the rear of the hostel and I alighted to enter through a small dining room door to the reception. It was a quaint almost canal level platform with one level above and a couple of room for accommodation. The proprietor took my passport, placed it in a safe behind the counter. I enquired as to why he was holding it instead of returning it to me. He suggested I check out the notice board opposite before he responded to my question. Every article on the noticeboard was a local newspaper headline: "Australian damages property," "Australian youth in drunken brawl." "Australian couple caught stealing in San Marco Jewellery store." It was all written in Italian but I understood and the photos of the guilty parties were added proof. I had no cause to question the proprietor any further as he promised he would return my passport when I check out of the hostel if I remained on good behaviour. I had a mental reminder of the security guard at the boarder and understood why he had such a hard line with me crossing into Italy. After a brief rest, shower and change of clothing, I made my way to the Central Square of the Piazza San Marco facing St.Mark's Basilica, one canal bridge crossing away from my hostel.

The doves of the Central Square were making their last adventure skyward before settling in the nooks and crannies of the surrounding architecture. The square was still wet seemingly given the impression of being hosed down and clean at the end of a busy foot traffic day. In point of fact the square had been some centimetres under water in the afternoon high tide which so often is the case.

From it beginning in the 5th century, the weight of the city of buildings pushed down the dirt and mud that it was built upon, squeezing out water and compacting the soil. This phenomenon, together with the natural movement of high tides cause periodic flooding in the city, creates a sinking sensation. As a tourist I felt safe and assured, like being on board a ship with lifeboats in the case of an emergency, as waiting gondolas stood as taxies throughout the main lagoon and in every side canal awaiting a potential customer to exit and enter the main arena.The water bound cities on flat ground of Piazza San Marco rectangle design reminded me of its centuries old legacy as powerful maritime republic. I gazed out from my vantage point before descending the stair level to the Square. To the far end stood the Byzantine Basilica of San Marco which I intended to explore the very next day. Gazing out to the open waters, the main canal from its entry point the stunning Basilica dominates the east entry were two inviting large Roman pillars stood. Napoleon himself had remarked "the drawing room of Europe" as he entered Venice via the Square. My mind was distracted by the sound of the Basilica's bell tolling as I gazed up at it. The sound rang across the square, once more disturbing the doves and the madding crowd who began flocking into the Square from all points of the compass. The beauty and splendour of the surrounding buildings reeked of the renaissance period with a whiff of Islam and Nordic influences thrown in. I was yet to see the tomb of San Marlo located under the altar in the Church which I had earmarked to visit the very next morning.

It began to drizzle light rain as I finished the last of my coffee having had my fill. It had been a night worthy of remembering. The Square was still in full swing as I left, fireworks lit the sky once more and small children amused themselves with throw-downs making indiscriminate bangs on the stone entry point of the pathway to the canal crossing near my accomodation. It had been a grand evening; one to remain in living memory but not one to die bye save for my sweet peaceful slumber.

My intent to take the tour through San Marcos the next morning had been noted by the night desk clerk before I ascended the stairs to bed. He warned of a huge crowds of tourist lining up for hours each day to visit the Church and suggested I get there early to avoid the crowd. I thanked him as I headed to bed but woke just on dawn and decided to make an even earlier start to be in the line at or near the front. As I crossed the canal bridge in the early morning rain I noted a small group of nuns making their way towards the Square. Getting step with the parading nuns a few metres behind them, we entered San Marco through a small passage way and I followed. The nuns exited stage left to a small chapel where no-doubt they were intent on prayed before the morning Mass. It was a golden opportunity for me to pay respects to the Lord of all and check out this amazing Cathedral of wonder. I had the place to myself and began to wander and take in the glory of it all as I had done on many occasions visiting many a Church and cathedral throughout the world to this present day. No sooner had I commenced my free tour than a security guard appeared from the shadows of a stone pillar nearby. I had caught his reflection on a glass panel containing a mosaic of the Virgin Mother with child. Without any sigh of surprise I quickly fell to my knees facing the altar in a mocked version of prayer, holding my hands together giving the impression of great piety.

The guard walked behind me and around, checked out my d'amour of an illegitimate love child and slowly passed me by. Relieved of the burden of my deception as quickly as I had found it, I justified to myself that as a now pilgrim of some limited means I was doing nothing wrong save not paying for the pending tour and lining up outside with the rest of the pilgrims. For a brief moment I did pray to Jesus via the Virgin Mary thinking Mother knows best. As luck would have it, the Priest arrived with an entourage of altar boys leading him towards the Chapel of nuns. I remained rigidly upright on my knees still acting pious as the sacred host in a Chalice of gold carefully held by the Priest with intent to serve communion to the nuns passed me by.

I quickly took the opportunity to have a look around, noting that the tomb of San Marco still had a sash across its entry point, so I just blessed myself for some unknown reason and left the Cathedral to the sound of the singing nuns. Outside a long line of pilgrim tourists wound its way from the front entry of San Marco around the corner to infinity. I was pleased now that I had achieved my goal despite it being deceptive. To my mind it wasn't so, for I had been educated to the religion, been an altar boy for to many a long day, given my fair share of hard earned pocket money to the will of the nun and priests and never ever had to pay to enter a catholic place of worship before. I wasn't about to start now. I made my way to the Galleria de Academia viewing the works of Leonardo de Vinci's Annunciation, prophets and Saint Lawrence and the Madonna enthroned with Child. My primary purpose thou was Leonardo's 'The Vitruvian Man' in which the great Master represents the ideal proportions of the human body, depicting a man inscribed inside two perfect figures, a circle representing the Universe and a square, symbolising the earth. This work alone had influenced the renaissance period and ever since art critic, artist and intellectuals to this very day.

I did not see myself in the company of a ghost possessing self superior knowledge or having artist ability, but it was the influence on this ordinary man none the less. Reportedly both de Vinci and Michelangelo had dug up newly buried dead in the middle of the night to dissect and examine the eternal workings of the human body from the inside out so to speak. It made sense to me that these men of such creative genius would have inside information to further their talent. I applauded their intuition at time; justifying what would have been then considered a deplorable act of sacrilegious proportion during their lifetime. This is what drew me to their work. My passion was not Leonardo de Vinci and his creative genius on this visit to this watery land mass of the living and the dead, it was the torn soul of Michelangelo, the leading figure of the Renaissance. The Academia Museum of Florence had loaned their prized unfinished statues of the tortured souls of the Master and his conception of carving in stone to the Venice Academia. Michelangelo believed sculptor was a tool of God and the stone held the body, mind and spirit of what he needed to release from captivity. The stone he chose for the David was a discarded quarried tall block weathered over 40 year, deteriorated and rough from the elements.

I stood at the foot of this near 5 metre (seventeen foot) statue, structured perfectly with adoration of the Master. In the shadow of my mind I visualised the battered face of Michelangelo, dressed in dirty, dusty worn clothing. The stench of his sweating body still covered in plaster from his duty to the Pope in completing his later masterpiece of paintings within and on the ceiling of the Sistine Chapel in Rome.

Remembering the gargoyles he painted around the holes of the ceilings that held the cross beams for him to lay upon as he painted. I could almost hear him speak as he frowned upon his paintings, looking up at the David: "I am not a painter, I am a creator of sculpture." As I made my way along the corridor of the gallery, I soaked in the withering and straining image of the Awakened Slave seeking to be liberated from the stone. Across the corridor the young slave seemed almost bound within himself. With prior knowledge of Michelangelo's grave digging expeditions,I wondered if he had actually removed a young child's body from the earth and anatomical study. The profound study of the Master was highlighted to me in the left elbow and careful lined bent biceps and triceps. The face seemed so youthful as it began to emerge from the hidden position under his bend arm. The image chiseled out from the rough rocky surface of the marble block still showing the rough tracks of the chisel.

The beard slave was just along the corridor and as I approach it seemed to be almost free from the marble with only his hands and part of his arm still enslaved by the rock; seemed to reveal even more of the Michelangelo's mind. The Masterful sculpture who had such a deep knowledge of anatomy. Down the corridor the Atlas slave seem to carry a huge weight on his head and shoulders but the head had not emerged from the stone leaving the unrevealed burden still encased there. The energy of the figure expressed the energy of a figure struggling to emerge from the marble. I had noted on the front door of the museum that the exhibition was finishing that day and was being moved back to Academia Gallery in Florence, so the ushers were keen to close up in readiness for the logistic transfer of the priceless works. I left the museum content to visit the works of the Master in Rome and in Florence as I continued my journey through Italy. Looking back I visualised the old Master-looking at me harshly with half angry eyes at the doorway. A curiously envious expression on his face, like he wished to carve me out of my apathy, wake me up to my creative self. I pushed the image back in to my logical mind, released to the confinement of my lot in life but for that moment being quietly disturbed about my future fate and lot.

In a natural state I had surmised that one must give up the things of youth and grow up, follow a career path ruled by money and do all the ordinary things in an extraordinary way. I had set in motion a pathway to the future of family and accept the curbing of my creative imagination, channeling such creativity into the life of business to serve the Master of the money machine. It so hap pened to be my lot for the majority of my life, that is until all my world turned upside down. Now in old age, after much personal pain and sorrow I have turned back time to those days in Venice. My journey then was of bold ambition, giving the appearance of being a free spirit but in point of fact being a slave to my folly for work, money and power, sex, alcoholic and tobacco. Now, thank God I have let go some of those vices. More to the fact of reality than of choice, for I am   getting older and my health could not maintain the pace of my lower nature passions and I now believe my time is best spent in pursuits tampered with love, forgiveness and giving. To some degree a roadmap of creation for my fellow man where I may be of best use. The thought for a moment now passing that it is all just a whiff of smoke and all that really matters is peace with ones own God of my own understanding within my nature and that of the universe of mankind.

I can no longer be habitually counterfeit as the real Doug is being himself, not the egotistical whole but the spirited self aware-ness, using my talents for the good of all concerned. Not letting the ego take control but letting Doug the unselfish drive my cre-ative nature for my own spiritual wellness. I left the Venice of sym-bolic struggle of man against the elements of time, as they man-age to master a hostile nature. The Venice of a middle aged mas-terpiece of sculptor, paintings and architecture. The city of 118 small islands that seemingly floats on the waters off a lagoon composing an unforgettable landscape of beauty that inspired powerful popes, emperors and explorers and the common man of adventurers of the likes of me. Arteries of canals and channels consolidated and organised into the greatest capital in the Me-dieval world was and is still sinking. There was so much that I did not see back then and so much that I still have not seen despite my return to Venice many decades later. For I am still on my ad-venture and do not intend to make Venice my last port of call be-fore I die. No,I have already engraved in my mind the image of that unknown climber buried on a snow clad mountain."He died climb-ing" is written on his head stone. That is my quest, to die climbing and I am not fussed if it is climbing a women or a mountain. Of course, God may have some other idea before I am through to the other side.

Arriving at Rome by rail I was pleasantly surprised to receive a phone call from Ian to meet him and Peter at the Trevi Fountain I about 10 am, as they had already found accomodation fo us all. I had an hour to kill and it was still peek hour, with crazy traffic jams of honking cars, busy pedestrians and beggars alike on the way.

I stopped to buy an apple at a street vendors cart, realising two block away later that, having consumed half of my purchase I had mistakenly paid seven times its value. I was still thinking in German marks and not Lira. Thirteen hundred lira equalled One dollar Australian I kept repeating in my brains I walked. I was now determined not to make the same mistake twice. I had not noticed the young women with the small baby who thrust the child at me demanding money so she could feed it. I felt sorry for her but was not game to open my cash belt around my waist for fear of being robbed by some other prying eye. I did not appear to be the typical mark in my untidy appearance, but obviously these daily street beggars could see that I was better of than they were. perhaps it was the half eaten apple I had in my mouth or maybe the women had followed me from the street vendor noticing how easily I parted with excess monies for my purchase.

Leaving the area in haste I was blocked on my way by a well dressed middle aged Italian with shining pointed toe shoes supported by a smart brief case. He spoke politely in perfect English asking if I could spare a few lira fo a much needed cab fare home to collect the wallet of monies he had left there. He sounded desperate in his plea for help but I declined with a firm "No," hurrying to the crowded area at the Trevi fountain. I felt I needed to redeem myself and in the tradition of good luck, I turned my back on the flowing waters of the Trevi and the crowd, retrieving a coin from inside my waist wallet and tossed the ten lira coin over my head into the water. Children a little older than Bambinos' were already in the fountain up to their waist in water collecting the coins. I felt the freedom of being relieved of my earlier lack of generosity that I may now be helping some poor family to benefit in some small way from my 'donation.' I was relieved also to see my good friends Ian and Peter who both embraced me like long lost brothers and I quickly forgot my guilt of the past hour as we wound our way through the street of Rome to our accommodation near the centre of the city.

The events that followed for the remainder of my time in Italy comes in flash backs now, as the power of my recall is somewhat surprisingly fading as I write these lines. I have now recollections of not so important events in a kind of slow motion rewind of the memory bank, which tells me that I am approaching the end of this saga of a past life and my story in the telling is of little relevance in the scheme of things. The memory of being on a crowded morning peak hour bus heading towards Vatican city jolts back to mind. We three intrepid travellers standing between old women dressed in black with a shopping bag in one hand, firmly gripping the overhead rail as the bus swayed into corners. It was on this journey that I recall Peter calling out from down the bus corridor: "Breath in, smell the arm pits." He was always coming out with some funny spur of the moments comments. Ian on the other hand was taking in the legs of a dark haired beauty gently rubbing up against her thigh as the bus rocked he was getting a horn.

For my part, I was observing all the comings and goings of the lonely commuters heading to who knows where, who knows why. We had wandered Vatican city as free spirits, amazed at the vast wealth of Di Vinci, Michelangelo and Raphael masterpieces and little pure gold treasures locked away in glass cages. Once having observed the splendour of The Sistine Chapel, we entered a corridor with a winding staircase of no particular destination observing a raining down of coin between the surrounding walls in a continual flow to a collection Well below. Coins thrown from above by the masses of Pilgrims in their desperate bid for some grace from the Lord. Secretly I was figuring how to find the way to the vault of wealth flowing down like water, but I never did find it.

I returned to St. Peter's Square on a guided tour in 2012 to a small area of the Vatican now open to view for the public. Apparently the teaming millions of tourist of the past and their donations did not warrant the right to the freedom to wander holy places. Damage to the paintings and artefacts from the rising steam of sweating bodies cost more to maintain the treasures than it was worth. The tour I took on my more recent visit was only one corridor of the prized collection and a viewing of the Sistine Chapel. The brochure I had in hand indicated the tours were worth nineteen million net profit Euro per annum to the Vatican so I could see the wisdom of the money men of the Vatican Bank's evaluation of their profit and loss account. They had lost much more than that in the most public revelations surrounding the Vatican bank's dealings with Milan's Banco Ambrosiano, one of the most high-profile bank collapses in Italy's history, as the Vatican bank was one of its main shareholders. It began with the power of money over the power of the spirit and demise in 1982, of Roberto Calvi, the bank's CEO who was found hanging under Blackfriars bridge in London, a ritual death by the Sicilian Mafia. It was May 1971 when I first walked across St.Peter's Square with my friends of the road Ian and Peter; a decade before the attempted assassination of Pope John Paul 11 in that very location. The Pope was struck four times and suffered severe blood loss, but he did recover. The Mafia, the CIA and the KGB were all accused of the plot to kill the

Pope. He on the other hand, upon his recovery was more concerned with the soul of his would be assassin Mehmet Ali A'gca. The Pope visited and prayed with him in prison and offered his forgiveness.

I was contemplating this as I stood once more in that Square in 2012, thinking back on my time there before the trouble and strife that seem to emulate across Christendom since that day. Lucia, in the Apparitions of Fatima had detailed the shooting of the Pope way back in 1917 when the Lady of the Rosary had appeared to her and her young cousins in a field. The events that have since followed reeked of a pending Armageddon, but at the time it was the last thing on my mind. I was thinking back once more of the event that followed my first visit.. It was just six years after my initial youthful carefree visit to the Vatican, when a new Pope was inaugurated. He rained for just 33 days and it was rumoured that he was poisoned. The Church's of politics and power has been on a downward spiral ever since in my opinion. Especially the controversy that surrounds the litany of lies and cover ups, not only in matters of monetary importance but that of its very priesthood and links with pedophilia. Such despicable acts have rained since the the times of the Spanish Inquisition, when sexual acts on children go so far out of hand within the Church, Vatican Canon law was changed so that the age of reason was reduced to seven instead of eleven. This then put the 'blame' at the foot of the child in lieu of the Priest, as it could from then on be reconciled that a seven year old child would know his or her own spiritual conscious in maters of right from wrong.

The current Pope Francis has taken the bull by the horns so to speak and sacked many a priest and bishop for lack of acting on the knowledge of knowing priest who commit pedophilia or participation in such acts. Slowly the Church is no longer able to overrule its canon law over that of the law of common man and in the long run this must prove to be a good thing. An old mind must be forgiven for a somewhat digression from my own path towards and ending of my story herein. So, to continue with my youthful wanderings to draw some conclusive meaning   to my narrative thoughts, feelings and behaviours in these snippets of my past life, there is a hope dear reader that you may gain some benefit. We three young travellers in the latter days of our youth meandered our way to the Roman Forum to examine the excavated heart of the Roman Empire. Our minds distracted by the creative genius of the architecture of the Romans in the era of the Caesars as equally as we were mindful of the distraction of the gladiatorial arena of the Colosseum. A time of great wealth, power and pride of Empire decaying in the killings of the innocent for the want of keeping the masses entertained to relieve boredom.

We too were bored after a couple of days, having visited St.Peter's Basilica, the Pantheon and its historic tombs. we filled in our time eating and drinking around the Pizza Navona and meeting others at the Spanish steps for coffee and a chat. By the time a week had passed we were relieved to catch the fast train to Florence to take in the highlights of the capital of the Tuscany region. I, with my fascination for renaissance art and architecture, was keen to continue my journey of exploration of iconic sites as was fellow travellers. It was a repeat of the Renaissance art of Michelangelo and De Vince; the Cathedral Dome,Giotto's Campanile, Palazzo Vecchio, walking across the Ponte Vecchio and overlooking the Basilica of Saint Croce as we climb the nearby hill. Not unlike viewing the Vatican from the seven hills of Rome or viewing the Leaning Tower of Pisa from a distance. We did it all and with the fading memories of climbing old stone stairways and ghostly images of doors and windows alike, all just fading memories now.

Perhaps the most memorable events of my remaining days in Europe were three embedded tapes in my brain. The first of these was making my way into a forest to relieve my bowels after finding the refuge we stayed in had a sewerage explosion flooded the communal bathroom. I was seated in the squat position in a nearby forest in the quiet of a summer morn listening to the silence. The sound of a rustling leaves on the ground nearby attracted my attention. Looking around I found myself in close contact with a young doe grazing on the undergrowth staring back at me. It was one of those beautiful moments of share bliss; that is until I let go an almighty fart which frightened my gentle friend who quickly vanished into the thick of the forest. The second was the memory of having lumps all over my body from sleeping in another refugee opposite the leaning tower of Pisa. We three had bed bug infection in our long haired scalps and lumps all over our bodies. We had no recourse but to vacate the premises in the early morning hours and make our way to a Pharmacy to purchase copious quantities of Calamine lotion.The third experience but indeed not the least was when we returned to London and visited an out of city university for a Jeff Beck Group concert. It was the next best thing in Peter's mind to listen to the Master guitarist as former member of the Yardbirds.

Peter had done his homework and we arrived at the University just in time to mingle with the audience whilst seated on the floor on the floor to hear Beck in action on stage. Peter could not get to see John Mayall on our European crossing but he got another wish with Beck in his finest hours after the Yardbirds demise.Ian had the pleasures of the dancing Lipizzaner horses in Vienna, Peter his Jeff Beck group and I, whilst not getting to meet Michelangelo Antonioni the film director did get to absorb the passion and artist ability of the great master Michelangelo. This was only part of my experience. The third one was the *'piste de resistance'* of that time. It was whilst directly after the Beck concert that I met the beautiful young jew, Sally. We had a crazy romantic fling for the remaining time in the UK but it was cut short due to her tour agenda to Scotland before returning home to the family. she came from an extremely wealthy dynasty in the health industry. I had already made up my mind to return to follow my plan of a career path in Australia. Besides, I was broke and had not even the plane fare home and would have to rely on my Father's generosity to lend me the money for the flight to Australia. I made my way to Victoria London to see Sally off on her next leg of her journey. Sally looked at me with big brown eyes enquiring if I would continue our romance and travel back to USA with her. I declined and gave her the only address I had in Australia, that of my parents, so that she could communicate with me. As the train pulled out from the station I wave her goodbye. Walking away I had a change of heart and jumped the turnstile to run to the departing train. My hand could not reach the back carriage door and the train departed without me. If I had reached that door and climbed on board who knows what direction fate would have taken me. Perhaps I would be a resident of the USA working for her families Jewish Empire raising the offspring of star-crossed lovers. I never heard from her again but found out she had written to me on serval occasions, but my mother in her wisdom had torn up the letters and never told me until many years after I had raised and educated my own brood to my then wife. Like all things that seem the natural course of events for my life both then and now, they all came to nothing in the end.

It was May 30, 1972 as I boarded the New Jumbo 747 aircraft looking forward to the return flight to Sydney. Dad had sent me the money for my flight which I promised to repay him on my first commission pay check on my return to my sales career. An announcement from the Captain the seated passengers on board the Jumbo was startling.

The Lod Airport near Tel Aviv had been attacked by crazed Japanese members of the Popular Front for the Liberation of Palestine and reportedly they had killed 26 people and injured 80 others. Two of the attackers had been killed and a third member was captured after being wounded. This was to be the story of terrorism for the remainder of the 20th century and is still happening from time to time with the rise of ISIS and other crazed fanatics. As it so happened the Jumbo jet I had boarded had at least a third of its passengers Japanese heading for Hong Kong on there destined stopover. It took another two hours for all those passengers to be cleared by the British Home Affairs and Customs before the flight taxied out for takeoff. It was the longest flight I had ever taken, apart from the stopover in Hong Kong and then Darwin, the plane had a two hour detour away from the war zone of Vietnam were the US were bombing.

A weary hippie type, unclean with shoulder length hair and a beard was a dead set target for Customs to do an extra baggage check. It had been a 22 hour flight not counting stop overs and another two hours to clear customs. I made a note in my head to make sure on my next journey to the Northern Hemisphere to be neat and tidily dressed with a short back and sides haircut. My youthful experiences lay dormant then until my ageing years now as I look back on the years that have transpired since that then journey to Europe as a last hurrah to my youth and the sowing of wild oats. At least that is what I thought but life has taken the cycle around again and it is this second journey in the afternoon of my life that has proven even more challenging and in a somewhat painful but memorable way, more exciting. It has been a long road with many a twist and turn for me incorporating a rise to power, some fame and fortune and the loss of it all again. In a worldly sense I have made it many times over only to see it all slip through my fingers again and again. Not to be discourage, I have climbed the ladder of money, prestige and power many times since only to find now that I had perhaps had my ladder of my designated path leaning against the wrong wall all along. I cannot change what was and what is now makes me more attuned to what is the meaning of my life, that has taken me over a lifetime from ego me to a more in tune we.

A thirteen year career in the Insurance industry followed my return from the days of my youth. I had set the goal and the plan on those distant shores of Germany behind the Cologne Cathedral way back on my first visit to that fair city in those days of youth in the 1970s. The path I had chosen back then came to a reality as I climbed the ladder of Corporate Management in the Insurance industry gaining all the awards and rewards that an enslaved soul strive for. It gained for me money, prestige and power beyond what I had bargained for. It came at a price with my ever increasing intake of alcohol and a forty a day cigarette smoking habit. I smoked like that for more than a decade and finally kicked the habit due to continual chest infections in the first year of the birth of my eldest son. Little did I know then the drink would get the better of me eventually. My only regret now in that regard is that I did not give up the booze when I stopped smoking. Also, that I had not taken a long hard look at my work ethic in lieu of the fact that I was heading down the same life cycle that led to my fathers's ultimate demise.

In my early married years I was away from home a lot due to job commitments for I was responsible to a host of country representatives and took it upon myself also to recruit, train and motivate an ever growing team of new agents for the company throughout the North West of the State. This put much strain on my relationship with my then wife and whilst I remained a good provider for my growing brood of three sons and a daughter, I was more interested in my personal goals than the family lifestyle. I left the every day things to the mother of my children far too much and settled for the life of a travelling recluse manager, having excepted the carrot from my superiors of going places up the ladder in the company. The pressure of the job and the fact that I got bored with living in motel rooms and living out of a suitcase prompted me to resign with the intent to be more devoted as husband and father in the future.

So I accepted a new challenge of being a self employed newsagent in a small country town. I was not content however to run a small business and renovated the shop, extending it to include the sale of guns, ammunition and explosives, a gaming location with teller box for the purchase of Lotto, Pools and lottery tickets, electronics and computer supplies, a jewellery department area and an ever growing plethora of novels, educational books and magazines. I was back soon enough on a of a seven day a week bent of work, expanding the business and finding the best way to relax after working in the pleasure of alcoholic beverage. My wife of the time handed over the kids to child care at my insistence to relieve me of duties from time to time so that I could focus on the further growth of the business. It is fair to say that I had a staff thieving problem and it took me three years to unwind it all. In the process I had unwittingly funded the purchase of a new home for one of my staff members, the well hidden retirement package for another and the inventory for another towns News-agency business. I finally got to the bottom of it all, sacked staff and began to rebuild the business in the worst drought of its time in the New England.

Not counting the amount of inventory that was being loaded on a truck and transported out of town in the wee small hours by an enterprising staff member, I had been loosing over $200,000 per annum in turnovers as a consequence of theft. An added bonus to the sacking of the guilty parties was that I caught the other town business owner and one of my staff member red handed in the act of stealing another truck load of my stock. It was one afternoon when it was suspect that I was out of town that I had sprung that trap. Despite trading through a drought for the next three years, the business turnover increased to levels were I had enough good profit on my balance sheet, profit and lost statements to gain a tidy sum for the business and I sold it at the first opportunity. I was exhausted with a bleeding stomach ulcer obviously brought on by the added stress of dispelling the wicked ones from my employment and having worked myself to the bone.

The incoming owner struck it rich for he doubled the turnover in one year. The day he signed the agreement for sale with me the drought broke and everything including land prices doubled within weeks. I still kept the building for a time, leasing it to the next owner but on the next renewal of the lease he decided not to sign again and moved to small premise in a nearby street. I was left with an empty building for one year and finally sold it for its original purchase price including the extended shop renovation. The business taught me a lot about staff management of retail business and keeping the books in order. The biggest lesson thou was the dishonesty of some staff and customers. The old saying of my Mums "Love many, trust few, always paddle your own canoe,"comes to mind.I filled in my time after the sale of the business in trading the stock market and spending time on horseback rounding up ranging cattle in the mountains. It was that experience that laid the seed for my 'Boundary Rider' song some years later that and thoughts of my Grandfather's adventures on horseback rounding up herds of ranging cattle in the New England Ranges

The next adventure saw me return to the Insurance industry for a number of years doing regional and Australia wide duties for various Insurance companies before returning to my own business ventures again. The opportunity came with the purchase of a quantity of office merchandise from an auction of receivership stock. I gained some knowledge in bidding at auctions, importing container loads of stationery items from mainland China and eventually buying a second business of an Australia wide paper merchant business. The timing of the purchase was at beginning of an upward surge in paper products and I sold that business for a tidy profit after only 18 months. We as a family had the best of everything: A waterfront home on the Harbour, cars, a boat and home entertainment for many hangers on. The children got the best of private school education and annual resort holidays. The cash cow of the business was at a crescendo when the rot set in and all that I lived for and depended upon came crashing down in a continual spiral.

The financial year ending 30th June 2002 saw the passing of my most financially successful year of my life on paper. Everything I touched that year seem to turn to gold, like I had the Midas touch. At the time, with two businesses under my belt, I noted that I had completed 40 group certificates for employees as a proof of the pudding on the need for employees to help run the show. A typical say at the height of success in the retail side of the business was probably summed up by one of my customers. In the shop I had a two lane walk way that customers walked through to purchase products. It was the Christmas rush, and I had two cash registers manned by staff ticking over full time. Both lanes to the counter on this particular day had customers lined up to pay for their chosen products from the back door to the front of the shop. I was rushing back and forward attending to the customers on a one to one basis and one of the customers pulled me up with an insightful comment. He was a little old Jewish man who had a serious but friendly look on his face as he commented: " This is very good, the way of this business, it is a little bit below expensive." That made my day and really summed up where I was at with my material success.

All seemed rosy in the family garden, but it would not prove to be so as fate would soon dictate. On reflection, I was working far too hard, spending what should have been quality time with family but instead I was engaged in the hands on running of the businesses day and night. Also, I was drinking far too much on a daily basis and whilst I never drank on the job I was on a downward spiral with the drink and could not see it. The habitual after-hours drinking was the only way I seem to be able to unwind. I was always in a state of exhaustion, had constant chest pains and was on a treadmill of the never-ending pursuit of business ideas and actions. It had not occurred to me to take time out to give myself peace of mind. I mistakenly believed I was fulfilling my duties as husband and father in the giving of my all too the material way of life to which we as a family had become accustomed. My work a day week I reduced to six to content myself with some sort of normality and relaxed on a Sunday morning bush walking with friends. This outdoor activity was always followed by catching up on lawn mowing, cleaning the swimming pool, taking a swim or washing the cars or the boat when the need arose. Other than this it was limited time with the children with a good red wine always at hand. I was back into my work pattern of the past Corporate era. The last real family holiday we had together was when my two eldest boys were in early primary school. Once I got into the treadmill of either working in leadership roles or running my own business, the idea of an all family holiday went out the window. It became a week a year away with one of my children followed by my ex wife taking one or another of our children away for an equal time in a resort location. A decade of more materially in my efforts had the equal and opposite effect of the death of my spiritual wellbeing. I resigned   myself more into what was an external stroking of my ego at the expense of my spiritual wholeness.

Drink seemed to sooth the savage beast that raged within and at the time it all seemed normal. On the surface, if glanced at by an outside observer, all seemed right with the world and our family. It was not so as I had buried my inferiority complex with alcoholic beverages which for a time quelled the real me. Measured by the standards of society we had all the trimmings of a perfectly happy, affluent and stable family unit. The crack in my armour began to show as I reached out more and more for external proof of my worthiness. The measurement measure was money, the egocentricity was the actions of what on the surface was to all intents and purposes a benefit to both my family materially and my customer base with the provision of personal service. I can not recall if I was ever happy in my past life as discontent drove me even more in my efforts to fulfil ill-conceived goals. Fate would have it that my time was up and whilst I was at the top of my pathway of apparent success, the downward spiral was just around the corner. It was a cloudy winter's day when the crunch came and our 28 years of marriage reached a stalemate on 2nd July 2002. I was no longer the loving attentive husband she had married and raised four children with. The common goal had turned to dust and she knew it and a better offer in a new relationship beckoned her. As for me I was too blind to see the wood for the trees, caught up in my own business world and attempting to fulfil the financial commitments that I had accepted as my lot in life for the benefit of my family. My life was already coming unstuck and booze was the bandaid to my holding it all together. This was just the beginning of what would prove to be my worst nightmare. The year proceeded with one nightmare after another as my ex, the mother of my children left with the children in toe one dark clouds Saturday . The divorce proceedings continued and with tightened credit my staff arrangement reduced from forty a year, back to ten and finally, it was I alone running the show and doing my best to stay afloat. I knew the business could not continue on its downward spiral so when the lease come up for renewal I didn't renew it. Fate took its hand once more and I was given little choice in the end but to close it all down.

My Mum had fallen and broke her hip for the third time just months after the separation and I had to move her into full time care. In the meantime a Kiwi mate had arranged to come to stay with me but died on the way to visit. I was his only Australian friend and the Police came knocking at my door to come and identify his body. The opportunity to do this went out the window, when I soon after received a call from New Guinea that my second eldest son Peter had committed suicide. All my world collapsed at that point and the only recourse for me was to drink away the pain. Perhaps the alcohol killed the pain somewhat but not completely. Some days and nights I just drifted through the world upon awakening, lost in a void of sorrow exhaustion and mental pain. My nights were long and I didn't sleep much preferring to do renovation activities to prepare the home for sale or perhaps, I hoped at the time, the return of my family.

I accepted my ex wife solicitors pay out ratios on the divorce settlement, cleared all indebtedness to the bank and closed down business interests in my attempt to do my best to recover. It didn't work as I needed the booze to keep me stable. Ultimately, I cracked and fell into a deep depression. It was then that my then partner Christine advised me to go bush to recover and so I packed up what had left of my material possessions, loaded my car and headed north. Thus began the life of a recluse for the next six months. My out of control screaming episode under the influence of alcohol in the presence of Christine had reduced me to a shell of my former self. It was there in my depressed state that I ceased drinking. Not that I knew it at that time that I was alcoholic, but more to the point, I was scared that if I drank I would have possibly done myself in or gone down the same downward spiral with alcohol and prescription drugs that my father had finally taken, resulting in his sad ending. I had enough to survive for the remaining six months as each day marched on and I finished with a pill that had me sleep through the night until dawn. My routine upon awakening was to put on a pair of shorts, T shirt and walking shoes and walk to the beach before I had time to think. I was determined, despite feeling in the depth of despair to walk away my blues so to speak. It was my routine to walk the three kilometre along the beach, wave to a couple who sat together every morning waiting for the sun to rise, say hullo to a man walking his dogs and give them a pat. I would on my return pick up a smooth stone from the beach, take it home and toss it in a dish. This was followed with some breakfast, household chores and the writing of a dark poem or two, then a short meditation. I had no specific plan other than to take my back-pack, toss in a tin of baked beans, a spoon to eat with and a bread roll and fruit and return to walking the day away.

Mostly I did not make contact with people, preferring to kept very much to myself. When the dish of stones was piled high, I began to return one stone a day to the beach as part of my routine. One morning I took the dish to the front door and threw the remaining stones into the front garden packed up my worldly possessions and headed south to Sydney. I was still depressed but I needed to find a job before the funds ran out. I took on a business development role in the industry I knew best with the intent to stay for perhaps a year or two until I was strong enough to start my own business again. The contract finished at the end of 12 months but I stayed for the next decade until the owner sold the business. In truth I had a lot of relapses from depression after I gave up the booze for good, but the pain of remorse and the unfulfilled spirit yearned to let go and find a new direction set me on a new journey of discovery.

It came in walking the French route of Way of St. James on the Camino de Santiago in 2013 at age 68. I returned again to walk the Portuguese route in 2015 and the French route again in 2017. All of these journeys released in me a lotus flower of creative idea resulting in the writing of poetry books, novels and albums of songs of my own inspiration. It has given me the balance of living that I could not find on the psychiatrist's couch and help me think more about the benefit that others may gain having read this journal in my world of matter and that of the spiritual quest that follows. It has been more about what had happened in my past life, what changed and what it is like now. So in the final analysis the past of me taught much that may benefit another and for me nothing more than a letting go. The highs and lows of my existence to this very day I can but sum up in a final brief of a statement of fact. I have studied my life and in retrospect seen all the things that the world had to offer and find it now has no meaning and like a whiff of smoke came, went and faded to nothingness.

I found in my wisdom, folly and madness that I had inherited the wind and nothing more. Through my sorrow and grief I learnt to cry but the more I cried the more sorrow came and the study of knowledge and grief just brought me more grief. And so I turned to pleasure in wine, in women, in song. I wanted so much to see what was worthwhile in the embracing of my folly, it all faded into the past of nothingness too. Not content with my lack of progress in living this life I through myself into great projects of building, restoration of houses and even agriculture. I built much wealth in stocks and shares only to see it all lost in the Stockmarket crash of 1987. So I rebuilt my portfolio to once more see it reduced in the divorce settlement of 2004 and and further diminish in the GFC downturn between 2007 to 2009. So I set to working hard in contact work, rebuilding my material wealth again to once more feel the pain of financial loss in the market due to the stock market turndown in the current Corvid-19 pandemic. It is different now to some degree for I have lost the fear of financial insecurity. But of all my rebuilding of the material assets it has gained me little but experience and more of nothing than something. The plan of a young man's dream to leave behind more than a headstone still plagues me. It matters little what I leave behind in the material sense, but more to do with the giving of We of me than the taking.

For if I have gained any wisdom at all it is in the knowledge of letting go and handing over to the nothingness of the spiritual. The nothing, the no thing wherein is the void. It is that centre that place of God instinct even if it is only in the manifestation of my belief. It is in my acceptance of what The Master of my being has built in my subconscious, the whole of me, my duty from here on in until my end comes too. And for that matter it is for, with and in you my dear reader. It is my belief now that the God of this Universe will one day bring into judgement every thought, word and deed of my life, including the hidden things whether they be good or bad. But I am not fearing now, I am not holding on to anything for what I have done nor what I have failed to do. I can only look back without regret and move forward with the begetting of wisdom for a better future for those I have loved, those I do love and those I have lost along the way.

No! No regrets
All the things
that went wrong
for at last I have learned to be strong

No! No regrets
No! I will have no regrets
For the grief doesn't last
it is gone
I've forgotten the past.

And the memories I had
I no longer desire
Both the good and the bad
I have flung in a fire

and I feel in my heart
That the seed has been sown
It is something quite new
it's like nothing I've known

No! No regret
No! I will have no regrets
all the things that went wrong
For at last i have learned to be strong.

No! I will have no regrets
For the seed that is new
It's the love
that is growing for you.

About the Author.

Doug McPhillips, poet, singer, songwriter, author, commenced his journey of discovery over a decade ago after life changing experiences.

The many tracks he has traversed though the Northern Hemisphere and down under in New Zealand and Australia have resulted in the facts and fictions of this novel.

Doug has recorded and sings songs interrelated to this work with unique majestic melody in true Australia style.
Doug has written four novels, two books of poetry, a travel guide and two albums of his songs inspired by his adventurers.

www.caminoway.com.au

" A journey of the Spirit."

Doug is an adventurer who divides his time between creative pursuits, love for family and friends, and those who may benefit most from his efforts and experience.

In the Latin Mass of the Catholic faith of my childhood there was a statement that the priest made to the congregation which simply interpreted states "It is a holy and a wholesome thought to pray for the dead that they may be loosed from their sins."

At the end of a difficult day I am reminded of that statement and before I close my eyes I often handover to the spirit of my ancestors the works, joys and sufferings of my day. it is not unusual for me to focus on my grandparents, parents and blood kin that have passed. In particular, I asked them to take care of the troubled spirit of my son Peter who died by his own hand to be there for him in his heavenly hours of need.

As for me I do not pray in a conventional sense but rather hand over to a Power Greater than me, the God of my own understanding, to guide me in all my waking hours and my Guardian angel whilst I sleep of course!

This book is available on line at www.caminoway.com.au/books

International at Ingram Sparke Publications In Australia, New Zealand, Canada, Europe and the U.S.A. as a paperback and eBook.

Printed in Australia.

Milling printers
c/- Fine Impressions
69 Granville Street,
Pymble 2073